CROCKETT'S DEVIL

The Mississippi Territory
and
Southern Tennessee

The Scene of the Action in "Crockett's Devil"

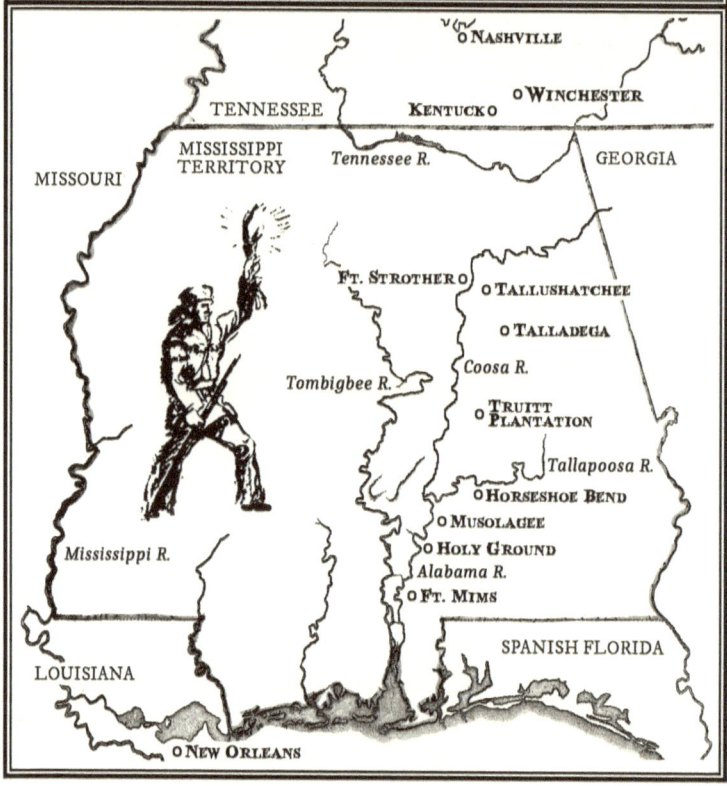

o NASHVILLE

o WINCHESTER

TENNESSEE   KENTUCK o

MISSOURI   MISSISSIPPI   Tennessee R.   GEORGIA
            TERRITORY

            FT. STROTHER o   o TALLUSHATCHEE

                              o TALLADEGA

                     Coosa R.

            Tombigbee R.   o TRUITT
                                PLANTATION

                              Tallapoosa R.

                              o HORSESHOE BEND

                              o MUSOLAGEE

            Mississippi R.   o HOLY GROUND
                              Alabama R.
                              o FT. MIMS

                              SPANISH FLORIDA

LOUISIANA

            o NEW ORLEANS

CROCKETT'S DEVIL

EVAN LEWIS

COVER BY
ROBERT STANLEY

STEEGER BOOKS • 2021

*Davy and I are much obliged to everyone to helped out
on this. They are, in mostly alphabetical order:*

Drew Bentley, Jackie Blain, Christine Finlayson, Kassandra
Kelly, Becky Kjelstrom, Nancy LaPaglia, Doug Levin, Ann
Littlewood, Marilyn McFarlane, Matt Moring, Cap'n
Bob Napier, Angela M. Sanders, Brian Trainer and most
of all—my wife Irene, who was there for whole journey.

A special tip of the coonskin cap to is also due to:

Walt Disney, Fess Parker, Buddy Ebsen, George Bruns
and Thomas W. Blackburn, Tennessee Ernie Ford, John
Wayne, Allen Wiener and William R. Chemerka.

PART I
RED EAGLE

CHAPTER I

"I should have you both shot."

I WAS A DEAD man. The only question was which of the three Creek warriors would make it official. My bet was on the squint-eyed fellow with the crude painting of a four-legged animal on his chest.

"Is that a possum," I asked, "or a polecat?" But he merely scowled, circling for a clear shot with his bow.

A close contender, a burly giant with a war club, took a swing at me and missed. I kicked him between the legs and he bawled like a castrated bull, exposing three black teeth and half a tongue. If his club didn't get me his breath surely would.

All the while, I danced a jig with the third savage, a human jackrabbit with a grip on my hair. He'd likely draw first blood with his scalping knife, but I'd heard scalping, while highly unpleasant, was not always fatal.

One of them, though, would surely get me. Pennsylvania McCoy, my tombstone would read. Born 1789, died 1813. In vain.

I didn't mind dying. That's what I'd come here to do. But I'd sworn to trade my life for that of the man who had taken everything from me. That man was Red Eagle, leader of the warring Creeks and the most hated Indian in the Mississippi Territory.

I'd had my shot at him, but the ball merely clipped an eagle feather from his reddish-blond braids. He sat high in the saddle, with alarmingly wide shoulders, and his skin, though streaked with warpaint, was as fair as my own. Like many Creeks, he was of mixed parentage and hardly looked Indian at all. Laughing at my poor marksmanship, he'd ridden off to the far end of the battlefield, leaving his three friends to pull me from my horse and snuff my candle.

While we struggled on, Red Eagle and his thousand warriors swirled about the small trading post and stockade known as Leslie's Fort. The Creeks' incessant war cries were punctuated by booming volleys of rifle fire from General Andrew Jackson's infantry. Powder smoke blanketed the field, the rotten-egg scent fouling the morning air. Men met death on every hand, and there would be no aid for one unlucky stranger at the mercy of three bloodthirsty savages. At least that's what I thought.

The possum-or-polecat was about to loose his arrow when a bay dun slammed into him, knocking him ass over teakettle. A rifle stock smacked the skull of the black-toothed giant, and a moccasined foot mashed the face of the scalp-hungry jackrabbit.

"Hate to spoil your fun," an amused drawl informed me, "but thirty more of them rascals are comin' to join the party." A lanky man in well-worn buckskins and a long-tailed raccoon cap leaned from his horse, offering a hand. And despite the gravity of the moment, he grinned.

I needed no further invitation. Grasping his arm, I swung onto the dun behind him. He'd not exaggerated the number of approaching warriors. Arrows whizzed past my ears as my rescuer kneed his horse and raced for the trees skirting the clearing. I marveled that none of those arrows found my back and could only guess that some higher power had further use of me.

Deep into the trees, behind squads of roaming foot soldiers, the rider wheeled his horse, and we saw the Indians had given up the chase. I dropped to the ground and checked myself for holes. I was amazed to be alive, let alone unharmed. My hand strayed to the St. Christopher's medal beneath my shirt, and the face of my mother came unbidden to my mind. I jerked the hand away. I could not afford tears. Not while Red Eagle lived.

"You're either the bravest jasper I've yet to meet," my savior said, "or the most foolish." He studied me with eyes as deep and blue as the sea. He had a ruddy, red-cheeked complexion, a long inquisitive nose and a mouth made for grinning. His reddish-brown hair was unruly as a bear's. I judged him a few years shy of thirty, scarcely older than me.

"Penn McCoy," I said, extending a hand. "I'll settle for most determined."

"Most determined to be scalped?" He took my hand in a firm grip. He was far stronger than he looked. "I'm David Crockett," he said, "but folks call me Davy. I'd admire to know what you was doin' out there."

"Same as you," I said. "Fighting redskins. This is a war, isn't it?"

Davy lost his grin. "Some call it that." He gazed back toward the battlefield. The war whoops and gunfire were only slightly dampened by the trees. "In any case, you'd best catch another mount and get back yonder with the rest of the volunteers. We're s'posed to prevent the Injuns from escapin', not dance a hornpipe with 'em. Old Hickory-face wants a clear field of fire for his infantry."

"Look, Mr. Crockett. Davy. I'm more grateful to you than I can say, but I don't give a fig what Andy Jackson wants. I'm no volunteer to be ordered about. I'm here on my own hook."

Davy's eyebrows went up. "You're stormin' about in the middle of the battle, and you ain't even enlisted? I reckon that answers the brave-or-foolish question."

"In point of fact," I said, "I was doing fine until your army arrived. If they hadn't complicated matters my business would be finished."

"And what business is that?"

"Purely my own." It sounded churlish to my ears, and I smiled to take the sting off.

Davy frowned. "Whatever you intend, you'd best pull back to the perimeter. If the Indians don't catch you here, the gen'ral surely will."

I peered deeper into the woods. Through gaps in the trees, the line of mounted frontiersmen looked solid and imposing. Turning in a circle, I saw they truly did have the field surrounded. "If the Mounted Volunteers are supposed to be on that line, how is it *you're* out roaming about?"

Davy sat back on his horse. "You got me there, Penn McCoy. But if you won't tell, I won't neither."

"Deal."

"Just take care, will you? When I save a feller's life, I prefer it to stay saved."

I NEEDED ANOTHER horse, but those now loose in the woods were half mad from the crashing gunfire, and skittered away at my approach. My own chestnut was no doubt among them, but I had scant hope of finding her.

Most of all, I needed a weapon, so I bolted back into the clearing and fell to my knees, searching the trampled grass for my longrifle. That rifle had been made by my father's hand and was my best link to him. It was also my best chance of killing Red Eagle. But it was gone.

Reduced to robbing corpses, I soon had two knives, a steel-bladed tomahawk and an iron-headed war club. The only firearm in sight was an old French musket with an effective range of less than thirty yards, and its former owner was nearly out of powder.

Clutching my primitive weapons, I roamed the edge of the woods, desperate for another chance at Red Eagle. He was easy to spot. His great black stallion dwarfed the ponies of his followers, raising him head and shoulders above the pack. The eagle feathers fastened to his braids streamed behind him as if he might take flight and soar over the field of battle.

Once, on the far side of the clearing, I saw Davy Crockett crash through a ring of warriors to rescue a soldier cut off from his company. Apparently, Crockett made a habit of that sort of thing. He was a strange man, and, had I the time, one that would be worth knowing. But I'd chosen another path in this war, and there was no turning back.

The battlefield was on a hillside near the Indian village of Talladega, in the eastern half of the Mississippi Territory. The large clearing had been cut from the woods and a stockade with a trading post built near a small stream. The surrounding trees—tall black oaks, maples and beeches—formed a canopy over the sparse underbrush.

The battle between a thousand rebel Creeks, now calling themselves "Red Sticks," and a like number of Tennessee regulars and volunteers had begun in orderly fashion. Jackson's infantry formed lines on either side of the clearing, while the mass of Creeks ebbed and flowed between them, loosing arrows, screaming their defiance and taking heavy losses from rifle volleys. Now, with Indian dead littering the field, smaller bands of hostiles broke off into the woods, ambushing the infantry and probing deeper toward the ring of Tennessee Mounted Volunteers.

Atop the high walls of the stockade, friendly Indians waved their hats and cheered Jackson's men. Until the arrival of the army, these 150-odd peaceable Creeks and their families had been under siege by Red Eagle and his horde. Their only offense, from what I'd heard, was refusing to join the fight against their white neighbors.

Back in Philadelphia, many blamed this uprising on President Madison. He'd rashly declared war on England, and the British, with their troops already fighting Napoleon, had responded by sending provocateurs to incite Indian violence along the northwest frontier. Whether by luck or design, that violence had spread into the South, precipitating the attack on Fort Mims, where the Red Sticks slaughtered over five hundred souls—men, women and children alike—with my parents and sister among them. That attack had been led by Red Eagle, and I had come to repay him.

At last a large group of Creeks veered away from the infantry and galloped in my direction. My heart leapt to see Red Eagle himself at their head. I knelt behind a stand of black oaks, musket at the ready. This was my moment. Firing a ball into Red Eagle's black heart would be worth any price.

My target was within fifty yards when he reined in and brought the band to a stop. I cursed my luck. With my father's longrifle, he'd be a dead man, but this old musket would merely alert him to my presence.

A quiet voice behind me said, "How old are you, Penn McCoy?"

I stiffened. I'd sensed no approach. But the voice was Davy Crockett's.

"Twenty-four," I said. "Why?"

"It plumb amazes me how a body can live so long and acquire so little sense." He stood an arm's length away, holding the reins of his dun along with those of a chestnut mare. *My* chestnut mare.

"You found my horse."

Davy shrugged. "Figured you'd be needin' her to ride on home."

"I have no home." I eyed the rifle butt in the scabbard aside his dun. "That's a fine weapon you have. Might I borrow it?"

He flicked his head toward Red Eagle's band. "There's at least eighty of them red devils within spittin' distance. You figure to get 'em all with a single shot?"

"Just one," I said. "Red Eagle. Please, Davy. I must do this."

He frowned. "Killin' Red Eagle wouldn't stop the fightin'. It'd likely make it worse. On the other hand…" He paused a moment, looking over my shoulder.

I turned to follow his gaze. Red Eagle and his men peered deep into the woods, scanning in all directions. They were no doubt looking for a break in the ring of volunteers. After a moment Red Eagle shook his head, barked a command and led the whole party off to the other side of the clearing.

I pounded a fist on the tree trunk, swearing long and loud.

"If you can rein in that temper of yours," Davy said, "we might save a good many lives."

"By killing Red Eagle?"

"No. By talkin' peace with him. If he asked his friends to lay down their weapons, they just might listen."

Talking peace? The idea was ridiculous. Impossible. And he thought *I* was foolish. "It would never happen. They're like rabid dogs. Once they've tasted blood they have to be put down."

Davy shook his head—a bit sadly, I thought. "You and Old Hickory-face ain't far apart in your thinkin'. But I've a notion it could work. You willin' to help me try?"

I hesitated. Deceiving the man who'd saved my life came hard, but I'd have sold my soul for another shot at Red Eagle. I sighed, feigning surrender. "What do you have in mind?"

TEN MINUTES LATER, Davy and I perched in the branches of twin maples overarching a wide pathway. The path led straight through the woods from the clearing to the ring of mounted soldiers. Davy waved his coonskin cap, and right on cue, the ring parted, leaving an inviting gap. If Red Eagle sought an escape route for his surviving warriors, this should prove irresistible.

Or so Davy hoped. His Tennessee neighbors had been eager to help, and the fact that his scheme was contrary to General Jackson's orders made it all the more attractive to them.

Now it all depended on Red Eagle.

We'd barely got settled when a small party of Creeks appeared at the edge of the clearing, staring open-mouthed up the path. They raced off, returning moments later with Red Eagle himself and a much larger party. Red Eagle raised his hand, shouted a command and galloped forward, his warriors streaming behind.

Our two trees were well chosen. Their thick branches overlapped, so we could position ourselves at any point over the path. As it now appeared Red Eagle would ride nearer to my side, Davy crawled to the end of his branch to meet me.

"Just remember," he said, "we need him alive. If he dies, we'll be shakin' hands with ol' Saint Pete."

I nodded, knowing this was true. My hand crept to the knife at the back of my belt. I hated misleading Davy as to my intentions, but took solace in his conviction that our deaths would be quick.

Then the Indians were nearly beneath us, and we jumped.

I looped an arm around Red Eagle's neck, wincing as his teeth sank into my forearm, and my knife went skittering off into the brush. Davy landed full in his lap, straddling the stallion backwards, and I heard him shout, "I come in peace," before we all crashed to earth in a tangle of flailing limbs.

Hooves pounded around us as the other Creeks swerved to avoid trampling their leader. I clung to Red Eagle's braids, scrabbling closer as he and Davy thrashed about in the grass. The closest Indians shrieked in alarm. Arrows were nocked and war clubs raised. I drew my tomahawk, desperate to make my kill.

"Stop!" Davy's shout rang above the hubbub. He sat on Red Eagle's chest, his knife tickling the war chief's throat. "Stop your fussin', and listen!"

The warriors hesitated. Red Eagle glared up at Davy with raw fury. Close up, he had wide black eyes, a firm-set mouth and a forehead with a fine collection of worry lines.

An Indian shouted in his own tongue and pointed ahead through the woods. Everyone looked. The gap in the volunteers' line was gone. The Creeks now knew they'd been tricked.

"There's been enough killin'," Davy told them. "Lay down your arms, and we'll talk treaty."

Several warriors growled. Evidently a good number of the heathens spoke English. Red Eagle laughed. "Your treaties mean nothing. Kill me now and have done with it."

That was enough for me. "Gladly," I said, and swung my tomahawk at Red Eagle's head.

"No!" Davy twisted, meeting my blade with his own, and sparks flashed between us.

Free of Davy's grip, Red Eagle threw him aside and made to rise. My last chance slipping away, I lunged for Red Eagle, but Davy grabbed my arm, squeezed, and the tomahawk fell. I aimed a fist at Davy's chin, but he dodged, caught my arm and threw me sprawling onto my back. In an instant he was upon me, pinning my arms.

The Red Sticks must have thought us the two craziest white men on earth. Several moved closer, spears lowered and clubs raised. Red Eagle snapped a command, and no one moved as he climbed to his feet.

Davy said, "I spoke truth, Red Eagle. Ain't nobody else has to die."

For a moment, the murderous savage seemed to consider the idea. But a rifle barked, then another, and two warriors plunged from their horses. A band of Mounted Volunteers came pounding toward us. Davy's friends had abandoned their line and ridden to our rescue.

Shouting commands, Red Eagle leaped astride the black stallion. A great host of warriors came thundering from the clearing, then split ranks, crashing left and right into the woods to veer around the volunteers. Red Eagle grinned, made a mocking by-your-leave gesture to Davy, and joined them.

Davy's friends reined up around us, and when he finally let me up I saw the mass of Indians galloping through the gap in the volunteers' line. The stunned Tennesseans dropped more than a few with their rifles, but it was far too late.

Red Eagle and his army had escaped.

"I've recalculated my opinion of you," Davy said. "You're brave *and* foolish."

GENERAL JACKSON'S BASE of operations, "Fort" Strother, was merely a collection of tents along the Coosa River.

Davy and I stood rigid in the command tent as the general marched back and forth, his mane of sandy-red hair giving him the appearance of a lean and hungry lion. His uniform was all brass buttons and gold braid and his bearing ramrod straight.

I'd seen him from a distance, and there'd been a good many caricatures in the Philadelphia papers, but this was our first meeting. He was tall, with a high forehead and a long, horsey face. He had a nose like a knife-blade and a blunt protruding chin, both designed for poking into other people's business. His deep-set eyes spit blue fire.

"By all accounts," the general said, "Red Eagle had well over a thousand hostiles at Talladega. Thanks to my planning, we had them completely surrounded and stood a fair chance of exterminating them all. Instead, you two rockheaded idiots turned Red Eagle and seven hundred of his warriors loose to commit further atrocities."

I was here against my will, escorted the thirty miles from Talladega with my hands tied behind my back. Displeased as I was, the soldiers were no happier. Jackson had promised food and blankets, but supplies had yet to arrive from Tennessee. The men were starving, the night was cold, and few had thought to bring winter clothing.

Jackson's left arm was in a sling, but army scuttlebutt said the injury had nothing to do with Indian fighting. Word was he'd been shot on a Nashville street in an argument over his wife's honor. Even in Philadelphia it was common gossip he'd married a woman not yet divorced from her previous husband. The sordid affair had damaged his political career, and he'd already killed one of his wife's detractors in a duel.

Jackson's jaw twitched. "For your interference, I should have you both shot."

"I'm powerful sorry, Gen'ral, but you can't do that."

Jackson bristled like a rooster. "Spare me your excuses, *Private* Crockett. I've heard all about your plan to capture Red Eagle. It was both ill-advised and insubordinate."

"That ain't it, Gen'ral. I'm just sayin' you can't shoot us both."

"Any why, pray tell, can't I?"

"On account of Penn here ain't under your command. He ain't even a volunteer."

Jackson's mouth opened and snapped shut. He shifted his scorn to me. "Is that true, McCoy? You are not enlisted in this army?"

I set my jaw and nodded.

"Then what in blue blazes were you doing in the middle of my battlefield?"

"That's simple, General. I was trying to kill Red Eagle."

Jackson blinked. "A laudable goal, I admit. But not when you interfere with the plans of your superiors."

"Pardon, Gen'ral, but you ain't exactly his—"

"Shut up, Crockett! Now tell me, *Mr.* McCoy, why your claim on that red devil's head should take precedence over mine."

I chewed my lip. It was none of his business. None of anybody's. But if I said nothing, I'd likely be under military arrest. I hung my head, fighting to keep my emotions in check. "Four months ago, my folks bought land down on the Alabama River. My father had been a gunsmith up in Philadelphia, and figured there'd be plenty of call for his trade here in the South. He brought along my mother, my young sister Maggie, and me."

"Mr. McCoy, I don't want a family history, I want to know—"

"I'm getting to it, General, in my own way." My mouth tasted of bile. "When the Creeks started killing one another I was up north gathering more of our belongings. So my parents and sister took their new neighbors' advice and headed for cover." My voice sounded brittle. "The cover they chose was Fort Mims."

Davy sucked in his breath. "Sweet Jesus."

Jackson's expression did not change. I saw now why Davy called him Old Hickory-face.

Fort Mims was no longer just the name of a place. It had become a curse and a rallying cry for civilized men across the southern frontier. When the young bucks of the Creek tribe had gone mad and began butchering their own people, inno-cent settlers and their families sought refuge in an old stockade near the border of Spanish Florida. The gates had not yet closed behind them when Red Eagle's warriors streamed in, leaving hundreds of charred and mutilated bodies amid the smoking ruins. News of the massacre flared through the South, prompt-ing politicians like Jackson to form armies, and settlers like Davy to volunteer. And men like me, who had lost everything, to seek their own private vengeance.

Jackson still stared at me. He seemed to want something more.

I got control of my voice and looked him straight in the eye. "When I went to recover the bodies, there was scarcely enough to bury."

The silence in the tent was oppressive. Jackson stood for a full minute before speaking.

"What you fools fail to appreciate is that the eyes of the nation are upon us here. I've just received word that the British have been driven from Detroit. That rascal Tecumseh is dead, and his Indian confederation is finished. The Red Sticks are the last obstacle preventing the effective prosecution of the war against Great Britain. If not for your interference, we'd have nipped this Creek uprising in the bud and been hailed as heroes."

When Davy opened his mouth to comment, Jackson scowled him down.

"Private Crockett, I'm sending you on a scouting mission. You are to locate Red Eagle and report back so that I may lead my army against him. You are under no circumstances to attempt his capture or to negotiate treaties." He fixed Davy with an icy stare. "Do I make myself clear?"

"You bet, Gen'ral. Sir."

"Understand me well, Crockett. I would execute you, but I'm told you're uncommonly popular with the men, and the last thing I need is a mutiny on my hands. But if you ever disobey me again, I will deal with you without hesitation."

Davy nodded, hiding a grin.

"As for you, McCoy, I don't give a hoot in Hell's hollow where you go, as long as you stay out of my way." His eyes met mine. "You have my condolences, but not my approval." For a moment, I almost saw the man inside, but he turned quickly away, showing us his back. "Now get out of my sight, before I shoot you both myself."

CHAPTER 2

"That's no ordinary Indian."

THE ROAR OF the bear startled me out of a nap. I was up on one knee in a flash, musket cocked and ready. The roar sounded again, throaty and plaintive and shockingly close. It came from a tangle of holly bushes not more than twenty feet to my left.

"Davy!" I whispered. "We got a big one. Where are you?"

"Here."

Squinting, I still couldn't spot him until he waved a hand. He lay prone in the scrub grass ten feet to my right, his stained buckskins and coonskin cap making him nearly invisible. Motioning me down, he pointed off across the small creek fifty yards away. His rifle, too, pointed in that direction, nowhere near the location of the bear.

"You lost your senses?" I jabbed a thumb at the holly thicket. "That beast could eat me alive."

Davy eyes twinkled.

A new voice issued from the holly thicket, that of a young girl. "Don't you fret none, Penn McCoy. I don't find you at all appetizing."

I rose to my knees, about to give Davy a piece of my mind, but he again motioned me down and pointed across the river. Instead of dropping flat, I scuttled to his side behind the huckleberry bush. "My fist and your jaw have things to discuss."

"That can wait," he whispered. "And button your lip. There's a big he-bear in those woods yonder, and I'm fixin' to lure him out."

"So you found some little gal to hide in that thicket and growl? What if you miss, and he gets her?"

Davy gave me a pitying look. "There ain't no gal, Penn. And no bear in the thicket. I was throwin' my voice." When I just stared, he added, "A trick I learnt from a Cherokee medicine man."

Davy chuckled to himself, and my face burned. I didn't like playing the fool. Besides, I was already peeved at him. Instead of hunting Red Eagle as ordered, he'd wasted the past three days hunting bears. The other volunteers warned me it would be like this. Once Davy Crockett made up his mind to do a thing, they said, no power on earth could turn him around.

Came another roar, this time from across the creek, with plenty of anger in it. Bushes quaked, branches snapped, and onto the bank burst a great black bear, snarling like a catamount.

"For a fellow going courting," I said, "he looks none too sociable."

Davy's cheeks grew redder than usual. "'Pears I had my boot on the wrong foot. She ain't a feller. She's a lady-bear who don't welcome the competition. Still, she's table meat, and we got hungry soldiers back at camp." He raised his rifle and eased the hammer back.

And I heard something, or more rightly felt and heard it at the same time. The pound of distant hoofbeats. Lots of hoofbeats.

Davy'd heard them too. With a sad shake of his head, he withdrew his rifle. Keeping out of sight of the bear, we ran half-bent thirty yards to a stand of gum trees overlooking a shallow valley. Davy peered intently toward the northeast, but all I saw were scarlet and gold treetops, and the distant slopes of Mount Cheaha, the highest peak south of the Appalachians. A cool wind blew up the valley, and I knew the first frost was not many weeks away.

Well behind us, the she-bear crossed the stream and circled the holly thicket, looking befuddled. I didn't blame her. I felt the same way. After a good deal of sniffing she gave a parting growl and lumbered off into the woods.

The pounding hooves were louder now, though I still saw no riders. Davy pointed, and I caught movement a good quarter mile away. A small party of horsemen came boiling over a rise and plunged into the valley. They weren't heading towards us after all, but following a wagon road angling roughly north to south. If they held to the road, they'd pass within five hundred yards of us.

I counted only a dozen riders, surprising for all the noise they made. But a moment later a larger party burst over the rise, galloping in the wake of the first.

"What do you make of it?"

"Red Sticks," he said without hesitation. "Chasin' a troop of militia."

"You can tell that from here?"

Davy made no answer, and after another minute things came into focus. Most of the first party wore dark green uniforms, while their pursuers were naked but for paint and feathers. The redskins numbered at least forty.

My blood raced. If Red Eagle was with that group, I'd have another chance to avenge my family.

"Come on," I said, starting for my horse. "Let's kill some heathens."

"If you're itchin' to commit suicide," Davy said, "there's a heap o' easier ways to do it."

"So you'd let them slaughter those soldiers, like they did my family?"

The militiamen were now passing as close as they were going to get. They leaned forward, hastening their horses, but it wouldn't be long before the Indians ran them to ground.

Davy raised his rifle. It was long, nearly as long as he was tall, but he handled it like an extension of his body. He'd even given it a name. *Betsy*.

The Indians were nearing their closest approach, still better than five hundred yards away. A full two lengths ahead of the others rode a light-skinned, fair-haired warrior on a huge black stallion. Red Eagle.

Davy cocked his hammer. He couldn't hope to hit anything at this distance. Maybe he planned to attract their attention and lure them away from the militia. Betsy barked. I waved the smoke away with my hat and gasped as the black stallion crumpled, sending Red Eagle flying. As he struck the dirt, the others reined their ponies, scanning the slopes for the shooter. Red Eagle was quickly up, but the militia kept riding and was soon lost from sight.

"A hell of a shot," I said, which was faint praise. I'd been to many a shooting match, but never seen anything like this. "Too bad you missed."

"Betsy don't miss."

"You were aiming for the horse? What kind of Indian fighter are you?"

"The kind who's tired of killin'," he said. "I learned somethin' 'bout myself at Tallushatchee, somethin' I wish I hadn't."

I'd heard about Tallushatchee. In my short time in the South, I'd heard little else. A week before the battle at Talladega, while I was busy stalking Red Eagle, Davy and the Tennesseans had surrounded and killed close to two hundred hostile Creeks.

"You sent a lot of savages to Hell," I said. "Isn't that what this war's all about?"

"No," Davy said, "it ain't. But for a while there at Tallushatchee, I plumb forgot that." He paused, not meeting my eye, and his cheek began to twitch. "My cousin Caleb was there. Not yet fifteen, and a lad so likable he could make a possum sit up and grin. He was right at my shoulder when a arrow took him through the eye. Don't recall much after that, 'cept Old Betsy kept buckin' in my hands, and Injuns kept dyin', but it was like someone else was squeezin' the trigger. Women and children died there, Penn, and I can't say but what I had a hand in it."

I didn't know what to say to that.

"Ma always said I had a devil inside me, an' I'm commencin' to think she was right."

"All mothers say that," I told him. "Look, if you've no stomach for killing redskins, what in the world are you doing here?"

Davy faced me. His eyes were dull, their normal twinkle gone. "I joined up with Jackson's army to do so some good, and I hope I done it. Now I'm just yearnin' to get back to my wife and young'uns before I'm forced to take another human life."

This declaration left me speechless. He had a home and a family who loved him, but was too squeamish to fight for them. I'd have fought to the last drop of blood for Maggie and my parents, if I'd only had the chance.

Down in the valley, Red Eagle mounted one of his warriors' horses while the displaced man hopped on behind a companion. Wheeling his new pony to face us, Red Eagle shaded his eyes and peered straight up the slope to where we stood.

"He's found us. How is that possible?"

"That's no ordinary Indian," Davy said. "And no ordinary man."

The other warriors pointed angrily in our direction, anxious to charge.

I longed for my father's longrifle, lost at Talladega. With that gun I'd have plugged three of those savages before they reached us. The musket I carried now was so worthless I might as well throw rocks.

"Appears we'll get that fight," I said, "whether you like it or not."

Davy shook his head. "Not just now. Red Eagle's hot-footin' it after them militiamen. And he'll no doubt catch 'em."

I opened my mouth to argue, but he was right. The band was already streaming off to the south. Disappointment washed over me. Another opportunity lost.

Davy said, "Reckon I have somethin' to report to Old Hickory-face now."

"Fine. Give him my regards." I felt more empty than ever. Despite Davy's strange aversion to killing Indians, I'd come to enjoy his company and rely on his skill as a woodsman. Pursuing Red Eagle on my own would be a much tougher chore.

Shouldering my rifle, I trudged toward the stand of maples where we'd left the horses. Once mounted, I turned my chestnut south after the Creeks.

Davy called, "Wait, Penn. Somethin' you oughta see."

Mounting his dun, Davy rode down the slope into the valley, where the black stallion still lay on the ground. I urged my mare forward. "Don't tell me you mean to haul that horsemeat back to camp."

"In a manner of speakin'." And without further explanation, he kicked his horse into a run.

I followed, cursing under my breath. Anxious as I was to be after Red Eagle, when Davy asked me to do a thing I felt strangely compelled to comply.

The stallion lay sprawled in the dirt. Davy knelt next to him, and I pulled up short. If he was set on butchering that animal, he could damn well do it alone. But instead of drawing a knife, he opened his canteen, poured water into his palm and held it under the stallion's nose.

This was pure foolishness. Offering water to a dead horse was an odd ritual, even for Davy.

I heard a snort. The stallion's body rippled from neck to rump and his chest began to heave. Davy spoke, too soft for me to hear, but his tone was soothing. Finally the horse flipped up his head, got legs under him and climbed to full height, shaking like a wet dog.

I stared, dumbfounded. After making an impossible rifle shot, Davy had done himself one better by raising a horse from the dead. I felt a prickling along my spine.

"Told you Betsy don't miss," he said. "The ball just creased his skull."

"Sure," I said, my mouth dry. "I knew that all along."

I slipped off my mare and approached. The stallion's eyes were bright and expressive, betokening unusual intelligence. His jet-black coat was shiny as a lake under a full moon, and a splash of white on his forehead, half the size of a hand, formed the rough shape of an arrowhead. Fastened to his mane with strips of rawhide was a long eagle feather. I almost pitied Red Eagle for losing him. Almost.

"Well," I said, "it's time we parted ways."

Davy seemed not to hear. He took hold of the stallion's reins and gazed off toward a clump of trees set back from the road. "You can come on out now," he called. "We ain't gonna bite you."

I'd no idea who he was talking to, and wasn't sure he did either. But he stood waiting, and eventually a thin young man leading a silver-gray horse emerged from the trees.

The lad's striped trousers and vest were too form-fitting to be store-bought, and his white shirt, though soiled, was obviously of silk. Pale yellow hair curled beneath the brim of his beaver hat. Compared to me in torn woolens and Davy in soiled buckskins, he was the very picture of sophistication. His horse, while smaller than the black stallion, was equally well bred and adorned with a silver-mounted saddle.

"I feared at first you gentlemen might be Indians," the young man said. "Was it you who shot Arrow?"

I said, "Arrow?"

Davy said, "You was ridin' with the militia. Why ain't you still?"

Close up, the lad's jaw looked fragile and his eyes pale. He was likely no more than sixteen. "Once we were out of sight of our pursuers, I slipped into the trees, waiting for them to pass. Then I spotted you two and worked my way back to investigate. I mean to rescue my sister, even if Captain Zane does not."

I said again, "Arrow?"

"That is Arrow." He pointed at the black stallion. "A beautiful creature, is he not?"

"He belongs to Red Eagle," I said. "How do you know his name?"

Davy said, "Who might you be? What's this about a sister? And who's this Cap'n Zane?"

The young man blinked. "So many questions. I shall endeavor to address them all. My name is Nathan Truitt. My father is Colonel Thaddeus Truitt, of whom you may have heard. Three weeks ago a party of Creeks led by Billy Weatherford invaded our plantation and kidnapped my sister Lacy. Billy was riding Arrow here, as he always does. Soon after, Father sent Captain Zane and his men to search for her."

I took this in. I had indeed heard of Thaddeus Truitt. He'd ridden with Francis Marion in the War of Independence and was now one of the richest planters in the South.

"By Billy Weatherford," Davy said, looking at me, "he means Red Eagle."

Nathan nodded. "That's one of his Indian names. The other is Truth Teller. He's hardly Indian at all, you know—just a fraction on his mother's side. Prior to this trouble he was our neighbor, and always kind to me. But for what he did to my sister, I have sworn to kill him with my own hands."

"You'll have to wait in line." I gazed again toward the south. If I left now, I might still catch those Red Sticks.

Davy said, "What'd you do to rile Weatherford's fur?"

Nathan shrugged. "Nothing at all. When Zane and his men failed to find Lacy, Father sent us to seek General Jackson's aid. A mile north of here we stumbled onto the war party and were forced to run for our lives. I am most grateful for your timely intervention."

Davy waved that aside. "I suspect the gen'ral will be right eager to help. I'll take you to him straightaway."

Nathan shook his head. "That will no longer be necessary."

Davy was about to mount his horse. He looked at Nathan sideways. "And why might that be?"

"Because now that I have located Billy Weatherford, I cannot risk losing him again. You two gentlemen must assist me in recovering my sister."

Davy said, "Didn't you get no schoolin' in numbers? If a dozen men weren't enough, what can three do?"

"You two are real fighters, not posers in uniform, like Zane's militia. We have merely to follow his trail and force him to release Lacy. That should prove easy to men as resourceful as I perceive you to be. I propose we set forth at once."

Davy laid a hand on Nathan's shoulder. "My apologies to your pa, for I've a tolerable lot of respect for him. But we need more men. Red Eagle won't release your sister on just our say so."

Nathan's eyes narrowed. He was not used to being refused. "If you will not assist me, I will rescue my sister alone. And General Jackson shall surely hear of your cowardice."

Davy tightened his grip on the lad's shoulder. "You can tell him to his face. 'Cause you're goin', even if I have to hogtie you."

Nathan and Davy glared at each other like a pair of bantam roosters.

I spoke up. "What about me? You going to hogtie me too?"

Both turned to stare.

"I had a sister too," I told Nathan, and that familiar ache began to swell in my stomach. "Her name was Maggie, and she was barely sixteen when Red Eagle attacked Fort Mims. My parents were there as well. Red Eagle has much to answer for."

Davy removed his cap, ran fingers through his shaggy hair and stared at the ground.

Nathan said, "My condolences, sir. I would be honored to know your name." He extended a hand.

I took it. He had a firm grip for a boy. "Pennsylvania McCoy, at your service. I'll go with you, even if Davy won't."

Davy shook his head. "I'm forced to admit," he said, "that

forty bloodthirsty Creeks won't stand a chance against you two
fire-breathers. I s'pose I'll have to tag along and beg you to be
merciful."

DAVY RODE POINT, leading the stallion Arrow. We'd
expected the big black to be headstrong, but he followed Davy
like a faithful dog. Nathan Truitt kept pace, proving himself a
fine horseman. His mount's coat shone like polished silver in the
sun, and we learned it was a thoroughbred raised in his father's
own racing stables.

After a mile or two the Creeks' tracks left the road, passing
within rifle shot of three cabins with smoking chimneys, and a
small plantation with horses in a stone corral. Nothing had been
molested. I couldn't figure it. In my experience, those two-legged
jackals never missed an opportunity to loot and burn.

We'd been riding close to two hours when we crossed a small
stream and stopped to water the horses.

"Red Eagle's still followin' the militia," Davy said, "but it's
mighty peculiar. He ain't just chasin' 'em, he's *huntin'* 'em." He
gave Nathan Truitt a keen look. "Why you s'pose that is?"

"Billy Weatherford's lost his wits. At least that's what Father
says. Six months ago Billy had a fine home, plenty of land and
plenty of friends—both Indian and otherwise. Those who know
him can hardly believe he's the same man."

I felt myself getting hot. "He was a savage six months ago,
wasn't he? If someone had shot him then, Fort Mims would
never have happened. Those five hundred innocents would still
be alive."

"And I would be home playing whist with Lacy," Nathan said.
"Your point has merit, Mr. McCoy. Perhaps we should never
have allowed the Creeks to live among us."

My respect for Nathan continued to grow. For a lad of gentle
breeding, he possessed a surprising amount of common sense.

Davy slid off his horse and knelt to fill his canteen. "No sense
frettin' over shoulda dones. Assumin' we ever catch up with them
varmints, what you aim to do about it?"

"Cut out Red Eagle's heart," I said.

"No," Nathan said. "Not until he releases my sister."

"Sure, that's what I meant," I said. Even though it wasn't.

"I was referrin'," Davy said, "to the matter of bumpin' up against forty Creek warriors and keepin' our hair on."

Nathan and I exchanged looks. I shrugged. Nathan said, "We'll deal with that when the time comes. Are we gaining on them?"

"Just the opposite." Davy nodded at the deep hoofprints where the savages had jumped the stream without allowing their horses to drink. "They're pushin' their ponies hard. Too hard. But they got to bed down eventually. Just now we got another problem." He flicked his eyes back the way we'd come. "Appears we're bein' follered."

"Can't be." I felt stung. "I've been keeping close watch."

Nathan peered back along our trail. "Who is it?"

"Someone mighty good," Davy said. "I only caught on a couple miles back."

I managed to swallow my pride. I'd yet to kill my first Indian, and was eager to start. "Some of Red Eagle's bucks? Let's set an ambush for them."

Davy handed me the reins to Arrow and his dun. "Wouldn't work." He pointed at a beech grove twenty yards off the road. "You two make camp over thataway. I'll slip back and see if I can catch 'em with their britches flappin'."

Nathan frowned. "You said Red Eagle was pulling away from us. Can we afford to fall farther behind?"

"If those are hostiles on our tail, we can't afford not to."

IT WAS CHILLY in the shade of the beeches. I dearly hoped this war would be over before winter arrived. When we had a small fire going, I got fixings from my pack and started coffee boiling.

"I'd like to meet your father someday," I told Nathan. "I've heard he's a real ring-tailed roarer."

"He was once. When he had two legs." Nathan drew an oil-wrapped packet from his vest and extracted a thin cigar. He offered me one, which I declined. "Father was fox-hunting three summers ago when his horse stepped into a gopher hole. He was pinned, and his right leg turned yellow as lemon custard. When they sawed off his leg, I swear they took a piece of his soul along with it."

I poured boiling coffee into a tin cup and handed it to Nathan. I'd met few rich people in my life, and felt kinship with none. Until now. Apparently great wealth was no proof against family hardship.

Nathan sipped at the coffee and sputtered. "What did you put in this, horse droppings?"

So much for kinship.

A retort was on my tongue when Davy reappeared and helped himself to coffee.

"Did you kill them?" Nathan asked.

Davy sniffed at his cup, grimaced, and poured it on the ground. "There's only one of 'em. Slipped away afore I got a good look."

I squinted at him. "Then why do you look so all-fired happy?"

"I admire a worthy opponent," he said. "Appears I got one."

CHAPTER 3

"I will surely blow your brains out."

THREE HOURS LATER, we crouched on a gentle rise under a stand of white oaks, a bed of acorns at our feet. The sun was a red glow on the horizon, while a three-quarter moon peered down from the darkening sky. A good ways to the south, in a bend of the Coosa River, a small fire flickered through the trees. Davy professed to see Red Eagle's men moving about before the fire, but I barely saw flames.

"What's the plan?" Nathan's voice was eager.

"Penn and me will sidle up there and inconvenience two of them lookouts. Other two are on the far side of camp, so they don't signify."

"You're going to kill them?"

Davy smacked his palm with the blunt end of a stone tomahawk. "Not if we can help it."

Speak for yourself, I thought, but said nothing.

"With the lookouts nappin', we'll scatter the horses. Then while the Injuns are out chasin' 'em, we'll take a run through the camp, see if Lacy's there."

"How? You don't even know what she looks like."

"If there's more'n one white gal held captive, we'll fetch 'em all. That do?"

"I'm going with you." Nathan drew a silver-chased pistol from his belt.

Davy shook his head. "This won't be no frolic. You stay here and guard the horses. I expect we'll need 'em in a hurry."

"I won't. Lacy's *my* sister. I should take the biggest risk."

"Who says you ain't? Whoever's been doggin' us is still out there, you know."

Nathan's eyes grew large in the moonlight.

"Just keep your wits about you, and you'll be fine as frog hair. Trust me."

Nathan nodded. He really did trust Davy, and I'll be hanged if I didn't too.

IT WAS BLACK as pitch under the trees, and Davy moved so silently I kept losing track of him. Every few moments I had to stop, bewildered, and wait for a *pssst* to beckon me onward.

A hundred yards from camp, Davy stopped me under a paw paw tree. This close, I saw their fires quite clearly. A few dark shapes moved about the camp, but most of the Creeks were apparently sleeping.

"I'll take the one watchin' the horses." Davy pointed to a line of trees along the river. "Yours is purt' near dead ahead, restin' beneath that gum tree. 'Stead of mindin' to business, he's gazin' up at the moon. Should be easy as pie."

"Sure," I said, drawing the tomahawk I'd acquired at Talladega. "Pie."

"Once them bucks go chasin' their ponies, you drift into camp from the left. I'll start on the right and meet you somewhere in the middle." Then he was gone.

I reversed the weapon in my hand, making the sharp edge ready. It was time these snakes starting paying for Maggie and my folks.

I crept forward, my heart thundering. Every scrape of dirt and rustle of leaf seemed loud as the crack of doom. I began to fear I'd passed my quarry by when something moved under my boot. My leg went one way and my body another, the air burst from my lungs, and next thing I knew I lay sideways on the ground with my arms pinned behind me. My tomahawk was gone.

I kicked backwards, putting every ounce of fear and frustration into it, and heard a grunt. My right arm popped free. I twisted onto my stomach, got my knees under me, and found my opponent straddling me like a horse. I snapped my head back. My skull connected with something equally hard, producing a gasp.

Scrambling up, I whipped the knife from my belt. The Indian sprang up too, half-bent and growling. Unlike the near-naked braves I'd seen on horseback, this one wore a loose buckskin shirt and breeches. One evil eye glared through a tangle of dark hair.

I lunged with the knife, hoping to end the contest quickly, but a strong hand caught my wrist. The Indian dove forward and sank sharp teeth into my hand. The knife fell. I let out a silent scream, fearful of waking the entire camp. Angry now, I put a bear hug on him and squeezed, aiming to crack him like a nut. He squirmed. He was smaller than me, but wiry, and had the strength of a wildcat.

Squeezing harder, I lifted him off his feet and his body went slack. Relieved, I loosened my grip. And got a head butt smack in the nose. I'd never felt such pain. My arms fell away and he kicked my feet out from under me, toppling me onto my back.

He commenced to kick my ribs and stomp my brisket. I got hold of his foot, and he hopped about trying to free himself, but I yanked him down on top of me. Hands clawed at my windpipe. I released the foot and returned the favor. We were busy choking the life from one another when I heard Davy's voice.

"Tarnation, Penn, you raised more fuss than a weasel in a henhouse. In another minute them Red Sticks'll be on us like hornets."

Shouts in the distance told me he was right. I shook the Indian by the neck. "What about him? Aren't we going to kill him?"

Davy grabbed my elbow, along with that of the Indian's, and dragged us to our feet. He parted the savage's hair and pulled it back, exposing a face in the moonlight. "You mean *her*?"

Beneath the dirt I beheld a delicate chin, full red lips and a dainty nose, now bleeding freely. And beneath the buckskin shirt heaved a womanly bosom. I'd been wrestling a girl. I jerked my hands from her throat.

"She ain't one of them," Davy said, "or she'd have screamed for help afore now. Time we all vamoosed."

Tasting blood, I wiped at my face. My hand came away wet.

The shouts from the camp were louder. Feet trampled the brush. Needing no further encouragement, I snatched up my fallen tomahawk and bolted for where we'd left Nathan and the horses. Footsteps thumped close behind me, and I assumed it was Davy until I chanced a look. That Indian girl was staying with me stride for stride.

Squeals and snorts filled the night air—the unmistakable sounds of a razorback hog—then a crackling of brush, receding off toward the river. A coarse voice laughed and others joined in, full and hearty. I slowed our pace, treading easier. I had to smile. The Indians had blamed our racket on the hog. That beast had come along just in time, as if guided by the hand of Providence.

Reaching the white oaks, we found Nathan bug-eyed with worry.

"What happened? Where's Davy? Who's that with you? Did you find Lacy?"

"Plenty—don't know—a redskin hellcat—and no," I replied in the order asked. "We're leaving. Now." And got a ferocious slap to the back of my head. I spun, made a grab for the girl, and missed.

"Go if you like, coward," she said in perfect English. "I go nowhere until Red Eagle is dead."

"Appears you two got somethin' in common." Davy was suddenly between us. "You oughta kiss and make up."

My cheeks burned. "What happened to you? Get chased off by that hog?"

Davy grinned. "Shucks, Penn, I *was* that hog."

THE GIRL'S NAME was Little Fawn. Her dark eyes shone in the moonlight, and once she'd wiped some of the dirt from her face, her skin was clear and smooth. Her hair was long, shiny, and bound with a beaded leather band. Around her slim neck hung a leather cord with a white-tufted deer tail. Taken altogether, she had a wild sort of beauty, and it made me oddly uncomfortable. She denied following us. She'd been trailing Red Eagle, she claimed, and we just got in her way.

The girl focused all her attention on Davy, and her voice sweetened when she addressed him. After less than an hour in his presence, she'd already set her cap for him. Nathan Truitt, meanwhile, blinked at Little Fawn like a love-starved puppy. It was downright disgusting.

At Davy's urging, we'd moved a good ways back from the camp to regroup. I insisted we sit in a patch of moonlight. If Little Fawn turned back into a wildcat, I wanted to be ready. Davy took a loaded pistol from her belt, along with an evil-looking butcher knife, but refused to search her person. He also refused to let me bind her, which rankled greatly. After all, I knew her considerably better than he.

"You're treating her like a woman," I complained, "not an Indian."

"She's a human bein' first, Penn. Then a woman. Just 'cause she's Creek don't make her our enemy."

What about my broken nose, I wanted to say, *and the claw marks on my neck?* Instead, I said, "In case you forgot, we're at war with the Creeks."

"Not with all of 'em. That white deer tail marks her as a friendly."

"Or asks us to think so. If you're really on our side," I said to the girl, "why'd you jump me back there?"

"I did not jump you, you stumblefooted oaf. You stepped on me. And when you broke my nose, I lost my temper." Her nose no longer bled, but it did have a slight kink in it. Every now and then she touched it, winced, and returned the hand to her lap. I wanted to touch my nose too, but refused to give her the satisfaction.

Davy's assertion that only half the Creeks were on the warpath was probably right, but that didn't make him right about Little Fawn.

The whole Creek War thing was so complicated it made my head hurt. As I understood it, the conflict started as a civil war within the tribe. The bunch calling themselves Red Sticks had become ungrateful for all the courtesy white settlers had shown them, and beat the drums for war. Other Creeks, having prospered through farming or commerce, resisted this return to savagery. But it was still blessed hard to tell one side from the other.

Davy removed his cap and scratched his head. "I'll beg you to forgive Penn here," he told the girl. "He had kin at Fort Mims."

Caught off-guard, it was like being kicked in the stomach by a mule.

Little Fawn went stiff. After a moment she turned to me, her eyes soft and dewy. I crossed my arms over my chest and scowled.

"You have my deepest sympathy, Mr. Penn. My family was butchered there as well. That is why I have sworn to kill Red Eagle. For that, and other crimes committed against my blood."

I swallowed, empty of words.

Davy said, "How long you been shadowin' Red Eagle?"

"Nearly a week. I watch and await my moment. It will come. I will kill him slowly, so that he may know the pain he has caused."

"You must not," Nathan Truitt said. "Not until we've questioned him. He holds my sister captive, and we must learn where."

Little Fawn seemed to notice him for the first time. "You are the son of Thaddeus Truitt. Your sister is the one called Lacy."

Nathan sat bolt upright. "You've seen her?"

"Only near your home, before this trouble began. My family and I often camped on Billy Weatherford's fields, and saw you and your sister ride by. She is quite lovely."

"But I never saw you there," Nathan blurted.

"We were Indians camped in the fields. Why should you?" When Nathan hung his head, she continued. "As to your sister, I have watched Red Eagle's camp for several nights. I have seen no women, and none ride with them by day. If he has her, she is elsewhere."

I forced a hard edge into my voice. "You were one of Red Eagle's tribe. You must know where he keeps his women."

Nathan's hand flashed to the pearl-handled knife at his belt. "Lacy is not *his woman*."

I shrugged.

Little Fawn pursed her lips. "Before the attack on Fort Mims, Billy Weatherford married my cousin Sopath. I was proud, for I considered him a fine man. Now I hear she is with child, but is nowhere to be found. No, Mr. Penn, I do not know where he keeps his women."

Davy slapped his knee. "Then there's only one thing to do. We'll ask ol' Red Eagle himself."

LITTLE FAWN AND I lay flat on our bellies fifty yards north of the Creek camp. Though within arm's reach of me, she was nearly invisible in the grass.

"Can you see him?"

"Of course," she hissed. "Can't you?"

I swear I heard her snicker. Could she really see Davy, or was she just trying to annoy me? Annoying me was something she was uncommonly good at.

I peered at an ancient live oak near the edge of camp. Its thick branches spread out as much as sixty feet, some directly over the sleeping Creeks. On one of those branches, if things went according to plan, Davy would be in position above Red Eagle.

Little Fawn had sparked the idea, claiming she'd seen him spread his furs and blankets beneath that live oak. Davy'd got that devilish gleam in his eye and asked Nathan to fetch the eagle feather we'd found fastened to Arrow's mane. The feather was ordinary enough, but the quill was decorated with red and black beadwork, and both Nathan and Little Fawn swore they'd seen it on the stallion in times past. It was a thing Red Eagle could not fail to recognize.

Davy's plan was to sneak past the lookouts and sleeping Indians, climb the live oak, and crawl out on the branch above him. Employing a horsehair fishing line fashioned by Little Fawn, he would lower the feather to within inches of Red Eagle's face and commence to tickle his nose. Once Red Eagle awoke, Davy would wait until he'd again closed his eyes, drop the feather at his side and make a silent retreat.

Then, assuming that went well, it all depended on Red Eagle acting precisely as Davy expected.

I was by no means pleased with this addlepated scheme, but Little Fawn and Nathan Truitt—both familiar with Red Eagle's character—had declared it sound.

Still, a sense of foreboding clawed at my vitals. At any moment, I expected a shout of discovery, followed by the bloodthirsty cries of forty wild Indians. That's why Little Fawn and I were here. At the first sign of trouble we were to raise a ruckus, creating a distraction so Davy could escape.

And while that was worrisome enough, I was far from convinced the girl could be trusted. Even if she'd spoken true about Red Eagle's location, she might still let out a whoop and bring the whole band down upon us.

"What's he doing now?"

"Waiting, Stumblefoot, and keeping silent. As should you."

I bristled. The nickname was less than endearing.

And waiting was becoming increasingly difficult, as I seemed to have half the insects in the territory climbing up my sleeves and trouser legs. I needed to scratch something fierce, but dreaded a fresh helping of derision from the girl.

To make matters worse, we were just downwind from a patch of moonflowers. They'd been my sister Maggie's favorite, and the heady fragrance brought me torment. I concentrated doubly hard on my desire to kill redskins.

"He's done it," Little Fawn said, admiration thick as honey in her voice.

Moments later, we heard the distant whinny of a horse. Having grown accustomed to the voice of the stallion Arrow, I'd have sworn it was his and no other's. But this, too, was part of Davy's plan. This meant he'd made his way clear, and now imitated the call of the stallion in hopes of summoning the chief to investigate.

We waited, ears perked for the slightest sound. After another minute Davy whinnied again, slightly louder. The call was haunting, as if carried on the wind. It came from north of camp, where a rise of ground stood bathed in pale moonlight.

"It worked," Little Fawn whispered. "Red Eagle is taking the bait."

Straining my eyes, I saw movement in the shadows beneath the live oak. I hoped she was right.

The "stallion" called again. Little Fawn and I looked to the moonlit hill, and right on cue Red Eagle's horse came prancing into view. Bathed in the moon's rays, Arrow's black coat glistened with a ghostly aura. Even I, knowing the animal to be flesh and blood, felt icy fingers running up my spine.

Arrow reached the top and reared up, hooves flashing. The breath from his nostrils looked like smoke in the cold night air. Nathan Truitt, guiding the horse from the other side of the hill, had played his part to perfection.

The hoot of a great horned owl drifted toward us. That was Davy, signaling that Red Eagle had left the camp.

"Time to go," I said. But Little Fawn was already up, darting toward a stand of elms just this side of the hill. Like her, I crouched low and ran a zigzag pattern, keeping to the shadows. My boots sounded loud in the grass, but I heard not a rustle from the girl speeding away from me.

My path took me gradually up the rise. I soon caught sight

of Red Eagle, striding tall and bare-chested, red-blond braids trailing over his broad shoulders. In his right hand was Arrow's eagle feather, and fastened in his hair was one that might have been its twin. He wore only a buckskin breechcloth and leggings, but showed no sign of being cold. His expression was reverent as he watched the stallion on the hill. I slowed my pace, fearful of attracting his attention, though at the moment I suspected a herd of buffalo could have traipsed past and escaped his notice.

The closer I got to Red Eagle, the hotter my blood flowed. Here was the murderer of my family, ripe for the killing. The pistol Davy'd loaned me was primed and ready. One well-aimed shot, and Red Eagle would bring no more sorrow to the territory. Even as I fought the urge, my hand drew the gun. My thumb twitched on the hammer. But I thought of Nathan Truitt, and hesitated. My own dear sister was beyond help, but his might still be saved. Fighting every natural instinct, I forced the pistol back into my belt.

Reaching the elms, I leaned against a trunk, my heart pounding. Though I'd seen Little Fawn enter the trees ahead of me, there was no sign of her. Neither did I see Davy, who had promised to meet us here. I was about to call out when a strong hand gripped my arm, and Davy appeared beside me, a finger pressed to his lips. I held my breath as Red Eagle passed within a dozen feet, heedless to all but the stallion.

The elms now stood between Red Eagle and anyone watching from the camp below. Motioning me to stay put, Davy slipped from the trees and flitted in the big savage's wake. His tomahawk rose for a knockout blow.

Quick as a rattlesnake, Red Eagle spun and caught Davy's wrist in his left hand. The tomahawk fell to the grass. As Davy struggled, Red Eagle reached for his throat, but Davy ducked under the arm, braced a foot against Red Eagle's leg and thrust himself away, bouncing to a wrestler's stance.

Davy was a good-sized man, all of six feet tall, but next to

Red Eagle he seemed a stripling. The Indian towered half a head above, and likely outweighed him by at least thirty pounds.

Davy gathered himself for another attack. Red Eagle simply stared, as if wondering whether this stubborn frontiersman was real or part of his vision. If he recognized Davy from our encounter at Talladega, he gave no sign.

Davy lowered his head like a bull. Red Eagle spread his arms, waiting.

Determined to help, I drew my tomahawk and was about to sally forth when Little Fawn spurted from the elms, running at Red Eagle from the side. She leveled her pistol, shouting something in Creek.

Red Eagle's head turned, his mouth gaping, just as Davy charged. Davy buried his head in Red Eagle's stomach, and the two went down in a tangle of flailing limbs.

I burst out of the trees, feeling foolish for having waited so long. While Little Fawn danced about seeking a clear shot, I pushed past her, gripping my tomahawk. I saw an opening and raised the weapon. *Blood for blood*, my father's voice roared in my head.

I sank to one knee, pinning Red Eagle's head to the ground, and brought the tomahawk flashing down. Then my mother's voice came: *Think of Lacy!* And almost of its own accord, the weapon turned in my hand and whacked Red Eagle with the flat of the blade. He grunted and struggled no more.

A DOUSING FROM my canteen brought Red Eagle back to life. His muscles heaved against the rope binding him to a black oak, and I feared he might break free, but eventually he gave up and glared at us, chewing his rawhide gag.

He dismissed me with the merest glance, but showed great surprise at seeing Little Fawn and utter bewilderment at the presence of Nathan Truitt. His inspection of Davy took longer. The anger in his eyes was mixed with frank curiosity. He then looked farther afield, apparently seeking his spirit horse, but

went unrewarded. Following instructions, Nathan had secured
Arrow with our own horses out of sight beyond the hill.

"We'd best hurry," Davy said. "He'll soon be missed."

Red Eagle grunted, clearly wanting the gag removed.

"Not just yet," Davy told him. "I ain't hankerin' to kill you,
despite the evil you done. But I can't say the same for my friends.
If you act reasonable-like, I'll do what I can for you."

I didn't like the sound of that. Judging by Little Fawn's growl,
she didn't either. Red Eagle arched his eyebrows. Nodding at
Nathan and Little Fawn, he made questioning grunts.

Little Fawn answered with a stream of Indian talk that nearly
singed Red Eagle's eyebrows. Nathan drew his fancy knife and
waved it under Red Eagle's nose. "What have you done with
my sister?"

Davy's hand shot out, gripping Nathan's wrist. He squeezed,
and the knife fell to the grass.

Red Eagle shrugged, feigning ignorance.

"If you don't tell us" I said, "you'll die right now." I judged
my distance. With three quick steps I could split his skull with
my tomahawk.

"Penn," Davy said. "No."

We locked eyes. And while we were so occupied, Little Fawn
darted between us, an upraised knife catching the starlight.

I reached for her and missed. Davy grasped her arms.

"Help me. Get that toadsticker away from her."

I wavered. This was my chance. But once again I heard my
mother. *Lacy! Lacy!* I wrapped one hand around Little Fawn's
wrist, straining to pry the knife loose with the other. She was
amazingly strong.

But we'd forgotten Nathan Truitt. While Davy and I struggled with the girl, Nathan pressed the barrel of his silver-chased
pistol against Red Eagle's temple. "When I remove this gag,"
he said, "you will swear to release Lacy. Otherwise I will surely
blow your brains out."

Davy said, "Nathan, don't! It's too late. His friends are comin' on the jump."

I wondered if that was true. I'd heard nothing but our own labored breathing.

"Choose, Billy." Nathan gripped the rawhide gag. "Lacy's freedom or death."

I groped for Little Fawn's knife, but my focus was on Nathan, fearful he'd rob me of my vengeance. From beyond the elms, feet tramped the earth, and a body crashed through the brush. Someone was coming fast.

"Tell me where she is!" Nathan tore the gag from Red Eagle's mouth. "Now!"

A painted Creek warrior with an old British musket hove into view, not five yards away. I released Little Fawn and tugged at my pistol.

The warrior took in the scene—Red Eagle tied to the tree, Nathan's gun at his head—and leveled his musket.

Red Eagle screamed a word in Creek. It might have been "Kill!" or it might have been "No!"

The warrior hesitated only a moment. Then his musket flamed and Nathan was blown aside, limp as a rag doll.

I felt sick. The pistol wobbled in my hand.

Davy cocked his gun, leveled it at the warrior's grinning face. His cheeks were flushed, his jaw twitching, but he seemed unable to fire.

I steadied my pistol and squeezed the trigger. The warrior's face vanished in a spray of blood.

More savages were storming up the hill. Davy scooped up Nathan, hoisting him over one shoulder. "The whole band'll be here in seconds. Back to the horses, now!"

I stood looking down at my first kill, my first taste of vengeance. I should have felt joy. Instead I felt nothing, nothing but the emptiness that was already mine. I turned to Red Eagle. I still had my tomahawk, and to finish him would be the work of a moment. But he didn't look so murderous now. He looked grief-stricken, a thing I could not account for. I heard Davy yell-ing, but still I wavered, until Little Fawn tugged at my sleeve.

"Come, Penn. Quickly. There will be another time."

Penn, not *Stumblefoot*. She was feeding me sugar, like she did Davy.

Snarling, I turned and ran with her to the horses. Davy had already draped Nathan over a saddle and was tying him down.

There would indeed be another time, I promised myself, promised my parents, and promised my sister. And glancing at Nathan Truitt, praying he still lived, I promised him as well.

CHAPTER 4

"Up jumped the devil."

DAVY KNEW MORE ways of avoiding pursuit than
I'd ever dreamed of, and Little Fawn knew more than
Davy. We splashed through stream beds and climbed rocky
crags, laying false trails until I was dizzy as a June bug. Nathan
Truitt, unable to support himself in the saddle, rode slumped
against Davy's chest, while I led the thoroughbred. By the break
of dawn, we were hidden in a canebrake along the edge of a
small creek.

The canebrake was like nothing I had ever seen. The wall of
great green stalks, each thick as a man's arm, soared twenty feet
into the sky, marching along the creek as far as the eye could
see. Little Fawn had steered us to this particular hidey-hole, cut
with axes quite recently by friendly Creeks seeking refuge from
the Red Sticks. The curving path into the brake was just wide
enough to admit our horses and the clearing inside was all but
invisible from without.

Davy had spoken only when necessary during our flight, and
not at all since our arrival. His shoulders were hunched and he
moved in fits and starts. I twice inquired if he was wounded, but
he said nothing and refused to meet my eye.

We lay Nathan Truitt gently on the ground, where Little
Fawn examined the gaping hole in his chest. She looked up,
eyes wet, and gave a small shake of her head.

"Penn," Nathan said between gasps, "Davy. Promise."

We knelt between the cut stalks on the damp earth. "I promise," I said. "Red Eagle will pay for this. For this and much more."

Nathan coughed, blood running from the corner of his mouth. "Save Lacy. Promise."

"We'll find her," Davy said, his voice brittle, "and fetch her safely home. I swear it on my sacred honor."

"As do I," I said.

From Nathan's nose and mouth came a long, slow hiss, accompanied by small red bubbles. Then he was still, staring up past the cane stalks into the pale sky. He had gone to join Maggie, and my folks, and so many others.

Without a word, Davy rose and strode into the narrow passage leading from the canebrake. He was immediately lost from view.

I passed my hand over Nathan's face, closing his eyes.

We *will* save Lacy, I told his departing spirit. And then, by God, we will make Red Eagle pay.

I felt a gentle hand on my shoulder. *Yes, we will,* said the voice of Little Fawn, but whether I heard it with my ears or with my heart I could not say.

THE DAY'S LIGHT had begun to fade when Little Fawn said, "We should bury him."

I studied the horizon in all directions. That Red Eagle's braves had not found us already made it likely they had given up and moved on to further deviltry. Davy had not returned, nor had we any idea when he might. The horses had long since gnawed what little grass the confined space had to offer, and were growing restless. As was I. And try as I might, I found no reason to disagree with Little Fawn.

So, draping Nathan's body over the saddle of his thoroughbred, we led the horses through the passage of cut stalks to the grassy bank of the creek. Just across the trickling water an ancient longleaf pine overlooked a small clearing. It seemed such a natural resting place that Little Fawn and I merely exchanged nods and set to work.

The earth was rocky and hard, but Little Fawn found two lengths of cut cane whose sharp, hollow edges made good shovels.

"Your friend Davy is an unusual man," she said after a time. "Is he a chief among your people?"

I bit back a retort. After the way she'd been shining up to him, I'd expected her to broach the subject. I resolved not to make it easy for her.

"No," I said, and kept digging. We had now cleared away perhaps a foot of the stubborn soil.

Several minutes passed before she tried again. "Where did you meet him?"

"On a battlefield."

"And did he save your life?"

I missed a thrust with my makeshift shovel and nearly stabbed my foot. I stopped to glare at her. "Told you that, did he?"

"You did." She continued digging. "Just now."

"Think you're pretty clever, don't you?"

"No more than I have to be."

Why did everything this girl say have to annoy me? "What the blazes is that supposed to mean?"

"I am of the Wind Clan. We are the leaders among our people."

"I thought Red Eagle was the leader."

Little Fawn leaned upon her cane shovel and flicked her head, clearing the hair from her face. Though she'd been working as hard as I, she was not sweating. Another Indian trick, no doubt, meant to annoy me.

"Red Eagle's mother was also of the Wind Clan, so he once had a certain standing. But true authority is passed only through the women."

"That makes no sense."

"It does not have to. To you."

Another insult. I wondered what horrors might befall me if I took a member of the Wind Clan over my knee. I resumed digging. "Why do you call your tribe the Wind Clan? I thought you were Creeks."

She clucked her tongue as if amazed at such ignorance. "You call us Creek, but our true name is Muscogee. A clan is not a tribe. It is more like a family, a bloodline. My cousin Sopath, Red Eagle's new wife, is of the Fish Clan. There is the Bear Clan, the Potato Clan, the Polecat Clan, and several others. We of the Wind Clan alone are privileged to punish wrongdoers, as I have sworn to punish Red Eagle."

I let out a snort and laughed. "There's really a Polecat Clan?"

She eyed me as if I'd lost my wits. "Of course."

I bit my tongue and resumed digging.

She frowned at me. "Where do you think Davy has gone?"

I'd been thinking on that all morning. "I suspect he just needed to be alone." I glanced at her, expecting another question, but she was too contrary to ask it. "Partly, I think he blames himself for Nathan's death." I put my makeshift shovel aside to lift several large rocks from the hole. If she wanted more, she'd have to ask.

The scrape of our digging seemed louder. For the first time, I noticed the buzz of insects, the soft music of the creek and the cold wind whistling through the canebrake. From somewhere in the distance came the double-rap of a woodpecker and the call of a wild turkey.

Several minutes passed before Little Fawn said, "Very well, Stumblefoot. What is the other part?"

I grinned at my small victory. "Davy's having a hard time. He lost a cousin at—" I was about to say Tallushatchee, then realized she would have heard of the atrocities, "—at one of the earlier battles. He lost himself for a time, and now he's afraid there's some sort of devil in him, just waiting to get loose."

I checked to see how she was taking this. She returned my

gaze, perfectly calm, as if I was talking about what we'd have for supper.

"Nathan's death made it worse. Davy dearly wanted to avenge him, but feared his devil might get loose again. Now he's unsure he can do what's necessary to save Lacy Truitt."

"Oh. Is that all." As if that explained everything.

I thought at first she was merely trying to irritate me, but the more I thought on it, the more sense it made that these wild Indians would understand the concept of an inner demon. Their own devils, after all, lurked quite near the surface, and were doubtless invited out on a regular basis.

"He's married," I said, just to jar her. "That's what you really want to know. Has two fine sons and a baby daughter up in Tennessee, and he's aching to get back to them."

Little Fawn stared at me a moment, her eyes large, and I realized my voice carried more heat than I'd intended. I looked away, feigning interest in our horses, tied to cane stalks across the creek. Then I studied them in earnest, for they'd begun to whicker and snort.

A low growl brought me spinning back. Twenty feet away, where we'd left Nathan's blanket-wrapped body at the base of the pine tree, four bristly wolves regarded us with hot yellow eyes. Their lips curled back, baring rows of wicked teeth. They smelled Nathan's blood and planned to feast.

Little Fawn appeared calm, though her hand was on her pistol butt.

My hand went to my waist, finding only knife and tomahawk. My pistol lay on the grass near my musket, propped against that pine tree. Still, I had no intention of abandoning Nathan to these scavengers.

Three of the wolves were mottled gray, crouching with ears back and tails extended. They were defending Nathan's body, which they seemed to consider their prey. The fourth wolf, with massive shoulders and a coat of purest black, took a more aggressive stance. He stood with head lowered, hackles raised, teeth bared and ears flared wide. For him, the pack's obvious leader, Nathan was only the first course.

Little Fawn eased the small pistol from her belt. She cocked it, the sound bringing a round of snarls from our guests. She might get one of them if she were very lucky, but what of the others?

I drew my knife and tomahawk. Drawing her butcher knife, Little Fawn crouched low and bared her teeth. She looked almost as menacing as the wolves.

The leader growled deep in his throat. His eyes grew smaller. He arched his back and fell into a crouch. This was the moment. Little Fawn leveled her pistol on the center of his chest. I gripped my weapons tighter and prepared to rejoin my family.

And from behind the pine tree stepped Davy Crockett. Scooping up two grays by the scruff of their necks, he cracked their heads together with such force that blood splattered his face and shirt. As the black leader and the third gray turned toward him, he gripped one of his victims by the tail and whirled it above his head. He swung it like a mace, and the remaining gray tumbled back under the impact. Little Fawn darted forward, her knife flashing. As she danced away, the wolf's lifeblood spilled from its jugular.

Davy still held the senseless gray by the tail, watching as the black leader advanced upon him. Instead of dropping the gray and drawing his pistol, as any sane man would do, Davy leapt to the attack. As the black wolf sprang for his throat, Davy brought the gray's body crashing down upon the animal's back. The black wolf scrambled up in an instant, jaws snapping, but Davy pressed on, bludgeoning the beast with great sweeping blows from left and right.

From Davy's lips came a cry so terrible I could hardly credit it as human. Flinging the bloody gray aside, he raised a mocassined foot and brought his heel slamming down upon the black wolf's skull. The crack of bone was sharp as a rifle shot. The beast's body twitched and lay still.

The only sound now was a low-pitched growl. Gripping my tomahawk, I moved toward the other wolves, trying to determine which still lived, and realized with a start the sound was coming from Davy. Little Fawn strode forward, wrapped arms around his waist and pressed her head to his chest, but he seemed not to notice. His face was dark with fury, and I knew he was back at Tallushatchee with his dead cousin Caleb.

"Up jumped the devil," I said into the wind.

OVER A SMALL fire, Little Fawn made coffee and boiled sweet potatoes produced from her knapsack. Spurning my help, she wiped the blood from Davy's face and rinsed his buckskin shirt in the creek, stretching it over a rock to dry. She was quite the little wife when she wanted to be.

Once we got some of the coffee and potatoes into Davy, he began to look more human.

"That devil of yours," I said, "he have something in particular against wolves?"

Davy hung his head. "I'm right sorry you had to see that. He's been fightin' to get out since Nathan was shot, and when I saw them wolves after you…"

"You saved my life," Little Fawn said. Then, as an afterthought, "And Stumblefoot's as well."

Davy's eyes roamed to the body of Nathan Truitt. His meaning was clear—he had *not* saved Nathan, just as he had failed to save his cousin—and for a time no one said anything at all.

I shivered and hunched closer to the fire. Most of the birds had gone silent and the sky had turned gray. It would soon be dark.

"With your help," I told Davy, "we can finally get Nathan in the ground." I nodded at the half-dug grave. "The earth hereabouts is unreasonably stubborn."

He looked up at me, his eyes fully clear. "That's a dandy hole you dug, but we won't be needin' it." He rose and approached the body.

Little Fawn and I exchanged glances, wondering at his meaning.

Davy said, "The notion of leavin' him here just don't sit right. We're takin' him home to his pa."

"What about our promise?" I said. "We swore to rescue Lacy."

"And I must kill Red Eagle," Little Fawn said.

"Only if you beat me to it."

Davy gave us the sort of look normally reserved for squabbling children. "We'll get to both them tasks. But just now, we got no idea where Lacy might be. I'm hopin' her pa can point us in the right direction."

"But should we not follow Red Eagle?" Little Fawn asked. "It may be difficult to find him again."

"We got no worries on that score. He's almighty determined to catch Colonel Truitt's militia, so I calculate we'll be headin' the same direction. 'Sides, he knows we got his horse, and he'll have a bone or two to pick with me. 'Long as we don't hide too hard, Red Eagle will find *us*."

CHAPTER 5

"We got them outnumbered."

NATHAN WAS STARTING to stink. We'd lain his body in the creek overnight, and the cold water helped, but we'd been riding since sunup and it was now well past noon. Davy led the thoroughbred with the blanket-wrapped corpse tied over the saddle, while Little Fawn and I did our best to stay upwind. Trouble was, the day was perversely warm for mid-November, and the breeze weak and fickle.

The hills hereabouts were steep and craggy, with moss-covered outcrops on every hand, but the rocks concealed many inviting glades and valleys. Passing one such, I said, "Look at this peaceful little grove. A man couldn't find a more suitable spot to spend eternity."

Davy looked at me slantwise. "When your time comes, Penn, I'll be shore to remember that. Any special words you want said over you?"

I doffed my hat and held it over my heart. "Here lies Penn, his time all spent, laid low by Davy's good intent."

Davy exhibited a very small smile.

Little Fawn said, "Just this once, I must agree with Stumblefoot. This is foolhardy, and Nathan does not deserve this indignity."

Davy kept riding. He pointed at a cluster of persimmon trees at the side of the path. "Looky there. Fruit of the gods. Got some near our cabin up on Bean's Creek." He took a deep breath, as if he could smell the fruit over the stench of the body. "Makes me wish even harder to be home."

Little Fawn and I exchanged looks. Like it or not, it appeared we were taking Nathan to his father.

Davy plucked a few of the golden-orange fruits and tossed one to each of us. The skin was wrinkled and the meat soft. I devoured one, reveling in its rich, tangy sweetness. No wonder the gods loved it.

Not far ahead, Little Fawn claimed, lay a friendly Creek village. She hoped they'd have news of Lacy or her cousin Sopath, and vowed it would be a safe place to spend the night. I was not at all eager to put myself at the mercy of an entire village of Creeks. We had only her assurance they were friendly, but Davy accepted everything she said as if it were straight from the Book.

Little Fawn reined her pony alongside Davy's dun. I veered wide around the other side. This put me slightly downwind of Nathan, but I wanted to hear what she said.

"Are you in truth so anxious to return home?" she asked. There was something of the coquette in her tone.

Davy fidgeted in his saddle. His cheeks looked redder than usual.

"I have… enjoyed our time together," Little Fawn said, "and would be saddened to end it."

Davy's back stiffened. "My Polly is expecting me. And the young'uns, too. Hope this tussle with the Red Sticks don't drag on too long, 'cause I'll need to lay in enough stores to see 'em through the winter."

Little Fawn nodded as if confirming a suspicion. "You are a good provider. And Stumblefoot tells me your seed is strong."

Davy fixed me with a look that would have fried bacon.

I widened my eyes and shook my head with vigor.

"Got me two likely boys," he said to Little Fawn, "close as two coats o' paint. John Wesley, the eldest, turned six this past summer. And little William is four. Both borned with rifles in their hands, and each can knock a squirrel out of a tree at a quarter mile." Davy's voice had softened as he spoke of his children, and his Tennessee drawl became more pronounced. "Baby Margaret—our Little Polly—is cute as a kitten, but squalls like a wildcat."

Little Fawn's shoulders slumped. For a time she rode in silence. Finally, she said, "Your wife. Polly. She is in good health?"

Davy's head jerked. The question had caught him off guard.

"Strong as a snappin' turtle," he said without looking at her, "though a tolerable lot easier to look at."

This, I thought, would put period to the subject. I was wrong.

"It is said that among certain faiths of your people, a man is allowed to take more than one wife. Is it such with you?"

I nearly fell off my horse. This was brazen, even for a savage.

Davy tugged hard on his reins, bringing his dun to an abrupt halt. Taken aback, Little Fawn turned her own pony and looked up at him from a half-bowed head.

I stopped close behind. If she was about to get her comeuppance, I wished to miss none of it.

"Smoke!" Davy stretched an arm toward the south. "And not far off."

Little Fawn stared high above the treetops, where plumes of dirty gray coiled into the bleak sky.

"No! Please, no." Little Fawn's voice was tight. "Not the village."

I felt strangely calm. Did I care if a Creek village burned? I tried to feel anxious or sorry, but somehow the concern would not come. I pictured Maggie crouched in a burning building within the walls of Fort Mims. The terrified faces of my parents. The wild Red Sticks storming the compound with flaming brands. I was full to the brim with sorrow, but wasn't sure any of it was for Little Fawn's friends.

She kicked her pony's ribs and shot off toward the rising smoke.

"Penn!" Davy's voice was sharp as a blade. "Take the reins!" He thrust a hand at me.

I urged my chestnut forward, taking charge of Arrow and Nathan's thoroughbred. I caught a whiff of the body and wrinkled my nose.

"Come quick as you can," Davy said, then went pounding after Little Fawn.

"Sure thing," I said to his dust. "Nothing I like better than riding through an Indian uprising with the war chief's horse and a rotting corpse."

The dust did not reply.

Arrow wanted to run, but Nathan's horse was balky. This rocky country was no place for a racehorse, and he was likely disconcerted by his master's unfamiliar scent. Still, I urged the horses along at a fair clip.

Reaching the top of a rise, I saw the village tucked between two sloping hills in the crook of a small stream. Tilled fields stretched into the valley before it. The dark cloud now covered half the sky, and was fed not by one fire, but many. At least a dozen buildings were ablaze and others already reduced to ashes. Villagers buzzed madly about while twenty riders with torches spread the terror.

I urged Arrow and the silver-gray down the hill. It was not steep, and the going was easier. From below came the distinct crack of a rifle, and one of the torch wielders plunged from his horse. I spotted Davy sitting his dun a good four hundred yards from the village, already reloading Betsy.

The riders looked wildly about, seeking the source of the shot. Even as the fallen warrior staggered to his feet, Old Betsy sang again, and a man dropped his torch, his right arm falling limp. It appeared Davy was keeping his demon in check.

Dragging the horses behind me, I thundered on. I scanned the warriors for Red Eagle, finding he was not among them. This band was only half the size of the one we'd seen earlier.

Little Fawn, riding hard, had nearly reached the village. Her pistol spoke, knocking a rider from his horse. This one did not get up. Davy's next shot made a warrior clutch his shoulder and slump over his pony. The Red Sticks looked at one another and decided their work was done. Turning their horses toward the south, they scampered into the woods like oversized jackrabbits.

Davy was just sliding Betsy into his scabbard as I reached him.

"A man might call that good shooting," I said, "if a man liked redskins."

"Just meant to discourage 'em," Davy said. "If we made 'em mad enough to fight, we'd have our tails in a crack."

"You, me and that hellcat?" I said. "Not a chance. We had them outnumbered."

THERE WAS NO heroes' welcome. A number of Indians gave us suspicious looks and went back to what they were doing—throwing water on the fires, caring for the wounded and wailing over the dead. Three of the cabins still burned furiously.

Scattered about the village were the bodies of hogs and cattle, bristling with arrows. Near the smoking remains of a wagon lay a smashed spinning wheel.

A plump young woman in blue gingham crossed our path and ran screeching toward Little Fawn, who crouched over a wounded man in woolen trousers and a linsey shirt. Unlike Red Eagle's savages these people wore civilized clothing, as if play-acting at being white settlers.

Little Fawn surged to her feet, peppering the screaming woman with questions. Then she addressed the villagers. Her voice rang with authority, cutting through the crackle of flames. Most of the Indians shook their heads, but a young boy cried out, pointing toward the nearest of the burning cabins.

Everyone gasped. The plump young woman fell to her knees, stricken. Men snatched up buckets and dashed to the stream, then raced with frenzied faces for the cabin.

Davy leaped from his horse, took Little Fawn by the shoulders. "What's wrong?"

Little Fawn's face was white. "This woman's mother, Mary Elk, was last seen entering that cabin. She may be there still."

Davy spun toward the cabin, snatching up a red wool blanket as he ran. Men flung water without effect into the roaring fire. The windows and doorway were sheets of flame.

Intercepting a man with a full bucket, Davy snatched it away and doused his blanket, then ran full tilt for the burning cabin. At the last moment he draped the dripping blanket over his head and plunged through the fiery doorway.

The Indians cried out, shocked and amazed. Mary Elk's daughter continued to wail. All eyes were on the cabin door.

I cursed Davy for a fool. In the short time I'd known him, he'd become the closest thing I had to family. Now I'd be burying him too.

Little Fawn started for the cabin. Keeping a firm grip on the horses, I slipped off my mare and threw an arm around her. Small fists beat against my chest.

"Let me go!"

I pivoted, allowing us both a view of the building. "It's in Davy's hands now, and the Almighty's. There's nothing we can do."

With a whoosh, one end of the cabin's roof crashed inward. A new crop of flames gushed into the sky.

Little Fawn screamed.

The men with buckets shook their heads, clenched their fists. Mary Elk's daughter fell forward and clawed at the earth. The others stared at the cabin with hollow eyes. I kept watching the doorway. I had nothing else to do.

The side wall of the building crumbled inward, throwing sparks and ash into the air. Little Fawn pressed her face to my chest, sobbing.

A patch of darker red burst through the flaming doorway, wobbled, and smashed to the earth before the cabin. The last section of roof fell in, followed immediately by the remaining walls.

Releasing Little Fawn, I walked stiff-legged toward the dark red heap on the ground. My heart punched at my ribs as if trying to escape. My chest was wet with Little Fawn's tears.

I stopped. The lump at my feet was covered with a scorched red blanket. Stretched out behind it were singed buckskin leggings. Steeling myself, I snagged an edge of the blanket and peeled it back. Whatever lay beneath it was blackened by flame and ash. I was about to turn away when something moved. I caught a flash of teeth and one gleaming eyeball.

"Howdy, Penn," said the voice of Davy Crockett. "Meet my new friend Mary Elk. She and me would look right kindly on a dram of corn whiskey."

AN HOUR LATER, we were digging graves. Five villagers had perished in the attack, and Davy and I worked with three Indians to put them in the ground.

The Red Stick raid had caught the friendlies by surprise. They knew Red Eagle was in the area, but believed he'd passed them by. Then, without warning, this smaller group of warriors had swarmed out of the south. Along with all the killing, the raiders destroyed a score of houses, a blacksmith shop, a small trading post and a storehouse containing the community's winter provisions. The sole remaining structure of any consequence was the corral. It was assumed the Red Sticks had saved this until last, planning to take the horses with them.

Saddened as the villagers were by the five deaths, they rejoiced that Mary Elk had not been the sixth. Davy was the recipient of much hugging, and they fed us a stew made with hickory milk and sweet potatoes, which was altogether the best meal I'd had since leaving Pennsylvania.

And now we dug graves. Davy whistled softly as he worked. One of our companions, an older man in suspenders, toiled in silence, while the other two—a striped-shirted fellow with his hair chopped short and a fleshy young giant in a porkpie hat—exchanged occasional grunts and growls. I focused on my digging, trying to keep my mind blank. Every time I caught myself thinking, I considered the same question. Did these dead Indians really deserve better treatment than Maggie and my folks?

Across the clearing, Little Fawn and the other women tended to the wounded. Little Fawn had prepared a concoction of herbs and mud that Davy pronounced exceedingly soothing to burns. Several villagers bore wounds from arrows or musket balls. One old man had lost an eye, and a young girl had a trampled leg, but the general opinion was that we would require no more graves.

The individual most in need of a grave, our late friend Nathan, was once again in the river, just downstream from the village.

Little Fawn had quizzed all and sundry about the possible location of Lacy Truitt. One old fellow had heard several women were held in a place called the Holy Ground, but either didn't know or wouldn't say where that might be. No one had news of Little Fawn's cousin Sopath, save that she was said to carry Red Eagle's child.

The women clucked away in their peculiar tongue, their voices rising and falling according to their interest in the subject at hand. I'd caught several sneaking glances at Davy, who worked shirtless in his singed breeches. He was solidly built, but rangy, and thinner than I'd have guessed. After his performance with the wolves, I'd expected the bulging chest and biceps of a modern Hercules.

Nodding at Davy, Mary Elk's plump daughter posed a question, causing the other women to giggle. Little Fawn looked up, smiled knowingly and rattled off a few words in Creek. At this, the women all cackled, gazing at Davy with open admiration. As the fuss died down, Mary Elk's daughter spoke again, flicking her head toward me. Little Fawn responded in a mocking tone, ending with a word that set the women chattering like chipmunks.

My cheeks burned. I had no doubt her final word had been the Creek equivalent of *Stumblefoot*.

A derisive snort issued from the young gravedigger in the

porkpie hat. His small piggish eyes and petulant mouth were almost lost in a large flabby face. I fixed him with a glare, signaling I was not to be trifled with. He puffed up his chest, returning the challenge. He was perhaps the biggest Indian I had ever seen, taller even than Red Eagle, but his muscles were not fully defined. He seemed a man who'd gotten by on sheer size without doing the hard work necessary to bring his body under control.

Failing to scare me, the big buck shifted his disdain to Davy, and had even worse luck. Davy went on whistling, paying him no heed at all. The Indian's face grew red, and he spat a stream of words that sounded highly uncomplimentary. His voice was odd and low-pitched, almost a croak. In the moments that followed, Davy's whistling seemed quite loud, and I recognized the tune "Yankee Doodle."

Making a show of throwing his shovel into the half-dug grave, the big brave climbed out and lumbered across the clearing. The women grew quiet as he approached and I leaned on my shovel to watch. Halting six feet from Little Fawn, he crossed beefy arms over his chest, glaring down at her. Davy stopped whistling, and the only sound was that of Little Fawn grinding herbs in a small bowl.

Mixing the herbs with mud, Little Fawn applied them to a young boy's burns. Though the big brave's shadow fell directly across her patient, she made no acknowledgment of his presence. I almost felt sorry for him.

The man spoke, his tone halfway between a question and an accusation. Little Fawn continued working.

The big fellow spoke again, at length, and with more heat. He turned once, shook a fist in our direction, and continued his tirade. His anger made the croak more prevalent. Still ignoring him, Little Fawn rose, helping the young boy to his feet. The lad muttered thankful words and shuffled away.

Little Fawn faced the big man squarely and spoke. Her voice was not loud, but the words sounded final, almost brutal. As he stood quivering, she turned away, motioning a woman with a gunshot wound to approach.

Angry words poured from the brave, causing the wounded woman to shy away. The other women clucked their tongues and looked embarrassed. Little Fawn turned upon him, fists jammed tight against her hips. Though half his size, she was clearly in control.

She nodded toward Davy and me. "If you would speak ill of these men, Big Frog, have the courage to use their language."

Big Frog? I stifled a laugh.

The brave half turned, sneered at me, and returned his attention to Little Fawn.

"You are meant for me, little one. It has always been so. Now you spurn me for this—" he shook a fist at Davy, "—this farmer. He and his kind are the cause of our troubles, the reason our people died today."

"They are *not!*" Little Fawn's passion flared. "Those killers, like those who slaughtered our people at Fort Mims, were Red Sticks. They have let hatred consume them and lost their way."

"It is *we* who have lost our way." Big Frog now addressed the entire village. "Each year more white men come from the north, and each year more of our lands are taken in so-called treaties. The whites will not be satisfied until we are homeless or dead. Red Eagle and the others are right. This is our last chance to save ourselves."

"Big Frog speaks nonsense," said the old man in suspenders. "We prospered in cooperation with our white neighbors. Our bellies were full and our larder well stocked. Until this Red Stick madness, we enjoyed the peace our ancestors always wanted."

Big Frog scowled at him. "And look what we have lost. Great hunters and warriors till the ground like women. We huddle in white men's cabins, wearing white men's clothing, raising white men's crops, and using white men's tools to bury our dead." Striding back to the half-dug grave, he plucked the shovel from the earth, raised it high and snapped the handle over his knee. "I will have no more of it."

Tossing the broken shovel aside, Big Frog removed his porkpie hat, tore it with his teeth and ripped it in half.

Davy addressed the villagers. "There's truth in Big Frog's words, but a heap less than he'd like." He leaned on his shovel, voice as calm as if discussing the price of furs. "Some white men are your enemies, but not all, not by a long shot. Most of 'em don't want war no more than you do."

Big Frog spat. "You speak thus from one side of your mouth, while with the other you seduce my woman."

Davy grinned. "Little Fawn's a right nice gal, and no mistake. But I got me a fine wife back in Tennessee, and she's all I want or need."

Little Fawn looked at her feet.

Big Frog stepped closer. "You lie, like every other white man. You have no honor."

Davy's hair bristled at the nape. This was not talk he would normally tolerate. I moved to his side.

Little Fawn stalked toward us. "It is you who lack honor, Big Frog. Any feelings I once had for you are gone."

Big Frog ignored her. Raising a hammy fist, he shook it in Davy's face.

Davy continued to grin.

Big Frog looked perplexed. He was no doubt accustomed to men being afraid of him. Then a crafty look came into his eye. Still looking at Davy, he threw a punch far to Davy's left, catching me square in the ribs. I went down as if kicked by an ox.

Once I found my breath, I tried to rise. A firm hand clamped my shoulder, holding me down.

"Easy, Penn. I believe Mr. Frog missed what he was aimin' at."

Mad as hell but equally curious, I stayed where I was.

Big Frog leaned his face close to Davy's and growled. "You are a coward. All white men are cowards. And you have stolen Red Eagle's horse. I will return it to him and be greeted as a hero."

" 'Fraid not," Davy said.

Big Frog glared at him. "You think to stop me?"

" 'Fraid so."

With a huff, Big Frog wheeled and strode stiff-legged toward the small corral. He threw a blanket over a dappled pony. "I ride to join our brothers. Who goes with me?"

The other young grave-digger ripped off his striped shirt and ran to the corral. Two more young braves, one who looked no more than twelve, moved to join them, but were surrounded by jabbering women. The older one shook free and spurted through to his pony, but the youngster surrendered and stayed put.

Mounted, the three braves paraded defiantly from the corral. Big Frog looked pointedly at Arrow, tied with our horses to an oak on the edge of the village. He glanced back at Davy.

Grinning, Davy shook his head.

Big Frog glowered at him, but Davy's grin just got wider, and the big brave finally looked away.

Arching his back, Big Frog addressed the village. "We are Red Sticks now. When next we meet, we will kill you all."

And with a parting sneer, he and his friends galloped off to the south.

Davy leaned down to help me up. His grin was gone.

CHAPTER 6

"You must think us very stupid."

THE VILLAGERS BEGGED us to spend the night, but Davy insisted we move on. If Big Frog returned with Red Eagle, he feared we'd wake up with our heads missing.

Despite the fact that most of their belongings had gone up in smoke, the Indians tried to press all manner of gifts and provisions upon us. Davy refused all but the scorched red blanket he'd used to rescue Mary Elk, while Little Fawn accepted a knapsack of undisclosed articles from a crowd of giggling women. A group of sly-eyed youngsters tried to present me with a walking stick and showed great amusement when I declined.

We made camp at dusk under a rocky outcrop some miles south of the village. Davy made a point of proclaiming how warm the red blanket was, while I shivered on the hard ground. Little Fawn, as ever, took no notice of the cold.

Next morning, she excused herself to wash in a hillside creek while Davy and I prepared to quit camp. We were retying Nathan's body to his horse when a vision in white emerged from the trees.

Davy said, "Jumpin' catfish!"

I was struck dumb, wondering if I'd died in the night and the Lord had sent an angel to escort me through the Pearly Gates. The angel's gown shimmered like white fire in the bright cold sunlight. Her feet were dainty, her bare arms slender, her waist trim and her bosom full. Her eyes shone like stars in the night and her lips glistened like rubies. Her shining black hair was bound with a ribbon of gold.

Her lips parted, and I prepared myself for music from the heavens. She said, "Whatever is wrong, Stumblefoot? You look like a fish gaping for a worm."

I tried to scowl, tried to look away.

Davy said, "Ma'am, you're the second-prettiest sight I've seen on this earth."

Little Fawn's smile turned brittle. "*Second* prettiest?"

"Next to my Polly, of course, on the day we jumped the broom."

Little Fawn's eyes clouded. She spun away and vanished into the trees.

Davy's movements were lethargic as we finished with the horses. When Little Fawn returned she was clad once more in her baggy hunting shirt and buckskin leggings. The rouge was gone from her lips, and except for brushed hair and a clean face she was precisely as before.

Except that she wasn't. I had seen the butterfly, and the caterpillar would never be the same.

WITH NO ROAD or path, we relied on Little Fawn's reckoning to guide us toward the Truitt plantation. She rode far ahead, disinclined to conversation. I struggled to avert my eyes. Looking at her now made me sort of ticklish all over, and it didn't seem right feeling ticklish over an Indian.

At least now I knew the secret of the knapsack. The Creek women had given her the dress and the warpaint to help turn Davy's head. That she'd failed was no fault of theirs, or hers either. They'd all underestimated the devotion a strong man has for his loved ones. But the more I dwelled on that subject, the worse I felt. The fact that Davy had a family longing for his return emphasized the sad truth that I had naught but memories and nightmares.

I needed to get my mind on another track. The landscape had begun to flatten, and there was room to ride two, or even three, abreast. Breathing through my mouth, I guided my chestnut past Nathan and his thoroughbred, into step alongside Davy's dun.

"Care to explain your behavior with that Big Frog brute? Why wouldn't you let me defend myself?"

Davy offered no sign he'd heard. I was about to turn away when he said, "There's a time to fight, Penn. And a time not to."

"Afraid that devil of yours might pop loose again?"

"It wasn't that. Big Frog's a bully, and none too bright, but his words had teeth. And those villagers were judgin' twixt him and us. Some were tempted to join him. We had to show 'em there's hope for peace."

I didn't know what to say. Forgiving and forgetting may be fine for someone whose family was safe back in Tennessee, but not for me.

Little Fawn had halted her pony and sat awaiting us. "You show great wisdom for one of your years," she told Davy.

"And you have big ears," I said, "for one so small."

She ignored me. "Many of my people think as Big Frog does. If the fighting does not end soon, more will join Red Eagle."

Davy nodded. "Then the fightin' must end. Soon."

"I am thankful," Little Fawn said, "that men like you and General Jackson have come to help us."

Davy chewed his lip, saying nothing.

Little Fawn watched him closely. "General Jackson *is* here to help us, is he not?"

Davy fidgeted in his saddle. "I'm just a lowly private, Ma'am. Ain't for me to say."

"I am not a *Ma'am*. Are you saying your general cannot be trusted?"

"Right pretty country hereabouts," Davy said. "How much further to the Truitt place?"

Little Fawn huffed. "What of you, Stumblefoot? Do *you* have the courage to speak the truth?"

The truth, I thought, was that Jackson saw this Creek conflict as an opportunity to build his own reputation, in hopes of gaining a more prestigious command in the war against the British.

That was certainly the prevailing opinion back in Philadelphia, and I'd seen no evidence to refute it. But such talk would surely be beyond Little Fawn's understanding.

"The truth," I said, "is that I don't know Jackson's heart, and neither does Davy. But I'll say this. If he ever came for supper, I'd hide the silver."

We rode awhile without speaking. An eagle glided high above us, its cry sharp and shrill. It seemed to be laughing at us. It was not a good omen.

Little Fawn sat straight and still, her face tight. "I have been a fool," she said. "And perhaps my people have been fools as well. I must think on these things."

Davy said nothing. His cheeks were white.

Little Fawn pointed to the south. "Ride until you come to a creek flowing from the east. Follow the creek upstream and you will find the home of Thaddeus Truitt. I wish you luck in rescuing Lacy." She kicked her pony into a run.

I couldn't help myself. I shouted, "When will we see you again?"

She looked back over her shoulder. "Perhaps soon, perhaps never."

And I gazed after her, unsure which to hope for.

AN HOUR LATER, crossing a broad valley, we heard gunfire. It came from dead ahead, on the far side of a tree-covered hill. We urged speed from our horses. Compared to the landscape further north, the hill was not steep, but the woods were thick and difficult to navigate, especially leading the thoroughbred and the stallion. Davy reached the top well ahead of me and halted, hand raised in caution.

The gunfire was louder. The sharp crack of pistols mixed with the deeper bark of muskets. When at last I reined in at Davy's side, we sat on the edge of a bluff overlooking another valley. At the far end ran a small creek, likely the one leading to Truitt's plantation.

Below us, within a circle of prone horses, lay a dozen men in green military jackets. Colonel Truitt's private militia. Crouched behind rocks and trees on every side were bare-skinned Indians shooting arrows and musket balls. The militiamen fired and reloaded their weapons at an impressive rate.

Between us and the militia, conspicuous for his fleshy bulk, stood Big Frog, flanked by his friends from the village. And far to the left, upon a speckled pony, sat Red Eagle himself, calm as if enjoying a picnic. He was perhaps sixty yards away, too far for my musket, but an easy shot for Davy's rifle.

Davy knelt at the edge of the bluff, studying the scene below. I eased closer to the horse behind him and stretched a hand toward Old Betsy.

Davy said, "Hate to have to whup you, Penn, now that we've become friends and all."

I snatched my hand away. "Just admiring the workmanship. But even if I wasn't, what's the harm in killing Red Eagle? With him dead, his young braves might lose heart and make peace. They might even help us find Lacy."

"The Red Sticks got other leaders. Not so smart, maybe, but meaner, and more determined to kill. Red Eagle's our best bet, and that's a guaranteed natural fact."

"Then what are we to do? Sit here and watch him slaughter Truitt's militia?"

Davy turned and tapped his head. "I've been thinkin' on that. Old Thad Truitt, you'll recall, rode with the Swamp Fox."

"Truitt was one of Francis Marion's men. So?"

"My pa ran a tavern when I was growin' up, and travelers told many a tale of Marion's exploits. He pulled some downright glorious tricks on the Redcoats."

"And?"

"And I recall one that might work on these Red Stick varmints. You're gonna hate it, but I'm hopin' Red Eagle will hate it more."

HE WAS RIGHT. I hated it.

I led Arrow back down the hill and circled wide to approach the Red Sticks from the west. Davy left Nathan beneath the trees at the top of the bluff and led the thoroughbred in the opposite direction, to come at the Indians from the east. Once we were both in position, according to Davy's thinking, we'd have them surrounded.

Scattered gunfire still sounded from the valley, but it was less frequent. Having felt each other out, the two sides had reached an understanding. The Creeks understood they couldn't get within bow or musket range without exposing themselves, while the militia understood they were going nowhere as long as the Indians remained. All the redskins had to do was wait until the whites ran out of ammunition.

Flanking the valley on both sides were stands of oak and long-leaf pine, concealing us from Red Eagle and his warriors. Sooner than I wished, I was in place behind the trees. My musket and pistol were primed, and the fixings to reload close to hand. I now had nothing to do but wait.

The wait was short. I barely had time to count my misgivings before I heard a distant bugle call, followed by galloping hooves.

"First Company, form up!" The commanding voice rang from beyond the Red Sticks' position. "Cavalry to my left, Infantry to my right!" Other voices shouted, mixed with the tramp of more horses.

I bent low in the saddle, trying to peer through the trees. But I couldn't even see the Indians, let alone an approaching army.

"Platoon A, muskets at the ready! Platoon B, fix bayonets!" The beat of horses' hooves went on and on. Another bugle sounded. Then a voice I recognized. "Second Company, take your position!"

I shook my head in wonder. It had all been Davy. I knew that, but still had trouble believing one man and two horses had made all that noise.

Had Francis Marion really employed this crazy scheme? In the unlikely event I lived to meet Colonel Truitt, I meant to ask him straight out. But Davy's call for the Second Company was my cue to begin. "Second Company to me!" I bawled, feeling foolish. I raced the horses through the woods parallel to the Red Sticks, tromping on stones to make as much racket as possible. "Form three lines and prepare to fire! Sergeant, take that laggard's name!" I added more shouts and curses as I kept up the steady clomp of the horses.

From the far side, the "bugle" sounded again, and I marveled that Davy was able to make such a noise with his lips. I fired my musket and pistol. "Bring up more ammunition! Gunners, load that cannon!" Finally warming to my task, I rode back and forth like a madman, whooping and hooting and shouting any order that came to mind. "Clear the decks! Make way for the artillery! Take no prisoners!"

Feeling heady, I tried to picture the actions of the Indians and militia. The Red Sticks, according to Davy's reckoning, should be on the verge of hopping the creek and scooting off with their tails between their legs, while the militia should be feeling its oats and preparing to hurry them on their way. By the time Davy and I emerged triumphant into the valley, the dumbfounded militia would greet us as saviors and our names would go down in history aside that of the Swamp Fox himself.

Things had gone remarkably well, but the horses were beginning to labor and my throat was raw. I listened hard for Davy to sound the charge, his signal the Indians were truly on the run. Instead, a twig snapped. I looked to my right and nearly soiled myself.

Six painted Creeks stepped out of the woods and aimed their weapons at me. I veered left, away from the valley, and faced another group. Still more, including Big Frog and his friends, blocked my escape from behind.

Big Frog waggled a finger at me. "For shame, Stumblefoot. You must think us very stupid."

I had no time for a retort. The only route left to me was straight through the woods into the clearing, and I took it.

Holding tight to the reins of Nathan's horse, I kicked my chestnut and burst through the trees with the Red Sticks howling at my heels.

As I raced into the clearing, I saw Davy, leading Arrow, gallop from the woods on the far side and point wildly toward the small ring of militia. The men were on their feet, waving and cheering, still thinking they'd been saved. They'd been fooled, even if the Indians hadn't. Muskets banged behind me. Arrows hissed past my ears. I leaned low over the chestnut's neck, and she thundered the last few yards to leap into the ring, pulling up short just as Davy arrived from the other direction.

Davy leaped from his dun, rifle in hand. He took aim at a screaming warrior less than forty yards from the circle. Betsy spoke, and the Indian collapsed with a yelp, clutching a bloody knee. More Creeks charged, and the militia finally got into the spirit, leveling their muskets and clearing the field.

Two minutes later the Red Sticks were under cover, out of bow and musket range, and things were much as they had been before. Except that now Davy and I were trapped along with the militia, and equally likely to die.

I turned to Davy, ready to spit poison. But his grin was sheepish, and I softened. "You sure that's how the old Swamp Fox did it?"

"Could be I overlooked one detail," Davy said. "Maybe that trick only works in the swamp."

Despite myself, I laughed. It was that or cry.

"What the hell happened out there?" A tall, broad-shouldered man with a satiny brown beard and captain's bars glowered down at us. "Where'd the army go?"

"Back to the taverns and campfires," I said, "where legends belong."

The captain eyed me like I was loony, and I couldn't call him wrong.

CHAPTER 7

"Providence is fickle."

MILITIA CAPTAIN GABRIEL ZANE looked to be about forty, with a finely-chiseled nose and a hard, straight line for a mouth. He had dark, piercing eyes and startlingly white teeth. His healthy, ruddy complexion was marred only by a jagged scar on his left cheek.

He listened irritably as Davy explained how our trick on the Red Sticks had failed. Nothing about it appeared to satisfy him. I think he half believed Jackson's army had truly come and gone, and that Davy and I were either fugitives or deserters. When the telling was done he frowned and walked the perimeter of our small defensive circle, peering into the woods on either side of the clearing.

While he was occupied, I took stock of our position. We had no real cover here, but the nearest trees offering cover to the Indians were seventy yards away. At that distance their muskets were all but useless, and only their strongest bowmen could propel an arrow with any accuracy.

One of Zane's men was not within the circle. He lay on his face twenty yards away, his neck twisted at an impossible angle. Two gaily-feathered arrows protruded from the back of his green jacket. He had been scouting the rear when the Creeks attacked, and moved too slow to escape their bowmen. The other men did not speak of him, but I caught their eyes straying occasionally in his direction. He was an all-too-blatant reminder of the fate in store for us all.

Returning, Zane said, "If I believed this story of yours, and I said *if*, one thing would still puzzle me. Why would you risk your necks to aid a company of complete strangers?" He narrowed his eyes as if expecting some further deception.

"As it turns out, you and your men ain't *completely* strange." Davy grinned, enjoying Zane's ruffled feathers. "We sorta crossed paths a couple days back, when Red Eagle got his horse shot out from under him."

Zane's eyes widened. "That was you?"

I aimed a thumb. "Meet Davy Crockett, Captain. Best shot in Andy Jackson's army. Maybe on the whole frontier."

Davy shrugged this off. "We'd have helped out anyway, Cap'n, it bein' only neighborly. Then we found out you was friends of Nathan's."

Zane had so many questions he seemed ready to pop. "Young Truitt? You've seen him? Where is he?"

Davy hung his head. "We bring sad tidings, I fear. Nathan Truitt is dead. We cached his body up yonder on the bluff."

Zane's face froze. He turned away, his back stiffening. The nearest militiamen swore under their breath and leaned to pass the news to their companions.

When Zane turned back there was a twitch in his jaw. He squatted and sat cross-legged before us, hands resting on his knees. "Tell me about it."

Davy did, simply and accurately, but made no mention of Little Fawn or our stop at the village. Whether he was embarrassed by her attentions or simply feared Zane would disapprove of friendly relations with Creeks, I could not tell.

Zane asked occasional questions, his eyes betraying doubt at some of the more outlandish details. It was clear he thought us mad as March hares.

"Colonel Truitt is a strong man," he said when Davy finished, "but this news might be the death of him. Not that he's likely to hear it." He gazed out at the surrounding Indians, and I took his meaning. The Red Sticks had only to wait until we ran out of ammunition. Returning his attention to Davy, he extended a hand. "I guess we owe you a debt of thanks for taking down Red Eagle's horse. Even if it did buy us only two more days of living."

Davy shook his hand. "Things do look bleak, Cap'n, and that's a fact. But Providence is fickle. You never know what she'll spring on you next."

Zane exhibited a grim smile. "I suppose that's so. And the worst we can do is take a good many of these red devils along with us."

Davy said, "If you don't mind my askin', what's Red Eagle got against you? That band chased you nigh onto sixty miles, passin' up homesteads and a nice fat village. Didn't even pause to chase us, and we caused him a considerable amount of grief. Must be wantin' you almighty bad."

Zane turned to stare out into the clearing, his features shadowed by the broad brim of his hat. "Best I can figure, he wants to destroy the Colonel. Jealous of his wealth, maybe, or the respect due him. This company is Colonel Truitt's strong right arm. You might even call it his legs. With us gone, Nathan dead and Lacy in the hands of Red Eagle, the poor man will have nothing left but his life. Then the Red Sticks will take that too."

As afternoon drained into evening we kept close watch on the Creeks, preserving our powder and firing only to discourage those coming too close. As long as we kept them pinned to their current cover they were of little danger to us. Six men kept watch for an hour, then rested while the other six took their positions. Davy, Zane and I were part of the second rotation.

Zane's men were a rough lot, but handled their muskets well and gave him no backtalk. The brass buttons of their uniforms were polished, their campaign hats brushed and worn level with the eyebrows. Nathan had called them posers in uniform, but what he took for pomp I saw as discipline. That discipline served them well now that their backs were to the wall.

A burly militiaman with gray-streaked dark hair cast occasional looks in Davy's direction, brow furrowed in puzzlement.

I said nothing to Davy, but felt certain he sensed the man's attentions also. In any case, I resolved to keep an eye on him. He might simply be uneasy at the prospect of imminent and grisly death, but it was equally possible he bore some unknown grudge against Davy, or suspected us of collaborating with the Red Sticks.

Under the guise of camaraderie, I asked Zane to introduce us to the men, but he merely nodded at each in turn and named them. Three were called Smith, one Malarkey, one Buzzard and the others less memorable. The burly man was one of the Smiths.

Davy said, "How 'bout that other one?"

Zane gave him a questioning look.

"That young feller sittin' by hisself," Davy said. "The one nobody talks to."

I blinked at this. I'd noticed him earlier myself, and promptly forgot about him. Apparently Zane had, too. The lad in question sat hunched at the other end of the circle, as far from the others as he could get.

Zane's mouth twisted as if swallowing something sour. "That," he said, "is my sister's son, Ned. He's the company's all-purpose dogsbody. Caring for the horses and emptying slop-buckets is pretty much all he's good for." And that was all he would say.

The young man looked up then, revealing a sallow, puffy face with watery eyes and a weak chin. His shoulders were narrow and his legs thin as sticks. It was hard to argue with Zane's assessment. He was certainly no one's idea of a soldier.

The Creeks kept trying to get at us, but not hard enough to risk their skins. Every few minutes some young buck would run a jagged pattern to fire his musket or loose an arrow. But their musket balls whizzed harmlessly overhead, while their arrows thudded into the ground ten or more yards outside the circle. On such occasions the two nearest militiamen teamed up to make things hot for them, and the Indians slunk back out of range. Zane's men carried muskets of recent British make, and the men had been well trained in their use. The Creeks' muskets, like the one I'd acquired at Talladega, were French-made relics of the Revolution.

On one occasion, a Red Stick brave snaked close enough to send an arrow solidly into the circle. He jumped up, running, and I fired, cursing as my ball went wide. Davy drew a bead with Old Betsy, and the militiamen cheered, thinking the Creek a goner. But by the time Davy squeezed the trigger, the rascal was a hundred yards away and already celebrating his escape. Davy, I knew perfectly well, could have trimmed the redskin's eyebrows at that distance, but his shot went wide, zinging against the rocks beneath the bluff.

"Shucks," Davy said. "Missed him."

Zane grumbled, "Why didn't you fire sooner? He was close enough."

"Had a gnat in my eye," Davy said.

Zane stomped away, shaking his head.

I glanced at the Smith who had seemed so interested in us, and caught a feral gleam in his eye. It was the look of a man who had just confirmed a suspicion.

ONCE DARKNESS CAME, we piled more wood on the fire. The flames cast a ghostly illumination over the clearing, making it less likely the Creeks would attempt an attack. And because the blaze was at our backs, our vision would be better than that of the Indians looking into the fire.

Davy took up a position next to Captain Zane. After a few casual remarks, he said, "How'd you come to work for Colonel Truitt?"

Zane hesitated. He seemed a closed-mouthed man who would normally ignore such questions. But Davy had a way of making folks open up and tell him things, so I was not overly surprised when Zane said:

"We met at the race track after one of his horses gave mine a trouncing. He came to know I'd done a bit of soldiering, and when those damned Red Sticks made off with his daughter he sent me and my friends here to get her back."

"And how's that goin' so far?"

Zane eyed him closely, as if deciding whether to take offense. "I've an idea where she might be held, but the Colonel insisted we seek help from General Jackson before attempting her rescue. You know what came of that."

Davy said. "You did get more men." He pointed at me, then himself. "You see, Cap'n, Nathan asked us to find Lacy for him, and we sorta promised to do it. Might be wise if we joined forces."

Zane shook his head. "Aren't you forgetting this pickle we're in?"

"I ain't forgot. But I ain't give up hope, neither."

"So," Zane said, "if by some miracle we survive this, you two wish to join my company?"

" 'Fraid I'm already spoken for, and Penn here ain't much of a joiner. But we'd surely like to help. We was on our way to the Truitt plantation, hopin' you or the Colonel might have an idea where Lacy'd be found."

Zane barked a laugh. "You two have brass, I'll give you that. You risk your lives on a damfool scheme to save us and get yourselves trapped. Now you talk about saving a girl you've never met, when you don't have a chance in hell of saving yourselves."

"That chance is small, I'll allow," Davy said, "but maybe it'll grow some."

"You're a strange duck, Crockett. Where are you from, anyway? Kentucky?"

"Tennessee," said a hoarse voice behind us. "He's from Tennessee." The burly Smith lay watching us with red-veined eyes, a finger on the trigger of his musket.

Without looking, Davy said, "How do, Myers. You owe me seven dollars, as I recollect."

"I owe you shit."

Zane looked from the burly man to Davy and back again. "Old friends, I see. What about it, Smith? You owe this fellow money?"

Myers—for that now seemed his true name—had a beefy red face and a wide, loose-lipped mouth over a stubbled chin.

He spat out of the side of his mouth. "Other way around. Done him a good turn once, when he was in need, and he lit out with my best horse."

Davy said, "It's bad enough, Myers, being a bald-faced liar. But there's a special corner of Hell reserved for them that steals from children."

Myers said, "Shit," stretching it to at least three syllables.

"Enough. I'll have no quarrels here." Zane drew a fancy pistol from a black leather holster. "On the odd chance we get out of this alive, you two can pound each other senseless. But until then, I'll shoot the first one who so much as sneers."

Davy said, "Fine by me."

Myers's lip's twitched, cold hatred in his eyes. Zane cocked his pistol. Myers grimaced and flopped over, staring out into the night. Zane watched a long moment before lowering the hammer of his gun.

"It's full dark now. Those heathens won't dare attack until morning." Zane moved across the circle to his bedroll, squatted, and began laying it out. "We'll take three-man shifts, two hours each, until dawn. The Smiths go first." He pointed at Myers. "And that includes you, whatever your name is. The rest of you get some sleep."

A Smith on the far side of the circle said, "Aye aye, Cap'n."

Myers farted.

Zane glared at Davy as if daring him to comment.

Davy licked a finger and held it above his head, gauging the direction of the wind. After a moment he nodded, drew an imaginary line from Myers to Zane, and said, "Pleasant dreams, Cap'n."

THOUGH I WAS bone tired, I slept badly, dreaming first of burning buildings, then of Little Fawn. I wasn't sure which was worse. Following a particularly vivid sequence involving both burning buildings *and* Little Fawn, I awoke, unable to breathe. The cause was immediately apparent. Someone had a hand over my mouth.

I was about to bite the hand when a face appeared, inches from mine, and a finger cautioned me to silence. The face and finger belonged to Little Fawn. Her lips moved closer, and she whispered in my ear. "Make not a sound, Penn. I must speak with Davy." She called me Penn, not Stumblefoot, so I knew I was still asleep.

I whispered back, "Get out of my dreams," and rolled over, clamping my eyes shut. I was not disturbed again, and the burning buildings soon returned.

I came full awake with a boot kicking me in the ribs. Attached to the boot was Captain Zane, and above him a purple-tinged sky.

"Damn you, McCoy. Where the hell is Crockett?"

I sat up, extending a hand to discourage further kicking. It took a moment for the words to sink in. *Crockett. Where is Crockett?* A stupid question. He was right there beside me. I looked up at Zane, grimaced at his ignorance, and shifted my gaze pointedly to Davy.

Except that Davy wasn't there. His scorched red blanket lay abandoned on the ground. Blinking, I peered around the rest of the circle. The other men were awake now, or nearly so, and all watching me. Davy was nowhere in sight. I looked to the picketed horses. Davy's was still there, as were the others we'd brought.

"I asked you a question, McCoy. Where's Crockett? What game are you two playing at?"

"Crockett's a coward," Myers said. "Scarpering off in the night is what he does. I suggest you gents check your valuables."

Several men did just that, while I said, "I don't know. I truly have no idea. He was there when I went to sleep, and now he's not."

Zane didn't like it, but my words rang true. Hell, they *were* true. I was mystified.

There was no more sleeping. Everyone kept watch on the clearing and surrounding territory as if fearful Davy would come howling out of the darkness with a pack of bloodthirsty savages. I forced myself to go about my business, packing my meager bedroll and cleaning my musket in preparation for what would surely be my last day above ground.

I felt betrayed. I'd expected to face death with a man I considered a friend. Now I was stuck with these strangers. And since Davy's disappearance, they were worse than strangers, for all now eyed me with suspicion. Maybe they wouldn't wait for the Red Sticks to kill me. Maybe one would slit my throat when my back was turned.

Dawn arrived without further incident, offering no clue to Davy's whereabouts. The Creeks were already up, laughing and capering about like schoolboys. Outside our circle, the dead militiaman still stretched on the grass where he had fallen. But he looked different this morning, white instead of green, and I realized he no longer wore his militia jacket. The two arrows that had pinned it to his back lay in the grass next to the body. One of the Red Sticks must have snaked out during the night and claimed the jacket as a prize, a form of counting coup that would gain him respect among his tribe. The dead man looked even more dead, lying there in his undershirt, and I shivered with the knowledge his fate would soon be mine.

My thoughts drifted to Little Fawn. I'd hoped to see her again—nearly as much as I'd hoped not to. Now I would never have that chance, not even in dreams. I couldn't even look forward to seeing her in the hereafter, for surely Indians went to a different place.

Zane's men made coffee, and the aroma was all the sweeter with the knowledge it could be my last. But no one offered me any, and when I moved toward the fire two men snarled and reached for their muskets. I chose to go without.

It was another hour before Red Eagle made an appearance. He'd probably slept late and enjoyed a sumptuous breakfast—maybe even bathed and had his hair braided—before coming out to slaughter us. He *did* look regal, posing with hands on hips beneath the bluff, surveying his own private killing ground. His braves, now numbering well over sixty, lurked behind trees on three sides of us. I spotted Big Frog trying to hide his bulk behind a cottonwood and snapped off a shot at him, just by way of saying good morning. The ball chipped bark off a tree two feet to his left and he laughed, answering with obscene gestures.

I was still worried about Davy. I refused to believe he'd run away. Wherever he'd gone, it was for our benefit. To doubt it meant I had not known him at all, and that I would not accept. Maybe he'd gone for help. And maybe—just maybe—he'd been captured.

Unable to shake this thought from my head, I peered into the trees, studying each warrior in turn for some sign Davy had been caught. A coonskin cap, perhaps, or buckskin jacket. I'd completed a first pass and seen nothing when my knees wobbled and nearly collapsed. A painted Creek warrior jogged toward Red Eagle toting a weapon too long and sleek to be a musket. A longrifle. Was it Betsy? At this distance, one long-rifle looked much like another, and there was every chance the chief possessed a better gun than his followers. But he'd carried no such weapon on the battlefield at Talladega, and I feared the worst.

Accepting the rifle, Red Eagle raised it above his head and addressed his braves. He spoke in Creek, but I needed no translation. It was the same speech commanders had given their warriors since time immemorial. Fight bravely for your homeland, fight for your wives and families, think of the songs that will be sung of you. And, of course, plunder your enemies' bodies and ravish their women. When his voice faded, the Red Sticks shook their weapons and screamed, raging about like so many savage beasts.

Red Eagle had driven them into a frenzy. Clearly, he was no

longer willing to wait for us to starve or deplete our ammunition. After hounding the militia for two full days he was willing to sacrifice a handful of followers to overrun our position and erase us from his sight.

Red Eagle thrust the rifle high a second time. The order to attack was coming. I felt it. So did the crazed Red Sticks. And so did the militiamen, who cursed and readied their muskets.

"Fire in groups of three," Zane snapped, indicating which three would go first. "Aim for the closest savages, then retire and reload while the next three fire." It was classic military strategy. Zane really *had* done some soldiering. "If we don't take at least half of them with us to hell, I'll be kicking your asses for eternity."

His orders didn't include me, so I moved to one side and checked the load of my musket. I longed once again for the rifle my father made me. If it was time to die, I wanted that gun in my hands, just as I wanted Davy at my side. Now I'd see neither again in this life, but might see Davy quite soon in the next.

Zane's nephew Ned, I noted, had also been excluded from the firing parties, and sat with head hung between his legs. As a fellow outcast, I felt a certain kinship, and, keeping my head down, crab-walked over next to him.

His head jerked up, eyes full of alarm. Then, seeing it was me, they narrowed in suspicion. Close up, he was even more unlovely than I'd thought, with mottled skin and a single scraggly eyebrow. "What d'you want?" His voice was somewhere between a whine and a growl.

"As long as we're about to die," I said, "thought we might do it together."

The noise that came from his mouth was like a horse breaking wind, and the smell wasn't much better. I turned my head and pretended a cough.

"That mean you don't think we're dying, or don't want company?"

The pale eyes studied me so long I began to feel prickly all over.

"Ever kill a redskin?" he asked.

I was about to say yes, but stopped. The subject, I had recently learned, was more complicated than I'd imagined, and this held no promise of a thoughtful discussion. I was still seeking a proper response when I detected a new odor, more subtle, but even more unpleasant than the first.

Ned had opened the carry-sack looped over his shoulder, and was rummaging about inside. The odor, I suddenly realized, was that of death, and I instinctively covered my nose and scuttled away from him. I did not want to know what he had in that bag, and any pity I'd felt for him was gone.

Red Eagle had paused in his speech, and his men answered with yips and shouts of approval. They too were smelling death, and it was not their own.

The moment had come. Red Eagle stretched out his arm, aimed a finger at us, and opened his mouth to issue a command. But another voice beat him to it. A voice speaking English.

"Stop!"

The Creeks exchanged bewildered looks. Red Eagle's head swiveled, seeking the source of the interruption. He threw an angry glance in our direction, though it had clearly not come from us. The Creeks buzzed with confusion.

"Red Eagle!" The voice quieted them.

I saw movement atop the bluff and pointed. Everyone looked.

Sixty feet above, a man in a green militia jacket and broad-brimmed campaign hat held a slender Indian woman by the neck. I thought for a moment the woman was Little Fawn, but her hair was shorter and adorned with an eagle feather, and her white gown of a different style. This woman's shoulders were exposed, her breasts heavy, and her protruding stomach proclaimed her to be with child.

"Leave this place," the militiaman shouted, "or your wife

dies! And with her, your baby!" Sunlight flashed on a blade at the woman's throat.

Zane's men uttered oaths of astonishment. Zane himself said quietly, "Who the hell is that?" but received no answer.

The Creeks grumbled and hissed until Red Eagle silenced them with a hand. He strode a few paces out from the bluff, affording himself a better view of those above. He spoke loudly in his own tongue.

The woman answered. Her voice was soft and musical, not at all like that of Little Fawn. She was putting up a brave front, but the catch in her voice betrayed her. Red Eagle posed a question and was quickly answered. For a moment there was silence.

My heart hammered like a drum. Was it possible we were going to live? My first thought was that I might have another chance at Red Eagle. My second was that I might once again see Little Fawn. My third was a niggling suspicion, a possibility I didn't dare express even to myself.

"Enough talk!" The man on the bluff bent the woman backward over his knee. A flick of his wrist would slit her jugular, and he had merely to release her to drop the bloody body at Red Eagle's feet. "Take your men and go!"

Red Eagle hung his head. His great shoulders quivered as if he might explode. The Red Sticks looked from him to the scene above and stirred uncertainly.

The man on the bluff said, "Now!"

Red Eagle looked up, his face white as bone. "For this indignity, you shall suffer above all others. I, who am called Truth Teller, swear it upon my ancestors. I will find you and drain your life's blood one drop at a time." Turning, he addressed his warriors in his own tongue. The Red Sticks stared, their shoulders slumped, and they trudged toward their ponies. Red Eagle walked among them, but more slowly, and the warriors veered wide around him.

The man on the bluff kept his knife at the woman's throat. Her sobs were so pitiful they touched even me. When the Creeks were mounted, Red Eagle climbed astride his own borrowed pony, cast a final scowl at the man above, and led his men thundering off toward the south.

Zane and his company watched them go. The man called Buzzard, a gawky fellow with a scraggly mustache and slack chin, cheered, while the others were still too stunned to celebrate. As the last of the Red Sticks vanished, Zane turned to stare at the couple atop the bluff. Muttering, he marched stiff-legged from the circle. His men followed, as if in a daze, and I trailed along behind.

The man on the bluff had sheathed his knife. He gazed down upon us with arms crossed over his chest. The woman, no longer sobbing, stood calmly at his side.

Zane reached the spot Red Eagle had occupied and craned his neck at them.

"Don't think me ungrateful," he shouted, "but who the blazes are you? Did Colonel Truitt send you?"

The man above clacked his heels and snapped off a crisp salute. In a voice quite different from that he'd used with Red Eagle, the man said, "Private David Crockett of Tennessee reportin' for duty, Cap'n." He removed the broad-brimmed hat and sailed it out over the bluff.

Myers said, "Shit."

Zane stood dumbfounded, but no less than I. Once again, I'd underestimated Davy's ability to pull rabbits out of hats. There was much I wanted to say to him, but could wrap my tongue around none of it.

Zane still stared at Davy. "One thing I don't understand, Crockett. Where in seven hells did you get Red Eagle's wife?" Under the circumstances, Zane's voice seemed surprisingly harsh.

Davy sensed it, too, and his grin grew tight. Meanwhile, the woman reached under her dress, extracted a round bundle and tossed it off the bluff. It fell directly toward me and I had to either catch it or step out of the way. I caught it—stained buckskin leggings wrapped around a soiled hunting shirt.

The woman shook out her hair, letting if fall to her shoulders. "Good morning, Stumblefoot. Did you miss me?"

CHAPTER 8

"You are afraid to live."

AS WE MADE preparations to leave, I spotted Ned kneeling at the side of the dead militiaman. His shoulders moved, and I thought for a moment he might be crying. Was it possible he'd had a friend?

But as I wondered this, Zane strode angrily up and cuffed him on the side of the head. Ned let out an animal-like bleat and flopped to his side, clutching his ear.

As the lad lay whimpering, Zane returned to his horse, and I could not resist creeping forward to see what Ned had been up to.

I was immediately sorry. The head of the fallen militiaman was a gory mess, and before averting my eyes, I realized his scalp had been peeled back. I turned away, sickened, and found Zane's hard eyes upon me.

"He collects scalps," Zane said woodenly. "White, Indian, man, woman or child. It doesn't matter, as long as they're dead, and someone else does the killing for him." He shook his head. "My sister should have strangled him at birth."

We were soon underway, and I finally managed to put the gruesome incident behind me.

For we who had just cheated death, the world seemed freshly made, brilliant in every detail. It was an exhilarating experience, and made for jovial comradeship.

The road east followed roughly the path of the stream, and the farther we traveled, the more the ground leveled out. To the south were gently rolling hills, and to the north rose the foothills of the Appalachians, hazy blue in the cold sunlight.

In the distance I saw wild turkeys and white-tailed deer. Sparrows soared overhead in flocks, moving south. We passed farmhouses with livestock in small corrals and fields with winter corn. A man chopping wood before a cabin waved a straw hat above his head and drew answering waves from the militia. Gradually the corn and wheat gave way to cotton. While many of the plants had been picked clean during the fall harvest, a shocking number of white tufts remained—testament, no doubt, to fear of marauding Red Sticks.

The further we traveled, the more the high spirits seemed to dissipate, and I observed Myers in guarded conversation with others of the company. Unseen by Zane, who rode well out in front, Myers spoke with one or two men at a time, then moved on. After each discussion, he and the others turned in their saddles to cast disapproving glares at us.

Little Fawn and I, leading Arrow, trailed ten yards behind the militia, while Davy, at the insistence of everyone, rode much further back, leading the silver thoroughbred. Nathan's body was now ripe almost beyond endurance. While I'd become somewhat accustomed to breathing through my mouth, the odor had caused a near-revolt among the militia. Only Zane's firm hand prevented them racing ahead without us to the plantation. And judging by the expressions of Myers and his friends, the body was not their only cause for discontent.

Little Fawn rode close at my side. Despite collaborating with Davy to save our skins, she was apparently still uncomfortable in his presence and found the company of Zane's men even more objectionable than my own. I was less than flattered, but somewhat soothed when she passed me a handful of hickory nuts. I had not eaten since leaving the Creek village, and devoured them at a gulp.

Little Fawn was eager to share the details of our amazing rescue. The white dress, she explained, was the same she'd worn earlier, but altered to resemble Sopath's wedding gown. And since she and her cousin had been childhood playmates it was no great feat to imitate her voice and mannerisms.

I nodded. I was curious what artifice she had employed to make her breasts appear heavy with milk, but not so imprudent as to ask.

"I don't mean to sound ungrateful," I said, "but after the way we parted company, why did you come back at all? And why take such a chance to save us?"

I felt sure I knew the answer—her obsession with the man riding silently behind us—but was curious how she would deal with the question. Her answer nearly knocked me out of the saddle.

"For you," she said simply.

For a long moment I was afraid to look at her. When I finally stole a glance, I found her watching from the corner of her eye, a small smile touching her lips. She was making sport of me again. The only surprise was that she had not called me Stumblefoot. Bitter words coiled on my tongue.

"We wish the same thing," Little Fawn said. "The death of Red Eagle. Perhaps it is time we joined forces."

I tried to grasp the meaning of this. I held my voice to a whisper. "You and I. Without Davy, you mean?"

"Davy is a good man, as we both know. But he has worked to spare Red Eagle, rather than take his life. We cannot be certain of his loyalties."

At this, I was speechless. I wasn't above misleading Davy, but conspiring against him was unthinkable. Little Fawn obviously sensed my feelings.

"He does not approve of killing," she said. "If the time comes that he must choose, will he aid us or thwart us once again?"

I thought hard about that, and felt I knew the answer. But Davy was nothing if not unpredictable.

All the while we talked, Myers had continued moving among the militiamen. The looks he cast us became ever more offensive. Feigning an itch in my side, I moved my pistol butt slightly closer to hand. The movement was not lost on Little Fawn. She shifted her reins, positioning her own right hand closer to her knife.

"If you don't trust Davy," I said, "what makes you think you can trust me? I have less reason than he to like Indians."

"You are less complicated. You want one thing and nothing else. For that reason, you are well suited to my purposes."

I almost feared to ask. "And what purposes are those?"

"To rid the world of Red Eagle and the other leaders of this rebellion, so that my people may move on with their lives."

"How do you know I want only one thing?"

"You are like an arrow, Penn McCoy. Once loosed, you will fly straight to the mark, but then you will be spent, without purpose."

My cheeks burned. "That's enough. I won't be turned into one of your quaint Indian fables. Yes, I will gladly trade my life for that of Red Eagle. I will do it because it needs doing, and because I am not afraid to die."

Little Fawn looked smug, as if she'd won some sort of victory. "No," she said, "you are not afraid to die. You are afraid to live."

That statement was too ridiculous to merit comment. Still, it irked me. I knew I was being mocked, but wasn't sure how.

SHORTLY BEFORE NOON we came to a spot where a large oak trunk lay partway across the stream, forming a pool. The ground on either bank was trampled and muddy from long use as a watering hole.

Zane called the company to a halt, and we took turns allowing the horses to drink. Some of the men simply flopped onto their backs, leaving the work to young Ned. Myers drew Zane aside and spoke to him in low tones. I watched sharply, hoping to glean some of what passed between them. Davy was less circumspect. He pushed his horse up next to Zane's roan and leaned in for an earful.

Zane looked up, annoyed. "Give us a moment here, Crockett. This doesn't concern you."

"Glad to hear it. Then you won't mind my listenin'."

Zane's brow knitted tight. "I command here. I'll ask you to remember that."

Davy nodded. "And as you may recollect, I get my orders from Old Hickory-face. Your coat has a powerful lot of shiny buttons, but his has more."

Zane set his teeth.

Myers said, "You may as well know, Crockett. The men aren't comfortable hauling that squaw of yours along. As long as Red Eagle thinks she's his bride, he'll be hot on our trail."

"He's been hot on your trail for three days now. What's changed?"

Zane let air hiss between his teeth. "We're nearly on Colonel Truitt's land. It's one thing to have those savages chasing us, but I don't want that woman bringing them down on *him*."

Davy took this in. "You reckon they'll attack the Truitt place?"

"I do."

"So," Myers put in, "we figure it's time we rid ourselves of the squaw." He looked back at Little Fawn, licking his fat lips. "Fact is, me and a few of the boys have volunteered to see her off, while you and the others ride on ahead."

Several men laughed.

Little Fawn stiffened. Something snapped inside me. The chestnut bolted forward, stopping squarely in front of Myers. "You're going to say you were joking," I said. "Then you'll promise never to joke that way again."

Myers glared at me, his face growing red. His eyes shifted to the rest of the company, finally back to me. Some of his confidence returned. "Or what? You'll shoot me, here amongst all my friends?"

I was surprised to see my pistol in my hand, fixed squarely on his burly chest. I felt the hard eyes of the other men upon me. I said, "With the utmost pleasure."

The men watched me. Several laid hands on their weapons.

Davy's drawl broke the silence. "S'posin' she did leave us. What would stop the Red Sticks from attackin' the house anyway? Seems to me we're better off *with* her than without. If Red Eagle gets too troublesome, she and me can do more play-acting."

Zane stretched his neck, scratching at his silky beard. After a moment he said, "Crockett's right. The girl stays with us."

"Just one thing," I said. "Little Fawn's not ours to keep or cast away. Whether she stays or goes is entirely up to her."

Zane frowned.

"That's so." Davy leaned slightly in his saddle, a hand on his rifle stock. "She decides."

I kept my eyes on Myers and Zane, but heard the smile in Little Fawn's voice. "I choose to stay. For now."

Myers's lip curled. "We still got unfinished business. Me and the Crockett whelp." He turned to Zane. "You promised, Cap'n. If we got loose from those redskins, we was free to scuffle."

Zane rubbed his beard with the back of his hand. "So I did. Crockett?"

"I want my seven dollars," Davy said, "plus interest. This here's as good a time as any."

Myers eased his bulk from his horse, flexed his arms and neck. "How'd you rather die—knife or tomahawk?"

Davy leaped to the ground. "I'll trust to bare knuckles. No holds barred."

Myers sneered. "You always were squeamish. But so be it. I'll twist your head off with my bare hands."

Davy pulled out his knife, pistol and tomahawk and handed them to me. I stuffed them into my belt along with my own. I felt like a human arsenal.

Zane's men quickly backed away, forming a circle. Their eyes were bright, their movements quick with excitement. I tied the horses to a tree downwind of the watering hole and took position on the edge of the circle next to Little Fawn. Her gaze was warm on my cheek, but I dared not look at her. I was still at a loss to explain my behavior. I'd had no intention of springing to her defense, at that or any other time. It was just something that happened—one of many recent occurrences I could not explain. All I knew for sure was that her attention made me uncomfortable.

Davy was still removing his canteen and powder horn when Myers charged, head down and body heaving like a bull. Davy hardly seemed to move, but when the big man was nearly upon him, he turned sideways and dropped the loop of his canteen strap over the fellow's head. As Myers roared past, Davy gripped the strap and yanked backwards. Myers's head snapped back, his great belly continuing the forward rush, and his feet whipped out as if climbing invisible steps. His body hung a moment in the air before crashing to earth with such force that the jolt ran up the chestnut's bones and into my own.

Davy casually unhooked the strap from the man's neck, tossing both canteen and powder horn to me. "There," he said. "Now we can get this frolic started."

Myers lay flat on his back, sucking air into his lungs. Davy waited.

I said, "Seeing as how you have a moment, what's the tale between you two?"

Davy glanced around at the rest of the company. Their faces were eager. "I was light of foot as a lad," he said, "and by the time I was twelve I'd traveled all the way to Virginia. Eventually I got a longin' for home and resolved to work my way back to Tennessee. Trouble was, I was five hundred miles away, with only four dollars to my name."

Myers flopped about like a turtle on its back, trying to right himself. The little man called Buzzard stepped forward to lend a hand, but Davy stopped him with a scowl.

"That's when I fell in with this scoundrel," Davy said, "who called himself Adam Myers. Said he was a wagoner from Tennessee, and that after haulin' a load of flour to its destination he planned to return there. As this suited my needs, I went along. He seemed a tolerable enough companion, then, but that was before he got his hands on my money."

Myers finally found his legs and swayed to his feet. His eyes were hot enough to melt steel.

"Myers kept delayin' his return to Tennessee, and was soon haulin' loads from one place to another. I took a job plowin' fields for another feller, and after earnin' enough to buy decent clothes I resolved to join Myers on a trip to Baltimore. My mistake, it developed, was trustin' him to hold my money—now amountin' to seven dollars—for safekeepin'."

Myers had his steam up now, and circled Davy at arm's length, his balled fists big as cabbages.

Davy watched, turning only when necessary to keep the man in sight. "In Baltimore, a ship's cap'n invited me on a journey to London. I was all-fired eager to go, but when I asked for my money, Myers refused, offerin' to horsewhip me instead."

Myers threw a roundhouse right at Davy's head. Davy leaned backwards, watching the punch sail by, and Myers buried his left fist deep in Davy's stomach. The right had been a feint. Davy folded over the punch and sat down hard. Yanking his hand free, Myers raised a boot above Davy's head. One good stamp would crush Davy's skull, but Davy grabbed the boot, twisting, and Myers toppled sideways. Up in a flash, Davy pinned an arm and a leg behind Myers' back and sat on him.

"At length," Davy said, "I had to get away at all hazards. So one mornin' I gathered my gear and cut out without a farthing to my name. I met another, more kindly, wagoner who put my case to Myers, but this skunk claimed my money was already spent."

A pistol banged, startling everyone, and Davy clapped a hand to his neck. On the far side of the circle stood Buzzard, a smoking weapon in his hand. I drew my own pistol, cocked the hammer and leveled it at Buzzard's chest.

Storming across the circle, Zane delivered a backhand blow that drove Buzzard to his knees. "I'll have no interference here."

Davy brought the hand from his neck and examined it. It was red with blood, but the wound appeared slight.

Myers wiggled out from under Davy and staggered to his feet. "The whelp lies. There was no money. He repaid my kindness by stealing a horse and I never saw him again."

Zane said, "This contest will continue. If Crockett wins, he'll get his seven dollars."

"Plus interest," Davy said. "He cost me that trip to London."

Zane glared at him. "Plus interest. But if 'Smith' here wins, he's the new owner of Crockett's dun."

"That's robbery," I said, my pistol still cocked. "Better we part company here and now."

Davy waved me off. "Cool your boilers, Penn. I agree. The money against my horse."

Myers smiled, broken teeth showing through his mud-caked lips. He extended a paw. "Shake on it."

Davy eyed the hand with distaste. Finally he took it, gave a perfunctory shake.

"And once you're dead," Myers said, "I'll pay court to that redskin gal, before I feed her to the colonel's hogs."

Still gripping Myers' hand, Davy yanked him forward, pulling him toward a vicious head butt. Myers twisted, avoiding the collision, and a bleating cry smote my ears, but with their heads locked together I couldn't tell from whom it came.

Myers freed his hand and flailed his arms. Davy growled, shaking like an enraged bear, and I saw he had his teeth clamped onto Myers' ear. The big man's screams reached new heights.

"I believe," I yelled above the noise, "that Myers is hollering 'Injun!'"

Zane bent over, hands on knees, peering into Myers' face. "That so, 'Smith'?"

"Yes, damn it! I give! Make the bastard stop!"

Davy's growling grew more fierce. Thrusting my pistol into Little Fawn's hands, I raced forward and clutched him by the shoulders. "Enough, Davy, you've won!"

He peered sideways at me, his eyes smoking hot. And he still had hold of that ear. The devil had him sure. The threat to Little Fawn had been too much.

"Beat that devil back," I told him. "Tamp him down. Show him who's in charge!"

Davy made a sound between a snarl and a growl, with nothing human in it. I tried to pin his arms, but he easily slipped my grasp. Little Fawn appeared, speaking soothing words into his other ear.

"Davy!" I said. "It's Penn. Penn and Little Fawn. You've won. Time to let go."

Davy's eyes closed. His body tensed, quivered. With a savage growl he pushed Myers away and spat blood onto the ground.

Myers' ear was torn half off his head.

Zane said, "God Almighty."

"Nope," I said. "Not even close."

BY THE TIME the fighters were cleaned and bandaged, Davy's eyes were clear, his breathing easy. All that time, Buzzard had knelt nearby, regarding him with eyes big as turkey eggs. The little fellow seemed near tears, like a boy who'd just lost his dog. Davy stepped toward him, extending a hand.

"By and large," Davy said, "I'm a forgivin' sort of man. Promise not to shoot me again, and we'll be friends."

His face now all aglow, Buzzard allowed Davy to pull him up. "Yessir, Mr. Crockett, sir."

"Davy."

"Yessir, Mr. Crockett. Davy. Whatever you say."

A hubbub arose as Zane demanded Myers' money. The big

man produced two dollars, claiming it was all he had, but a search of his kit bag revealed thirteen more, all of which was transferred to Davy's pockets.

Myers said, "You'll regret this, Cap'n. Crockett can't be trusted. He's a tricky bastard, as we've all seen. I'll lay odds he knows more than he's telling. Hell, he may even know—"

Zane smacked him across the face. "You're the one I can't trust, Smith. Or is it Myers? Consider yourself discharged."

Myers said, "But—"

"Another word from you, and I'll have you shot." He motioned to Buzzard and another man. "You two get this jacket off him. It belongs to the colonel." He turned back to Myers. "You can keep the hat. Maybe it'll keep the flies off that ear."

Myers sputtered as he was led in shirtsleeves to his horse. Once mounted, he glared hatred at Zane, then shifted it to Davy. Unspoken words poured from his eyes like venom.

Davy said, "Ride long and hard, Myers. Next time we meet I'll take a horsewhip to you."

With a snarl, Myers kneed his horse around, jumped the creek and galloped off toward the south.

"The rest of you mount up," Zane said. "It's time we reported to the colonel."

Buzzard piped up, "Beggin' your pardon, Cap'n, but it may be too late for that."

Once he had everyone's attention, he jabbed a thumb at the eastern sky. There, boiling above the treetops, was an all-too-familiar sight.

Smoke.

CHAPTER 9

"There is blame enough for all."

THE FLAMES WERE visible half a mile away. If it was only one building, it was a big one, and burning like merry hell. Huge cypress trees lined the road, forming a leafy canopy, and it was like riding down a chute into a fiery furnace. We thundered past storehouses, slaves' quarters and a score of smaller buildings. The Truitt plantation was larger than many towns I'd seen.

Emerging from the trees at last, we beheld the fire in all its glory. Only the outlines of the building were visible through the flames, but the slanted roof and rising peak signaled it was either a barn or a very large church. The great number of grooms and servants clutching the reins of frightened horses in the surrounding fields argued for a barn.

Fifty yards to the left stood another building, mostly brick, with a roofed portico and marble columns rivaling those of Independence Hall back in Philadelphia.

Clouds of black smoke billowed from the barn, blotting out the afternoon sun. No one fought the blaze. The barn was too big and the fire too far out of control. Hostlers, slaves and servants in livery simply stood watching, their faces lit orange by the flames. Cows, pigs and chickens ran in aimless circles in the fields beyond.

Zane led his men galloping across the lawn of the mansion. Davy veered instead toward the barn, where he leaped from his dun and ran to the horse-handlers, shouting questions. Little

Fawn and I followed, arriving in time to catch the answers. Yes, all the animals were safely out of the barn, though one wrangler had died in the effort. The heat, even at a distance, was blistering, and I was quickly bathed in sweat.

As there was nothing to be done at the barn, Davy led us toward the house. Under the portico sat a white-haired, white-bearded man in a wheelchair. His face was craggy, his nose long and sharp, and his eyes, as they flashed over us, pierced me to the bone. His shoulders were wide as an oxen yoke. Even confined to the wheelchair, he exuded power and authority. This, I had no doubt, was the renowned Colonel Thaddeus Truitt.

Zane stood at the colonel's side, shouting over the whoosh of flames. Whether Truitt heard him I could not say, for the old man's attention was fixed on the silver thoroughbred and the blanketed burden tied across its saddle. He seemed no longer aware of the great flaming pyre of his barn. After what seemed an age, the old man turned to scrutinize each of his militiamen in turn. Most dropped their heads or turned quickly away. Zane alone held Truitt's gaze, but his cheek twitched like he had a mouthful of grasshoppers.

Raising a hand, the colonel ordered a groom to lead the horse and body away, and for a moment I saw the officer who had helped Francis Marion harry the British from the Carolina swamps. How that much man fit into the wheelchair, even with one leg missing, was a puzzle.

As questions were asked and answered, we learned the fire had indeed been the work of the Red Sticks. Truitt's servants had seen only three painted Indians, and one sounded exactly like Big Frog. I snuck a glance at Little Fawn. Her head snapped sideways, her eyes challenging, and I quickly turned away. I wondered if this evil had been done at Red Eagle's order, or on Big Frog's own initiative.

I felt the weight of Colonel Truitt's gaze upon me only once, though I noticed he devoted considerable attention to Davy. At no time did he betray the slightest interest in Little Fawn.

Eventually, when it was clear there was no chance of the fire spreading to the house or other buildings, Truitt spoke to a liveried servant, who invited us into the mansion. This invitation included Davy, Zane and me, while the rest of the militia were to help the grooms care for the displaced stock.

The colonel's instructions made no provision for Little Fawn. She turned away without a word, but Davy threw me a look. I touched her shoulder, ducked under the expected slap, and said, "Davy would like you to join us."

She eyed me sternly. "What about you?"

"Me too," I said to placate her.

Whether she believed me or not, she took my arm. The servant's eyes widened as we passed through the great double doors, but no one tried to stop us. Another servant took our hats and hung them on a rack. Truitt's main hall was big enough to accommodate Jackson's army and fancy enough to awe the crowned heads of Europe. The floor was a checkerboard of black and white marble stretching half an acre to a grand staircase, and above it all hung a crystal chandelier the size of a small house. Lining the walls were pedestalled statues of Greeks or Romans, some lacking heads or arms. A great number of these were naked. I felt Little Fawn's eyes on me and quickly averted my gaze.

Higher up were paintings in gilded frames. The largest, a good thirty feet wide, depicted a band of men battling an army of Redcoats. At the center of the action, an officer with a fox tail adorning his hat flourished a pistol in one hand and sword in the other. Next to him, a powerfully-built man with black hair and a craggy face shouted encouragement to a group of rough-clad patriots. The black-haired man was Colonel Truitt himself, at the side of Francis Marion, the legendary Swamp Fox. One of Marion's men waved a war-torn Continental Army flag, and I was almost moved to salute.

The servant guided us past these wonders to a large sitting room with windows overlooking the burning barn. Zane and the colonel sat facing the flames. Having more than my fill of burning buildings of late, I led Little Fawn to a maple divan with its back to the window. Davy sat on a straight-backed chair next to my end of the divan.

Colonel Truitt's eyes lanced out at Little Fawn, then focused on me, pinning me to the seat back. Scowling, he turned his attention to Davy. "I will not have that... *creature* in my house."

"If you mean Little Fawn," Davy said, "I'm right sorry to hear it. Means Penn and me will be leavin' too." He stood, shooting a glance at me, and I scrambled up as well. Little Fawn remained in place.

Truitt's neck swelled as if he'd grown a goiter.

Zane said, "To be fair, the girl helped save us from the Red Sticks. I believe she's a friendly."

"William Weatherford was also a *friendly*, until he became Red Eagle." The colonel's voice was a knife scraping stone. "He sat at my table, shared my whiskey. Then he kidnapped my daughter and murdered my son. I've come to believe it was a mistake to hope these savages could adapt to civilization."

"A belief I've long held," Zane said. "Indians are little better than animals, and the rich lands of this territory are wasted on them."

"So," Little Fawn's tone was scathing, "you believe my people should be forced from their land and pushed into the wilderness?"

Zane was unfazed. "The wilderness is where they damn well belong. I've no doubt they, and *you*, will be happier there."

"And you, Colonel. Is this your feeling as well?"

Ignoring her, Truitt turned to Davy. "You have honored me in returning my son's body. It could not have been pleasant. And I wish very much to hear of Nathan's final moments. For those reasons, the woman may remain, provided she does not speak again. My forbearance has limits."

Davy looked a question at Little Fawn.

She said nothing, but I heard a small *hmph*.

Truitt said, "Now. Please. What happened to my son?"

No one was eager to speak. Davy and Zane exchanged glances. The colonel said, "Gabriel. You first."

Zane wet his lips, stretched his neck. "We were seeking Jackson's camp when the Red Sticks appeared out of nowhere. Outnumbered, we retreated, but they'd nearly overtaken us when we heard a gunshot and Red Eagle's horse went down. We later learned that was thanks to Mr. Crockett here. As we made our escape, Nathan apparently dropped out of formation and worked his way back to meet Crockett and McCoy. We failed to notice his absence for several miles, at which point the Indians were again hard after us."

Truitt said, "You *failed to notice.*"

Zane squirmed in his chair. "Your pardon, Colonel. I ride at the front of my men. Your son was in the rear, and the man nearest him was Buzzard."

Truitt sighed, as if this explained it. He shifted his fierce gaze to Davy and me. "You two were there when he died?"

"We three," Davy said, "but the blame is mine. It was my plan that went catawampus, and—"

"There is blame enough for all," Little Fawn said. "Even Stum—, even Penn here will admit that is so. We must all accept responsibility."

I braced myself for an outburst from Truitt. His face was grim, but his voice calm. "I wish to hear it. All of it."

Davy told it truthfully, though perhaps emphasizing Nathan's accomplishments at the expense of his own. When he was done, Truitt turned to me.

"You killed the savage who murdered my son?"

I nodded. Strangely, I took no pride in that fact.

"Then I would like to shake your hand."

I sat staring until Little Fawn jabbed my ribs, then crossed the room and took his hand. It was big, like the rest of him, and coursing with strength. I fought the urge to flinch.

"I am in your debt, Mr. McCoy. Any favor you ask I shall endeavor to grant."

I considered this. As Little Fawn had said so plainly, there was only one thing I wanted. But before I killed Red Eagle, we had another task. "There is one thing," I said, watching for some sign he regretted the offer. "We seek news of your daughter Lacy. We promised Nathan to bring her home safely."

Truitt's eyes glistened. He turned to Davy, and for the first time glanced briefly at Little Fawn. "You are unusual people. You do me a great service, and all you ask in return is to do me another."

Davy said, "After losin' your son, I'd understand you not trustin' us with Lacy."

Truitt waved that away. "What's done is done. Nathan was headstrong, a quality he inherited from me. I've no doubt that had he followed your instructions, he would be alive today." I saw why this man had been such a great leader. Davy had not mentioned Nathan's disobedience. The old man deduced that on his own. "My answer, of course, is yes. Captain Zane will guide you to the Creek village where Lacy is rumored to be held. He will provide whatever assistance you require."

Davy looked at Zane, receiving a brisk nod. "If I ain't bein' too nosy, Colonel, there's one thing I been puzzlin' on. Why would Red Eagle snatch your daughter? Is he wantin' ransom?"

Truitt's wide shoulders stiffened. This was not a new question. "No. No ransom. Nor any other outright declaration that he has her." The colonel stared at his lap.

"Then what makes you so all-fired sure he does?"

"My good friend Gabriel here." Truitt looked up at Zane. "We were playing cards in this very room the night it happened. The Indians approached the house quietly enough, then began screaming like all the devils in Hell. Gabriel rushed out in time to see Red Eagle pull poor Lacy across that black stallion of his."

Zane gave a somber nod. "That's so. Same horse you brought in, Crockett, with the arrow mark on its forehead."

"And you went after 'em?"

"Of course. But by the time the servants had my horse saddled, the savages were well out of sight. I searched half the night and failed to find sign of them. Next day I took a few of the colonel's hands and followed their trail. It led west, through that clearing where they ambushed us yesterday, but soon split in a score of directions."

Little Fawn said, "What village is this where you believe she is held? And what makes you believe she is there?"

Zane hesitated, glanced at Truitt. The colonel looked directly at Little Fawn for the first time. "Reasonable questions, I think. Answer her, Gabriel."

"I've made it known there is a standing reward for information as to Miss Truitt's whereabouts. We were told by friendly Creeks, or Creeks *professing* to be friendly, that a number of young white women were taken to a place called the 'Holy Ground,' near a village at the confluence of the Coosa and Tallapoosa rivers." Zane's tone was condescending, and he pointedly addressed his remarks to Davy rather than Little Fawn.

Little Fawn said, louder than necessary, "Thank you."

"Pardon, Colonel," I said, "but back to Davy's question. What would Red Eagle have to gain by taking her?"

Truitt rubbed his forehead. "He may still make demands. Barring that, my best guess is that he was warning other settlers not to interfere with his activities—showing them how easily their wives and children could be taken."

Davy said, "Hm."

"But we can't judge his motives as if he were a civilized man," Truitt continued. "His actions at Fort Mims proved that. He's a killer of women and children, a mad dog that must be put down before he can do further damage."

I clutched my stomach. The mere mention of Fort Mims gave me convulsions. I glanced sideways at Little Fawn. Her face was stony.

Truitt said, "Are you ill, Mr. McCoy?"

I forced a smile. "Only sick at heart. My condition will be much improved by Red Eagle's death."

A coffee-skinned young woman entered without a sound and waited, head bowed, near the door.

Truitt said, "What is it, Maylissa?"

"Supper's ready, Colonel, sir.'

"Thank you, my dear. And bless you." His voice was surprisingly gentle. Truitt turned back to us. "The British have beguiled many of my slaves with promises of freedom and even great riches. Those who remain do so because they *choose* to serve me."

No one said anything to that.

"I have dwelled too long upon my own misfortunes," Truitt said. "I sometimes forget that others have suffered as much or more. I will be pleased to have you gentlemen as my guests at table. You too, Gabriel."

Davy cleared his throat, nodded toward Little Fawn.

"If she behaves herself," Truitt said, "she is welcome to dine in the kitchen. If not, she can eat outside with the other animals." He flicked a finger, and the servant whirled his wheelchair about.

Davy and I remained seated, awaiting an explosion from Little Fawn. Instead, she sat staring at her lap. "He has lost a son to my people, and perhaps a daughter. I cannot judge him until he has time to grieve. Go. Eat. This task of *behaving* will require all of my attention."

AT DINNER, DAVY did his best to lighten the mood by regaling us with a series of colorful yarns. I found them all quite amusing, but he got no reaction from Truitt until telling of a bear named Deathhug. His wife had raised him from a cub, he claimed, and the beast now sat at table and dined with the family.

"You're making that up," Zane said.

"Not a bit," Davy protested. "Trouble was, that poor old feller had a delicate stomach. I was obliged to shoot an Injun and boil him up with vegetables, lizards and a crocodile's tail. We fed the critter half a peck every two hours, and he was soon right as rain."

At this Colonel Truitt had to smile, Zane let out a snort, and the ice was finally broken.

Two hours later, our bellies full and spirits warmed with brandy, Davy and I were back in the main hall. Rooms had been prepared for us upstairs, and I, for one, was anxious to retire. Over dinner, the colonel had shared his assessment of the Creek War, and my head swam with names and events.

Red Eagle, he'd explained, was only one of several Red Stick leaders. Some went by Indian names like High Headed Jim, while others sounded decidedly non-Indian, like Josiah Francis. There was even a black shaman who called himself the Prophet Abraham. And Andy Jackson was not the only commander intent on quelling them. Georgia had sent General John Floyd across the Chattahoochee with fifteen hundred men, supported by friendly Creek chiefs William McIntosh and Big Warrior, while Mississippi sent General Ferdinand Claiborne up the Alabama to join forces with large numbers of Choctaws and Chickasaws.

In Truitt's view, this conflict was about many things—among them the efforts of officials in Washington to transform the Creeks, traditionally hunters, into merchants and farmers; the fact that the Indians were deep in debt to trading companies under control of the Spanish; and the machinations of the British in what he called "Mr. Madison's War."

Like my father and other learned men of Philadelphia, Truitt felt President Madison's declaration of war upon Great Britain had been the height of folly. The root of the problem was England's war with France. Having nearly doubled the size of their fleet—to as many as six hundred ships—they required many more sailors to man them. In their view, every British-born American was fair game, and they'd sent press gangs into the States to collect them, scooping up a good many American-born citizens in the process.

And things had only gotten worse. In retaliation for the British stirring up Indian trouble along the northwest frontier, U.S. troops had made several attempts to drive them out of Canada, most of which met with dismal failure. Now the British had cut off trade with the States, and were blockading U.S. ports to prevent commerce with France.

Many in New England had become so discouraged with Madison's efforts that they insisted on withholding troops and money. Truitt vehemently disagreed. Though most of the fighting thus far had been confined to Canada, he was certain England would soon turn her attention to the South, particularly while American armies were occupied with the Red Sticks. It was time, he believed, for all of us to rally together and support the cause.

It was all too much for me, and in any case irrelevant to my purposes. To me, this war was about Red Eagle murdering my family and kidnapping Lacy. It was a contest between him and me—a contest I planned to win.

While Zane remained behind to discuss plans with the colonel, Davy insisted we explore the wonders of the main hall. A portrait on the wall opposite the painting of Truitt and the Swamp Fox caught my attention and drew me across the room. Unlike the austere images of Martha Washington and Dolly Madison I'd seen in Philadelphia, this canvas depicted a young woman who enjoyed life and didn't care who knew it. She smiled playfully, as if daring me to take her hand and pull her through the frame into the hall.

"Gentlemen, allow me to introduce Miss Lacy Truitt." Between us stood Little Fawn, face freshly scrubbed and eyes a-twinkle. She had evidently behaved well enough to merit dinner.

Lacy Truitt had masses of honey-blonde curls and deep blue eyes that shone like sapphires. Her chin was ever-so-dainty, and her nose a trifle less pointed than her father's—an imperfection that enhanced rather than detracted from her beauty.

I gasped as an elbow jabbed my ribs.

"Pull in your tongue, Stumblefoot. There is drool on your chin."

I half-raised a hand to my mouth. Little Fawn saw me and smirked. I arched an eyebrow at her. "Jealous?"

"Piteous. Such a lady would think you dust beneath her feet."

Stung, I could think of no proper retort. "Is that so."

"It is," she said. "And she would, of course, be right."

A door at the rear of the room creaked open a few inches and stopped. After a moment it opened further and Buzzard's half-bald head appeared. "Mr. Crockett," he whispered. "Where's Mr. Crockett?"

"Here I be." Davy came around the staircase. "What's ailin' you?"

The little man peered carefully around the hall before beckoning us to follow. His sallow, nervous face was paler than ever. "This way. Quickly."

We followed a narrow hallway past many closed doors, through a pantry and finally to a windowed door opening into the night. At Buzzard's urging, we stepped onto a dark patio at the rear of the mansion. He closed the door behind us and we stood in the light of a three-quarter moon. The air was cool enough to show our breath.

Davy said, "What?"

Now that he had us here, Buzzard seemed reluctant to speak. His mouth was grim and his eyes darted about as if every shadow held danger.

"Easy," Davy said. "You an' me are friends, remember? Why'd you bring us here?"

"The dogs," Buzzard said. "Beware of the dogs."

I'd seen no dogs since we arrived. I was cold and ready for bed. I snorted and turned back to the door.

Davy said, "We're almighty grateful for the warnin'. Just where might these dogs be found?"

Buzzard pointed out into the night, across the rear lawn of the mansion toward a line of moonlit trees.

A voice sounded inside the house. Male, with authority, and coming nearer. We moved away from the patio door, and out stepped Captain Zane. He was not pleased to see us.

"I'm hunting Buzzard," he said. "One of the servants said he was about."

I turned, amazed to find the little man no longer with us. He'd vanished as surely as if he were a ghost.

"Sorry, Cap'n," Davy said. "It's just us three."

Scratching his beard, Zane regarded Davy a moment before turning back to the house. "You should get some rest. We set out at first light."

"There a message?"

Zane stopped halfway through the doorway. "Message?"

"For Buzzard," Davy said. "Case we sees him."

"No message." The door snapped shut.

CHAPTER 10

"You're a willful cuss."

MY FEATHER MATTRESS was soft as a cloud, and I would have happily remained abed for a week. But when Davy woke me, urging me into my clothes, the moon was still high in the sky. The servants had not prepared a room for Little Fawn, so Davy'd snuck her into his and stretched out on the floor in mine.

Not until we'd crossed the lawn behind the house and stood in the shadows of the trees did he stop to explain himself. "Them dogs," he said. "I aim to find them dogs."

I was still shaking the sleep out of my head. "Pardon my ignorance, but aren't we leaving in few hours to find Lacy? Do we really need dogs more than sleep?"

"Buzzard's all het up about 'em."

"Ah, yes. Buzzard. Who am I to question the ravings of a halfwit?"

"Knew you'd understand. Step lightly now. Best they don't hear us comin'." Then he was off, and I had no choice but to follow.

The tall cypresses created deep shadows, but there was little or no undergrowth. After perhaps fifty yards, I caught glimpses of other buildings in the distance. One was long and low with a lamp flickering in the window. Davy led that way first, but stopped well short, and I bumped into him from behind.

"What the hell."

He stood silent a moment. "Bunkhouse for the militia."

"And how do you know that?"

"Snorin'. Don't you hear it? Same snores we heard last night."

I was still shaking my head over the notion of identifying men by their snores when Davy was off again, and I ran to catch up. Our next destination was a smaller building, hardly more than a shack. This time I was alert for a quick halt, and was not disappointed. "What now?"

"Smithy. Smell them warm coals?"

I did, and the scent brought memories of my father's forge. "Yes," I gulped.

"Good man. Now this way." He nodded off into the darkness beyond the blacksmith shop.

We'd covered another thirty yards when the land began to rise, and we'd reached the top of a small hill before I spotted the windows of another building glinting through the trees. "Overseer's cottage," Davy said. This appeared to be a two-story structure with a chimney.

Wary as I was, he fooled me again, stopping in the trees well short of the house. Motioning me to stay, he melted into the woods and was lost from sight. I listened hard for barks, growls, snuffling or the pad of canine feet. Nothing. My nose tickled and I pinched it to prevent a sneeze.

"You." Davy's voice startled me, and the sneeze escaped. He was now somewhere in the darkness behind me. "I might 'a' knowed."

"You brought *him* and not me?" The new voice was Little Fawn's. "He could not sneak up on a rock."

I sniffed, clearing my nose.

Davy said, "This could be a might dangerous. I meant to spare you."

"So. You seek the dogs."

How did she know that? I felt like an actor who had walked on stage during the wrong play.

"I'm thinkin' we'll find 'em," Davy said, "at that house out yonder. I'll be grateful if you and Penn stay here, coverin' my retreat, whilst I take a closer look."

"Stay with him?" Little Fawn stepped out of the shadows, her eyes flashing in the moonlight. "I may as well stand here and shout, 'Hello the house! Intruders in the woods!'"

"Much obliged," Davy said. "I shan't be long."

Little Fawn and I glared at each other. The night was getting colder. I peered through the trees toward the overseer's house, but saw no sign of Davy.

Little Fawn said, "Penn…"

I felt ticklish again. I said, "What did you mean earlier, saying I was afraid to live?"

She was quiet a moment. I waited.

"Suppose you met Red Eagle here, tonight, and killed him. What would you do tomorrow?"

I opened my mouth, but no words came out. I thought furiously. "I would… I would keep looking for Lacy Truitt." I turned to face her, proud to have proved her wrong.

"That does not count. Suppose you killed Red Eagle and rescued Lacy at the same time. Then what would you do?"

I peered into the night, wishing Davy would return.

"You are afraid to live, Penn McCoy, because you have not allowed yourself to grieve."

Her words conjured up images of Maggie and my parents. The familiar ache began in my chest, expanded into my stomach.

A dog barked in the distance. Then others. Around the side of the building galloped Davy. "Run! Make for the mansion!" He tore through a patch of bright moonlight, and I saw four large, ominous shapes bounding along behind him.

I turned and ran down the hill, Little Fawn close beside me. The barking grew louder. The dogs were gaining. I picked up my heels.

Before we'd covered fifty yards, Davy had pulled even with us. My legs wobbled and my chest felt close to bursting. Little

Fawn ran as effortlessly as a deer, and I wondered if that ability had prompted her name. Far to our right, the bunkhouse door crashed open, disgorging militiamen in various stages of undress. Over my shoulder I saw the lead dog—a dark, spotted brute half the size of a horse—close upon our heels.

We darted through the cypress trees, the mansion now less than a hundred yards away. But it might have been a mile. Two of the dogs, the spotted hound and a shaggy-haired monster with a white or yellow coat, quickly flanked us, then pulled ahead. As we burst from the woods onto the lawn, the two leaders turned on us, snarling. I clawed the tomahawk from my belt. Little Fawn drew her knife.

Davy said, "Stop! Let 'em surround us."

Pressing our backs together, we brandished our weapons. The two leaders took positions in front of us, while the other hounds, black as shadows, completed the circle. These animals had been well trained, an accomplishment I might in other circumstances have admired.

The spotted one, apparently the pack's leader, did most of the barking. His spine was rigid and a row of fur bristled from the nape of his neck to the base of his tail. His bared teeth glistened. My hand crept toward my pistol.

"No, Penn." Davy's voice was barely a whisper. "Wait."

Lights were coming on in the mansion. I swiveled to see the militia advancing slowly from the trees. Their long woolies gave them the appearance of ghosts in the moonlight.

The spotted hound lunged at me. I swung my tomahawk, but the blow glanced off, and the beast's foul breath filled my nostrils. Then I was bumped aside and Davy stood in my place. He held the dog's legs at shoulder height, his face bare inches from the gnashing fangs. And he began to grin.

I sucked in my breath. Davy looked so almighty happy you'd have sworn he was holding one of his own beloved children rather than a snarling beast from Hell.

The hound lunged, snapping at Davy's nose, but always just

out of reach. Giving this up, the animal fell to growling. Davy grinned on, looking steadily into the dog's eyes. And when the hound at last fell silent, Davy opened his mouth, extended his tongue and licked the beast on the snout.

I wrinkled my nose. Little Fawn emitted a soft laugh.

The dog's huge tongue lolled out and lapped Davy's face, first tentatively, then with enthusiasm, and Davy patted its spotted hide.

A collective gasp came from the servants gathered on the mansion's patio. The militia halted twenty yards behind us, eyes wide and mouths agape.

Davy released the dog, and it stood once again on four legs, looking up at him and panting. Ten feet away, the shaggy yellow growled, a sound echoed by the others. Davy's new friend bared its great teeth and faced each of them in turn, making a sound that chilled me to my heels. The two black dogs sat back on their haunches and whined. The shaggy one put up more of an argument, but after a few halfhearted snarls it too bowed to the spotted hound's dominance.

"You three are supposed to be in bed." Captain Zane stood behind us, squarely between the two black hounds. "Why are you disturbing my dogs?"

I said, "*Your* dogs?"

"Penn and the lady here were just taking a moonlight stroll." Davy gave Zane a broad wink, intimating just what kind of stroll it had been. Little Fawn giggled, and my face flushed. "I began to fret the Red Sticks might be about, and came to check on 'em. Those hounds of yours musta figured we wanted to play."

A low buzz of conversation came from the militia. Zane quieted them with a stern look. Buzzard, I noticed, stood in the rear, peeking between two larger men.

Zane said, "I'll post men here in the yard. They'll guard against savages, and protect anyone compelled to take another *stroll*."

"Uncommon kind of you, Cap'n."

Zane seemed about to say more. Instead, he made eye contact

with each of the dogs, put two fingers between his lips and whistled. The two blacks sprang up immediately and trotted back toward the trees. The shaggy yellow glared at us, skirted wide around us and fell in at Zane's side. The spotted hound remained at Davy's feet.

Zane scowled. "Samson. Come!"

The hound glanced at him with casual interest and returned his attention to Davy.

Zane clapped his hands. "Samson!"

Davy reached down and scratched Samson behind the ears. The dog closed his eyes and rolled out his enormous tongue. "You oughta go with your master," Davy said.

Samson nuzzled his hand.

Davy pointed toward Zane. "Go," he told the hound.

Samson lay down and rested his head between his legs. He peered up at Davy, his tail wagging.

It was hard to tell in the moonlight, but Zane's face appeared as red as his beard. Davy turned to him with an elaborate shrug.

The militiamen laughed, earning a withering look from Zane. "We leave at dawn," Zane said through clamped teeth. "Be ready." He spun on his heel and marched stiffly out toward the overseer's house, the yellow hound close at his side.

Davy looked down at the spotted brute and shook his head. "You're a willful cuss, ain't you."

Panting happily, the animal flopped onto his back, stretched his hind legs and exposed his belly. His front paws made a stroking motion that said, quite clearly, *Indeed I am. Pet me.*

WELL BEFORE SUNUP, we mounted our horses and assembled in the yard before the mansion. The colonel, Zane said, wished to address us before we left. His dozen-odd men joshed each other and laughed, pleased to be on the offensive at last.

Davy still refused to explain the previous night's dog hunt.

He'd been chewing on a hunch, he said, and was not ready to spit it out.

Samson, after a night of whining on the patio, was there to greet us. The daylight showed his coat to be a grayish blue, punctuated with black spots. Davy tossed him a slice of bacon he'd saved from breakfast and the hound made it vanish. Davy seemed resolved to let the hound accompany us. I suspected he saw in Samson a free spirit akin to his own.

A servant in livery emerged, pushing Colonel Truitt's wheelchair. The colonel was swathed in blankets, and I was suddenly envious. My trousers were thin and the morning air cold.

"I wish you all luck," Truitt said, "and will pray for your success. For men such as yourselves, I understand that honor is its own reward. Nevertheless, I wish to offer further incentive." This got the attention of the militia. They quieted their horses, waiting. "I will pay one thousand dollars to the man most instrumental in freeing my daughter." When no one spoke, he continued, "I offer a further thousand for Red Eagle's scalp, and twenty dollars each for those of his warriors."

The militiamen let out a whoop.

Zane said, "Pardon, Colonel. But if for some reason Miss Lacy is not found, does the offer for the scalps still stand?"

"It does. Red Eagle's deviltry has gone far enough. He must be snuffed out, along with all who support him."

"Your pardon, Colonel." Little Fawn's voice was hard as ice. "How will you tell the scalp of a Red Stick from that of a *friendly?*"

Truitt chewed a lip, and a few men snickered. After an awkward silence Truitt said, "Good luck to you, men, and godspeed."

Zane led the procession onto the tree-lined road. Davy followed with Arrow. He was hopeful the stallion might prove valuable if we were forced to bargain for Lacy's freedom.

Little Fawn's face was tight, and Davy appeared thoughtful.

I urged my horse up next to his and said, "The colonel's words remind you of anyone?"

"Sadly, yes."

"Old Hickory," I said.

"Now that you mention it," Davy said, "that's so. But I was thinkin' more of you."

I was so stunned I dropped the chestnut's reins, and she ambled to a halt. Had I really sounded that bad? Did Little Fawn see me in the same light? Gathering up the reins, I started after them, but remained well behind, feeling small.

With the notable exceptions of Buzzard and Ned, Zane's men remained jubilant. The half-bald halfwit seemed more jittery than usual. He cast repeated looks over his shoulder, and seemed to be trying to catch Davy's eye. More than once, he slowed his horse and drifted toward Davy's dun. But in each case another of Zane's men intercepted him and nudged him back into the pack. Zane's nephew Ned, meanwhile, rode well apart from the others, neither speaking nor spoken to.

The sun was just peering over the horizon when we stopped to water the horses. Before too many hooves had trampled the earth, I saw the red-stained spot where Davy's devil had nearly devoured Myers' ear. Samson prowled the banks of the stream without drinking, and I began to wonder if he feared the water. Then came a great splash, soaking two nearby soldiers, and the dog was lost from sight. An instant later he burst onto the bank with a fish between his teeth. He shook himself from head to toe, dousing the rest of the company, and laid the fish proudly at Davy's feet. It was a shovelnose sturgeon, nearly a foot in length.

Davy dropped to one knee, ruffling the hound's fur. Samson's tail whipped back and forth with such enthusiasm that two horses bolted off into the brush. Buzzard approached, patting Samson's side, and said, "Good dog." Davy looked up, and the little man seemed about to say more when Zane cut the break short.

"Let's move. With luck, we may catch those red devils napping."

At the word *devils,* Davy's shoulders twitched. Fear of his own demon still plagued him. I only hoped he wouldn't hold back once we reached the Red Stick camp. I did not expect this rescue of Lacy to be easy, and Davy's demon may be our best chance of success.

"You too, Buzzard." Zane slapped a quirt into his palm. "Mount up while we're all still young."

Buzzard scuttled off. Davy remained on one knee, stroking the hound's neck. Only after Zane stomped off did Davy take up the sturgeon, wrap it in leaves, and place it carefully in his saddlebag.

We continued west, past the site of the siege beneath the bluff, and on into new territory. The farms here were fewer, the fields less tilled. We saw little game, and no settlers. All the cabins we passed appeared abandoned, and some were merely charred remains. "The homes of my people," Little Fawn explained. "Those who refused Red Eagle's call."

The sun rose, pale and cold. Further west, the landscape grew rocky and uneven. A thirty-foot bluff rose above a shallow creek on our right, and directly ahead, a path between two hills appeared to lead into a valley.

Davy nodded toward the gap. "Rider comin'," he said just loud enough for Little Fawn and me. Squinting, I saw nothing, but knew better than to doubt him. With an edge to his voice, Davy added, "It's Myers."

And it was. The man Zane had dismissed from the company reined in at the head of the column and executed a sloppy salute. He still wore his broad-brimmed militia hat, and had a dirty bandage over the remains of his right ear.

"What the hell," I said.

Davy nodded. "My feelin's, exactly." He urged his horse forward, me following, until we were within hearing distance.

"No one on guard but old men and boys," Myers was saying. "It'll be a cinch."

Zane turned to face us. "Good news, gentlemen. Red Eagle's warriors are not in camp. We will have free rein to search for Miss Truitt."

"And you will have free rein to take the scalps of women and children." Little Fawn said.

"You misjudge us," Zane said. "We do not make war upon noncombatants." His expression seemed sincere, but the grins of the men said otherwise.

Davy said, "What snake pit did you crawl from, Myers?"

"I've forgiven you your trespasses," Myers said, "and I'm hoping the cap'n will forgive mine."

Zane slid from his saddle, dropped to one knee and drew two lines in the dirt with his quirt. He pointed to one end. "We're here, at the opening between these hills. The camp lies here," he jabbed the earth at the opposite end of the lines, "at the far end of the valley." He traced a route around the hills. "I'll take half the men around the southern end and strike from the southwest." He glanced up to see that we understood. "The rest of the men will accompany Mr. Crockett and his party straight through the valley, attacking from the east."

Zane quickly named seven men who would follow him, including Buzzard and Myers. Buzzard's eyes met mine. They were wide with alarm.

"Give us ten minutes to get in position," Zane told Davy. "Then trot your horses quiet as you can. We don't want pounding hooves to scare them off." Buzzard and the others he'd named took positions behind him. "Within the hour, victory will be ours."

Davy said, "Nothin' wrong with victory. Providin' we mind why we've come. We're rescuin' Miss Lacy."

"Mr. Crockett is correct," Zane said, "but if any Red Sticks stand in our way, we'll remind them this is a good day to die."

He raised his quirt like a sword, turned his horse and led his contingent off around the southern edge of the hills.

I examined the militiamen left to accompany us. They were six of the biggest and hardest-looking of the bunch.

"Ten minutes," Davy said. "Any o' you gents got a timepiece?" None of the men responded.

I dug into my saddlebag, pulling out a silver-cased pocket watch.

"Haven't used this since I left Pennsylvania."

Little Fawn leaned over, watching as I wound it. I opened the cover with a thumbnail and showed it to her.

"What does it say?"

"Ten thirty-seven." I was surprised she couldn't tell time. "Not accurate, of course, but it'll tell us when ten minutes are up."

"Not that," she said. "What does it say *here?*" She pointed at the words inscribed inside the case.

"Never mind." I snapped the watch shut. The words were those of my father, words I could not bear to read in front of others, particularly Little Fawn and Davy. "So," I said to change the subject, "you can't read."

She sniffed. "I can read what matters. I can read the trail of a marsh rabbit, the signs of coming snow, the entrails of a rattle-snake. And with rare exceptions," she flicked a glance at Davy, "I can read what is in a man's heart."

I didn't like where this was leading. I snuck another look at the time. Nine minutes to go.

"Also," she said, now in a whisper, "I can read a map. And the one Captain Zane drew is a lie."

Davy joined us. The man had the hearing of a sparrow hawk. "How so?"

"That passage through those hills leads to no valley. It is a box canyon, sometimes used to train horses or keep cattle. You will find no Red Sticks there."

WHEN THE TEN minutes had passed, Davy insisted we proceed as instructed, just as if we did not at any moment expect to be shot down like dogs.

"We'll watch your backs," one of the militiamen said, an idea I found less than comforting.

"Hope you have a plan," I whispered to Davy.

"Me too."

We loped along so slowly that if my nape hairs had not been standing at attention I might have dozed off. Samson ranged from side to side and far out front, sniffing and snuffling at everything in sight. We were quiet. There was plenty I wanted to say, but feared I might betray our awareness of the trap, spoiling our chances to turn the tables.

We were thirty yards from the canyon mouth when a ruckus broke out behind. Horses stomped and snorted, men swore, and above it all rose the cackling shriek of a raccoon. I was so keyed up I nearly jumped out of my saddle. Samson, who at that moment had been leading the procession, tore through us in a blue streak, and was instantly among the militiamen, snapping, snarling and chewing up the landscape in search of the coon. The hound's booming bark, mixed with the coon's ferocious snarls, stirred the madness to new heights. The horses reared up, squealed, and sunfished, sometimes all at once. Men yelped and cursed, and two spilled backwards from their saddles.

I scarcely had time to wonder what a raccoon was doing here in the open, and in full daylight, when Davy shouted, "Now!" and kicked the flanks of his dun. Leading Arrow, he shot off, veering to the right around a hill to avoid the canyon mouth. Little Fawn was close behind, with me in the rear. We splashed along the creek bed with the hill on our left and the bluff high on our right.

By the time the barking stopped, we'd covered a good deal of ground. We pressed on, not daring to slacken our pace. It was unlikely our escorts would catch us now, but the whereabouts of Zane and the others was unknown. From far behind us came a volley of muskets. A signal?

I wondered how Samson had fared against the coon. I'd once seen two raccoons kill a dog, and knew them to be vicious fighters. Little Fawn must have divined my thoughts, for I caught her eyeing me with a most piteous expression. Then she laughed, and I realized what she must have known all along. The raccoon was Davy.

I ground my teeth. Samson, too, had been fooled, but that only meant I was no dumber than a hound dog. Curious as to his fate, I glanced over my shoulder. Far back along the trail, I caught a flicker of motion. I looked again, and sunlight flashed on something blue. It was the dog, surging towards us like a whirlwind.

Turning to share this news, I saw Davy's hand raised, ordering a halt, and relief rushed over me. He must believe us safe from Zane's trap. But my joy was short-lived. Square in our path were six men in green jackets. And right between them, wearing a triumphant smirk, was Zane. Myers and the rest sat their horses calmly, each with a musket trained upon us. There was nowhere to go but back, and this we tried, wheeling our horses madly. But we'd no sooner turned than our six beleaguered escorts thundered into sight.

Zane said, "You people don't know what's good for you. We'd picked a peaceful little canyon for you to spend eternity. Now you'll rot here in the mud instead."

"That's as may be," Davy said. "But we won't be lonely."

Zane scowled over his gunsight. "What's that supposed to mean?"

"Means we got company." Davy turned his gaze slowly up the bluff, where a score of painted Red Sticks stood poised with bows and arrows. "And they look plumb delighted to see you."

CHAPTER 11

"You have consorted with demons."

MY STOMACH FLOPPED like a trout on a string. Arrows would kill us no deader than musket balls, but they looked infinitely more painful.

One of the Creeks said, "Drop your weapons," but the words were still leaving his mouth as Zane swung his musket and shot him off the bluff. The militia followed suit, filling the air with lead and smoke, and the Indians responded with spears and arrows. The atmosphere was alive with death, and I was set to bolt in either direction, awaiting Davy's lead.

Instead, he grasped my arm and shouted, "Stay!"

Little Fawn struggled in a similar grip. Our eyes met, and words passed between us as if we'd spoken aloud. *Davy knows best.*

When the smoke lifted, three green-jacketed men lay on the ground. The rest, with their horses, were gone. Red Stick warriors came clambering over the bluff, while others covered us with their bows.

"We surrender." Still gripping our arms, Davy raised them high overhead. "We brung news for Red Eagle." A few Creeks cocked their heads at this, but the rest merely growled. "Tell them," Davy asked Little Fawn. And apparently she did, for after a few words of her gibberish, they seemed slightly less eager to kill us.

News for Red Eagle? The only news I had—that I planned to cut out his heart and make him eat it—would hardly endear us to his followers. Davy was likely just stalling, playing for a chance at escape.

Two of the downed militiamen lay before us, and one behind. Sadly, Zane and Myers were not among them. A group of warriors approached the two in front, jabbing them with spears to no effect. But a shout went up from behind, where Big Frog and his friends from the village had found a survivor. The green-clad man lay half on his side, legs curled, hands up to deflect further abuse.

"Either kill me or stand downwind," the soldier snarled. "I can't stand the smell."

Big Frog's skinny friend fell upon him, a wicked knife gleaming in his fist.

I turned away, not wishing to see the rest. Davy and Little Fawn watched without flinching, though their faces were grim. When the screaming stopped I chanced a look. The slim young warrior wiped his blade on the man's green jacket and stood.

Big Frog and his friends looked to us, smiling like vultures. Would we be next?

One of the Indians on the bluff was older and sported a wispy beard decorated with beads. Facial hair was unusual among the Creeks, even those who appeared to be of mixed blood.

"Take us to Red Eagle," Davy said to him. His voice betrayed no doubt or fear. "We got words for his ears alone." Little Fawn spoke in Creek, parroting Davy's tone.

The bearded man curled a lip at Davy, but his manner toward Little Fawn was respectful, almost subservient. Davy and I were pulled from our horses and our hands roughly bound, while Little Fawn was unmolested. A man gave a happy cry as he discovered Davy's rifle, but this was quickly passed up to the leader.

Minutes later, after we'd been prodded back onto our mounts, the procession started up the creek toward the west, moving parallel to the party on the bluff. Arrow remained riderless, and was accorded even greater respect than Little Fawn.

I was miserable. We had not only failed to rescue Lacy Truitt from the Indians—but were now in need of rescue ourselves.

As we rode, I occasionally heard crackling leaves in the brush under the bluff or among the trees to our left. The Red Sticks heard it too, and one or another frequently nocked an arrow, only to turn away with a shaking head. It was some small comfort to know that Samson, at least, was enjoying himself.

The trail got rougher as the creek bed rose to meet the bluff, but we eventually joined the rest of the war party. Hands still bound, we proceeded single file through forests and gullies for well over an hour. Then the Indians' mood began to change. Their weariness fell away and they sat lighter on their ponies. A few even looked at us and smiled.

The reason became apparent as we topped a rise and saw a large town sprawled out in the valley below. I'd expected a rude collection of lean-tos and cook-fires. Instead, this community looked far larger and more permanent than many villages in the Pennsylvania countryside. A hundred or more small buildings congregated, without benefit of streets, around a vast open field and several larger structures.

"The Holy Ground?" I whispered to Little Fawn.

She shook her head. "If it were, you would not be permitted to see it. Lightning bolts and hailstones would fall from the sky were you to set foot on sacred ground. This is merely a town—one among many where the Red Sticks hold sway."

Lining the road into the valley were fields partitioned into large garden plots. Each plot showed signs of recently harvested corn, and beneath the leaves were patches of bright orange or green where pumpkins and melons still grew. The fields gave way to clusters of buildings, each with a tiny garden growing tobacco and beans.

Women and old men peered at us from around the buildings, while small children scampered forward to watch us pass. Some of the youngsters were clad in furs, some in scraps of European clothing or blankets. Most offered only taunts, but several were so bold as to toss small stones. One lad, no more than six, ran up, struck me on the leg with his fist and darted away. Some adults laughed, but others made approving noises. Little Fawn shot me a look, and, with ill grace, I groaned and adopted a pained expression, making the little demon's face gleam with pride.

Most of the open area at the town's center was devoted to a huge sunken field with man-made banks around the edges. At one end were poles decorated with human scalps, while a taller pole at the center was topped with a skull.

Next to the field, four long buildings with clay walls and slab roofs faced each other like primitive grandstands around an open square. Beyond this squatted a large circular building with a cone-shaped roof that looked vaguely like a church.

As we neared the square, a number of Indians emerged from the grandstands to await our arrival. One was a head taller than the rest, with flowing red-blond hair and impossibly wide shoulders. I growled, straining at my bonds, but the rawhide merely bit deeper into my wrists. This was not the way I'd pictured my next meeting with Red Eagle.

Without his warpaint, his skin was shockingly fair. If not for his rough dress—a blue woolen sash over a buckskin breechcloth and leggings—he could have been taken for a white man. Unlike many of his followers, he wore no rings in his ears or nose. The only primitive aspect of his appearance was the large eagle feather braided into his hair.

If Red Eagle recognized us, he gave no sign. He had eyes only for Arrow, and strode briskly forward to stroke the stallion's head and pat his flanks. He seemed to be asking gentle questions of the horse, after which he nodded, as if receiving answers. Next he examined the scar left by Davy's rifle ball, and checked Arrow's legs and hooves for cuts.

After treating the horse to some tidbit from a pouch at his waist, Red Eagle turned to the leader of the war party and received an animated account of what was surely the battle below the bluff. For the grand finale, the man gestured dramatically at Davy, Little Fawn and me. He no doubt considered us the icing on his cake.

Red Eagle eyed us only briefly before turning back to the bearded man. At Red Eagle's barked questions, the fellow's head bowed, his shoulders slumped, and he pointed toward Big Frog and his friends.

Under Red Eagle's gaze, the three warriors blanched and shriveled. Big Frog tried to put up a bold front, but the others appeared ready to wet themselves. Scowling at the thin young warrior who had scalped the last of the soldiers, Red Eagle barked a command. Eyes wide, the fellow oozed off his pony and crab-walked forward. A moment later he lay groaning in the dust, felled by a backhand clout from Red Eagle's fist.

Red Eagle began to speak, and the warrior's body spasmed as if each word were a blow. Finished, Red Eagle raised an arm and pointed back the way we'd come. Then he spun away, paying no further heed as the wretched youth mounted his pony and loped away.

I looked a question at Little Fawn.

"He wanted one of Zane's men taken alive," she whispered. "For questioning."

Red Eagle now turned his attention to Davy. "You are an obstinate fellow, Mr. Crockett. That is a trait I admire. And you have treated Arrow well. But if you believe that will save your life, you deceive yourself." Turning his back on us, he marched majestically toward the town square.

I stared after him, hatred coursing through me. The murderer of Maggie and my parents had been so close I might have leapt from my horse and strangled him—were I not trussed up like a turkey. There would be another time, Little Fawn had assured me. I hoped this had not been it.

FROM OUR VANTAGE point, on our knees before the grand pavilion, the town square seemed enormous. Each of the four structures had open fronts and contained three levels of benches, now stuffed with Red Sticks. Their mood was jovial, almost festive, and I had little doubt our deaths were to be the entertainment of the day. I wondered if it would be some elaborate ceremony—a savage mockery of Romans feeding Christians to the lions—or if they'd simply slit our throats and add our scalps to the poles.

While the roofs of the other structures were supported with plain wooden posts, those of the building before us were carved in the form of great serpents coiling up toward the heavens. Crudely-executed paintings adorned the inside walls—men with the heads of beasts and beasts with the heads of men. The Creeks seated in this building were more gaudily clad than most, and I judged them to be tribal bigwigs.

Front and center sat Red Eagle himself, occupying a partitioned area all his own. He had donned a white cotton shirt, and about his neck he now wore a large silver gorget, evidently some mark of rank. The only other signs of ostentation were the eagle feather in his hair and the brightly colored beads decorating his buckskin leggings.

Across Red Eagle's lap lay a longrifle. It was immediately recognizable as a fine weapon, and I assumed it was Old Betsy. But as Red Eagle raised the rifle to quiet the crowd, I leaned closer, so close I nearly lost balance and fell on my face. Then I saw no more because my eyes were wet.

"Penn!" Davy whispered. "What's wrong?"

I shook my head, unable to speak. This was the weapon my father had presented me on my thirteenth birthday—the one I'd lost at Talladega and feared was gone forever. Now it was in the hands of my father's murderer.

"Buck up," Davy said. "We ain't sunk yet."

I wanted to answer, wanted to explain it was grief, not fear, that had me in its grip. Since Little Fawn's scolding, the need to grieve had never been far from my thoughts, and this turn of events had all but unmanned me.

Red Eagle eyed me with distaste. No doubt he, too, mistook

my emotion for cowardice. With a curl of his nose, he shifted his attention to Davy. "Where is my wife?"

I blinked, amazed. By this time, I'd assumed he'd have found his wife safe at home and realized he'd been bamboozled. I peered sideways at Davy. He too was surprised, while Little Fawn's expression was an unreadable as ever.

Red Eagle said, "Do not pretend ignorance. You were with Truitt's militia when one of his greenjackets held Sopath at knifepoint. You will tell me where she is or I will feed you, piece by piece, to the hogs." His southern drawl was only slightly less cultivated than that of Colonel Truitt, and despite the threatening words, his tone almost cordial.

"I'm almighty sorry we was forced to hoodle you," Davy said. "That was me up on the bluff, and the woman warn't your wife."

Red Eagle snorted. "Do I not know my own bride? Did I not speak with her and hear her voice?"

"No," Little Fawn said. "You do not, and you did not. The woman in the white dress was me."

Red Eagle snorted again, his brow growing dark.

"Save me, husband! Spare these men, or they will surely kill me." Little Fawn's voice was suddenly musical. Her features had softened, and her head canted at a different angle. Had I not seen the change, I'd have believed her a different woman.

Red Eagle rose to his feet, swung my rifle around and pointed the muzzle at Davy's chest. "So. Your treachery knows no depths. But the question remains. Where are Truitt and his mercenaries holding my wife?"

This was thickheadedness beyond belief. Even while acknowledging the deception, Red Eagle persisted in the belief his wife had been taken.

"If you wish to speak of missing women," I said, "tell us what you've done with Lacy Truitt."

Red Eagle's gaze slid to me, his nose wrinkling as if I'd just plopped from the rear of his horse. "I will brook no foolishness," he said. "Tell me of my wife, or I have no use for you."

The square was quiet. Far away, on the edge of camp, a dog barked. It was a friendly bark, and I thought little of it until the sound grew louder, mixed with the squeals of children. Red Eagle turned an eye toward the disturbance. We did likewise.

From between two of the grandstands raced a spotted blue hound. Samson. Though his teeth were bared and his demeanor utterly ferocious, I'd come to recognize that expression as a smile.

Red Eagle seemed to understand this, for he kept the rifle trained on Davy. Samson, meanwhile, paid no heed to the crowd. Bounding straight across the square, he skidded to a stop before the kneeling Davy and lapped his face with great enthusiasm.

"Good boy," Davy said. "I'm right glad to see you too."

After nuzzling a moment under Davy's chin, the hound turned, arched his back and snarled at Red Eagle. He paid no mind to the rifle mere inches from his snout.

Davy said, "Easy, boy. *Sit.*"

Samson growled. The hair along his spine stood straight up, and his legs tensed, ready to spring.

Red Eagle lowered the rifle, smiled, and pointed a long finger at the dog. "Sit," he said.

The growling stopped. Samson rolled out his tongue, lowered his rump to the ground and panted happily.

From somewhere over my shoulder, a harsh voice spoke in Creek. My nostrils twitched, filled with a sour stench, and Red Eagle glanced up, his eyes hooded. The man approaching was made up for a masquerade ball. Beneath a black-painted face, he was covered from neck to moccasins with a robe of feathers. The robe was outlandish enough, but paled beside his head-piece. This, too, was covered with feathers, but these had not been plucked. They were still attached to the body of a dead owl.

The owl's yellow eyes were fixed open in a parody of life. What primitive method had been used to preserve the body I could not guess, but this was apparently the source of the foul odor. Leather straps tied to the creature's legs were knotted beneath the old man's chin, and the owl swayed drunkenly from side to side as he walked. The effect was grotesque, if not comical, but the Red Sticks eyed the man with both respect and fear.

Samson sank to the ground, rubbing his nose in the dirt.

I raised an eyebrow at Little Fawn.

"A *hillis haya*," she said, barely a whisper. "What you would call a prophet, or shaman."

The shaman carried a five-foot staff with a cow tail tied to each end. Shaking the stick at us, he turned to address the tribal leaders. While his words were a mystery, his strident tone had the singsong quality of a preacher. He pointed his staff repeatedly at Davy and the hound, with sort of by-the-way gestures at Little Fawn and myself. When he finished, the murmur of a hundred voices flooded the square.

Red Eagle looked down at us. "The prophet believes this animal to be a demon," he said quietly, "and intends to prove it."

I said, "That's ridiculous."

"Should he succeed, it will go hard on you. Perhaps hard on me as well, as you still hold knowledge of my wife. But the will of the tribe trumps my own."

I looked sideways at Davy. I'd still had no chance to ask why he'd insisted we surrender to the Red Sticks. I hoped he was preparing to uncork one of his wild schemes, but his expression was not encouraging. He looked as worried as a man could be.

The shaman raised the staff high above his head, above even the head of the dead owl, and twirled it about. As the cow tails spun faster and faster, he began to chant. The stilted cadence was eerie and punctuated with yips and howls. After a good deal of this fol-de-rol the old man's body began to quiver, then shake with violent convulsions. The twirling staff flew from his hand to strike the dirt.

The Creeks watched his every move, their faces bright and expectant. Only Red Eagle himself seemed uninterested in the performance. Laying my rifle aside, he crossed arms over his chest and regarded us thoughtfully. Determined to give him no satisfaction, I glared back with every ounce of contempt I could muster, but he remained unfazed.

The shaman's convulsions were slowing. When the twitching finally ceased, his eyes popped open and he extended a bony finger at Davy. He pronounced a single word, bringing gasps from all corners of the square. Red Eagle's lips tightened. I needed no translator to tell me we'd been found guilty.

The shaman turned to address the tribe. His ringing words were accompanied by many gestures and expressions, as if telling a story. As the tale went on, his tone sharpened to raw fury and righteous disgust. His cow-tail staff stabbed again and again at Davy and Samson.

As he finished, the Red Sticks surged to their feet and howled their agreement.

Red Eagle leaned forward, speaking softly. "The prophet has consulted the Master of Breath and confirmed that you have consorted with demons. He has decreed you be staked out in the *chunkey* yard and flayed to death. This is not the fate I would have chosen, but I am bound by his decision."

Little Fawn said something in Creek, causing Red Eagle to wince. Davy said nothing at all, but his expression was grim.

The shaman raised a hand, quieting the crowd. For a moment the silence held, and into that silence came the hoot of an owl. It was faint at first, as if carried a great distance on the wind, but the Indians were immediately alert, all heads turning toward the sound. The hoots grew louder, closer. The Indians' faces shone with reverence, as if hearing the voice of God. Even Little Fawn seemed enrapt. The hooting was now nearly upon as, and the shaman's eyes were twin fires of mystic fervor.

The Red Sticks gasped as the great bird itself soared into sight above the buildings and circled the square. I gasped too, for I'd thought the hooting another of Davy's tricks. Davy saw me looking and winked, and I realized that rather than impersonating the owl, he had summoned it.

With a final hoot, the owl bent its wings and fluttered to a landing, sinking its claws into Davy's coonskin cap. Though still on his knees with hands bound behind him, Davy rose to his feet in the attitude of one receiving a great honor. The Indians, Red Eagle included, appeared awestruck. The shaman's eyes bulged near to bursting.

With the owl resting comfortably atop his head, Davy's neck swiveled, owl-like, to peer at the Creeks in the building to our left, then nearly all the way around to those behind us. He repeated this motion in the opposite direction until all within the square had felt his gaze.

Then Davy began to hum. The tune was slow and majestic, and it was only with great effort that I recognized the song as "Turkey in the Straw." Davy's body quivered and twitched, much in the manner of the shaman, but instead of dancing about, Davy remained bolt upright. His lips opened and owlish hoots came from his mouth. When he paused, the owl on his head hooted in return. In this manner they carried on a sort of conversation, while all assembled stared in wonder.

The owl itself had the last word, producing a screech that tickled my spine.

Davy opened his eyes and regarded the tribal leaders. "With the owl as my guide, I have visited the domain of the witches. This feller you call prophet," he swiveled his head to peer at the feathered man, "is a witch sent to sway you from the true path."

As Little Fawn translated for the crowd, the shaman's face mottled. Then he cried out in English, "He lies! His demon trickery has deceived even the owl. I will prove who is truly favored by the spirits." Canting his head to one side, he raised his arms and made claws of his hands. Fixing his gaze upon the owl, he said, "To me, messenger, the Master of Breath commands it." He let out a hoot, nowhere near as convincing as Davy's, and when the owl merely blinked, he tried again and again until he could produce merely a wheeze.

Regarding the old man calmly for a moment, the owl stretched his legs. After three short hoots, sounding very much like laughter, the bird spread its wings and soared off into the eastern sky.

The Red Sticks were stunned to silence. The shaman hung his head. Even his dead owl looked dejected.

Samson rose and sauntered to the shaman's side. Looking sinfully pleased, he lifted a leg and relieved himself on the old man's moccasins.

Red Eagle was first to speak. Stepping from the shade of the building into the sunlit square, he pointed down at us. "These three may be our enemies, but they are surely favored by the spirits. Go now, that I may meditate and seek further guidance."

As the warriors dispersed, heads shaking and voices hushed, two young men in feathered necklaces came forward to assist the shaman. The old rascal was in such a daze that it required both men to guide him away.

Only when the square was deserted did Red Eagle address us. His face was still stern, but a corner of his mouth curled, almost in amusement. "Do not think me simple enough to be deceived by such nonsense, but you have bought yourself time. We will speak further, and unless you have news of my wife, no amount of trickery will save you."

CHAPTER 12

"A thing unheard of."

FROM INSIDE, THE round building next to the square resembled both a church and a theater. Benches rose in concentric circles from the mat-covered floor to the outer wall, surrounding an open area with a fire pit. The fire was lit, and the smoke, instead of filling the room as you'd expect, trailed up through a hole in the cone-shaped roof.

It was easy to imagine the building packed to the rafters with Indians smoking, chanting and dancing around the fire. But at the moment only four us were present—Davy, Little Fawn, myself, and the man I'd sworn to kill. At Red Eagle's instruction, we sat cross-legged on the reed carpet near the fire. It was warm here, especially after becoming accustomed to the cold, and, if not for the presence of Red Eagle, the experience might have been pleasant.

The three of us sat in a rough quarter circle, me nearest the fire, while Red Eagle faced us, an arm's length away. Our bonds had been removed to allow us to climb over the portico, which was the only entrance to the building.

Red Eagle apparently considered us no threat to his safety, though I still hoped to prove him wrong. If we all attacked at once we stood a fair chance of strangling him. But while Little Fawn would gladly help, I knew Davy would not.

Red Eagle seemed to know it, too. He peered at Davy with frank curiosity. "You are a peculiar man, Mr. Crockett. You could have killed me on two separate occasions, yet you took pains to save my life. I wish to know why."

"Killin' don't solve problems," Davy said. "It makes 'em."

Red Eagle considered this. "You are wise for one of your years. I suspect there is Creek blood in your family."

Davy grinned. "A flatterin' notion. But Pa Crockett's a simple Irishman, and Ma's mostly English."

Red Eagle *tsked* as if this were a shame. "I was able to bring you here because the others believe you are favored by the spirits." He showed the hint of a smile. "A belief I do not share. But I required this opportunity to speak with you alone."

Davy flicked his eyes around the room. "What is this place?"

"It is called a *chokofa*. It serves as council house, sweat lodge, and simply a place to escape the winter cold."

"Not a church?" I said.

"Not in the sense you mean, Mr. McCoy. But to my people, all gathering places are sacred."

I sniffed. Just the answer I would expect from a heathen.

"We are here so that you may divulge what you know of my wife." Red Eagle's eyes brushed over Little Fawn and me, but it was clear he expected the answer from Davy.

Davy took this calmly. Too calmly, for a man who was surely bluffing. Any "news" he might have of Mrs. Red Eagle would be a lie, as he could have no more idea than I where the woman might be. Until arriving in this town, we didn't even know she was missing.

"I'll be plumb tickled to help," Davy said, "providin' you release Lacy Truitt. We swore an oath to young Nathan."

Red Eagle's features froze. "Nathan was a good lad. He should not have died."

"Your savage shouldn't have killed him," I said with heat.

"No, he should not. I ordered him to stand down." He looked briefly at me. "Had you not shot the man, I might have done so myself."

Davy cleared his throat. "About Miss Lacy."

"Nathan accused me of taking her," Red Eagle said softly, "just before he died. But I swear I know nothing of her fate. I do not make war upon women—not even the daughters of my enemies."

This was too much to bear. "What of my mother, my sister Maggie, and the others you butchered at Fort Mims?"

"My mother as well." Little Fawn's voice was strained. "And two aunts. All murdered. Does that not qualify as war?"

Red Eagle stared into his lap. "A mistake. A tragic mistake. One I would give my life to erase."

I rose to my knees, fists clenched. "Nothing will erase your guilt. But I will gladly take your life."

"As will I," Little Fawn said. "The Wind Clan cries out for blood."

Red Eagle raised his head. His face was so constricted he was hardly recognizable. "Then take it. I have lost everything else. My lands. My honor. And my wife."

I was sorely tempted, and glanced at Davy to see if he would stop me. His eyes remained fixed on Red Eagle.

"Why?" Little Fawn demanded. "Why did you join the Red Sticks? Why did you attack Fort Mims?"

Red Eagle winced as he'd been slapped. "Sopath," he said. "And Sopath again."

"You lie. My cousin would never have counseled such folly."

Red Eagle raised a huge hand, waved this objection away. "You misunderstand. After she was taken, her captors forced me to join the Red Sticks."

There was silence for a time, as we considered this remarkable statement.

Davy said, "What captors? Who?"

"I did not know at the time. They sent word I must declare for the rebellion or she would be killed. I knew this Red Stick movement would doom our people whether I joined or not. I had no choice but to comply."

Red Eagle looked so pitiful I almost felt sorry for him. Almost.

Little Fawn regarded him steadily, her features brittle.

"You didn't know who took her *at the time*," Davy said. "But later you did?"

"I learned she was taken by a gang of white men, and that two of them had taken refuge at Fort Mims." Red Eagle's voice had shrunk to a whisper. "We knew the stockade was well defended. I planned to demonstrate before the gates and demand those within surrender Sopath's abductors." He plucked a sliver of reed from the woven carpet and snapped it between his fingers. "Instead, the soldiers were drunk and the gate propped open with sand."

Little Fawn struck the mat with a fist. "So you killed them all."

Red Eagle shook his head, either in denial or regret. "Events moved too quickly. With no thought but Sopath, I rode screaming through the gate, seeking the men who had taken her. My braves followed, clashing with the soldiers."

"And you found the varmints you were seekin'?" Davy asked.

Red Eagle toyed with one of the beads adorning his leggings. "Before they died, they admitted working for Colonel Truitt."

"There's no chance they lied?"

Red Eagle's lips twisted. He turned to stare at the fire, and flames danced in his eyes. He crushed the bead between his fingers. "None."

"But you allowed the slaughter to continue." Little Fawn was relentless.

I fought back images of Maggie and my folks. The words spoken within the room were barely audible above the war cries, gunshots and the screams ringing in my head.

"I ordered the women and children spared, but the young

warriors' blood was up. They turned upon me, threatening my life if I remained."

"So you ran away."

"I went for help, returning with men loyal to me. We were too late to save most within the fort, but we stopped the killing and did what we could for the survivors."

This sounded self-serving to me. And despite Red Eagle's high-toned manners and appearance, he was still a war chief. I looked at Davy, my eyebrows raised, and he answered with a nod. I was stunned. Was it possible I'd been wrong—that the man truly responsible for my family's death was Colonel Truitt?

We were silent for a time. At last Little Fawn spoke, her tone considerably softer. "You were born of my clan, and I wish to believe you. But I would hear you swear this after taking the White Drink. I would hear you swear to the Master of Breath."

Red Eagle's brow darkened. "You have not told me what you know of Sopath. There are ways to extract such information."

Little Fawn nodded at Davy. "That knowledge is held by Davy Crockett alone, and his will has twice the strength of yours. Chop off his fingers and toes, sear his eyes from their sockets, strangle him with his own entrails, and still he would not tell. Not until he is convinced you speak the truth."

I peered slantwise at Davy. His expression remained calm, but despite the fire's orange glow, his face was tinged with green.

"Let's sample this White Drink," he said. "I'm feelin' a mite thirsty."

THE MOOD IN the town square was gay. Seasoned warriors thumped their chests and laughed, while younger braves scurried to and fro with buckets of water and bundles of holly branches. Samson capered freely about, and the Indians, who evidently deemed him a powerful spirit, tossed him strips of jerked venison.

This time, far from kneeling in the dirt before the main grandstand, Davy and I occupied seats on either side of Red Eagle. Little Fawn, relegated to the shadows on the bench behind us, had agreed to show her face as little as possible. Though the women of the tribe owned the land and wielded all power within their clans, she'd explained, the ceremony of the White Drink was reserved for men.

Aside from sitting peaceably beside Red Eagle, whom I did not yet trust, only one thing marred the occasion—the smell. A monstrous odor hung over the square like a dark cloud, burning my nostrils and stinging my eyes. It reminded me variously of unwashed feet, fried eels and boiled muskrat. My suffering did not escape Little Fawn's notice.

"That," she said brightly, "is the White Drink, and it is said to taste even better than it smells." It was a tea, she told me, made from the yaupon bush, which I gathered was a variety of holly, and considered a blessing bestowed upon the Creeks by the Master of Breath. Among other benefits, the drink was said to purify a man of all sin, return him to a state of perfect inno-cence, and make him immune to arrows and bullets. Visiting traders and missionaries, judging the tea only by appearance, had mistakenly dubbed it the Black Drink. I listened to all this with only half a mind, still horror-stricken at the notion of pouring such noxious brew into my gullet.

The crowd hushed as three young men carried large gourds into the square. One was Big Frog, and though he strutted under the attention of the assembly, he was clearly not pleased with the assignment. Little Fawn had told me the serving of the drink was a menial task, assigned to would-be warriors who had yet to take their first scalps. The three men high-stepped to a stop a dozen feet away and pivoted to face us, the gourds balanced shoulder high.

Big Frog stood directly before me, evidently assigned to serve me. Though his face was placid, his eyes brimmed with hate.

I glanced past Red Eagle to see how Davy was taking this. He appeared maddeningly calm, as if awaiting a mug of ale.

"Watch Red Eagle," Little Fawn whispered in my ear. "When

he and Davy begin to drink, you must also. And you must continue to drink until the gourd is lowered."

I grimaced. I was gagging already, and that was just from the stench.

Red Eagle nodded at the servers. Two of them shouted "Choh!" and Big Frog jumped in half a beat behind. Then all three approached, stepped into the grandstand and held their gourds close to our mouths.

I peered sideways at Red Eagle, which was slightly preferable to looking at Big Frog.

The servers sucked in their breath and began to sing. At the first note, a droning "Yooo," Red Eagle's lips parted. I followed suit. At the second note, "Hooo," the servers tipped the gourds and began to pour. I shuddered as the warm swill streamed down my throat. I could not help thinking *Yo Ho Ho*, and nearly choked from laughter alone. To make matters worse, Samson joined in, howling along with them, and proved himself the best singer of the bunch.

That second note went on interminably and when the servers finally reached the third, which sounded like "Laaa," their voices were spent. But just as I prepared to breathe again, the three launched into a second verse, same as the first. And once again Samson outshone them. It might have been funny had I not been drowning. Big Frog, whether from spite or sheer incompetence, allowed much of the foul stuff to spill over my cheeks and course down my chest, while more dribbled into my nostrils, forcing me to snort.

When the torture finally stopped, all I heard was my own gasping and gurgling. Light-headed, nauseous and bloated, I foresaw only two possible results. Either my stomach would burst, showering those around me with black slime, or I would begin spewing liquid from every orifice.

As Big Frog and the others stepped away, Davy and Red Eagle sat up straight in their seats, looking surprisingly normal. For my part, I feared to move. The stuff seemed to fill my entire body, and thanks to Big Frog's spillage, covered every inch of me as well.

Little Fawn whispered, "You did well, Penn. You have made me proud."

Before I could enjoy this first-ever compliment, my toes began to wiggle. The quaking motion continued up my calves and thighs, growing in force as it engulfed my stomach, chest and throat, and I erupted like a volcano. The liquid surged in wave upon wave from the bottom of my being, and it was all I could do to direct it forward rather than drench those around me. The retching went on and on, and I dimly heard laughter from around the square. When the tide finally quelled, I saw Big Frog a dozen paces away, his breeches spattered with goo.

And that was the only satisfaction I got from the experience. Red Eagle ignored me completely, Davy tossed me a sympathetic smile, and Little Fawn merely sighed.

Big Frog and the others moved on to serve others in the main pavilion. While they repeated the word "Choh!" before each serving, the attempted singing seemed to be over. With nothing else to do, Samson sat watching me, ears pricked forward and head canted as if awaiting a repeat performance.

The Creeks had no further interest in me. They focused all their attention on Davy, sparing only occasional glances at Red Eagle.

I turned to Little Fawn. "What's happening?" But she, too, kept steady watch on Davy, her eyes large and glowing. Even Red Eagle watched him.

What they were waiting for I could not fathom. Davy appeared relaxed, returning their looks with good-natured interest. He, too, seemed baffled by their attention.

A great noise from my right brought me spinning about in time to see a stream of black ooze shoot out into the square. In the next compartment a middle-aged warrior wiped his lips, looking quite proud of himself. The man next to him puffed his chest, lurched forward and expelled his own river of tea into the air. This effort traveled a good eight feet before touching down, considerably farther than the first man's, and shouts of approval echoed around the square. I stared as a third man readied himself to spew.

"I understand why they made Davy and I drink that slop, but why are these others doing it?"

"It is considered a great honor. And a way of communing with our gods."

Red Eagle and Little Fawn paid no attention to the other drinkers. They still watched Davy, as did most of those present, even when another contestant's vomit splashed into the dirt. Davy saw my confusion and winked, leaving me more at sea than ever.

I hissed at Little Fawn, nudging her knee. "What is it?"

"A thing unheard of. Only one man in recent memory has mastered the White Drink. That man is Red Eagle. Others must quickly expel it—though perhaps not as quickly as you."

At last the light dawned. Davy had taken the drink with Red Eagle and myself and shown no ill effects. He had equaled the Indians' best at this test of fortitude and astonished them all.

Before I could question Little Fawn further, she slipped from the pavilion into the square. She moved like a wraith. One moment, she was at Big Frog's side. The next, he writhed in the dirt while she held his gourd above her head. Squaring her feet, she tilted her head and drank. After a round of angry exclamations, the Red Sticks watched in silence as she drained the contents of the gourd. Then, with an impish grin, she opened her mouth and belched.

For a full minute, everyone simply stared. I found myself torn. While half of me rooted for her to hold the stuff down, the other half wished her to spew. So when nothing further happened, I was both pleased and mortified. The Red Sticks were clearly stunned. Not only had a white frontiersman managed to corral their sacred drink, but the same feat had been accomplished by a woman.

Little Fawn said in a clear voice, "Now, Red Eagle. I ask you here, in the presence of the Master of Breath—do you swear that all that you told us of Lacy Truitt, my cousin Sopath and the attack upon Fort Mims was true?"

All heads swung to Red Eagle. They had not been privy to his statements, but his honor had been questioned, and his answer was a matter of great consequence.

"I spoke naught but truth," he said firmly, "and trust I always shall."

The Red Sticks nodded, expecting no less.

Red Eagle sounded so sincere I almost believed him myself. But the ghosts of Maggie and my parents were not so easily satisfied.

"Wait!" The force of my voice startled even me. "You may take Red Eagle's word based on some barbaric tea ceremony, but I do not. My sister is dead. My parents are dead. I cannot absolve this man of guilt without further proof."

Outrage rumbled from the pavilions. A hundred savage warriors were now eager to lift my scalp, but the words were out and I could not get them back.

Swallowing my fear, I faced Red Eagle. "If you cannot provide proof of your innocence, I demand trial by combat."

Red Eagle's brow furrowed. He studied me long and hard, and I knew I was perilously close to death. "You are a man of hidden depths, Penn McCoy. I have no doubt you would be a formidable adversary, but I would not enjoy killing you, and dying at your hands would please me even less. Perhaps that sad circumstance can be averted." He turned to the drink servers and spoke shortly in his native tongue.

One of the young men nodded and ran from the square.

Little Fawn swung to face Red Eagle, her face alight with something between hope and fear. She put a question to him in Creek.

Red Eagle answered, his tone somber, and Little Fawn's mouth fell open in astonishment. Then she looked at me.

I looked from one to the other, wondering what the hell was going on.

A hubbub arose from the far corner of the square, and the drink server returned at the head of a small group of people. He was trying to hurry them, but the others trudged slowly along.

As the newcomers came nearer, I realized they were not Indians. A gray-bearded man shuffled along on a cane, while two tow-headed farm boys followed at his feet. There were three women. One was blonde, and dressed in ragged gingham. Damning my eyesight, I strained to see her more clearly. Was this Lacy, delivered to us at last? But as she came nearer, I saw she was too old, and her features less perfect. The second woman was brunette, and possibly of mixed blood. But the third one's hair was fiery red, and her slim figure stabbed at my memory.

I stared at her, my heart pounding, then leaped from the grandstand, running. The young brunette looked up in alarm, but I had eyes only for the redhead. I was nearly upon her when she too looked up, her face amazed, and I crushed her in my arms.

Her name burst from my lips like a prayer.

"Maggie!"

"One of your friends must die."

MAGGIE LIVED! I could not have been more amazed had the sky opened and rained angels. She had been lost to me—a ghost, a torment, a life unlived. And now she was here, warm, solid and lovely. My heart swelled near to bursting, and we cried together before my friends and enemies, and I was not ashamed.

I remember little of the next few hours, save for joy and tears and endearing words. I know I hugged Little Fawn, and probably others as well. It was now a different world, full of light and color and the sweet scent of days gone by.

Much later, as the three of us sat with Maggie in the simple house that had been her home since Fort Mims, I leaned close to Davy. "If I embraced you earlier, I trust you'll consider it forgotten. I was overcome."

Davy exhibited a most devilish grin. "Ain't likely I'll forget," he said, "but 'tain't me that matters. You was squeezin' Red Eagle, too. Shucks, you even hugged Big Frog."

Watching us, Maggie laughed, and all other thoughts were gone. She was here. We were together, and that was everything.

"This is hard," Little Fawn said, "but I must ask. Are you able to speak of events at the fort?"

"No, by God!" I was on my feet in an instant. "I'll not have it!"

Stone-faced, Davy and Little Fawn started to rise. Maggie stayed them with a hand.

She looked up at me, her eyes imploring. "It's all right, Penn. The other survivors and I have discussed it often."

"Are you certain?"

"Sit, Brother. I appreciate your concern, but you should hear this."

I sat, focused on Maggie, impressed with her calm. Was I trying to protect her feelings—or my own?

"Our time at Fort Mims was short," Maggie said, "because we arrived the evening before the attack. And we very nearly left that same night. They had just received a shipment of whiskey, and the soldiers were drunk. Some of the women too. There would be much dancing and lewd behavior, we were told, and Mama did not wish me to witness it."

"As was only fittin'," Davy said softly.

Maggie nodded. "But Papa's back was paining him—you know how it was, Penn—and I would not hear of us leaving so soon, especially after dark. We retired to one of the cabins within the stockade and were quite comfortable, except for the noise. Two soldiers tried to force their attentions on Mama and me, but Papa drove them off with his rifle."

I clenched my fists. "What two soldiers?"

She laid a hand on my knee. "Please, Penn. They're dead."

Little Fawn said, "A woman was there. Tall and graceful, with kindly eyes and a tongue like a whip. She wore a deer-tail pinned to her head like a halo. Her name was—"

"Mary Whitedeer," Maggie finished. "Yes, we met her next morning, and she made us breakfast. She was a strong woman, kind and generous, as were her two sisters."

"She was my mother," Little Fawn said. "Did she die well?"

Maggie's eyes welled, and she laid a hand on Little Fawn's. When she could speak again, she said, "When the Red Sticks came, she and her sisters returned to the cabin with us. While we cowered behind a table, your mother met the Red Sticks at the door. She stabbed one in the neck, taking his war club, and fought off several others. But brave as she was, the Red Sticks were too many. She died protecting us."

Little Fawn hung her head, and I saw her cheeks were wet.

Davy cleared his throat. "When the Injuns attacked, did you see Red Eagle amongst 'em?"

Maggie nodded. "Mary Whitedeer pointed him out, and I watched through a slit in the wall. He looked fierce and terrible, not at all as he does now."

"An' did he massacre women and children?"

"Many died," Maggie said, a sob in her voice. "More horribly than I can say." She broke down then, and we waited in silence.

We had all heard the stories—women scalped and mutilated, babies cut from their mothers' wombs, children's brains bashed out against the walls. That my young sister had been forced to witness such horror filled me with rage.

"Red Eagle himself," Maggie said through her tears, "avoided the women. And when children came in his path, he leaped over them. The only soldiers I saw him fighting were those Papa had driven off the night before."

"Them soldiers," Davy said, "were they wearin' green jackets?"

Maggie looked amazed. "How did you know?"

"He questioned 'em," Davy said. "Then he killed 'em."

Maggie nodded. "After that, he argued with the other Indians. That was the last I saw of him—until later."

"You were very brave," I said.

"Mama and Papa were the brave ones. Near the end, Mama forced me to lie in a corner beneath a blanket. She and Papa stood above me, fighting to their last breaths. When they... *fell,* the Indians failed to search beneath them. Only later, when I realized the cabin was on fire, did I crawl out and stumble through the door. Most of the Indians were gone, the fighting over, and I would have gone back for Mama and Papa. But Red Eagle rode in with a band of warriors. I was scooped up, along with other survivors, and brought here, where I have been ever since."

"Your parents died well," Little Fawn said, and I felt her eyes caress my face.

"Yes," I said, trusting myself to the smallest of words. "They did."

THAT NIGHT, THE heavens opened up. Thunder, lightning and the drumbeat of rain on the small cabin gave us little sleep. Maggie and I sat together, hugging, and our tears fell as freely as the rain. But the next morning, the world looked different. Red Eagle wore the same cotton shirt and beaded buckskin leggings. The same eagle feather adorned his head, as much a part of him as his hair. But he looked different to me now. He was a man, rather than a beast parading about in human skin. I cast about for a proper apology, finding none. At last I blurted, "I have wronged you in my heart. I no longer wish to kill you."

He offered a wide smile. "A great many men will be pleased to hear that, Penn McCoy. Their own chances have increased significantly."

I smiled back. I knew he was making sport of me, but could not help liking him.

Along with Davy and Little Fawn, we were back in the round building the Creeks called the *chokofa*, this time with half a dozen sub-chiefs and two medicine men. Thankfully, the black-faced shaman with the owl hat was not among them. In the shadows near the outer wall lurked two armed warriors, presumably to assure we were not disturbed.

Among them was a man whose bearing was almost as regal as Red Eagle's, but his hair was shot with gray, and he wore a strip of white cloth that covered his eyes like a blindfold.

"Another holy man?" I whispered to Little Fawn.

"My uncle," she said, "and father to Sopath."

Red Eagle's eyes were upon us. "When Lame Bull's daughter was taken, he tried to prevent it. Her abductors responded by thrusting a burning brand into his eyes. Such is the mercy of your friends Truitt and Zane."

I winced. Only yesterday we had sat at table with those men, in seemingly amiable conversation.

Red Eagle turned to Davy. "Will you now share what you know of my wife?"

"I'm purt' near sure she's bein' held at the Truitt plantation, but for you to attack now would be mighty bad medicine."

So there it was. Davy's whopper about Red Eagle's wife was finally out of his mouth. I dreaded what would happen when Red Eagle discovered he'd been flummoxed. And on a deeper level, I was strangely ashamed. Now that I entertained friendly feelings toward the man it seemed wrong to lie to him—even to save our skins.

From the expressions of several chiefs, I suspected they understood English. For the others, Little Fawn provided a translation.

"We are many," Red Eagle said, "and I could gather a thousand warriors within a few days. Truitt's men would stand little chance against us."

"You'd surely destroy 'em," Davy said, "but you'd lose a tolerable number of friends, and they might kill Sopath just for spite. And Colonel Truitt, whatever his sins, is much revered by my people. If he dies at your hands, they'll send even more armies to march against you. It's time to end this here war, afore all hope of peace is lost."

Red Eagle grunted. "I fear that point has already passed."

"Things are bad," Davy said, "but we ain't yet beyond the pale. Best course now is for us to return to Gen'ral Jackson and tell him of Truitt's crimes. He'll send back so many soldiers that Truitt and his varmints will be forced to free your wife. Meantime, you might be lookin' for Lacy Truitt. Her freedom'd go a long ways towards makin' peace."

Red Eagle seemed to consider this as Little Fawn relayed Davy's words to the chiefs. When she finished, he said, "You are bold to assume we wish to end this conflict." He met the looks of the other Indians. "We did not enter into this war to beg for peace on the white man's terms."

"There's some," Davy said, "who think you're aimin' to help the British. Keepin' our armies busy so's they can land troops on our shores."

Red Eagle bristled at that. "My people serve no master but themselves. We fight to rid our lands of white oppressors—both British and American—now and for all time."

The chiefs nodded agreement.

Davy turned to face them. "Don't forget, I hobnobbed with your spirits and seen the future. Your cause is noble, and you made the whites sit up and take notice. You been strong in war, but now you must be strong in peace. Bad as I hate to say it, there's greedy men lookin' for an excuse to steal your lands. Those rascals gotta be exposed, so's us honest folk can all treat fairly with one another."

This speech brought a thoughtful nod from Red Eagle, but the others seemed unaffected. They began speaking in their own tongue, while Davy and I watched and wondered.

Little Fawn followed their words closely, and various emotions flickered across her face. She was quite beautiful here in the fire's glow. If we two were here alone, and under other circumstances… But no, we were not alone, and things were what they were. Nothing else bore thinking about.

Judging by expressions, Red Eagle took one side of the argument, while the chiefs took the other. Red Eagle's tone was plaintive but not pleading, stern but not angry, cooperative but not conciliatory. I saw now why he had such influence.

When the talk finished, Little Fawn's face was white with shock. She spat a few harsh words in Creek. Immediately, the two armed warriors emerged from the shadows, awaiting orders.

"Silence, woman," Red Eagle said, "or your presence will no longer be tolerated."

She glowered at him, nostrils flaring, and spat upon the reed mat.

Red Eagle held her gaze a moment before turning to address Davy and me. "The chiefs believe you are strong of heart, but are unimpressed with your plans for peace. They, do, however, agree it would be safer for Sopath to be rescued by army troops."

Davy waited, his expression respectful. Little Fawn continued to squirm and scowl.

"The chiefs are willing to wait a short time for you to put your plan into effect."

Davy nodded toward the group. "Thankee, gents."

"There is one condition," Red Eagle said. "You three have fought on the side of our enemies. Many of our young men have died, including sons of those present. The blood debt must be paid."

Little Fawn snarled something in Creek. The nearest warrior laid a hand on his knife hilt.

"You, Crockett, may ride to your General Jackson and procure men for this undertaking. You and one other." Red Eagle looked pointedly at me, then at Little Fawn. "In payment for the lives taken from us, one of your friends must die."

I stared. Die? Surely I'd misheard. But Little Fawn's fury increased and Davy's expression grew to one of horror.

Red Eagle lifted a hand. The two warriors unslung their bows, nocked arrows and took aim at Little Fawn and myself.

"You fools," said Little Fawn. "We are trying to help you."

"Choose," Red Eagle told Davy. "One lives, one dies."

Davy's face was tight, his eyes hard. He had clearly not expected this. I saw his mind working furiously, but our situation seemed hopeless.

"Take Little Fawn with you," I said. "She'll be of greater use."

"No!" Little Fawn cried. "Take Penn. He has a sister to care for."

Red Eagle watched Davy. "An interesting dilemma. The woman is quite skilled, and has proven herself with the White Drink. But she has a sharp tongue and wields it too freely."

Little Fawn said something that sounded obscene.

"The man is fiercely loyal, of strong convictions, and is certainly less contrary. But he is hot-headed and compulsive." Red Eagle shook his head. "A difficult choice."

Davy's body had grown rigid. His eyes were darker, his features more angular. I recognized the signs. His temper was close to boiling over.

"The answer's simple." Davy's voice was grating almost beyond recognition. "I've sinned more against you than Penn and Little Fawn combined. If you're so all-fired eager for blood, take mine."

The Creeks just stared at him, eyes bright. They knew nothing of his devil, but could surely sense the danger. If they were half as wise as they pretended, they would end this now.

"Kill me, damn you!" I struggled to my feet, pressing my back into the arrow of the man behind me.

"Stop!" Red Eagle's tone compelled me to obey. He kept his eyes on Davy. "That is unacceptable. If you do not choose one or the other, both shall die. Decide quickly, or the order shall be given."

Davy's whole body trembled as he struggled to contain himself. He was likely seeing his dead cousin Caleb, and Nathan Truitt, too, with me or Little Fawn stretched out beside them. If Davy's fury was unleashed in this confined space, many of these Indians would die. We might escape the building, but there were hundreds more outside.

"Stop before it's too late!" I shouted. "You don't know what you're doing!"

Davy rose to his feet. His teeth were bared, his nostrils distended, and I swear I saw steam coming from his ears. His whole body trembled as if standing on an earthquake. A low growl issued from his throat, and from just outside the building came an answering howl from Samson.

Strangely, the Red Stick chiefs began to laugh.

"Enough," Red Eagle said. "A man so loyal to his friends is worthy of our trust. You are all free go."

So it had been a test! But the words came too late. Davy's demon was loose, and no longer listening. A moccasined foot soared above Little Fawn's head, knocked the warrior with the bow and arrow sprawling. Without pause, Davy bounded toward the man behind me.

I surged up, wrapping him in a bear hug, but it was like trying to grapple a tornado. "Red Eagle! Help me!"

Little Fawn arrived first, clinging fiercely to Davy's legs. The Red Stick chiefs scrambled back while the devil flailed out in all directions. A great weight slammed into us, and we spilled to the matted floor, a mass of churning and slashing limbs. A feather tickled my nose. Red Eagle had joined the fray.

"Davy!" I roared. "It's over! No one has to die!"

My words had no effect, for the devil continued to struggle, defying our combined strength. Red Eagle had his arms and legs fastened around Davy's body in a wrestler's hold, while Little Fawn and I clung to whatever limbs still boiled about. Mindful of what happened to Myers' ear back on the stream bank, I stayed well clear of Davy's gnashing teeth.

One of the shamans chanted, shaking his cow-tailed stick. The two warriors crouched with spears poised, awaiting the command to strike.

I refused to give up, but my hope was nearly gone. And that's when Red Eagle began to speak.

"Peace, Mr. Crockett," he said, his voice surprisingly calm, "if you desire peace, you must exhibit it yourself." Despite Davy's kicking, Red Eagle kept on, as if soothing a wild horse. And somehow his words got through. Davy's flailing gradually lessened until he ran completely out of steam.

For long moments we lay still, taking in great lungfuls of air. I began to ache in every part of my body.

"Is he finished?" Red Eagle asked.

I caught Davy's eye. I saw regret there, and relief.

"The genie," I said, "is back in the bottle."

"I misjudged him," Red Eagle said, "I had thought him a man who could take a joke."

TWO HOURS LATER, bandaged and sore, we were ready to depart. Little Fawn and I had been treated with herbs and poultices for scrapes to knees, elbows and other places too numerous to mention. Red Eagle wore a purple bruise from chin to ear. Davy himself, though embarrassed and contrite, was remarkably free of injury.

Red Eagle made light of the fight, assuring Davy he had more than passed the chiefs' test. They'd agreed to wait six days for our return, after which they would attack the Truitt mansion without us. Davy's pleas for more time fell on deaf ears.

Red Eagle had sworn to send riders to other Red Stick bands, demanding that Lacy Truitt be delivered to him. Finding her would not be easy, as war parties roamed the territory all the way to Georgia and into Spanish Florida.

Our horses were restored to us, along with one for Maggie. Indian women paraded back and forth from their homes delivering bundles of fruits, nuts and dried venison for our journey. The blonde woman and dark-haired girl Red Eagle had rescued from Fort Mims brought a basket of biscuits that smelled like heaven.

Samson still romped about, careful to miss none of the scraps offered by admiring children. But he seemed to sense we were leaving, and returned time and again to Davy's side.

Maggie arrived with a particularly large sack of food. "Please do not be angry," she said, her voice small, "but I am not going with you."

I could find no words.

"There is no place for me with the army, Penn. The soldiers I have met were far worse than the Indians. When you have prepared a new home for us I will gladly come, but until then I am better off here, with friends."

"No! I'll not part with you again. I'd be sick with worry."

A soft hand touched my arm. "She will be safe here, Penn. I promise."

I turned to regard Little Fawn. "You cannot promise that."

"I can," she said, "for I am staying also."

The morning air was suddenly colder. "Why?"

"I fear I might be tempted to slit your general's throat. Here I can look after your sister, and Red Eagle as well. I will see he does not forget his promises."

There was wisdom in her words, and in those of Maggie. They would be well treated here, and I could not vouch for the soldiers at Fort Strother. But the stinging in my eyes and emptiness in my chest was proof the heart cares little for wisdom.

Davy asked Red Eagle for the return of Old Betsy, and a runner was sent for her. Red Eagle himself carried the rifle I still considered my own. I longed to request its return as well, but his regard for it was obvious, and it was rightfully his under any definition of the spoils of war.

Betsy was delivered into Red Eagle's hands, and he laid mine aside to admire it. "I understand your attachment," he told Davy, "and envy you. This weapon has a rare balance, and a rare spirit."

Davy accepted the rifle. It was clear Red Eagle hated to give it up. "I was hopin'," Davy said, "that Penn's rifle might be returned too. But I s'pose that could be a pickle."

"Penn's rifle?" Red Eagle was confused. "I was told he carried an old musket."

"That's so," Davy said, "but only after losin' his rifle-gun at Talladega. Seems one of your bucks found it and give it to his boss."

It took Red Eagle a moment, but he got it. He plucked my longrifle from the grass at his feet. "This weapon was Penn's?"

"His pa made it," Davy said. "Got a fancy inscription and everythin'."

"It was a gift from Swift Elk, a warrior of renown," Red Eagle said. "I was greatly honored." He examined the copper plate affixed to the rifle butt. "I did not know it was Penn's, for I have no skill with letters."

I was shocked. For all his intellect and eloquent command of English, this man could not read.

A peculiar look passed between Davy and Red Eagle.

"I propose a wager," Davy said. "You and me'll throw the sticks. If I win, Penn gets his rifle back. If you win, you keep it, and take Old Betsy as well."

I could not believe my ears. "No. I will not permit that. You cannot risk Betsy."

"I can," Davy said. "And will."

"And I cannot resist," Red Eagle said. "I doubt two finer weapons exist anywhere in this land."

The Indians crowded about, excited to witness such a contest, and I was helpless to prevent it. I tasted elation and despair in equal measure. Much as I longed for my rifle, I couldn't bear the thought of Davy losing his.

The sticks, it developed, were pieces of split cane, each the length of a man's hand.

"The rules are simple," Little Fawn told me. "Each player throws four. The man with the most sticks landing curved-side up is the winner."

It sounded like a fine game, little different than throwing dice, but for Davy to risk his beloved rifle in such a match was downright reckless. If he lost I'd be doubly depressed.

The Indians formed a great circle around the contestants, allowing them ample room to throw. Little Fawn and I joined them. Excitement ran high, and I observed many warriors with their heads together.

"They are betting," Little Fawn explained. "Those few favoring Davy are receiving great odds."

Davy held his sticks clumsily, appearing befuddled as the rules were explained to him—twice. This brought groans from several among the crowd, doubtless those who had wagered on him to win.

One of the more gaudily attired chiefs stepped forward to referee. As Davy and Red Eagle fingered their sticks, waiting, the chief raised an arm high in the air. Absolute silence reigned. Even Samson was tense, his tail erect and quivering. The chief stretched the moment into an eternity, pushing the suspense to the limit before thrusting his arm toward the ground.

Simultaneously, Davy and Red Eagle tossed their sticks. Neither throw went more than a few yards, but the lengths of cane seemed to hang in the air, prolonging my torment.

The Creeks leaned forward, eyes huge, straining to see the result. I blinked, unable to focus. A man next to me screamed, as if in great pain. Another, on the far side of the circle, shrieked with joy. Then a great hubbub arose, everyone babbling at once, and I still did not know who won.

With a broad smile, Red Eagle raised my rifle over his head, and my heart sank. It was surely a signal of victory. But instead of demanding Betsy, Red Eagle lowered the weapon and extended it butt-first to Davy. With a tip of his cap and a modest bow, Davy accepted.

Most in the crowd groaned, a few cheered, and Red Eagle spoke, turning in a circle to address them all. "The spirits have spoken," he said, "and today they favor our good friend David Crockett."

At this, there was general approval. None, after all, could deny the will of the spirits. I advanced to Davy's side, and at last saw the sticks in the dust. Davy's four were all face down, with the rounded side up. A perfect throw. Equally remarkable, all of Red Eagle's lay on their backs, exposing the split edges. The worst possible result.

Davy held out my rifle, and I wrapped my hand gingerly around the stock. It was almost like shaking hands with my father. Maggie ran from the crowd and linked her arm in mine. She ran her fingers lightly along the rifle barrel, and I knew she felt Father's presence as well.

While the crowd still buzzed, Red Eagle approached Davy.

The two shook hands and I moved closer to catch their quiet words.

"Got me a confession to make," Davy said. "I learnt this game from a Cherokee medicine man. Taught me the secret of throwin' any score I want."

Red Eagle winked at him. "I possess the same secret."

CHAPTER 14

"There's low-flyin' comets tonight."

I MISSED MAGGIE. BACK in the Creek town, her argument had made sense. But a day's ride away, I began to doubt. Were the Red Sticks really as hospitable as they'd seemed? The burned-out farms, dead cattle and clouds of vultures we passed moving north told a different tale. Perhaps the Indians were only murderous when away from home. I only knew I would rest easier if Maggie had come along.

Little Fawn had promised to look after her, which should give me comfort. But capable as I knew her to be, she was surrounded by sworn enemies. And had she truly stayed to protect Maggie, or was that merely an excuse? Big Frog, a man to whom she had been betrothed, was there, as was Red Eagle. She had once hated Red Eagle with a passion, but now, with the hatred gone, did the passion remain? If his wife were found dead, would she set her cap for him?

"You miss her almighty bad," Davy said.

"Naturally. She's my sister. I'm still getting used to the idea she's alive."

Davy said, "Uh-huh," and I thought I detected a smirk.

"What's that supposed to mean?"

"Means that look on your face ain't the sort a man gets from missin' his sister. Leastwise, I hope it ain't."

Damn the man. Did he read minds, along with everything else?

"You really do have a devil inside you, don't you?"

His face darkened, and I immediately regretted my words, but they could not be unsaid. Davy kicked his horse, loping up the trail ahead of me, and we rode in silence for the rest of the day.

Samson roamed wide off the trail in pursuit of jackrabbits, turkeys and squirrels. I feared what would happen if he encountered a panther or bear, and would have said as much to Davy, had we been on speaking terms. As it was, I had to manufacture his response. *If them critters lack the sense to steer clear of him*, he'd likely say, *they'll have to take their medicine.*

We rode until well after dark, making camp next to a small stream. As we gnawed jerked venison I tried to get him talking again.

"I confess," I said, "I'm worried for Maggie and Little Fawn both. What will happen when Red Eagle discovers you made up that tale of his wife being held at Truitt's?"

Davy eyed me soberly awhile, probably still nursing my "devil" remark. Finally he sighed and raised an eyebrow. "Ain't much danger of that, 'cause I didn't make it up."

I snorted. "I was right there with you at the plantation. There were no Indian women about, least of all beautiful young captives."

"Ah," he said, taking a large bite of biscuit.

"Ah? That's all you have to say?"

"I didn't see no Injun maidens neither," he said after swallowing. "But I saw them dogs, and so did you."

"The dogs. You never did explain that."

"Had me a hunch. And when Zane tried to ambush us, he confirmed it. I'm dang near certain Red Eagle's wife is bein' held in that overseer's cottage."

"Dang near? You risk the lives of my sister and Little Fawn on *dang near*?"

"Red Eagle wouldn't hurt 'em," he said. "No matter what."

"And how do you know that?"

" 'Cause I wouldn't."

"*You* wouldn't? Of course you wouldn't. What kind of answer is that?"

"Best I got. You should eat one of them biscuits. Purt' near as tasty as my Polly makes."

I saw there was no use pursuing that particular subject, and bedded down mad. I didn't like thinking that Colonel Truitt, a man I'd long admired, had kidnapped a pregnant woman and ordered us killed to cover it up. But Nathan had said the loss of his leg had changed him, and the loss of his daughter, followed so soon by that of his son, may have driven him mad. As I well knew, grief had the power to change a man—make him do things he'd otherwise never contemplate.

Next day, Davy was on the lookout for game. He figured we'd hit Fort Strother by nightfall, and find a warmer welcome if we brought food. In less than the time it takes to tell, he'd shot two white-tailed deer, gutted them and slung them over our horses.

As hunting always seemed to lift his spirits, I made another stab at conversation.

"About Lacy Truitt," I said, "Did you believe Red Eagle when he claimed not to have her?"

"I did."

I'd come to believe him, too, after seeing Maggie. But now I was beginning to wonder. "So where does that leave us? She has to be somewhere. You think Truitt was lying about that too?"

Davy shrugged. "Don't rightly know how good a liar he is. But I'd bet my pants Nathan believed she was taken by Injuns."

"So where do *you* think she is?"

"Don't know," Davy said. "And that about sums it up. There's altogether too many things we don't know, but I aim to find them out."

AT DUSK OF the second day we reached the Coosa River, and spotted the fires of Fort Strother winking through the trees on the far bank. A picket at the bridge rose to challenge us with his musket, but at Davy's greeting of "How do, Clem. Still got the colic?" the man doffed his hat and waved us on.

Instead of heading straight for General Jackson, Davy skirted the tents of the regular soldiers, declaring we would first pay a visit to the Mounted Volunteers. Samson stayed close to us now, wary in the presence of so many strangers.

The smell of the place was like a fist to the nose. Sweat, urine, excrement, and the pungent aroma of never-washed clothes hung like a fog over the camp. Had it been this bad when we left? The Red Stick town, except for their mad shaman and God-awful White Drink, had been remarkably free of such odors.

One fire burned higher and brighter than the others, and was ringed by a score of raggedly-dressed men. Davy reined in and slid a deer carcass to the ground, motioning me to do the same. The volunteers clambered about, awestruck at the sight of so much food, and began peppering him with questions. But Davy begged off, saying his first duty was to instruct Old Hickory-face on the prosecution of the war. "By Gawd, someone oughta," roared one man, and we rode off to raucous laughter.

General Jackson's mood had not improved in our absence. The instant we were ushered into his presence he scowled up from the table serving as his desk, aimed a quill at Samson and said, "Get that infernal beast out of my tent! This is a command center, not a god-damned barnyard."

Davy looked at me and shrugged. "Samson," he said mildly, "mind the gen'ral and vamoose."

The hound sauntered up to Jackson's desk and sniffed among his papers in search of food. There was none in sight save for a half-full bowl of hickory nuts. Covering the bowl with a hand, Jackson roared, "Guards! Remove this animal at once!"

Two blue-clad men with muskets pushed through the tent flaps and stopped, eyeing Samson with scant enthusiasm. The dog curled a lip, exposing a dozen razor-sharp teeth, and growled.

A young fellow in round-rimmed spectacles and the bars of a second lieutenant, whom I remembered as Jackson's aide, entered behind them and said, "If you want him shot, General, we'd best fetch a cannon."

Jackson rose from his chair and peered down his nose at us. "Do none of you men know how to handle a dog?" Puffing up his chest, he strode around the desk and glowered down at Samson.

"Go!" he said in his most commanding tone. A bony finger pointed toward the tent flaps.

Samson turned his great head, following the line of Jackson's finger, and found nothing of interest there.

Jackson jammed clenched fists against his hips and stretched a few inches taller. Glaring straight into the blue hound's eyes, he belted out an order with the force of a hurricane. "Sit!"

Samson did nothing for a moment. Then he glanced at Davy, and I swear upon the Book he seemed to wink. He shook himself as if wet, turned around three times, strolled over into a corner behind Jackson's desk and plopped down next to a stool.

Jackson grunted and relaxed his stance. "That, gentleman, is how to handle a dumb beast. Ample evidence why I am a general and you are not." He waved a hand at his men. "You three, out."

They went, gladly, and Jackson turned his attention to us. Me he dismissed with a mere wrinkle of the nose, but he looked Davy up and down as if sizing him for a coffin. "I presume, Private, that you have fulfilled your orders to the letter, and are now prepared to lead me to the hideout of the rebel leader Red Eagle."

Davy cleared his throat. "Well, Gen'ral, it's like this…"

"I warned you, Private, that I would brook no deviation from your instructions. Did you find Red Eagle or not?"

"Most perzactly, Gen'ral, he found us."

Jackson's brow tightened. "But you can now guide me to his base of operations?"

"That'll be a tad difficult," Davy said, "as he moves around a lot. But if I had me a troop of soldiers to help rescue his wife,

I suspicion I might persuade him to quit the war an' bring his friends to the peace table."

Jackson's face turned purple, and his hand went to the butt of a holstered pistol. But after a moment he shook his head, pinched the bridge of his nose and returned to the chair behind his desk. "An extraordinary statement, Crockett. Before I shoot you, would you care to explain it?"

Davy launched into an abbreviated tale of our journey, listing what we'd learned and what we suspected. He made no mention of Nathan Truitt, his sister Lacy, or Little Fawn. Nor did he admit we'd visited Red Eagle's town, but implied we'd met him in a temporary camp next to a nameless stream. Otherwise, Davy's story was true, well told, and in my opinion quite compelling.

Jackson reacted with huffing jowls and bulging eyes, and by the time Davy finished he appeared to have aged ten years. "To summarize," he said, "you would have me believe that Colonel Thaddeus Truitt, one of the most beloved heroes of our War for Independence, should face military arrest for kidnapping the native wife of the butcher of Fort Mims. Then, his wife restored to him, this butcher should be pardoned for his atrocities. Perhaps you wish me to share a glass of port and a cigar with him as well."

Davy brightened. "That'd be uncommon kind of you, Gen'ral."

Throughout this exchange, I'd been watching Samson. He took no interest in the proceedings, peering instead at the stool beside him, upon which sat the general's fancy dress hat. This was a magnificent thing of blue wool festooned with gold braid and the yellow plume of some exotic bird. It was a hat worthy of the most extravagant Italian opera, and the way Samson eyed it made me increasingly nervous.

Jackson saw nothing of this. "By God, Crockett, I fear you are not only deluded, but may be dangerously insane. From all you've told me, Colonel Truitt deserves a medal for his actions. If all men were as diligent as he, this Indian trouble would be behind us, and we could focus on driving the British from our shores. In case you haven't heard, they have now recaptured Detroit, and are rumored to be moving south! From this moment, you are confined to camp pending possible court martial."

Samson chose this moment to rise up on his haunches and sniff at the hat's fluffy plume.

Davy cleared his throat, causing the dog to glance at him, and shook his head, *No!*

Jackson exploded from his chair. "No? Do you wish to add insubordination to the charges?"

"It ain't that, Gen'ral, not that at all, it's just—"

Samson's great jaws opened and snatched the glorious hat from the stool.

"Just what?"

Samson shook the hat as if breaking the neck of his prey, then sank to the earth and held it between his front paws as he chewed with great gusto.

"Just that I've seen the error of my ways," Davy said quickly. "I sees now why everyone wants you in the governor's mansion up in Nashville."

Jackson's shaggy eyebrows arched. "Everyone wants that, do they?"

"It's the talk of the camp," Davy said, " 'specially among the Mounted Volunteers."

Jackson grunted, reversing the beginning of a smile. "You are still confined to the fort." He swung to me. "As for you, McCoy, since you cannot keep your nose out of military affairs, you may now consider yourself a volunteer. You, too, are confined to camp. Should either of you attempt to leave you will be shot."

Davy hung his head. I did likewise, mostly to avert my eyes from Samson and the mangled hat. If Jackson discovered him now we'd all face a firing squad.

"Now get out," Jackson said, "and take that damned mutt with you!"

Samson rose and bounded through the tent flaps like a gust of wind. I saw with relief that the hat had vanished with him. Davy and I followed meekly, eager to be quit of the place.

My nerves clanged as we picked our way through the tents of officers and enlisted men, expecting angry shouts from behind. But none came, and we were soon back at the fire of the Mounted Volunteers.

I could have found the place with my eyes closed, guided by the sweet aroma of roast venison. Not surprisingly, the group huddled there had swollen to at least sixty. The two deer carcasses hung skinned and smoking upon spits above the fire, the focus of anxious eyes.

Davy's return brought ragged cheers, and men jumped up to clap him on the back, hailing him as their savior. He was given a seat of honor before the fire and insisted I join him. He was also offered the first steaming joint of venison, which he waved off, claiming we had recently eaten. That was untrue, of course, but I followed his example. Much as I desired hot, fresh meat, these scrawny souls looked far more hungry.

As we quickly learned, supplies from Fort Deposit arrived shortly after we had left to hunt Red Eagle, but were exhausted within three days. The men were back to a diet of acorns and hickory nuts—"living like savages," one man complained—and I bit my lip to refrain from telling them how much better the Red Sticks were faring.

Warming myself by the fire, I tried to relax. I was once again among honest men of my own race, and felt that should comfort me. But something was missing, and I realized with a start what it was. Little Fawn. At first I rebelled against the idea, telling myself it was Maggie I missed, but guilty feelings would not alter the truth. I had grown accustomed to Little Fawn's presence and felt strangely out of kilter without her.

The men pressed Davy to recount our adventures, but he insisted they first advise us of conditions in camp. The food shortage, it developed, was not their only problem. With the nights growing ever colder, they required winter clothing and far more blankets than the army could provide.

"And worst of all," said a man in a battered beaver hat, "our families needs us. Most of us only enlisted for sixty days, promisin' to get back and lay in meat and firewood for the winter. Them enlistments is up, but Old Hickory won't let us go."

"Says we'll be shot," said another, pointing his pipe at us like a pistol. "For desertion!"

After due commiseration, Davy bowed to their wishes and launched into his tale. This time he left nothing out, and the volunteers marveled at the pluck of Little Fawn, groaned at the death of Nathan Truitt, and swore oaths to restore sweet Lacy to her family. Captain Zane and his militia were painted in the darkest terms, to the point that their mere mention brought hisses and boos. Colonel Truitt was portrayed as a broken man, driven to desperate measures by personal tragedy. And Red Eagle was cast as a forest god who had been manipulated and defamed by evil whites seeking to steal the Indians' land.

Had I been one of his audience, my blood would burn to take Zane by the throat and shake the life from him. This, I suspected, was precisely Davy's goal, but what he hoped to accomplish while confined to camp I could not imagine.

Davy's voice trailed off as a young man in an officer's uniform appeared at the edge of the circle. He was flushed and nearly out of breath, and it took a moment to recognize him as the second lieutenant we had seen briefly in Jackson's tent.

"The general's hat!" he said. "Has anyone seen the general's hat?"

A few men snickered, which proved infectious, and soon there was universal merriment around the fire.

I peered into the trees where I had last seen Samson chewing on his prize. If the hat were discovered now, I feared Jackson would deem shooting too good for us. I quickly looked away, fearing the aide would divine my thoughts.

But the officer was not looking at me, or Davy either. He

stared open-mouthed at the half-stripped deer carcasses resting above the fire. "Meat! You have meat?" He seemed about to
swoon. "Wherever did you get it?"

"Light and sit," Davy offered quickly. "We'll rustle you up a
bite." Davy nudged me with his hip, and I nudged the man next
to me, allowing Davy to make room for the young officer.

The lieutenant sat. He had a lean, good-natured face, and a
wide, easy smile. "I haven't tasted meat since, since... leaving
home." And as one of the volunteers handed him a bloody slice
of venison, he sighed, "Oh, Lordy Lord."

Still nervous, I flicked an eye around the fire, finding no sign
of Samson. Hopefully he'd retreated into the woods beyond the
camp to bury the evidence.

"How you like waiting on Old Hickory-face?" Davy asked.

"A thankless task," the aide said between bites. "Nothing is
ever quite to his satisfaction. And when his hat went missing,
he was mad enough to eat bees. My God, this meat is good."

"The volunteers tells me he won't turn 'em loose, even though
their enlistments is up."

The aide nodded sadly. "He's determined to carve out a little
glory from this campaign. It galls him to see lesser men leading the real army up in Canada, while he's stuck here with you
unruly volunteers."

Davy puffed up his chest, jutted out his chin, and said, in a
dead-on impression of Jackson, "Give me a month, and I'll send
those damned lobsters scurrying across the ocean with their tails
between their legs."

The lieutenant laughed. "That's him to a 'T'. It's well known
he's set his sights on the governor's seat, but I believe his ambition runs even higher."

I caught movement in the corner of my eye, and my heart
all but stopped. Samson came trotting happily toward us, a
misshapen mass of blue and yellow between his teeth.

Planting his rump directly in front of Davy, the hound ogled
the lieutenant's venison and let the remains of Jackson's hat fall

to the earth. I stared in horror. The plume was gone, the braid tattered and the wool torn to shreds. Covering it all was a gooey mess of mud and saliva. Still, there was no doubt it had once been an officer's hat.

Jackson's aide had stopped eating to gaze at the travesty before him. I got one leg under me, ready to bolt for my horse. Davy, meanwhile, appeared relaxed, even amused.

The lieutenant leaned forward to pluck the hat between two fingers. "A useful animal," he said. "Brings scraps of rubbish to feed your fire." He looked slantwise at me, an amused twinkle in his eye. And with a flick of his wrist, he tossed the pitiful thing into the flames.

I stared. Davy grinned. Samson accepted the last scrap of meat from the aide's fingers. "Well," the fellow said. "I should be getting on with my search. The general will be inconsolable if I can't find his hat."

"That'd be a blessed shame," Davy said.

"It surely would," the aide said happily. And then he was gone.

With the two carcasses now stripped of meat, some of the volunteers had wandered off. But a good number crowded closer. One said, "What you aim to do about this Zane blighter, Davy?"

"If the gen'ral'd give me a troop of soldiers, I'd go tie a knot in his tail," Davy said. "Instead, he got me confined to camp, just like you-all."

"Confined, hell," another man said. "I'm leavin' soon, no matter what the general says. I ain't lettin' my family starve just so's he can play tin soldier."

Others murmured agreement.

"I'm gettin' a notion," Davy said, "that maybe we can take care of Zane and our families both, and thumb our noses at Old Hickory-face in the bargain. What d'you fellers think o' that?"

The men exchanged glances. "We think," said one, "that you'd best tell us about it quick-like, afore we're forced to squeeze it out of you."

AN HOUR LATER, the volunteers had retired to their tents, while Davy and I bedded down near the smoldering fire. The thought of crowding into a tent with a dozen volunteers had set my nose to twitching, and Davy did not press the matter. He was soon snoring, and I was seeking the least rocky stretch of cold ground when two hulking shapes separated themselves from the darkness.

"Where's Crockett?" one of them growled.

"You found'im," Davy said, instantly awake. He made to rise, but a huge hand grasped his hair and held him down.

In the pale moonlight, I recognized the two as my least favorite volunteers. I'd made their acquaintance after the Battle of Talladega, when they'd reviled Davy and me for allowing the Red Sticks to escape Jackson's trap. Their names were Kyler and Hatch, and I'd since learned they were roundly hated by the other Tennesseans.

"So you're still an Injun lover," one said. This was Kyler, a lanky, knock-kneed man with a pock-marked face, a hooked nose and a spade-shaped black goatee.

"An' now," added his partner, "you plan trouble for old Colonel Truitt. 'Fraid we can't allow that." Hatch was built like a water barrel, with livid scars crisscrossing his face. He claimed it had been done by Indians, but was such a liar that men doubted him just on principle. His nose was mashed flat over loose, blubbery lips.

The two men stood scowling down at Davy, paying me no mind at all. I looked around for my weapons, despairing to see them on the far side of the fire pit. My next thought was of Samson, but he was nowhere in sight, likely on another of his nocturnal hunting trips.

Davy said, "Kyler, you ain't got brains enough to grease a skillet. An' Hatch, you're so ugly your ma musta fed you with a slingshot."

I was trying to form some plan of action when Davy kicked Kyler in the knee, producing a most wonderful howl. His hair now free, Davy sprang up, swinging a fist at Hatch's jaw. The man moved with surprising speed, dodging the punch and drawing a knife, while Kyler stopped hopping and produced a steel-bladed tomahawk.

"Now you done it," Kyler said. "Now you're going to die. And your big-city pal too."

Davy stood rock-still, but his face darkened and his cheek twitched. "C'mon," he said in a rasping voice. "If it's killin' you want, I'm you're man."

I gasped. I'd heard that voice before—most recently in the Red Sticks' council house. I damned Kyler for a fool. If he'd threatened only Davy we might have had a normal tussle. By including me he'd roused thoughts of Caleb and Nathan and sealed his own fate.

I scrambled up, clutching a heavy stick, and several options flashed through my brain. I could shout for help on the off-chance Davy's friends would awake in time to help. I could charge the two men with my stick, pitting it against the knife and tomahawk. Or I could try to circle around them and reach my weapons.

But the truth was, any of those actions would be too late to prevent disaster. Davy's blood was up, and unless I could stop him someone would surely die. Even if he killed only Kyler and Hatch, whom no one would mourn, Jackson would have an excuse to execute him.

There was only one course left to me, and I took it without hesitation. Swinging the stick, I charged forward and smacked it solidly against the side of Davy's skull. The crack of wood upon bone was ugly and loud, and I prayed I had not killed him.

Kyler and Hatch stood flatfooted as Davy crumpled, and I swung the stick at Hatch's face. But he found his wits in time to duck. Bobbing up, he slammed a fist into my ribs, sending me reeling. Kyler followed with a swing of his tomahawk, nipping my ear and slicing through my hair. Scowling horribly, Hatch advanced with his knife held low, prepared to gut me.

With assailants on either side, I feinted a swing at Kyler and spun about, throwing the stick full in the face of Hatch. It struck him square in the nose, but he merely smiled, a sight more horrible than his scowl, and thrust the knife toward my gizzard.

I stumbled back toward Kyler, flailing my fists in desperation. Hatch was nearly upon me, his knife hungry for my throat. Something flashed before my eyes, and I assumed it was my all-too-brief life. Then Hatch was gone. I shook my head, baffled, until I heard Hatch's shrieks and recognized the spotted monster snarling over him. Samson!

Kyler shouted, "Hey!" and rushed to his partner's aid, but I tripped him, stomped his knee and kicked the tomahawk from his fist.

"Samson!" I roared. "Stand down!" And to my amazement, he did.

I heard clapping then, and turned to find a dozen men in a half-circle around us. The ruckus had finally awakened the other volunteers.

Kyler clutched his knee, growling, while Hatch whimpered like a baby. The arm of his coat was in shreds and soaked in blood.

"Good boy," I told Samson, and meant it.

"Where's Davy?" someone asked.

I spun back to the dogwood, where he lay half-buried in leaves. I flipped him onto his back, alarmed by a trickle of blood above his ear.

"We need water!"

A man thrust a bucket at me, and I spilled the contents over Davy's head. *Wake up, damn you. Please wake up.*

Nothing happened. I slapped his cheek, shook him by the shoulders, and still got no response. I hung my head, my eyes welling with the realization I had killed not only Davy's devil, but the truest friend I had ever known.

Then a voice beneath me said, "Best keep your head down, Penn. There's low-flyin' comets tonight."

CHAPTER 15

"I'm not cut out to be a soldier."

I DREAMT SOMEONE WAS kicking me in the ribs. Then I opened my eyes, and wished I *had* been dreaming. The boot sending pain through my body was very real, as was the soldier attached to it.

Uttering several words never heard in church, I grabbed at the boot, but this merely brought more soldiers. It was still full dark, but I saw their ring of bayonets glinting in the moonlight. Davy, awakened in similar fashion, said, "Right neighborly of you fellers to call, but might you come back after breakfast?"

One of the soldiers snorted, and I saw sergeant's stripes on his sleeve. "We ain't had breakfast since this consarned war began. Now hop to it. The general craves the honor of your presence."

Minutes later we were ushered into a tent. Not Jackson's, as I'd expected, but one absolutely bare of furnishings. It sat squarely in the no-man's-land between the officers and the enlisted men. The sergeant detailed two soldiers to guard the entrance and two others to accompany us inside.

"Nice place," Davy said, sniffing. "Not much for creature comforts, but right handy to the latrine."

The guards regarded him stonily. Both had bayonets pointed at us, and appeared ready to use them. Davy and I squatted on the cold ground, awaiting further developments. A cool wind beat against the sides of the tent, whistling through gaps in the ceiling. I wished I'd brought my saddle blanket.

Davy gingerly touched the back of his skull. "Sure got me one hellacious headache," he said. "Don't s'pose you know where I catched it."

I was still fishing for an answer when General Jackson swept in, bristling with brass buttons and gold braid—but decidedly without a hat. That hungry young lieutenant had reported us after all.

A soldier behind him held a candle, casting a dim light over the interior. Jackson inspected us as if we were some particularly foul breed of vermin. "I should have trusted my instincts and had you shot after Talladega."

Yep. Definitely the hat.

"Instead, I showed leniency. And how do you repay me? By inciting mutiny and bribing my men with venison." Jackson waggled a finger at Davy's open mouth. "Then, when two loyal volunteers take you to task for it, you set your hound upon them."

So it was *not* the hat. I spoke up. "Kyler and Hatch said that? They lie. Is it not customary we be allowed to face our accusers?"

"At the moment," Jackson said, "they are in the infirmary. Private Kyler's knee may be shattered, and Private Hatch will be lucky to keep his arm."

"Beg pardon, Gen'ral," Davy said, "but—"

"Enough! You two will remain here, under guard, until I decide what to do with you."

"Gen'ral!" Davy's shout shocked Jackson into silence. "If we ain't at Colonel Truitt's by dusk tomorrow, them Red Sticks'll overrun the place, slaughterin' every man, woman and critter in sight. You want that on your head?"

"All I want on my head," Jackson said sourly, "is my hat, which mysteriously disappeared concurrent with your arrival. I'll brook no more of your nonsense, Crockett. Be thankful you still live." He turned on the soldiers. "See that you guard these men damned close. They're tricky devils. Especially Crockett." Then he stormed out, as haughty as a hatless man could be.

The soldiers followed and closed the flap, leaving us in darkness.

A chill went through me. It was a two-day trip back to Truitt's, and we'd planned to leave this morning, Jackson's orders notwithstanding. If we failed to return on time, I dreaded what might befall Maggie and Little Fawn.

An hour or so passed, my thoughts growing less comforting by the minute. Finally I said, my voice low, "Davy, we have to get out of here!"

"You're preachin' to the choir," he replied. "Now hesh up a mite longer. I'm still cogitatin'."

A tent flap opened, allowing moonlight to spill in, and a guard's head appeared.

"General said not to let you talk. Figures you'll get up to no good."

"Gen'ral's got a suspicious nature," Davy said. "We're innocent as newborn babes."

The guard snorted. "Babes with iron fists, from what I hear."

The flap closed, and we sat once more in blackness.

I scrabbled as quietly as possible closer to Davy's position. "Maybe they'll really shoot us," I whispered. "It would beat this worrying all to hell."

"We'll save that as a last resort," Davy replied, equally quiet. "Now we know how big their ears is, I got me a plan."

A short time later, Davy said, no longer whispering. "Holy Hannah! Where'd you come from?"

"Shush, darlin'," answered a sultry female voice, "don't let them soldier boys hear. I just slipped under the tent to comfort you."

"But you ain't got no clothes on!" came Davy's retort. "What if they catch you?"

"Well, I'm sure I just don't know. How handsome are they?"

The tent flaps flew open. Both of them, and two heads poked in.

I'd been standing in one front corner and Davy in the other.

As the heads appeared, we each grabbed the closest and bashed them together with a satisfying *clonk*.

"Oh, my!" said the woman's voice. "They're not very handsome at all!"

SOON AFTER, AS the sun came peeking over the mountains, two men in blue uniforms strolled casually toward the tents of the Mounted Volunteers. Each man carried a bundle of clothing as if heading to the river to do his wash. But they weren't headed for the river and had no intention of washing. Several paces behind them walked a blue-spotted hound.

The two men were us.

"I trust you won't tell Maggie we escaped because of a naked lady." I said.

"How 'bout Little Fawn?

"Her either. I swear, that lady sounded so real I was tempted to jump her myself."

"My, my," Davy said. "Such compliments. You're like to make me blush."

I resisted the urge to glance over my shoulder. Any moment might bring the hue and cry that our bound and gagged guards had been discovered.

But we reached the volunteers' fire without incident. They stiffened at the approach of two uniforms, but Davy called out, "How do, you pack of rattlesnakes," and their faces lit.

"Davy! We heared you was arrested."

"Idle gossip," Davy said. "We was invited to a costume party." He then turned serious. "Listen up, you know that plan we hatched last night. The one to ease all our woes?"

"We was ready this morning," one man said, "and right put out when they took you away."

"The time is now," Davy said. "And I mean all-fired sudden, before musket balls start buzzin' 'round our heads."

The men scattered, gathering up their belongings and lashing them to horses. Davy and I did the same, not even pausing to change back into our own clothing. Time weighed heavy on me. Even if we escaped camp immediately and rode all night, our chances of reaching Truitt's plantation before tomorrow evening were slim. Little Fawn's face came to mind, followed by Maggie's, and I pushed them both away, still unable to consider the consequences. Then I felt an extra stab of guilt, recalling that the safety of Lacy Truitt and Red Eagle's wife might also depend upon our timely return.

Minutes later we mounted up, a force of twenty-odd men, and trotted toward the bridge at the southern end of camp. The remaining volunteers stood, watching us go, and many shouted encouragement.

I still saw no activity around the tent where Davy and I had been confined. Ahead, though, the bluecoats at the bridge saw us coming and rushed about, taking up positions to block our crossing. The sound of the cannon being trundled onto the bridge gave me a hollow feeling in my stomach.

"Can't we ford the stream somewhere else?"

"I aim to make a statement," Davy said. "Gotta show everyone Old Hickory-face ain't God Almighty."

"I see. We're getting ourselves shot dead to expose Jackson as a tyrant. Is that the entire plan?"

"Not quite," Davy said. "If needs be, I'll bust out the old Crockett grin."

The hollow feeling spread from my stomach into my chest.

We were now less than thirty yards from the bridge. A man in sergeant's stripes appeared to be in command, and he stood directly behind the cannon, next to a young soldier with a burning torch. The other soldiers leveled their muskets at us, their faces set in grim lines.

I looked back through the trees towards Jackson's tent and saw the general himself emerge, still bare-headed, looking curiously in our direction. Even if he failed to recognize me and Davy in the blue uniforms, he must have thought it odd to see Samson frolicking along beside the column.

Davy kept us trotting steadily forward. I closed my eyes, saying a silent prayer, and the beat of our horses' hooves upon the bridge sounded like knocking on the gates of Hell. Then Davy called a halt, and we pulled up nose-to-nose with the cannon.

Davy addressed the sergeant. "Top o' the mornin', Hezekiah." He doffed the blue cap and bowed in the saddle, then nodded at the soldiers on the bridge. "Sorry to trouble you gents, but bein' as it's such a fine day, we got a notion to take a ride." He then commenced to grin. The soldiers stared at him, and more than a few answered with grins of their own. Even the sergeant was hard put to maintain a stern expression.

Everyone waited. Men on both sides glanced from Davy to the sergeant and back again. Dimly, I heard shouts from the camp. The trussed-up guards had finally been found.

"We'd admire to have y'all join us," Davy added, "if'n you like."

Galloping hooves sounded behind us, and I feared Jackson had sent reinforcements. But it was only one rider on a shaggy white horse. As he pushed past, I recognized him as the young lieutenant who'd come searching for Jackson's hat. My heart sank into my boots. Clearly, the general had sent him, and we'd be shot as deserters.

The lieutenant's spectacles reflected the pale sky, masking his eyes. "Private Crockett. Mr. McCoy. I'm surprised to find you two on the loose. And I see you've acquired more hats."

Davy nodded. "I reckon Old Hickory-face sends his regards."

"He does," the lieutenant said. "Sergeant, instruct your men to move aside. The general has changed his mind, and will permit these volunteers to leave."

Despite his astonishment—and ours—the sergeant gave the order. Relief flooded the faces of his men, and they gave us a ragged cheer, drowning out the noise from the camp.

Davy pranced us past them, and once across the bridge we broke into a gallop, heading south. After a time I glanced back, finding no pursuit, and saw two men split off from the rear of our column, galloping westward into the woods. The thin one had his leg wrapped in bandages and the fat one had his arm in a sling. Kyler and Hatch, taking this opportunity to desert. I said nothing to Davy. Any discussion of those two would recall last night's fight, and he might ask who'd brained him with a stick.

Just then Jackson's aide spurred his shaggy white horse from the bridge and raced after us. He fell in next to Davy and delivered a mock salute.

Davy looked sideways at him. "What in thunder got into the gen'ral? Never knowed him to change his mind."

The lieutenant smiled. "He didn't. He sent me with orders to light the cannon. Guess I'm not cut out to be a soldier."

CHAPTER 16

"Fate favors a fighter."

DAVY PUSHED US hard until dark. We'd have ridden all night, but the moon and stars, as if conspiring against us, remained behind the clouds. Then it began to rain, and when a horse stumbled, spilling its rider on the muddy ground, Davy called a halt.

I slept not at all, my head full of dire visions, while the company snored away the precious hours. I had come to believe Red Eagle a decent, even honorable man, but he was still a savage and subject to the whims of his chiefs and medicine men. Though reason told me Maggie and Little Fawn should be safe, I listened only to the voice of fear.

In the pale light before dawn, Davy at last roused the men, aided by Samson, who made a game of snatching away their wet blankets.

"Will we make it to Truitt's by dusk?" I asked.

"We'll sure as shootin' try," Davy said, refusing to meet my eyes.

"If anything happens to the women…"

"Yes," he said in that voice that was not his own. "I know."

I felt a chill, sensing that his devil lurked perilously close to the surface. But if anything *had* happened to Maggie or Little Fawn, I knew I'd make no effort to rein it in. Instead, I swore I would embrace his demon and unleash my own.

Jackson's recently retired aide seemed to sense my unease, for he made an effort to engage me in conversation upon other matters. His name was Aaron Yessler, and he'd been a law clerk in Nashville before the war. As it would now be perilous to return, he planned to head for Charleston, where he would ply his trade under a new name. But first, he promised, he'd accompany us to Truitt's and help free Red Eagle's wife.

The entire company had pledged the same. Few shared Davy's hope that this action might end the war, but their regard for him was such that they were determined to see his mission through before returning home to care for their families.

We pushed the horses as hard as we dared, but stops for rest and water grew ever more frequent. The sun sped across the sky, and at dusk we were still hours from our destination. By this time my brain was afire with worry and I could only ride on, urging Davy and the others to greater speed.

Thankfully, the land had leveled out and that night's moon took pity on us, pushing half its light through the clouds. But time passed all too quickly, and it was well past midnight when we reached the stream leading to Truitt's plantation. We turned east, but had not covered a hundred yards when Davy called a halt and slid from his horse. He fell to one knee, studying the ground.

"Red Sticks passed this way. 'Least an hour back."

"How many?" Aaron Yessler asked.

"A sight more than a hundred. Maybe a damn sight more. We'd best haul our britches."

This last statement I heard only dimly, as I'd already kicked my chestnut and spurted past. The other horses were soon pounding in my wake. Terror had me fully in its grip now, and my heart thundered in my chest.

I kept my eyes on the distant sky, dreading the sight of smoke. The Indians first act upon reaching Truitt's plantation would surely be set fire to the mansion.

After a time Davy caught up to me. We exchanged a grim nod, but he made no attempt to slow me, and we raced alongside by side through the night. Eventually Davy threw up a hand, signaling a halt. I hesitated, seeing no reason for delay, but when he grasped my chestnut's bridle I slowed my pace.

"What? Why stop now?"

For answer, Davy pointed on down the road. I squinted but made nothing of it.

"Fires," he said, and my fear quickened, assuming he meant the buildings of the plantation.

Davy charged past, and I reeled after. We covered another fifty yards before I saw specks of light in the distance. But before panic gripped me, Davy reined in, and I realized the fires were actually quite close.

"Red Sticks," he said to my questioning look.

Peering into the darkness, I discerned figures moving about the flames. What I had taken to be burning buildings were simply campfires. At their center was the dark outline of a cabin. And off to one side, what first appeared to be a lake shimmering in the moonlight resolved itself into a large group of grazing horses.

"Red Eagle's band?"

Davy nodded. "One of them horses is Arrow."

I judged we were now only a few miles from the plantation. The question was, were the Creeks still preparing for their attack, or—their deviltry completed—were they celebrating their victory?

Davy read the question as clearly as if I'd spoken. "Let's go ask 'em."

Yessler and the others were not eager to proceed. Despite Davy's assurance that Red Eagle was trustworthy, these were the very Indians they had fought so recently at Talladega. They must have thought it the height of madness to ride casually into the camp of their enemies.

"You men wait and watch," Davy told them. "If things go well for us, we'll be back directly. If not," he paused and shrugged, "ride north to your families and don't look back."

They regarded us silently. Finally one man turned his head and spat. "That what you'd do, Davy, if you was us?"

Davy just grinned, then kicked his dun and rode boldly forward, making no effort to disguise our approach. I felt considerably less bold, but was determined to discover the fates of Maggie and Little Fawn, even at the cost my life. Between us, ears cocked and tail erect, trotted Samson the hound.

A shout went up from the darkness, and in an instant we were surrounded by a dozen braves with war clubs and bows.

"Crockett," Davy said cheerfully, "and McCoy. Will one o' you gents kindly tell Red Eagle we've come to call?"

Evidently this request was understood, for one of the Indians grunted a command and another loped off toward the camp.

One of the warriors said something in Creek, pointing to Davy, and the others loosened the grips on their weapons. But just as I was feeling more kindly toward them, one pointed at me and mimicked a man spewing like a fountain. The others laughed heartily at my expense. I forced a smile. Davy looked slantwise at me, containing his mirth. Then he, too, began to chuckle, and I could not escape the contagion. In another moment I was laughing as hard as the rest.

But as the hilarity wound to a halt, the smiles of the Indians faded. Though they clearly knew us, their manner revealed a tension that did not bode well. Something had happened in our absence—something to change their feelings toward us.

A voice from behind said, "You boys require assistance?" In a curved line twenty yards away, Yessler and the others sat their horses, rifles handy across their laps.

The Red Sticks growled, their eyes flashing between us and the volunteers.

"Appreciate the offer," Davy said, "but we're gettin' along famously. You'd best back off a ways, so's not to make these red gentlemen nervous."

The men looked at Yessler, who nodded, and the company melted back into the night.

The runner soon returned from camp, beckoning us forward, and led us past the small cook-fires to the cabin. Close up, I recognized it as one of the abandoned homesteads we'd passed days earlier. Before this war began, it had no doubt been inhabited by settlers very much like my parents. Wherever these folk had gone, I hoped it had not been to the perceived safety of Fort Mims.

Grouped about the entrance were a score of grim-faced Creeks, some of whom I recognized as chiefs and medicine men. A big fellow in a beaded vest stepped forward, scowling, and I stopped short when I realized he was Lame Bull, Sopath's father—the man Zane's gang had blinded with a hot stick.

"You are late. Your word is broken."

"My watch may be broke," Davy said, "but my word's still tickin'. Where's Red Eagle?"

"Inside," Sopath's father said. "You should pray he is well."

Samson bared his teeth and growled. The blind man's face went white. He stepped back a pace.

Davy said, "Why wouldn't he be?"

The man said nothing, but his hostility was palpable. I strained my eyes into the darkness, seeking Maggie or Little Fawn, and my foreboding returned in full measure.

Davy dismounted and stepped onto the cabin's porch. Every nerve a-twitch, I followed. He pushed the door open and we peered into the dimly lit room.

Davy said, "What in tarnation?"

I stared in wide-eyed wonder.

Red Eagle sat centered behind a long rough-hewn table, hands bound before him with a strip of cloth. And at either end of the table, leveling cocked muskets at his breast, sat Maggie and Little Fawn.

Red Eagle said, "Welcome, gentlemen. Please join us."

Without turning to look, Maggie said, "That really you, Penn?"

"It is. But is that really *you*?"

She spun about, lowering the musket, and her smile was like a Sunday sunrise. "Thank the Lord."

Little Fawn, too, lowered her weapon. "We missed you," she said. The words addressed us both, but her eyes were for me alone. "All of us. Is that not true, Red Eagle?"

"Gentlemen," Red Eagle said, "the truth of that statement cannot be exaggerated."

THE STORY WAS quickly told. When Davy and I failed to return at the appointed time, the Red Stick chiefs insisted upon mounting their own attack on Truitt's plantation, and nothing Red Eagle said would dissuade them. The Creek medicine men were convinced we had betrayed them to General Jackson, and the shaman with the owl hat wished to flay and burn Maggie and Little Fawn in our stead. So when the war party reached this abandoned cabin, where they prepared for the attack, Red Eagle brought the women under his protection. Providing Maggie and Little Fawn with muskets, he instructed them to take him prisoner in hopes of confounding his tribesmen long enough for Davy and I to return. That we would indeed return, none of the three had harbored the slightest doubt.

I found the tale incredible, until Red Eagle admitted the idea had been Little Fawn's. Next to Davy, she was the most clever human I had ever known.

The sad news was that most of Red Eagle's scouts had returned, and he still had no news of Lacy Truitt. She had vanished as completely as if a hand had reached down from the heavens and plucked her from the earth. I began to fear that might be very near the truth.

While Davy and Red Eagle labored to smooth the feathers of the chiefs and medicine men, the ladies and I rode out to help the Tennesseans make camp. We spent the next hour warming ourselves at the volunteers' fire, while I did my best to pretend I had not been concerned for their safety. Neither woman was at all fooled.

The men were unsure what to make of Little Fawn, which suited me fine, but made no effort to hide their admiration for Maggie. She had grown considerably since leaving Pennsylvania, and I had to admit she was no longer the lanky girl of my memory—but a budding young woman. To see her amid a score of potential suitors filled me with a whole new breed of discomfort.

Still, nothing could dampen the pleasure of Little Fawn's company. Her hair shone in the moonlight, and her deerskin shift was resplendent with red and yellow beads. Had her words always held such music? Had her hip always curved in just that way? I tried to recall the bedraggled ruffian who had wrestled me in the dirt a scant week earlier, but the image would not come. The woman before me was enough, and all I could hope her to be.

We sat quite close as we talked, and Little Fawn occasionally laid a gentle hand on my leg. I was careful not to move, so as not to discourage this, and began to contemplate resting my own hand upon hers.

I was pursuing just such thoughts when a guttural voice called from the darkness. "Stumblefoot!" I knew the voice, a harsh croak more fitted to reptile than human, and turned to search the night for Big Frog.

"Stumblefoot," he said again. "It is time for a reckoning."

Several Tennesseans grabbed up their rifles and muskets. I stood, peering into the darkness. Big Frog strode boldly toward me, accompanied by three other Red Sticks. "Be at ease," I advised the volunteers. "This is a private matter."

"Private or not," Yessler said, "we'd best stay alert if we mean to keep our hair."

"A sensible precaution, but it's mine he wants." I looked into Yessler's bespectacled eyes. "When the ruckus starts, I'd be obliged if you'd look after my sister."

"Gladly."

"And if events go bad for me…"

"My hand upon it." His grip was firm and strong, and put me more at ease.

Maggie's face was white. I gave her shoulder a gentle squeeze. "Fear not," I said softly. "Fate favors a fighter, and I have much to fight for."

Little Fawn faced Big Frog with hands on hips. Her eyes flashed defiance. "Leave us, fool. You have no claim upon me."

"You have one upon me, witch. It seems I cannot forget you. Perhaps if I kill the one you call 'Stumblefoot', it will end the spell."

I put myself between them. "Are you challenging me to a duel, Froggy?"

"I am."

Things were stirring in the Red Stick camp. More Indians would soon join us. I pressed my rifle into Yessler's hands and stepped past Little Fawn, exhibiting a confidence I did not feel. "Appears we have business, then. Let's make an end to it."

I wished Davy were here to advise me. Big Frog may be a fool, but he was a very big fool, and had already proven his ability to down me with a single punch. Facing him man-to-man was not a thing to take lightly.

Big Frog stepped forward, and as the fire lit his face I saw the depth of his fury. In that instant I felt almost sorry for him. This was more than wounded pride. He was truly smitten with Little Fawn, and her presence in the Red Stick town must have rekindled his hope. My return had dashed that hope and driven him to desperation. I knew all this and understood it, because in his place I would have felt the same.

But no degree of understanding would prevent him killing me. That would require all my strength, all my skill, and a fair measure of luck.

"Your challenge is accepted," I said, "and the choice of weapons is mine." Good sense told me it should be rifles, a weapon I was more familiar with. But I felt I must beat him on his own terms. A knife or tomahawk would suffice, but these were not the weapons of a civilized man, and had likely been toys in his cradle. The war club and bow would likewise offer him great advantage, while a pistol would weigh too heavily to mine. There was only one way we would face each other as equals—and that was my only true choice. "Fists."

Little Fawn gasped. Maggie sobbed.

Big Frog broke into a hideous grin. He outweighed me by at least forty pounds, and his arms were half a foot longer than my own. And had he known I was raised in a city, rather than here on the frontier, his confidence would have soared even higher. Aside from a few boxing lessons from my father, I had only one advantage. My wits.

Our weapons were quickly disposed of. I passed mine to Little Fawn, while he threw his to the ground, demonstrating his contempt.

I shrugged out of my jacket and shirt. The fight would warm me, and I wanted nothing that would give him purchase. With a derisive snort, Big Frog peeled off his buckskin vest and flung it onto his weapons. His glistening chest was enormous in the firelight, and I began to regret forgoing firearms.

But it was too late for regrets. We now stood face to face, arm's length apart.

The three men behind Big Frog had grown to thirty, and more arrived by the second. Several newcomers brought torches, so that they might better witness my destruction. Some of the Tennesseans flourished torches of their own, making our private battlefield almost bright as day.

Men on all sides began to shout. Most of the shouts were in Creek, and I could well imagine their meaning, so did my best to shut them out. My father had taught me to focus on my opponent's eyes, saying they held the intent of his hands. I spread my legs, bent my knees and watched Big Frog's face. My best chance was to move quickly, in and out, striking like a snake, because to fall within his grasp would mean my doom.

Big Frog's eyes were focused just beneath my chin. When he

lunged, his outstretched arms went straight for my throat. Fore-warned, I spun left and darted past him, smacking a fist into his ribs. Or rather, where his ribs *would* be, were they not shielded by layers of fat. As it was, my punch bounced off, slowing him not at all. He lumbered back around, glaring, and I forced a laugh. In our first exchange, we had accomplished little more than trading places.

Big Frog charged again, this time with arms flung wide to prevent me darting past him. I feinted to his left, watched his weight shift and wheeled back to his right. Grasping his right arm in both hands, I spun him about like a turnstile. As he staggered, I kicked him soundly in the seat of his breeches. This provoked laughs from both sides. I had embarrassed Big Frog, but not hurt him, and he was now even madder than before.

I asked myself what Davy would do, and saw my possible salvation. Big Frog's greatest weakness was his brain. I would make him try to think.

"I'm confused," I whispered, for his ears alone. "Why do you want Little Fawn?"

The question surprised him, but he shook it off and took a wild swing at my head. I ducked, buried a left in his belly and clipped his jaw with my right. His head rocked back, but his body pushed forward and I barely escaped a death hug.

"Think about it," I said. "She's ill-tempered, bossy and head-strong as a mule."

He scowled at me, but was clearly trying to think. While he was thus occupied, I darted in and delivered two solid jabs to his nose. The volunteers cheered. Big Frog shook his head as if annoyed by an insect, but blood flowed from one nostril. He looked straight at me.

"She is all of that," he said, "and that is why I love her."

I was so stunned I dropped my guard. *God help me*, I realized, *that's why I love her too.*

A huge hand flashed out and closed around my windpipe. Wittingly or not, Big Frog had turned the tables on me, forcing *me* to think. Unable to breathe, I pummeled his body, but it was like punching a side of beef. My strength fading, I placed both hands on his chest and shoved. He shoved back, reveling in this test of main strength.

I was close to blacking out. When I could push no more, I lowered my head and let my arms go slack. Meeting no resistance, Big Frog bulled forward and I head-butted him squarely between the eyes.

The crack of skull upon bone was loud, even above the screaming crowd. Big Frog reeled back, squalling. The cheering volunteers lent new life to my limbs. I charged, bashing his face with a right forearm and a sweeping left hook. He crashed on his back with a great *whoof* and I pounced on him, pinning his arms with my knees. My thumbs dug deep into his throat, probing for his Adam's apple.

Big Frog made squawking noises, and after a moment I realized he was trying to speak.

I eased my grip, and the squawks became words.

"Kill me," he said. "Kill me, or I will surely kill you."

I was sorely tempted, for I had no doubt he meant it. But Maggie was watching. Did I truly want this sight fixed in her memory? And what about Little Fawn? She had once been promised to this man, and might harbor some small feeling for him.

"I'll kill you if I must," I said. "But I would rather bargain."

His eyes narrowed. He was trying to think again.

"What will it take?" I demanded. "Money? Horses?"

His piggish eyes grew shrewd. "No money. No horses. I have lost that which I most treasure, and must be repaid in kind."

A moment passed before this sank in. Then the muscles swelled in my arms, my hands dug in and I nearly snapped his neck. "You will never have my sister," gritted. "I will kill you first, a thousand times over!"

The breath hissed from his throat. The crowd fell silent, and through a red haze I heard Maggie cry, "Penn! Don't!"

Then a strong hand closed upon my shoulder, and a voice said, "Why not hear him out? Maybe he ain't so dumb as he looks." The voice was Davy's, and his calm demeanor had its effect on me. I loosened my grip.

Big Frog sucked air and coughed, then began to laugh. "Your sister? You thought I wanted your sister?"

Failing to see the humor, I nearly strangled him again.

"What I want…" he said, choking out the words, "… is your rifle."

"WHAT WERE YOU and that fat fool saying to one another?"

Little Fawn sat at my side before the fire, while the volunteers celebrated my victory. She eyed me strangely, and her questions were many.

"Just trading insults," I said.

"You defeated him, yet gave him your rifle. What did he give you in return?"

"He agreed to stop calling me Stumblefoot." I looked around, wishing to change the subject. Davy sat with Samson's great head in his lap, regaling the Tennesseans with tales of bear hunting. Across the fire, Maggie was in avid conversation with Aaron Yessler. I feared our talk before the fight may have given him the wrong idea. "Should I break that up?" I asked Little Fawn.

"Like me," she said, "your sister is a woman grown. She must follow her own heart, and not be ruled by her relatives."

She stood abruptly, brushing grass from her shift, and held out a slim hand. "Come."

Taking the hand, I rose awkwardly, conscious of those around us. But most gave us only a passing glance before returning to their conversations.

Tugging gently, Little Fawn led me away from the fire and into the darkness. She glided over the dark earth with such grace that I felt clumsy, and took great care not to stumble.

"You have grown, Pennsylvania McCoy." She smiled up at

me, her teeth gleaming in the moonlight, and my name sounded sweet on her lips. "The man I knew as Stumblefoot would never meet a warrior's challenge bare-handed, let alone present him with a fine rifle."

I had no words for that. Any growing I may have done had been purely accidental, and not a thing to brag about. Words in general had been hard to come by since our return from Fort Strother. Talking with Little Fawn had been a simple thing when we were adversaries, but now that I felt differently, I feared to say the wrong thing, and had no notion what the right thing might be.

"When you were away," she said, "Maggie spoke much of you. You were a good brother, Penn, and a dutiful son."

"Does that surprise you?"

For answer, she guided my arm behind her and wrapped it about her waist. The press of her body as we walked made my heart beat faster. Ahead of us, black against the dark sky, rose a stand of ancient oaks.

"When I was away," I said, "I thought of you often." My voice sounded strained, but I was greatly relieved to get the words out.

Reaching the edge of the woods, Little Fawn led me between two tall oaks. She turned to face me, put her arms around my neck and pulled herself closer. Her breath was warm on my cheek. "In these thoughts you had of me, was I perhaps unclothed?"

I stiffened, too shocked to reply. I had spoken from the heart, and her answer was to make sport of me again. She smiled wickedly now, and I steeled myself for another taunt. Instead, she crossed her arms over her body, tugged the deerskin shift up over her head, and let it fall to the earth.

I caught my breath. Enough moonlight filtered through the trees to show me she was completely naked, and completely lovely. With a growl, I gathered her into my arms. She pressed hard against me. And for a time, we had no need of words.

CHAPTER 17

"You been hornswoggled."

THE ROAD TO Truitt's mansion was as I remembered it—long and straight under a canopy of cypress trees. The plantation outbuildings appeared abandoned, and crows perched boldly on the fence posts. Somehow, Davy had convinced the Creeks to stay behind, giving him a chance to carry out his plan, and we rode with only the volunteers to aid us.

At last, a quarter mile ahead, we sighted the white pillars of the mansion, and Davy shouted, "Now!"

The company slowed, and the two men at the rear let Davy and I slide from the rumps of their horses. From the head of the column, Aaron Yessler tossed us a mock salute. He was in full uniform now, and, lending ceremony to his command, two other men wore the uniforms Davy and I had borrowed at Fort Strother. To all appearances, this was a delegation of regular soldiers and volunteers sent by General Jackson.

Yessler smiled. "Luck to you, gentlemen."

"To us all," Davy said. And the company rode on.

Davy and I slipped off the road into the trees. It was near mid-day, a time Truitt would be least suspicious of unexpected visitors. While Zane and his militia welcomed the new arrivals, Davy and I planned to circle the mansion and slip in through the back door. If all went well, we'd capture Truitt's men without firing a shot and be free to search the property for Red Eagle's wife.

This was the moment Davy had been waiting for, his chance

to enlist Red Eagle in the cause of peace. This was the chance I'd longed for as well—to confront the men truly responsible for the slaughter of my parents.

Davy and I ran easily through the grass, keeping the line of trees between us and the mansion. I hoped he was right—that no shooting would be needed. While he carried Old Betsy, I was stuck with the battered musket formerly belonging to Big Frog. Still, I did not regret my bargain. Little Fawn's scent was still with me, and I reveled in the memory of her taste and touch. We'd spoken little this morning, but the bond was strong between us.

Little Fawn had pleaded to come along, of course, but Davy would not hear of it. If Truitt's men saw a woman riding with the company, they would be instantly on alert. Samson remained behind for the same reason.

"She's a mighty fine gal," Davy said as we ran.

I looked sideways at him. Had Little Fawn told him what happened between us?

He turned his head and twitched his nose as if sniffing my clothing.

My cheeks burned. "If you say another word, we may come to blows."

"I've said my piece. But I meant it. She *is* a fine gal."

I let it go. We both knew which *she* he meant, and despite my embarrassment, his approval meant much to me.

"They're almost to the house," Davy said, "and Zane's men are waitin' with open arms. Zaney's got him a number of new recruits, too."

"Is everyone smiling?"

"So hard they're like to crack their teeth."

We knelt behind a bush to observe the proceedings. Yessler dismounted to shake Zane's hand. A moment later the volunteers stepped down, handing their reins to servants. Then everyone, volunteers and greenjackets alike, began filing into the mansion. Davy's plan was working.

But just as the great double doors closed, he said, "Oh-oh."

"Oh-oh? What's oh-oh?"

"My scalp's pricklin' something fierce. We could have us a problem."

"Two problems," said a voice behind us. A voice I knew and despised.

"Was I you," said a second voice, also familiar, "I'd be raisin' them hands."

Davy and I shared a glance and grimaced. We raised our hands.

"Now turn around, and be doin' it plenty slow."

We did that too. And there behind us, accompanied by two of Truitt's green-clad militia, stood Kyler and Hatch.

YESSLER AND THE two uniformed volunteers sat tied to the bases of statues in the mansion's main hall. Glowering down at them were a dozen members of the colonel's private army. And overlooking them all were the stately portraits of past and present Truitts.

"Where's the others?" Davy asked, and Yessler was about to answer when one of the greenjackets cuffed him across the mouth.

Our friends eyed us bleakly. We'd been their only hope of rescue, a hope now dashed. And Davy and I were to blame. If not for us, they'd all be safe at Fort Strother.

My sole consolation was that Kyler and Hatch still suffered from their wounds. Kyler walked with a pronounced limp, while Hatch's arm hung at an odd angle. I rejoiced at every grimace and groan.

Davy and I were prodded into a room with a large maple desk, a Persian carpet and a wall lined with books—clearly Colonel Truitt's study. The wall opposite the books was covered with a blue and white flag—the battle flag of the South Carolina militia during the War of Independence. Above the desk hung a curved cavalry saber with a worn brass hilt. The flag and sword were sad reminders that a once-great man had succumbed to bitterness and greed.

Colonel Truitt himself was not present. Instead, seated behind the desk, was Captain Gabriel Zane.

"Have a seat, gentlemen," Zane said, "and we'll make you less comfortable."

Two wooden chairs were pushed to the center of the room, facing the flag, and we were forced to sit. While Kyler covered us with Betsy, Hatch went about lashing our ankles and binding our wrists behind the backs of the chairs.

"Imagine my delight to discover you two still lived." Zane poured himself a glass of red wine from a cut glass decanter. "Now I can enjoy your deaths all over again."

Davy said, "Where's our friends?"

"With the other rats." Zane took a sip of wine and smacked his lips. "In the cellar."

"And where's Truitt?"

"The colonel has had quite enough of you. In his view, men who side with savages against their own race are no better than feral dogs. You will be disposed of accordingly." Zane preened, waiting for us to ask his meaning. When we did not, he supplied the answer himself. "Once it grows dark, you will be taken to the woods and slaughtered. There will be every indication you were killed by marauding Red Sticks."

Davy remained calm, giving Zane no satisfaction. I strove to follow his example.

"Ironic, is it not? Your deaths will be laid at the hands of those you wish to protect. The hue and cry will be nothing compared to Fort Mims, but it will further alarm the local settlers. Many have already sold out for a pittance and fled the territory. You may rest assured your deaths will serve a purpose."

The mention of Fort Mims made my hackles rise. Zane and his colonel were the men truly responsible for my parents' massacre, and I was powerless to act.

Hatch cracked Betsy's barrel against my skull, filling my head with stars. "Twixt now and nightfall, what say me and Kyler soften them up a mite?" The scars crisscrossing his face grew livid with excitement.

"That can wait." Zane drained his wine glass and set it down. "I don't want blood on this rug. It will be mine someday."

"Yours?" Kyler's eyebrows went up.

Hatch elbowed him in the ribs. "When he hitches up with that Lacy gal."

"Shut your mouth!" Zane slapped the desk with such force that the wine glass toppled, bouncing on the thick carpet. "You are not to mention her name."

"Gloat while you can," Davy said. "Old Hickory-face may've been raised on pickle juice and vinegar, but he's an almighty keen soldier. He's got a hundred men ridin' south as we speak."

Zane sneered. "I very much doubt that. These two gentlemen advised me of your mutiny, and the three in the hall confirmed it. You are merely a pack of deserters, presumably bound for Tennessee. Jackson has no fondness for you, and will be pleased to hear of your deaths."

Davy and I looked at each other and winced, knowing he was right.

ASIDE FROM GRAMMAR school, which I had sometimes enjoyed, I had spent twenty-four years on this earth without being held captive. Now, after two weeks in the South, I had been the unwilling guest of the Indians, the army, and the aristocracy. When this war was over, if ever, I was going to find a friendlier place to live.

Zane had left us in the care of Kyler and Hatch, who took every opportunity to torment us. Though careful not to make us bleed, they delighted in backhand slaps and short punches to the ribs. As this was thirsty work, they soon emptied Truitt's wine decanter and filched another bottle from his desk.

Davy accepted the beatings in silence. His eyes were narrow and his brow tight, and I judged he was plumbing his bag of tricks for some means of escape. I took it for granted he would find one, for he had not failed us yet. Of course, the only alternative was despair, and that would gain me nothing.

Kyler and Hatch had slouched on a purple sofa beneath the battle flag, where they could kick our shins without exerting themselves. At last, having drained the last of Truitt's wine, Hatch's head drooped until his chin pressed upon his chest. Kyler leaned back and was soon snoring.

I, too, closed my eyes, trying to envision a future with Little Fawn and Maggie. But all I could see was death.

Excited shouts erupted in the hall.

"Red Sticks!" someone yelped. "Boilin' up the road like a swarm of locusts!"

Kyler jerked up, face taught and fish-belly white.

Hatch cut short a ferocious snore and opened one eye, peering owlishly about the room.

"Watch them!" Kyler snapped. He rose painfully and hobbled from the room.

Across the hall, the dining room door slapped open and Zane raced out, a turkey leg in his fist. Ripping a napkin from his neck, he ran toward the front windows, out of my view. "Hell and damnation! Must be a hundred of the devils."

"And they got torches! They'll burn the mansion sure!" someone cried.

"No they won't," Zane said, "because we'll beat them to it. That will buy us time to get away. You men at the windows keep those savages occupied. The rest prepare torches. Now!"

Men scurried to their tasks. I saw Yessler and the volunteers still bound in the hall, their faces white with horror.

Hatch glared his hatred at us.

"You're itchin' to run, ain't you?" Davy said. "Go ahead. We won't miss you none."

"I'm goin' nowhere," Hatch replied, "till I see you burn."

In the hall, militiamen raced frantically about. I saw no torches yet, but hoped Davy would hurry his thinking.

"Hatch!" Zane's commanding voice came from just outside the room. "Untie those two, and be quick about it!"

Davy caught my eye and winked, and I understood. He was throwing his voice again. Hallelujah, we'd soon be free.

Hatch stared stupidly at the doorway. "Turn 'em loose?"

"Immediately. I'm tired of waiting. We're taking them to the woods."

Hatch rose from the chair and tugged a tarnished knife from his belt. Scowling all the while, he bent and began to saw at the rope around my ankles.

Davy and I exchanged the smallest of nods. Once free of our bonds, we had merely to overpower the half-drunk Hatch and arm ourselves. Then, hopefully, Davy had a plan to deal with the guards in the hall.

I was feeling jubilant until Kyler appeared at the door. "What the hell?"

Hatch peered up dumbly, the knife still working at my rope. "You gonna help me, or just gawk?"

"Help you what?"

"Cut these bastards loose, like Zane said."

Kyler stared at him. "Zane said that? When?"

"Just now, damn you. He was just outside."

Kyler looked over his shoulder into the hall. "Out here? Hell, you been hornswoggled. I been right across the hall, jawing with Buzzard."

Hatch looked daggers at Davy. "Zane wasn't there?"

Kyler laughed, an ugly sound. "Remember what we heard back at camp? About Crockett making his voice come from somewheres else? Gag the bastard before he has you believin' Napoleon Boney-part himself is at the door."

Hatch pulled a filthy handkerchief from his pocket, tied it roughly around Davy's mouth, and slapped him so hard his head rocked.

"You're too damned stupid to guard them," Kyler said. "I'll send Buzzard in. Come help me with the torches."

They left.

From beyond the walls came the wild cries of Red Eagle's warriors, and though my perspective had changed, they still chilled my blood.

"Davy," I began, "what in Hades are we—"

I stopped short as Buzzard appeared in the doorway, studying us with ferret-like eyes. After a moment of this he glided across the carpet silent as a cat.

Davy nodded a greeting. Buzzard placed a finger to lips, cautioning him not to speak, then noticed the gag and cautioned me instead.

Slipping a bone-handled knife from his belt, Buzzard moved behind Davy's chair. He was freeing us! My spirits soared, but as he bent over, a loud gurgle came from his stomach. Clutching his belly, he froze in place, his face a mask of terror. But no one came through the door.

Buzzard breathed deep, like a man reprieved, and knelt to apply his blade. But just as his knee touched the carpet, an ill wind burst from his britches. The disruption was long and loud and smelled of sour cabbage. I held my breath, for more reasons than one.

This time, Hatch's head appeared in the doorway. His face wrinkled, his nose twitched, and he stared at Buzzard as if unwilling to credit his senses. Then his expression changed to an odd mixture of rage and glee.

Buzzard seemed incapable of movement. "I wasn't doing nothing! Just checking his ropes!"

"I know what you was doing, turd." Rushing forward, Hatch lowered a shoulder and knocked Buzzard to the floor. He quickly bent and pried the knife from the little halfwit's grip.

Buzzard began to whine. "Please, you mustn't hurt me. Cap'n Zane likes me, he does."

"No." Hatch said. "He don't."

Davy glared up at Hatch, his eyes hard as rifle balls.

A smile opened beneath Hatch's flattened nose, displaying chipped and blackened teeth. Still smiling, he slid the bone-handled blade beneath Buzzard's chin and slit his throat. The little man's lifeblood spurted out onto Truitt's carpet.

Growling deep in his chest, Davy heaved against his bonds.

Hatch laughed, thick and ugly, and dropped the knife at his feet. "When the flames reach you," he told us, "you'll envy this bastard." With a last leer at Davy, he snatched Old Betsy from where she lay and left us to our fate.

Davy struggled so mightily I thought his chair would break. But it held firm, as did the ropes, and after a time he slumped back, thoroughly defeated.

I cudgeled my brain for some strategy yet untried, some last means to gain our freedom. But I lacked Davy's wit, and all my schemes went nowhere. Growing more desperate, I finally hit upon an idea—an idea so abhorrent I hated to consider it. But it seemed our only chance.

"Davy," I said, "Buzzard died because of you. Because he wanted to be your friend. Next it will be Yessler and the volunteers. All because they trusted you and followed you."

Davy looked stung. It pained me to continue, but it had to be done.

"Just like poor Caleb," I said, hating myself. "Just like Nathan."

Davy growled, gnawing at his gag. He lurched against his ropes, his chair scraping the floor.

Through the open doorway, I kept watch on the men in the hall. If anyone came in now, we'd be lost.

"Your Mounted Volunteers are trapped in the cellar. They'll all burn! There will be new widows and orphans all over Tennessee."

Davy's face darkened. His eyes were flecked with red.

Torches flared in the hall, casting weird and ever-moving shadows.

"You men at the windows keep those savages occupied!" Zane shouted. "The rest get some furniture piled here. I want a good blaze!"

Glass shattered. Muskets banged. The Creeks answered with war cries.

Men ran from the dining room with chairs, tables and a divan, shoving them together at the center of the room. Paintings were snatched from the wall and added to the pile.

"They're going to fire the place!" I shouted at Davy, "and we'll all die! What will become of Polly then? What of John Wesley, young William and baby Margaret? How will they survive without you? What if this Indian uprising spreads to Tennessee? They'll be butchered, along with a thousand others."

Davy's cheekbones gleamed through his skin. His breath came in snorts. His muscles corded and bulged and his chair rocked as if caught in an earthquake.

I bored on, relentless, sickened by my words. "Think of your family! William—dead! John Wesley—dead! Polly and little Margaret—dead!"

"The Red Sticks!" someone shouted. "They're fixing to charge!"

"Light the drapes!" Zane yelled. "And torch that pile. Then get the hell out of here!"

The whoosh and crackle of flames drowned out the Indians' war cries. Light flickered and flashed, casting grotesque shadows across the hall.

Davy twisted his wrists until his hands dripped with blood. Gathering his bound feet beneath the chair, he heaved upwards, his entire body shaking with the effort. At last, with a tremendous crack, the chair splintered beneath him.

Surging to his feet, Davy shook loose from the broken chair and tore his wrists free. Snatching up Buzzard's bloody knife, he slashed the rope from his ankles. His eyes were wild and his face contorted. Bathed in the flickering light of the fire, he looked like a demon fresh out of Hell.

"Davy, quick!" I yelled. "Free me too!"

But he was no longer himself. Heeding me not at all, he plunged into the hall and raced out of view.

Yessler and the others yelled his name, but their cries quickly turned to curses. The fire burned brighter and hotter. Smoke rolled through the open doorway, stinging my eyes and nose.

I strained against my chair, trying to mimic Davy's feat, but lacked his strength. If only he had cut my bonds. Then I remembered Hatch sawing at the rope around my ankles. Could he have weakened it? I twisted my legs so violently my chair crashed to the floor. Kicking and squirming like a madman, I at last heard a snap and my legs came free. Rolling to my knees, I got one leg under me and pushed to my feet, my arms still bound behind the chair. I was semi-seated and bent half over, but I could walk a little, and did.

I waddled into the great hall. The drapes were nearly consumed. Flames licked along the window frames and would soon be running up the walls. The blaze from the pile of paintings and furniture had now reached the chandelier. Yessler and the others struggled vainly against the ropes binding them to the statues.

"Where's Davy?" I shouted.

"He ran." Yessler's tone was bitter, and he jerked his head angrily toward the door at the rear of the hall.

"Sorry," I said, and scuttled after Davy. The three men pleaded for help, ignoring the fact I had no hands to free them, and every call was like a knife to my heart. These men had already seen Davy desert them, and now I, too, appeared bent on saving my own skin. But my only chance to aid them was to get free, and the only man who could help me now was Davy—a man I had driven beyond the brink of madness.

CHAPTER 18

"Pray that you are right."

THE CHARRED CORPSES of Fort Mims came unbidden to my mind, making the gorge rise in my throat. I could not endure such visions again. With new resolve, I twisted my arms, hoisting the chair further up my back and allowing my legs more play.

The door at the rear of the hall was half open. I kicked it back on its hinges and hobbled into the narrow hallway leading to the patio. The cries of Yessler and the others grew dimmer as I ran, but caused me no less anguish. I'd nearly reached the door when I heard a rifle shot—the distinctive bark of Old Betsy. I barged onto the patio, chair and all, and looked wildly about.

Two men were halfway across the rear lawn. One was Hatch, his back to the line of encircling trees, with Old Betsy smoking in his hands. The other, charging toward him with no sign of injury, was Davy. And beyond them both, scampering off into the woods, went Zane and his green-jacketed villains.

Hatch threw the empty rifle aside and clawed a tomahawk from his belt.

Davy continued his advance. He raised an arm, a knife blade glinting in his hand.

"Davy!" I shouted. "Come back! Our friends will die!"

Hatch screamed. What he saw in Davy's eyes I could only imagine, for the wrath of that devil had never been turned upon me. Hatch's tomahawk slashed the air between them, but the knife flashed down like winter lightning. Hatch's scream ended in a gasp. He crumpled and fell, to lay flat on his back with Buzzard's bone-handled knife buried in his breast.

It was like a knife to my heart as well. Davy had hoped to never take another human life. Now he had, and I was to blame.

I leapt from the patio and scuttled across the grass, the chair's back pounding the base of my skull. I was ten yards shy of Davy when he started off again, striding toward the tree line.

"Davy, wait! Your friends need you!"

His head turned briefly, and his glance chilled me to my heels.

"Please! Only you can save them!"

He strode on with a grim determination that meant doom for anyone in his path. If not for the imperiled volunteers I would have let him go, for the world would be much improved with Zane and Hatch consigned to Hell.

Summoning the last of my strength, I hiked up the chair and sped past him, turning to block his way. "I lied, damn it! Polly is safe! Your boys are safe. I needed your devil and I lied, but now I need *you*!"

Bent as I was, he towered above me. Staring into his face I saw what Hatch had, a fury so dark and terrible I nearly swallowed my tongue. But behind him, tongues of flame leapt from the mansion's windows, thick smoke boiling into the sky. I pressed on.

"Our friends will burn! Just like my mother and father. I couldn't save my parents, but I can save those men, if you'll only help!"

Davy's hands fell upon my shoulders, clutching me so hard my knees buckled, and I felt despair. From somewhere in the distance came the baying of a hound. It sounded like Samson, but reason told me it was probably one of Zane's guard dogs charging to the attack. The baying turned to barking, but I could not turn my head to look, and I was about to collapse when a great force plowed into us, toppling us over.

I crashed onto my side, still strapped to the chair. Next to me,

Davy lay on his back, pinned to the earth by a great blue hound, an enormous tongue lapping his face. It was Samson!

Pounding hoofs announced more company, and a dozen riders came galloping around the side of the mansion. Most were near naked and bristling with weapons, but at their head rode Red Eagle. And leading our horses, even more lovely than my memory of her, came Little Fawn.

I glanced at Davy, fearful what his devil might do, but found him smiling and ruffling Samson's fur. The madness had passed.

As the riders thundered to a stop, Little Fawn jumped to the ground and planted a kiss on my lips.

"So you are Stumblefoot once again. And you have tied yourself to a chair."

"Please," I said, nodding at the mansion. "Our friends are in the cellar, others in the hall. We must get to them at once!"

Little Fawn slashed my bonds. She pressed a big knife into my hands, and I saw it was her own.

"What of my wife?" Red Eagle demanded.

"Out yonder," Davy said, pointing toward the trees. "But we'd best go lookin' for her alone. If them varmints see your braves comin', they might panic an' kill her."

"I will help your friends." Little Fawn looked to Red Eagle, who spoke quickly to his braves. The men leapt from their ponies, following Little Fawn toward the patio, and I joined them. As if sensing my presence, Little Fawn swung about.

"No, Penn. Go with Davy. He needs you."

I glanced back. Davy was already astride his horse. He held the reins of my chestnut and beckoned me to take them.

"She's right," he said. "I surely do."

TREES WHIZZED BY, some grazing my elbows, as we raced past the bunkhouse and the smithy. And all the while, the roar of the burning mansion filled me with dread for the fate of Yessler and the others.

Reaching the top of a rise, Davy called a halt. "There," he said, pointing through the trees, and I saw the outline of the over-seer's cottage. Red Eagle kicked Arrow, about to spurt ahead, but Davy caught his arm. "Wait."

Red Eagle turned on him, his voice thick with menace. "Why?"

"Zane and his skunks are saddlin' horses. If they see us comin', they'll just skedaddle."

Scowling, Red Eagle peered off toward the cottage.

"I can't see 'em either," I said, "but Davy has the eyes of a hawk."

Red Eagle grunted. "What do you propose?"

"We'll blindside 'em." Davy led us off to the left, deeper into the woods and up the slope of another hill. Reaching the top, we gazed down onto the scene behind the house.

Sixty yards below us, Zane and a score of greenjackets bustled about strapping packs and bedrolls to their horses. The animals were tied to a rope stretching between the building and an ancient oak.

"Have you a plan?" Red Eagle's voice was hard as iron.

Davy drew Betsy from his scabbard and went about loading her. "Chewin' on one."

"In that case," Red Eagle said, "we'll use mine." And as we stared, he kicked Arrow's sides and tore down the slope, his savage war cry piercing the sky.

The men below gaped in surprise. Their horses stomped and snorted.

I looked at Davy. He shrugged. In one smooth motion he swung Betsy to his shoulder and fired. And the horses below went mad, bucking and bolting in all directions, suddenly free of their tether.

My own rifle scabbard was empty, but my tomahawk hung from a saddle loop. I plucked it out, and Davy and I charged after Red Eagle, Samson bounding between us.

Zane bawled orders at his men. Some had already fled, fearing the Red Stick horde was upon them. But Zane jabbed a finger at us, and his meaning was clear. We were three against twenty. That was apparent to me as well, and made my stomach lurch.

A musket banged and a ball whistled past my head. More shots followed. The militia was rallying. Equally discouraging, Zane's three guard dogs bounded around the corner of the house and raced up the slope to meet us.

One of the black hounds charged Red Eagle, now scarcely twenty yards from the militia. Jaws stretched wide, the beast sprang for Arrow's throat. But the stallion, too, soared into the air, and a hoof smacked the dog in the chops, sending it yelping off into the woods. Red Eagle and Arrow plunged into the greenjackets, scattering them like geese.

The shaggy yellow hound charged at Davy, but Samson shot between them, catching the hound's hind leg between his jaws. He flipped the yellow onto its back and ran in a circle, spinning the animal like a top, then the two went snarling down the hill in a ball of blue and yellow fury. The third dog leapt at me, his black pelt glistening. I lashed out with my boot, but the chestnut reared and I missed, and went flying from the saddle.

I landed on my backside, jarred to the teeth, and the black beast pounced like a wolf. Flopping onto my back, I cracked a knee against his skull, but before I could scrabble up he sank his fangs into my leg, just below the knee. Through the blinding pain, I hammered his head with the tomahawk, but he had tasted blood and wanted more. He tore his teeth from my calf and went for my face.

Close up, his snapping jaws looked wide enough to swallow me whole. In desperation, I thrust the tomahawk between us, and his teeth closed upon the handle, nearly ripping it from my hand. I grabbed the other end, holding it like a bit between his teeth. He snapped madly at the tomahawk, his face inches from mine, my own blood dripping from his fangs. I could not hold him long.

The sounds of battle seemed far away. Muskets and pistols

crashed. Men shouted and cursed. Horses screamed, dogs yowled, and above it all rose Red Eagle's blood-chilling war cry. I struggled on, determined not to die flat on my back, my parents unavenged. But my arms were heavy and death was a heartbeat away when something crashed against the hound's skull, spattering my face with spittle and blood. The beast went limp and collapsed on my chest.

Davy stood above me, holding Betsy by the barrel. "Come on," he said, "Red Eagle's hoggin' all the fun." He shoved the stunned hound aside and helped me to my feet.

Below us, Red Eagle swung his war club like a scythe, breaking bones and bashing skulls, while Arrow knocked attackers aside. Several men managed to catch horses, and went pounding off into the trees, but at least a dozen still remained.

My leg wound throbbed, but this was no time for weakness. I drew Little Fawn's wicked butcher knife and clacked the blade against the head of my tomahawk. "Let's go," I said, and we raced down the slope toward the battle.

A war cry erupted close at my side. I looked about, thinking the Red Sticks had arrived, and realized the scream had come from Davy. I stared, fearing his devil had returned, but he grinned at me, nodded, and we charged on down the hill.

Zane's men sent musket balls singing toward us. One tugged at my shirt, another stole my hat and parted my hair. Then we barreled into the mass of struggling bodies, smiting left and right like madmen.

"Kill the bastards!" Zane bellowed. "Kill them!"

A tomahawk ripped through my sleeve to the flesh, and I sank my knife into the man's throat, warm blood gushing over my hand. Davy rammed his rifle barrel into the eye of a man aiming a pistol, ducking as the ball whizzed over his head. A man grabbed my throat, clawing at my windpipe, and I plunged Little Fawn's knife through his wool jacket, twisting the blade to rip muscle. The shouting, grunting and smack of blows dissolved into a great roar, and I hacked and slashed until blood hung about me like a mist.

Knees tight about Arrow's flanks, Red Eagle towered above the battle, his war club weaving a circle of death. A man rose before him with a pitchfork, and I saw it was Kyler. Arrow reared back, eyes huge and white, and Red Eagle dropped his club, clinging with both arms to the horse's neck.

Kyler limped to Arrow's side. His smile was hideous as he thrust the pitchfork toward the horse's chest. I shouted, "No!" but was powerless to help. Red Eagle leaned forward, his hand closing around one of the tines, and yanked back, wrenching the weapon from Kyler's hands. But the effort cost him his balance and he plummeted off the far side of the horse.

Seeing this, the greenjackets surged forward, eager for slaughter, but Arrow whirled about, hooves flashing to drive them back. Red Eagle rose to his feet, his face a mask of death. Drawing the pitchfork back over his shoulder, Red Eagle heaved forward and hurled it like a javelin. Straight toward Kyler it sailed, the center tines piercing his eye sockets and bursting through the back of his skull. He flopped backwards, pinned to the earth, his mouth still gaping in surprise.

The fighting slowed as men paused to stare. Even Davy watched, and as he did, a man ran from behind with a long-handled wood ax high above his head. It was Myers, the bully who'd robbed Davy as a boy, and nearly lost an ear to Davy's devil.

I shouted a warning, but Davy did not turn. Myers was nearly upon him now, the blade plunging toward Davy's back. At the last moment, Davy spun about, holding Betsy like a quarterstaff, and caught the ax on the barrel. The *thunk* of wood upon iron was loud, and the force of the blow drove Davy to his knees.

The ax head was now hooked over the rifle barrel. With a snarl, Myers jerked the handle back, yanking Betsy from Davy's grasp. I swung to help, but a militiaman kicked my knee and sent me sprawling. Myers' piggish eyes glowed with triumph as he raised the ax to split Davy's skull.

Then a bolt of blue flashed between them and the ax was gone. As Myers stared dumbly at his empty hands, Davy hauled a fist up from the ground to smash against the big man's chin. Myers' feet left the earth and his body hung in the air before crashing to the dirt, where it lay still as death.

At Davy's side stood Samson, the ax handle gripped between his teeth.

"Good boy," Davy said. Taking the ax, he caught Red Eagle's eye and flung it twirling end over end through the air. As those below watched in wonder, Red Eagle soared up to pluck it deftly from the sky. And just like that, the battle resumed in earnest.

Davy snatched up Betsy and swung her like a club, bashing heads and jaws. I hacked and stabbed at every limb that came within reach. Samson and Arrow rampaged about, knocking men aside like ten-pins. And Red Eagle, ax in hand, tore through the militia as if blazing a trail through a forest of saplings.

I marveled at Red Eagle, for the battle joy was plainly upon him. I'd heard of such a state, where your opponent's movements seem sluggish and dull, where every blow falls true, and every death makes you stronger. For me, that feeling had never come, not even now, in the fiercest battle of my life. For me, every thrust was an effort, every enemy a terror. I was powered by fear, not joy. My arms grew heavy, my leg throbbed, and my boot squelched with blood, no doubt my own.

The battle swirled wide around Kyler, a fearful sight with the pitchfork standing straight up from his head. But suddenly Zane was there, a boot upon the dead man's chest as he ripped the weapon free. "McCoy!" he roared, and rushed at me, his face distorted. I ducked, the fork's bloody tines just missing my head, and he was about to strike again when a savage cry swung us both about. Hacking his way through the remaining militiamen came Red Eagle, his terrible gaze fixed upon Zane. Red Eagle had at last found the man who'd taken his wife, and plowed toward him, inexorable as Fate.

Zane dropped the pitchfork and ran, knocking his own men

aside in his haste. I grabbed the weapon and glared about for someone to stab, but our enemies' ranks had thinned. At least a dozen greenjackets sprawled at our feet, while others scrambled for the woods. Zane reached the closest horse and hauled himself into the saddle.

Red Eagle raged toward him, but was still ten yards away when Zane threw us a final scowl and spurred the horse, pounding off into the forest. Red Eagle spun about, racing through the bodies toward Arrow, but before reaching the stallion he slowed, stopped, and turned to gaze back at the house. He was thinking of Sopath, I had no doubt, and weighing his priorities.

Samson tore after the retreating militia, while Davy and I just stood, chests heaving. The battle had lasted a lifetime and I could hardly believe it was over.

I looked closely at him. His eyes were clear and his cheeks bright. There was no sign of his devil, but beyond that he was a fright. His buckskins hung in tatters, the exposed flesh laced with knife cuts and scorched with powder burns. His hair was matted and his face smeared red, like he'd been doused with a bucket of blood. I had to laugh.

Davy looked back at me, grinning. "You think I'm a sight, take a gander at yourself."

I looked at my chest and arms, and nearly choked, for I too was spattered with gore, and must have resembled a corpse just risen from the grave.

"Is that the place?" Red Eagle stood before us, bare-chested, bleeding from a dozen wounds, his face grim and terrible. He gestured toward the cottage. "Is that where Sopath is held?"

Davy nodded. "If it ain't, I'll eat my hat."

Red Eagle's jaw twitched. His eyes smoldered. "If it is not," he said, "I will eat your heart." And he stalked off toward the door.

CHAPTER 19

"I heard the angels sing."

IN THE SUDDEN stillness, the overseer's cottage had an ominous look. The late afternoon sun splashed over a tiled roof and brick chimney, leaving the rear of the building in shadow, and I envisioned phantoms peering down at us from the second story windows.

The sky above the treetops was bathed in orange. Little Fawn and the others might be trapped in that burning mansion, and it required every ounce of will to stand my ground. But Davy and I had sworn to help Red Eagle find his wife and could not falter now.

Arrow grazed in the tall grass, the battle seemingly forgotten, while my mare and Davy's dun watched from a distance, swishing their tails. The yellow hound and his black companions crouched near the edge of the woods, eyes aglow.

Samson roamed from one green-clad body to the next, as if to ascertain which were dead. For my part, if any clung to life, they were welcome to it. With one exception, I'd had my fill of bloodletting. The only death I still desired was Zane's.

The rear door of the house was locked, but a single kick from Red Eagle sent it crashing against the inner wall. We edged into a dimly lit room, weapons ready. I slid a curtain aside, and a shaft of light spilled across the floor. We were in the kitchen, quite alone. We stood a moment, listening to the silence. Davy pressed a finger to his lips, and Red Eagle nodded. Anyone lurking within would know of our presence, but it would not do to advertise our precise location.

Red Eagle glided into the next room, where we found a table and four straight-backed chairs. Next came a gloomy parlor, with seating grouped about a fireplace. Above the mantel hung an old musket, another souvenir, no doubt, of the Revolution. I opened shabby curtains, allowing light enough to reveal a threadbare carpet and vases of withered flowers. Across the foyer lay a small study, empty of life, and a dark staircase leading upward.

Red Eagle ascended the stairs without a sound. Davy followed his example, while I found the squeak in every step. At the top we discovered a narrow hallway and three doors, all closed.

Tomahawk raised, Red Eagle turned the first knob and swung the door wide. The room contained only a small canopied bed and a wardrobe closet. The wardrobe was empty, and we found nothing under the bed but dust.

The second room was much the same, but showed signs of habitation. On a chair lay a green jacket bearing a captain's insignia, and beside the bed sat a pair of polished black boots. Zane's room, surely. A leather-bound book lay on a side table. Curious, I flipped to the title page. *The Song of Roland.* Was this how Zane saw himself—a valiant crusader leading the charge against the infidels?

Red Eagle had grown steadily more tense, seething at each failure to discover his wife. Approaching the final room, his features were as fierce and angular as a wolf's. He grasped the doorknob, turned his wrist, and grunted. This door was locked. "Sopath," he called, his voice amazingly soft.

A slight sound issued from within. A chair leg, perhaps, scuffing against the floor.

"Sopath." Louder this time. "Is that you?"

Muffled sounds reached us. None resembled words, but the message was clear. Someone was in distress.

All need for caution was past. Red Eagle leaned his shoulder against the door and growled. Though he scarcely seemed to exert himself, metal shrieked, wood splintered, and the door burst inward, wrenched from its hinges.

For a moment, we simply stared. The room's far corner held a broad-shouldered figure bound to a chair.

Red Eagle swore. Instead of crossing the room, he turned to a wardrobe cabinet and flung open the doors, finding it empty. He swung upon Davy, teeth bared, nostrils distended. "You promised me my wife."

Leaning hard upon his rifle, Davy said nothing.

I edged past them toward the bedraggled creature in the chair. Wild eyes regarded me through the tangled white hair. His cheeks were hollow and his skin tinged with gray. It was shocking to think this was the famous war hero I'd met only a week before—Colonel Thaddeus Truitt. Lengths of thick rope bound him to the chair, while a shorter piece served as a gag. He looked as miserable as a human could be.

Slipping behind Truitt, I worked at the knot of his gag, but it was tight and my fingers still sticky with blood. With a snarl, Red Eagle brushed my hands aside, grasped the rope and ripped it from old man's head. Truitt's wail died as Red Eagle clamped a huge hand about his throat.

"Where," Red Eagle said, his voice cold as death, "is my wife?"

Eyes frantic, Truitt gasped for breath.

"Speak, before I snap your neck."

Davy said, "He don't know."

Red Eagle scowled. "You said she was here. Now you say she is not?"

"I said he don't know. If he was in charge, why would he be trussed up like a turkey?"

Red Eagle's jaw twitched. He released Truitt's neck and sank to the bed, his features ashen.

Truitt coughed, red specks dotting his lips.

"What about it?" I asked. "Why were you held prisoner?"

"Zane," Truitt croaked. "Zane played me for a fool."

"We figured he'd snatched Red Eagle's wife," Davy said. "At your orders."

Truitt stiffened, but as he spoke to Red Eagle his words were soft. "I heard you had taken another bride, and that she was quite beautiful. But I swear to you, Bill, on the friendship we once shared, that I know nothing of your wife."

Red Eagle stared at the floor.

"However," an edge came into Truitt's voice, "that hardly excuses your kidnapping my daughter, or murdering my son."

Red Eagle's cheeks went taut. He did not look up. "I have been over that with Crockett and McCoy. I was unaware of Lacy's disappearance. And I might have saved Nathan, had I not been tied to a tree."

Davy winced. "That's so, Colonel. The fault was mine."

Truitt stared at each of us in turn. "Then where is my daughter?"

"And where is Sopath?" Red Eagle demanded.

No one answered, so I busied myself cutting Truitt's ropes. Davy hefted the old man in his arms and carried him downstairs, while I brought Betsy. Red Eagle followed, his movements leaden. With Truitt deposited on a divan, we looked blank-faced at one another.

Red Eagle turned to stare out a window. Davy sat on the piano stool and stroked his chin.

I propped Betsy against the wall and took a chair facing Truitt. "How long were you held in that room?"

"Four days," he said. "When Zane reported you and Crockett had been captured, I chided him for not continuing on to the Red Stick village to rescue Lacy. The damned rascal laughed at me. Said he was tired of taking orders from a one-legged fool. He vowed that my land, and much of that belonging to the Creeks, would soon belong to him."

That got a snort from Red Eagle, but no one spoke.

"Had you not come," Truitt went on, "I would surely have gone mad. Death seemed so near that last night I heard the angels sing."

"They gave you no food?" I asked. "No water?"

"Water, yes, but—"

Red Eagle's head whipped about. "What was that about singing?"

"I was out of my mind." Truitt clutched his stomach. "Hunger will do that."

"But you heard singing?"

"So I thought. Beautiful. So beautiful I cried."

Red Eagle's eyes were bright.

Davy said, "What?"

"Sopath is renowned for her singing. A visiting priest once compared her to an angel."

"So you think…"

"I don't know. I scarcely dare to hope."

Outside, a hound bayed. Samson. I had come to know his voice, and his moods. This was no friendly greeting, but a call to arms.

Davy was already racing for the door, Red Eagle and I quick on his heels. Truitt's shouted questions went unanswered.

Samson was not in sight as we burst into the back yard, but the baying came from the east side of the house, the side opposite the hill. Red Eagle matched Davy stride for stride as they sped for the corner. My leg shrieked with pain, but I clamped my teeth and followed.

Rounding the corner I spied three saddled horses tied to a tree twenty yards away. Samson crouched nearby, his attention fixed on the cottage.

Davy and Red Eagle had stopped. They too stared at the side of the building, where a rough door had been flung back, revealing the dark entrance to a root cellar.

"What's happening?" I whispered.

No one answered. Davy and Red Eagle were already moving silently toward the opening.

I was about to follow when a woman emerged from the cellar. Despite her tangled hair and filthy leather tunic she was dark and beautiful, and for an instant I thought I was looking at Little Fawn. Then I saw she was round with child.

"Sopath!" The name burst from Red Eagle, and he lurched forward, only to stop as Zane appeared, close behind the woman, a pistol in his hand.

"No one moves," Zane said, "or the women die."

Women? Then the word made sense as Zane dragged another figure into the light, thrusting her before him like a shield. She, too, was bedraggled and dirty, but her hair was blonde, and her dress adorned with ribbons and bows. I sucked in my breath. Beneath the grime were the proud lips and luminous eyes I'd admired on canvas in the mansion.

"My god," I said. "Lacy Truitt!"

Zane hustled both women out of the cellar, careful to keep them between him and us, and I saw their hands were bound behind their backs.

"We're leaving," Zane said. "If anyone tries to stop us, I will not hesitate to shoot."

Red Eagle growled, and I heard frustration mingled with the rage. He longed to rip Zane to pieces, but dared not endanger his wife. Davy, too, appeared flummoxed. For once, his wit was of no avail.

Zane started the women moving toward the horses.

"Lacy!" The shout came from behind us, and I spun to see Colonel Thaddeus Truitt hobbling forward, using Old Betsy as a crutch.

"Halt!" Zane barked. "Or your daughter dies."

"You won't harm her, Gabriel." Truitt's voice held its old confidence. "You've been too long in love with her."

Zane pressed the pistol to Lacy's head. "Don't try me, Colonel."

Truitt slowed not at all, pushing his huge frame past us, growing ever closer to Zane and the women. He was ten feet away
when Zane snarled and cocked the pistol. Truitt swung Betsy
up from the ground, leveling the barrel at Zane, but before he
could pull the trigger, Zane leveled his pistol and fired.

Colonel Truitt staggered as the ball caught him low in the
chest, but determination took him two more steps before he
collapsed at his daughter's feet. Lacy cried out as if she herself
had been shot, and fell to her knees at his side. At the same
instant, Red Eagle surged forward, stopping short as Zane
dropped the empty pistol and jerked another from his belt.

"I was fond of Miss Truitt," Zane said, "but I have no such
feeling for the squaw." With the barrel pressed to the base of
Sopath's skull, he edged closer to the horses.

Davy knelt next to Lacy, examining the colonel's wound.
When he looked up his face was bleak. He gave a small shake
of his head.

I said a silent prayer. We had found Lacy Truitt, as promised,
and restored her to her father just in time to witness his death.
She hunched over his body, her shoulders wracked with sobs,
only slightly more miserable than I.

Then some flicker of movement caught my attention, and I
glanced past Zane. Fifty yards away, in the woods between us
and the mansion, a shadow flitted from tree to tree.

"Lacy is lost to me now." Zane said. "I regret what I must do,
but your wife comes with me. Once safely away, I shall set her
free. You have my word."

Thirty yards behind him, a face peered over a bush, and I felt
a thrill. Little Fawn. Motioning me to silence, she continued
her advance.

"Your word is smoke." Red Eagle's eyes were slits. He stood,
chest heaving, clenching and unclenching his huge fists. "Release
Sopath. Now."

Little Fawn was almost within striking distance. Catching
my eye, she pointed at Zane and made a clubbing motion. She

pointed at me, then at Sopath. Her meaning was clear. When she struck Zane, she wished me to pull Sopath out of harm's way.

My heart began to pound. Little Fawn was putting herself in grave danger, and I was powerless to prevent it.

Zane backed toward the horses, pistol still at Sopath's head.

Little Fawn darted from the bushes and sprinted the last few yards, her war club raised to bash his skull. I held my breath, then cursed silently as Zane's eyes narrowed. Whether he'd seen something in our faces or heard her footfalls I could not tell, but he spun about, swinging his pistol, and fired.

Through the flash of powder I saw the gun barrel leveled at Little Fawn's chest. My heart fell into my stomach. My limbs refused to obey me and I could only stare as Davy and Red Eagle leapt forward. But Zane's hand whipped like a snake, snatching a knife from his belt and pressing it to Sopath's throat.

As Davy and Red Eagle stopped, I shuffled forward, my mind a red haze. A voice croaked, "Little Fawn," and I realized the voice was mine. Her body lay perfectly still at Zane's feet, a dark stain spreading across her shirt. I started towards her.

"Leave her!" Zane snapped. "She's buzzard meat."

Little Fawn's butcher knife sprang from my belt, slashing the air before me. My thoughts were a muddle, but I knew this was the man responsible for the death of my parents. He had done evil to Red Eagle, Lacy Truitt and many others. Now he'd taken Little Fawn from me, stolen the future I'd only begun to imagine. Zane's lips flapped, forming words, but I paid no heed. All I heard was my heartbeat, and the memory of the pistol blast. I had to kill Zane, had to prevent him harming Sopath. That was what Little Fawn wanted—the last thing she had wanted in this life—and I was determined to please her. Zane would be sent to Hell, I would save Sopath, and all would be as Little Fawn wanted, except that she was gone. I thought all these things, and I did not think them, as faces and feelings skittered through my mind. But all the while I kept walking, the knife poised to strike, focusing every ounce of my hatred upon Zane.

Zane backed away, dragging Sopath with him. His eyes bulged and his mouth widened. He was shouting, but I refused to hear. I felt hands on my arms but shook them off. I began to run, striving ever harder not to think about Little Fawn. Zane's blade twitched near Sopath's throat, but I steeled myself to do what must be done. I was nearly within arm's reach, about to leap, when Zane changed everything.

He thrust Sopath directly into my path.

I was so surprised I dropped the knife, stumbling as she fell into my arms. I blinked and stared, regaining my senses. It was only then I saw Zane racing for one of the horses. He had outwitted me, retreating for just that purpose. And now he seemed certain to escape, for no one was close enough to catch him.

Zane sprang into the saddle. I lay Sopath gently aside and ran toward him, emptiness and defeat stinging my eyes.

From somewhere behind me, Red Eagle shouted, "Attack!" I shook my head in despair, for I was trying my best. Then I heard a snarl and a streak of blue flashed by me. Samson!

The hound's jaws stretched wide, huge teeth glistening as he sprang from the earth, sailing straight for Zane. Zane kicked wildly at the horse's flanks, but the beast was frozen with terror. For a moment man and dog seemed to merge atop the horse's back. Zane screamed, whether from panic or pain I could not tell. But his pistol butt rose and fell, producing a dull *thunk*. Samson fell to the earth as Zane's horse exploded into action, bolting off into the distance. The other horses, terrified of the dog, also skittered away.

Red Eagle let out a cry of rage, but made no move to follow. He was too busy cradling his wife. Davy, too, stood rooted to the ground, haggard and exhausted. His own horse was on the far side of the house, and he could never reach it in time to catch Zane.

Samson rose unsteadily and shook himself.

Almost afraid to look, I glanced back to where Little Fawn

lay in the grass, and seemed to *feel* rather than hear her call my name.

Was it possible she lived? I dared not hope, but the mere chance drove vengeance from my mind and I ran to her, falling to my knees at her side. Cradling her head, I turned her face to mine and prayed for some sign of life. I saw none, and a tear slipped from my eye to strike her cheek. All at once her body convulsed, she coughed, and her eyes fluttered weakly. "Penn."

As I hugged her to me, overwhelmed with joy, she spoke again, "Sopath, and Lacy. Are they safe?"

The question was typical of her. She had nearly died, but was concerned only for the fate of others.

"Davy," I called. "Davy! Little Fawn's alive!"

At my words he turned, his features softened, and he broke into a broad grin. "Thank the eternal," he said. "There could be no better news."

We were all safe, at least for the moment, and I collapsed on the ground, overcome with relief, anger and regret.

CHAPTER 20

"I cannot go with you."

THE UPPER STORY of the Truitt mansion was gone and most of the walls had collapsed, but flames still licked at the skeletal remains.

Seated on the rear lawn, Sopath daubed at Little Fawn's wound with herbs, some plucked from a pouch and others gathered fresh from the woods. The pistol ball had taken Little Fawn high in the chest, thankfully missing her lungs. Sopath, who had much experience in such things, had removed it, and was confident she would heal.

Next to her, Lacy Truitt worked at Red Eagle's many cuts and scrapes. She and Sopath were never far apart. Such a bond had formed that Sopath suffered Lacy's pain, while Lacy shared in Sopath's joy.

The Tennessee Volunteers lounged nearby, passing wine bottles they'd snatched from the cellar. While glad to be alive, their mood was subdued. Aaron Yessler and the men in the main hall had been rescued, but two others, trapped in the basement, had succumbed to smoke poisoning. Their deaths filled me with a guilt and shame I would take to my grave.

Maggie, while washing and bandaging my swollen leg, had half her attention—and half her concern—on Yessler, who lay nearby, head propped on a bedroll. He was still gray-faced and weak, and no amount of wine would stem his cough.

Sopath, we learned, had been in the cellar for nearly three months. While not physically mistreated, she was fed only enough to survive, and feared greatly for the life of her unborn child. Lacy Truitt had no inkling of Sopath's presence until she too had been abducted. Three weeks before Davy and I met Nathan, she'd been out for an evening stroll when Zane and Myers bundled her up and tossed her in with Sopath. It was for her own protection, Zane said, promising life would be sweet once the war ended. Though Lacy feared to guess at his meaning, she knew he had pressed her father for permission to court her, and been steadfastly refused.

Sopath and Lacy rose from the grass, gathering bloody rags and clothing, and moved off toward the well, where many of Truitt's frightened slaves had gathered. After a moment, Maggie followed, providing my first opportunity to speak to Davy alone.

"What's next?" I asked him. "Are we going after Zane?"

Davy turned away, gazing off toward the north. "I've been thinkin' much of Polly and the boys. I miss 'em somethin' fierce, Penn. It's time I was huggin' 'em all and layin' in meat for the winter."

I stared at him. "You're leaving?"

"Just seeing to what's necessary. Zane has much to answer for, but I reckon he'll have to wait."

I swallowed my objections. Davy was a man who brooked no argument. "What of Red Eagle? Now that he has his wife back, will he help end the war?"

Davy hung his head. "'Tain't likely. On the face of it, the Red Sticks attacked Truitt's plantation, burned his mansion and shot him down like a dog."

"But the Indians didn't attack, they rescued our friends. The militia set the fire, and Zane killed Truitt himself."

"You and I know that, plain enough. But who'd believe us?"

"We have the testimony of the volunteers."

"Deserters," he said, "as are we. Indian sympathizers. Who'd listen?"

I looked away, sick at heart. "So Red Eagle will be blamed."

"Sure as shootin'. The colonel's death will be a tolerable strong argument for those fixin' to exterminate the Creeks."

"And the war will go on."

"Worse'n ever. Only good news is, the weather'll make it hard to fight. The killin' may slack off 'til spring."

I had no words for what I felt.

"Come with me, Penn. Polly'll be tickled to meet you, and Maggie too. An'if'n you decide to stay, everyone on Bean's Creek will help throw up a cabin."

I gazed off toward the well. Events had moved so quickly, I'd given little thought to Maggie. She was my responsibility now, and I must see to her well-being. We could return to Philadelphia, but that seemed a betrayal of our parent's dreams. They'd chosen a life on the frontier, and meant that for us as well. While this territory was still too turbulent, Tennessee seemed a likely compromise. At least it would give us time to plan our next move.

But there was another factor to consider. Someone else— someone in addition to Maggie—had become a part of my life, and I could not imagine a future without her.

The women would be returning soon. I knew it was time for me to act. I hobbled over to Little Fawn. Her eyes were closed and she lay with her head on a rolled-up blanket. Her face was deathly pale.

My leg throbbed where Zane's hound had bitten me, and I tried not to wince as I eased myself down beside her. But her eyes opened, and she smiled up at me.

"I am sorry," she said, "that I am not up for another *stroll*."

I felt my cheeks flush. "Neither am I. But I must speak to you." I leaned closer, lowering my voice so we would not be overheard. "Davy's going home."

Little Fawn nodded. "His family needs him."

I was surprised she understood so quickly, but should not have been. She understood many things more easily than I.

"He's invited Maggie and me to go along. Thinks we may even want to settle there."

"People say Tennessee is quite beautiful," she said. "Almost as beautiful as my own country—before the war."

"I wish," I said, and faltered. The words I wanted were lodged in my throat. "I want... I would be... would you consider..."

"I am sorry, Penn. I cannot go with you."

So there it was. Quicker than me, as always. And I had nothing more to say. A wind gust brought the sting of smoke to my eyes, and I looked away.

"You honor me, Penn McCoy. Truly. But my people need me now. I am of the Wind Clan, and we have much influence, even among the Red Sticks. If the Creek nation is to survive, we must heal our differences. I had feared we would be torn apart from within. Now I see the greatest danger is from without, from men like Jackson and Zane, who use us as pawns to further their ambition." There was great strength in her voice, and great sadness.

I could find nothing further to say.

She squeezed my arm. "I do want to come with you, Penn, more than I can say. Perhaps, when the war is over, if you still want me, you might ask again."

"I will ask again," I said. "Now. You may answer whenever you wish."

She smiled, sadly, and we watched the smoldering mansion in silence, the pain in my leg forgotten, but the pain in my heart profound.

PART II
KENTUCK

CHAPTER 21

"We been robbed!"

THE JOURNEY TO Tennessee was both jovial and somber. The Tennessee Volunteers rode with us, eager to see their families again. We were all grateful to be alive, but could not forget the men we had lost. Whenever we stopped, men drank toasts to them, recalling jokes they had told and small kindnesses they had done.

Maggie rode next to Aaron Yessler, hopes for the future dancing in their eyes.

My own thoughts were with Little Fawn, and each step farther away from her was harder than the last. Ordinarily Davy would have tried to cheer me up, but he too was sick at heart. His attempt to end the war had backfired, and he feared he had doomed the frontier to a lengthy conflict. Too many good men had died, among them Caleb Crockett, Nathan Truitt and Colonel Thaddeus Truitt—and rightly or wrongly, Davy blamed himself.

I carried my own share of guilt. Far from helping Davy rid himself of his inner demon, I had deliberately brought it to the surface. Though that action had saved our lives, I feared what it might mean if that devil raised its ugly head in the company of Davy's family.

We had, of course, done much good. Sopath had been returned to her husband and, God willing, would provide him a healthy baby. Lacy Truitt had been granted her freedom, despite having no family to share it with, and we had thwarted Zane's plan to steal the plantation.

I too had much to be thankful for. My dear sister, given up for dead, had been restored to me. And in Little Fawn I had discovered a love I thought existed only in the fevered minds of poets. That should warm me, I knew, but instead I felt empty, as if my heart had been ripped from my chest and buried in the Mississippi mud.

THE AIR TURNED colder, and we began each morning with frost on the ground. It sometimes snowed, though little clung to the earth except on the highest ground. We shivered in our blankets at night, as the wood we gathered was too damp to provide a good fire.

We veered wide around Ten Islands so as not to come within miles of Fort Strother. Those few travelers we met had no news of Jackson's army, save that it was still in camp, and still hungry. Each day we came nearer to Tennessee, and the men became ever more anxious. Some were apprehensive, fearing for their families, while others rejoiced in the coming reunions.

My first glimpse of Tennessee was a vast green ocean of trees framed by the distant blue mountains. I'd passed through the state earlier on my way south, but had been blind to its beauty. Davy sucked in deep breaths of air, calling it sweet as moonshine, while two of the volunteers actually fell to the earth and kissed the ground. To me, it smelled no better than the Mississippi Territory, though I was careful not to say so.

I sensed Davy's growing excitement. His normal calm gave way to a nervous energy. His eyes danced with warmth, and his ruddy cheeks burned scarlet.

Throughout that day our company dwindled, as men sought their own paths. Most vowed to return to the army in the spring, should they be needed, though many believed the Creeks would be crushed by then, and some felt their guns would be better employed against the British. There were rumors the Redcoats were even now sailing south around Spanish Florida toward

New Orleans. Should the British gain control of the Mississippi, there would be little to stop them from sailing north to destroy our nation from within.

Aaron Yessler was last to leave us. His parents lived to the east, near Lawrenceburg, and he was obligated to see to their well-being before considering his own. We turned our backs, allowing he and Maggie a private moment, and when we rode on, her cheeks were wet with tears. He had promised to visit as soon as may be, but that was hardly soon enough.

Next morning Davy led me up a hill and insisted I join him in climbing the tallest tree. Once high in the branches, we gazed over seemingly endless woods, broken only by the glistening bands of rivers. "There," he said, pointing, "just beyond that fork and maybe two miles northeast. That's Kentuck. That's home."

I smiled, nodding, but he must have sensed my confusion. "No, Penn, that's still Tennessee. But when I first laid eyes on this land, somethin' said to me, 'Davy, this here's how Kentucky musta looked to ol' Dan'l Boone, untouched and unspoiled, an' seen by no one 'cept wild animals and Injuns.' This here's my Kentuck, I thought, and she always will be."

As we moved on, his enthusiasm became catching. The land was thick with black oaks, post oaks and hickory trees, and winter-blooming moonflowers gave the air a heady scent. Those far blue mountains seemed to beckon us onward, with the promise of greater wonders. There was something invigorating about this land that made a man think all things possible. Even Maggie took notice, and on occasion her grief gave way to a wan smile.

There were signs of game at every turn. Within the space of an hour we saw raccoons, rabbits and beaver, along with signs of wolves and wildcats. Eagles and sparrow hawks soared high overhead, and at times the sky was dark with carrier pigeons. Late in the afternoon the scream of a panther sent three white-tailed deer bolting from the trees, crossing the path within easy rifle shot, but Davy ignored them. He sat up straighter, and even laid a hand on Betsy when a bear lumbered from the woods to peer at us. But this close to home, Davy was in no mood for delay, even to pursue his favorite pastime.

He seemed acquainted with every rock and tree. "Just yonder," he would say, "beyond that rise, is the trail to George Taylor's place." Or, "That stand of hickories is where me and Arch Hatchett come upon a bear bigger'n my cabin." We soon reached a stream, which Davy informed us was Bean's Creek. The water was a dazzling blue, and flowed briskly over the smooth rocks, producing a most comforting sound. Davy tilted his head as we rode, rocking gently as the river's music welcomed him home.

Reaching a fork in the creek, Davy halted his dun, nodding at the smaller stream. "This branch feeds in from Rattlesnake Springs," he said, and the catch in his voice made it evident this waterway led toward his own beloved Kentuck.

He raised his head, looking high above the treetops and I was surprised to hear him sigh. But I followed his gaze, and understood. There, bending to the mild breeze, was a thin ribbon of white smoke, barely visible against the pale winter sky. Someone was at home there, home and awaiting his return.

Davy was quiet as we rode along the creek, and I left him to his thoughts. I looked up often at that plume of smoke, and sure enough, I soon discovered the source—a small log cabin in a glade of green.

"Ain't she beautiful?" Davy's voice was thick.

I forced myself to see the rude cabin through his eyes, recognizing all it signified—home and family, his own piece of heaven on earth. All the things Maggie and I had lost.

Adjacent to the cabin, beneath an ancient elm, stood a small log corral where a mare and two colts pricked their ears at us. Two thin cows gnawed at weeds in the garden beyond, while a spotted hog rooted in the brush.

All this merited only a glance, for what commanded my attention were two shaggy-haired boys sloshing up from the creek with buckets of water. At sight of us the younger lad let his bucket splash at the other's feet and ran flat-out up the path toward us. In an instant the older boy was whooping and yelling in his wake. Davy kicked his horse, hurrying to meet them. But before he did, a slim young woman with honey-red curls darted from the cabin and dashed across the yard, waving and calling Davy's name.

I looked at Maggie, who beamed back at me, and we followed slowly, allowing the Crocketts their reunion, but staying close enough to bask in its glow.

Davy let the boys drag him from the saddle, where the three fell into a ball of churning limbs. The woman, whom I'd no doubt was Polly, soon reached them and dived into the tangle. Samson capered about, showing concern, but finally sat like a sphinx, waiting, and rolled out his enormous tongue.

Seeing Maggie's eyes glisten, I nudged my mare closer and gripped her shoulder. She hung her head, sobbing openly now, but pressed one hand over my own. I saw my parents, young and happy, rolling with me and Maggie in the grass. I saw Little Fawn welcoming me home with children yet unborn. Maggie, I was certain, saw much the same, but with another partner. Together, we watched and waited, as Davy's joy tempered our sorrow.

THAT FIRST NIGHT, Polly fried bear steaks and served them up with roast potatoes and hot biscuits, and I could not recall a meal half so fine. Remembering Davy's tale of the tame bear who joined them at table, I jokingly inquired as to his absence. At this, Davy's cheeks flamed, and Polly arched an eyebrow at him. But she said, quite casual, "Oh, you mean old Deathhug. Yes, we do miss him terribly. It pained my heart to lose him."

I blinked at her. "Lose him? Why, what happened?" I looked at Davy, who filled his mouth with meat and chewed industriously.

Polly shook her head, her eyes downcast. "Well, Davy was

away for quite a spell, you know, and supplies ran low. And since he brought home such honored guests…" As her voice trailed out, she turned her hands palms-up and spread her arms at the feast before us.

While I just stared, Davy choked on his steak. Maggie suffered a fit of giggles, and in moments the little cabin rocked with laughter.

The Crocketts welcomed us so warmly we felt like kin. Maggie and Polly took to one another like sisters born, and the boys called us Aunt Meg and Uncle Penn. Polly joked that her load was much lighter, with Maggie doing half the cooking, cleaning, and mending. She hoped we we'd still be on hand in the spring, so Maggie could help with her garden.

Polly herself was a delight to eye and soul. Green eyes and freckles complimented her red curls, pert nose and stubborn jaw. Her voice was light and warm, even warmer when her Irish was up, and she guided the boys with a firm, soft hand.

John Wesley, the six-year-old, was almost the spitting image of Davy, with the same bold nose and ruddy cheeks, while William had the striking eyes and curly hair of his mother. Both were good-natured and obedient, eager to hunt with Davy but equally disposed to farm chores. Baby Margaret, as advertised, was strong-lunged but cute as a button.

Samson was officially accepted into the family when we began our first hunt. At the call of Davy's horn, a baying arose from the woods and three sinewy coon dogs romped into the glade. At the sight of Samson, sitting coolly at Davy's feet, the three stopped short, fur ruffled and teeth bared.

"Boys," Davy said, "meet your new messmate, Samson." Yawning wide enough to swallow them whole, Samson lumbered to his feet and shook himself alert. "This here's Tiger, Brutus, and Soundwell," Davy went on, pointing out each dog. "They look a heap wolfish, I know, but that's 'cause they've been so long without tanglin' with a b'ar. We aim to remedy that this very day. And," he said, looking straight at Samson, "we trust you'll join us."

Samson barked once at Davy, then once at each of the dogs, and the booming sound echoed back from the mountains. Tiger, Brutus and Soundwell looked at Davy, looked at Samson, and promptly seated themselves, tails awag.

That country around Bean's Creek was so fresh and new we could hardly walk without tripping over game. Davy claimed the bear population had doubled during his absence, and the way he went about harvesting them I was inclined to agree. On that first hunt we took half a dozen bears in a single day, and when Polly could handle no more we delivered meat to the neighbors, who responded in kind, sharing vegetables for our table and grain for our horses.

In all, it was an idyllic existence. As one raised in the confines of a city, I found this life breathtakingly free. Maggie, too, flourished in these fertile surroundings, and by day she was once again the carefree girl of my youth. But often in the evenings she would draw apart, and her spirit went to Lawrenceburg.

Whether her pain or mine was the greater, I could not say. Sometimes at night I'd slip through the woods to the nearest hill, to sit and gaze deep into the southern sky. At such times I could almost feel Little Fawn's caress, almost breathe her warm scent, and it was comforting to imagine that she, even over such a distance, could feel the weight of my yearning.

We'd been in Kentuck only a few days when I asked Davy, "How long until you get those stores in for the winter?" He just looked at me, amused, and I added, "Red Eagle might be needing us, and God only knows what evil Zane's been up to."

"Dog my cats, Penn! You got it bad." He shook his head. "We'll be here a spell yet, but don't you fret. Our business there ain't done."

MAGGIE AND I had been enjoying the Crocketts' hospitality for about two weeks when the older boy, John Wesley, burst in from outdoors crying, "Pa! Someone's been in the shed! We been robbed!"

Davy was first out the door, with the rest of us close behind. The shed, which also served as shelter for the horses, sat between the cabin and the stream. It was where Davy cured his bear pelts and stored meat and foodstuffs for the winter. The door hung open, but before we could all rush through, Davy motioned us back.

Stepping in a wide loop to the doorway, Davy entered alone. He was back almost immediately, again stepping carefully, with his eyes to the ground.

"Someone took a big haunch of b'ar meat," he said, still scanning the earth, "an' a sackful of taters and corn."

He dropped to one knee, peering intently at the ground, and finally announced, "Footprints. Big ones, and deep."

"Was it Injuns, Pa?" John Wesley asked.

"Nope. An' that's a puzzle. Folks in these parts don't believe in robbin' their neighbors."

Before evening, the foodstuffs had been transferred to a corner inside the cabin and covered with bear pelts. No more was said about the robbery, but Davy's face was thoughtful.

CHAPTER 22

"More trouble than I thought."

DESPITE HIS JOY at being home, Davy continued to blame himself for the death of the two volunteers.
Three weeks after our return he resolved to ride north to the
county seat of Winchester, seeking word of the men's friends or
family. He hadn't known them well, but reasoned that any man's
life—and death—should count for something.

We hunted along the way, of course, loading the pack horses
until they could carry no more, and thus arrived in Winchester
with meat and hides to trade for such necessities as powder, shot,
tobacco, coffee and salt, with enough left over to secure ribbons
for the ladies and candy for the boys.

As county seats go, Winchester was still young, but they
did have a brick courthouse, of which they were exceedingly
proud. And the log jail they'd accidentally burned down while
celebrating the mustering of troops was now being rebuilt.

The bald man running the store had a beard thick as a bird's
nest. "I met young Jensen once," he said, naming one of the
men. "I recall he had a cabin up near Elk River." The Elk River,
it developed, was a two-day trip to the north, through hard
country.

"The other feller" the bald man said, "had folks up near
Clarksville, but that's a fur piece, too. If it's bad news you wish
to deliver, I've some closer to home. Your place is down near
Rattlesnake Springs, ain't it?"

Davy admitted that was so, and the man produced a letter with a broken seal. "This come for the widow Patton."

Davy looked hard at him. "*What* widow Patton?"

The man consulted the letter. "Elizabeth, her name is. Seems her husband James took a spear wound at Talladega, and finally expired down at Fort Strother."

Davy's face went white, and he turned away.

I shared some of his grief, for Maggie and I had already met the lady, who occupied a large farm not far from Kentuck. She was a strong, handsome woman with two small children, and considered quite well to do, but how she would fare on her own there in the wilderness was greatly troubling. And her story was becoming ever more common, as each new traveler told of a friend or neighbor who would not return from the war.

"I'll take that letter," Davy said, his voice flat, "if you'll send others north for us."

The bargain was quickly made, and as Davy bartered for goods, I wrote notes to each of the families, painting the men as heroes. Afterwards, we gathered what little news had come of the war.

General Jackson, by all accounts, was still hunkered down at Fort Strother, hungry and cold, awaiting his chance to deliver fire and brimstone to the Red Sticks. The British, meanwhile, who'd been blockading southern ports this past year, had extended their efforts in the north from Lake Erie to the Mississippi, making such goods as tea and silk impossible to come by. President Madison relied on Admiral Perry to build a fleet to harry our enemies in the North, but feared for our sovereignty should the British invade from the South, particularly now, when threatened from within by the Creeks.

We spent the night in Winchester, returning to Kentuck the following afternoon, and received bad news on the home front. The boys had been awakened in the wee hours by squeaking wheels, grabbed their rifles, and were about to sally forth when Polly stopped them, fearing for their safety.

"Once Maggie had the boys corralled," Polly said, "I took a rifle and went to investigate. I heard the wheels rumblin' way off down the road, but our wagon was already out of sight. I'm powerful sorry, Davy" she explained. "Not knowin' who or what mighta took it, I was afraid to give chase."

Davy hugged her close. "You done absotively right. That old wagon warn't worth much anyways."

He and I went out to examine the scene of the crime, and he once again paid close attention to the ground.

"Same tracks?" I asked.

"Same sidewinder as was in the shed," Davy confirmed. "Appears we got more of a problem than I thought."

OVER THE NEXT few weeks, Davy hunted bear with a vengeance. Some days it snowed, but Davy pushed on undeterred. The four dogs romped along with us, and it was a wonder how Tiger, Brutus and Soundwell worked in concert with him. They seemed to anticipate his every wish, even without commands. Samson, of course, remained a free spirit, but did his part as well.

Whenever Davy and I were alone, I tried to sound him out on our return to the Mississippi Territory. He listened with typical good nature, but his answers were vague. He enjoyed being back in the bosom of his family, a joy I could surely relate to, but not completely share.

On our first few trips, I'd accepted the loan of John Wesley's rifle, a fine weapon, though short for a grown man. But one day Davy said he had a surprise for me, and led me up Bean's Creek to a cave.

"Another bear?" I asked.

"Close," he said, grinning. "Not a b'ar, though. A Bean."

It was then I noticed smoke curling up from the cave mouth, and recognized the familiar scents of sulfur and saltpeter. Inside the cave, as I now expected, sat a smoking forge, smithy tools, and great iron tubs for melting metals. Pumping the bellows was an an iron-haired man in a stained apron, who at first glance looked much like my father.

Davy introduced him as Jesse Bean, one of the first to settle this country, and the man who'd named the creek. Bean was broad, stout and thick-armed, with a grip like a vice. His face was round, but his eyes shrewd.

"I've a favor to ask," Davy told him. "Penn here is a fine hand with a rifle, but finds himself, for reasons quite peculiar, bereft of a weapon." Turning to me, then, Davy said, "Jesse here is hands down the finest gunsmith in all of Tennessee."

Bean looked keenly at me, as if judging whether I was truly worthy of his attention. Then he exhibited a broad smile. "Be honored to outfit your friend, Mr. Crockett, though it may be a spell before I get to it. My fool son went and busted his arm, leaving me short-handed, and I have other commissions to complete."

I doffed my hat and looked at him in earnest. "If you'll permit me, sir, such work runs in my veins. With your forge and tools I could craft my own weapon."

He eyed me with new interest. "In your veins, you say? Your father a gunsmith?"

"Was," I said, managing not to choke. "A fine one."

"McCoy," he said, musing, "from Pennsylvania? Don't tell me your pa was Manfred McCoy."

I nodded, blinking, and he clapped my shoulder. "In that case, you're more than welcome. The honor, in fact, will be my own."

Over the next weeks, I spent long hours at the forge, working on my own rifle and helping Bean with his orders. Tennessee felt increasingly like home. When I wasn't in the cave, I was hunting with Davy, and, with one large exception, I was content.

Just before Christmas, Aaron Yessler arrived bearing gifts, and the life returned to Maggie's eyes. I was happy for her, but the writing on the wall was clear. I would soon be losing her again.

THE FIRST DISTURBANCE from the south came
in mid-February, on our next visit to Winchester. Word that
Red Eagle himself had butchered Colonel Thaddeus Truitt,
hero of the Revolution, had further inflamed the frontier. Davy
argued against the truth of this until his words ran dry, but the
storekeeper had heard the tale too many times to discount it.
Even more disconcerting was the news that General Jackson had
attached Truitt's former protégé Gabriel Zane to his command
and dispatched him to personally dispose of Red Eagle.

The storekeeper knew no more, but had heard of a fellow in
the next county who'd recently returned from the war. Naturally,
Davy would not rest until we paid this man a visit and wrung
him dry of news.

"You boys missed a little dust-up," the fellow told us. "Old
Hickory finally got off his rump when he heard Red Eagle
was gatherin' warriors down at Tohopeka. But them red rascals
outwitted him again, ambushin' us twice along the way. Jackson's
own nephew, young Sandy Donelson, took a bullet clean through
the head, and General Coffee got shot in the side. After that,
Jackson lost heart and high-tailed it back to Fort Strother."

"Two good men," Davy said, looking off toward the south.

"What of Red Eagle?" I asked. "Did you see him?"

The man spat tobacco juice between his teeth. "Doubt he was
even there. But you musta heard about his leap."

Almost in unison, Davy and I said, "Leap?" and the fellow's
eyes twinkled.

"General Claiborne cornered him down at a place called the
Holy Ground," he said, "right around Christmastime. The other
Injuns scattered like weasels into the canebrake, but Red Eagle
fought on 'til he was the last man in the village. The soldiers had
him trapped on a bluff more'n a hundred feet above the river, and
was pushin' in from three sides. There he sat, atop his stallion,
with no way out. And what do you s'pose he done?" The man
paused and wet his lips, clearly enjoying the drama. "He prods
that horse and leaps clean off the bluff, landin' smack in the

middle of the river, while musket balls splash around him like hail. When he goes under the soldiers think he's dead, but he bobs up, still in the saddle, and makes it to the far bank. Then, with nigh on a thousand soldiers watchin', he dismounts, cool as you please, and makes sure his horse ain't hurt. That done, he mounts up, rips out a partin' war cry and gallops off into the forest."

Davy and I exchanged a look. I shrugged. If it were any man other than Red Eagle—or perhaps Davy—I'd have thought this fellow a liar.

"You seen this with your own eyes?" Davy asked.

"Close enough," the man said smugly. "Heard it from a feller whose cousin knowed a man who was right there at the river, an' every word is gospel."

I had doubts about the gospel part, but it was cheering to know Red Eagle still lived.

"Wish we'd been there for that," I said, hinting once more at my desire to return, and this time caught a gleam in Davy's eye. At last, I thought, he was beginning to feel the same.

The storekeeper had news of the war in the North as well, and it was all bad. Within the past month, the British had taken Fort Niagara, leaving as many as eighty Americans dead, and—with their Indian allies—gone on to sack and burn the city of Buffalo.

On our return to Kentuck, we fell once more into the pattern of our lives. Winter was slowly giving way to spring, and the war seemed far away. But I grew more anxious by the day. Often after supper I'd retire to that nearby hill and keep watch on the South, where my longing for Little Fawn grew ever more intense.

CHAPTER 23

"Will you come?"

WE WERE RELAXING around the fire one evening when we heard whimpering at the door. Polly opened it to admit Soundwell, Davy's white hunting hound, his fur ruffled and streaked with blood.

Davy shot from his chair, knelt next to the dog and spoke soothingly as he examined the wounds. The rest of us formed a circle around them, eager to see, but careful not to spook the poor beast.

I had a good view of Soundwell's head, and what I saw sickened me. Most of the blood, it appeared, had come from his left ear, which hung limp, half-torn from his scalp. The hound's hind leg, too, bore a deep and ugly gash. Under Davy's ministerings, the dog's whimpering lessened, but his body still quivered, and shook with occasional spasms.

"Was it a bear?" I asked.

"No b'ar ever done this," Davy said, his voice thick, "nor a wildcat, neither. 'Least none that walks on four legs."

After Polly applied bear-grease and other salves to the hound's wounds, Soundwell rested at Davy's side near the fire, eventually finding sleep.

Next day, we searched the area, making ever wider circles around the cabin, until we found a patch of bloody grass. Davy spent a good while examining the ground before pronouncing his verdict.

"Some lowdown skunk laid a b'ar trap here, an'baited it with meat. Once the dog was caught, he took a knife to his ear."

"Who? Who would do such a thing?"

Davy stood, peering into the woods around us, and the fire in his eyes hinted that his devil was not far below the surface.

"Same footprints as before. This here game has gone on long enough. Time I brought it to conclusions."

"How are you going to do that?" I asked, but he was already walking stiff-legged back toward the cabin.

I feared for whoever dared do this, but at least that villain deserved what was coming to him. Mostly I feared for Davy himself, and what the return of his devil might mean.

When my rifle was finished, Jesse Bean declared it the finest ever to come from his forge. While I doubted this, I was greatly pleased, and felt certain my father would be proud. I continued working with Bean, but had come to a decision about my future. Much as Maggie and I cherished the Crocketts' company, their cabin was crowded with so many bodies. If I should be lucky enough to add Little Fawn to our family, we would need a home of our own.

"If the offer still stands," I told Davy, "I'd appreciate your help with a cabin."

Davy's smile was wider than his face, and that very day we began felling trees. The site was right there on Kentuck, less than three miles from his home. "Anyone else this close would make me ticklish," he said, "but as for you and Little Fawn—I'd want you no farther."

Neighbors appeared to help, neighbors I didn't know we had, and the task went quickly. Davy often helped, but at other times he was away on business he declined to disclose, and Maggie and I made many fast friends.

One morning, as I was heading for the new cabin, Davy called me back.

"How 'bout takin' a day off?" he said. "I'm in mind to gather a little firewood."

"Don't the boys do that?"

"They do," he said, "but a good pa shows 'em a good example."

So we picked up axes and went, and had reached a small clearing not more than a mile from the cabin when he stopped, smiling around at the trees.

"This here's a likely spot," he said, and laying Old Betsy down against a fallen log, he moved off toward the tree line. I placed my new rifle next to his and followed.

We set in on a couple of tall maples, and our ax blows soon fell into a steady, almost hypnotic rhythm. Thus occupied, I was oblivious to all else until a rough voice barked from somewhere behind.

"You can drop those axes," it said, "and raise yore paws high."

The voice was familiar—unpleasantly so—and even before I complied, I was certain who I'd see.

I was right. Standing next to the log where we'd left our rifles, and wearing the most evil smile I'd ever seen on a human, was Davy's old nemesis, Adam Myers. He held two flintlock pistols, both cocked, and aimed directly at us.

Davy said, "Thought you was dead, Myers, and rollin' the bones with Old Nick."

"Couldn't go quite yet," Myers said. "You an' me got unfinished business."

"Can't argue with that. You busted into my shed, stole my wagon, and sculped my dog."

Myers' smile grew. "That I did. And now comes the grand finale." He hooked a coil of rope with his foot and flipped it into the air. The rope fell at Davy's feet. He did the same with another coil directed at me. "Now, gentlemen, you're going to pick those up real careful-like and move close together. And don't try none of yore shenanigans. I can't hardly miss at this range."

As we moved closer, I tried to catch Davy's eye for some sign of hope, but he remained stone-faced, offering nothing.

"Now both of you sit. McCoy, you bind Crockett's legs. And

make that knot plenty tight. Any foolishness, and you'll be hearin' your Master's call."

I followed instructions, saying, "Sorry, Davy," as the rope bit into his ankles. Then Davy was forced to tie me, and Myers tossed another length of rope, making me tie Davy's hands behind his back.

This done, Myers approached me from behind and began on mine. Once I knew he'd laid down his pistols, I considered making a grab for one, but Davy read my intention and warned me off. Maybe he had a plan, after all.

Davy said, "I got one question, Myers. You think this up all by yourself, or did Zane send you?"

Myers shrugged. "He mighta suggested something, but I was already of a mind to see you again." He touched the remains of his left ear. "A man don't forget a thing like this." The ear, which still bore Davy's teeth marks, had been sewn on with rough twine, and stuck out from his head at a grotesque angle.

When we were securely bound and helpless, Myers finished the job by gagging us with shorter lengths of rope. He then stood back and admired his handiwork.

Davy and I shared a glance, and he nodded. Should we survive this encounter, Zane would have to pay.

"Now comes the fun part," he announced. "You got yourself quite a reputation, Crockett. Folks say you're the just about the deadliest bear-hunter in all creation. Well, I figger it's time for them bears to return the favor."

He grinned mysteriously, as if inviting us to guess his meaning.

I glanced at Davy, and thought I detected a twinkle in his eye, but for my part, I only knew it was going to be something extremely unpleasant.

Myers returned to the fallen log and picked up an oaken keg. "I borrowed this here honey from one of your neighbors. I aim to dress you gents in it, then let nature take its course."

He pulled a knife from his belt and pried out the cork. "You may have a disagreeable evening," he went on, "but within a day or two you should be back to your old selves. Two ugly piles of bear shit."

He laughed then, and I felt my bowels growing loose. Had we really survived all our travails in Creek territory, only to be devoured by bears?

I glanced again at Davy, and this time, even through the rope binding his mouth, I'd swear I saw a grin.

Myers stood over us now, gloating. He began to tip the keg.

"Hold it!" said a voice. A *female* voice. And I gaped to see Polly Crockett emerge from the trees at the far side of the clearing, a longrifle at her shoulder.

Myers' mouth fell open, and he turned to stare stupidly as more people stepped out of the woods. John Wesley, young William, Maggie, Jesse Bean, the widow Patton and several others who'd helped with my house-raising. And every last one of them had Myers in their gunsights.

ONCE DAVY AND I were free, there were many hugs, handclasps and backslaps. It had all been planned, I learned, a scheme designed by Davy. He had long ago divined who was behind his troubles, and been tracking Myers' movements until he determined the perfect time and place to spring his trap. And Myers had walked right into it.

Davy's friends and family had been with us all along, and we were never in real danger.

The only question left was—what to do with Myers?

As there was plenty of rope on hand, the general consensus was to string him up. But Davy demurred. "Despite the evil this varmint's done me, I ain't anxious to have his blood on my hands."

There was more debate, until Polly and Maggie got to whispering between them, and finally took their whispers to Davy. He looked shocked at first, and shook his head vehemently, but they kept after him without mercy until he finally surrendered.

Myers, now trussed up just as Davy and I had been, watched all this with growing alarm, and by the time it finished I saw he'd wet his britches.

"Adam Myers," Polly said, "it is the judgment of this court that what's good for the goose is good for the dadblamed gander."

She picked up the honey keg, removed the cork, and hoisted it over him. The rich honey began flowing, covering his face and chest. She continued down one leg and up the other, then did both his arms. That done, Maggie used Myers' own knife to cut the rope binding his ankles.

"Davy insisted we turn you loose," Polly said, "and that's what we're doing. Get up, and get out of here, before we set the dogs on you!"

Trembling like a six-foot earthquake, Myers rolled to his knees and struggled to his feet.

"Please," he said with a whine, "you can't just—"

Polly put two fingers between her teeth and whistled.

Brutus, Tiger and Samson came bounding out of the woods and stood snarling at Myers.

"Git!" Polly said. "I can't bear the sight of you no longer."

Myers gave her one last look, widened his eyes at the dogs, and took off running.

The hounds were eager to follow, but Polly stayed them with a hand, and we stood enjoying the sound of Myers crashing through the brush until we could hear him no more.

I stepped close to Davy and spoke quietly, but with some heat. "You reined all these folks in on your plan, but kept me in the dark? What kind of friend are you?"

Davy ducked his head. "I'm right sorry, Penn. I seen your play-actin' once before, and couldn't be sure it'd fool Myers."

I could hardly credit my ears. "You didn't trust me?"

He said nothing for a moment, and I felt the urge to punch him in the nose. Then he began to laugh, and I balled up my fist.

Davy raised a hand, palm forward. "I was gonna tell you, Penn.

Truly. But Maggie begged me not to. She figgered it was too good a joke to pass up."

I turned to see Maggie covering her mouth and giggling, and my fist fell open. Then she ran forward, enveloping me in a hug, and I felt the anger drain clean away.

WORK CONTINUED ON my cabin, and at the end of each day, it was easier to envision my life there. In those visions, Little Fawn was ever at my side. And that's when the dreams began.

At first I awoke with just a feeling, a gentle tug from the South. But as nights progressed, the feeling became a word, *Help!*, and before long I was hearing Little Fawn herself calling me, begging me, shouting for me to come.

"She's in trouble," I told Davy. "There can be no doubt. I must go to her."

I expected him to tell me I'd lost my wits, for many a man has been driven mad by love. Instead, he merely nodded. "You're right, Penn. You can do nothin' else."

We sat in rough-hewn chairs before my own cabin, which lacked only a roof, and I'd thought us alone. But Davy suddenly stood, and a voice behind me said, "You can't do this, Penn." I turned to face Maggie, who, as ever, had Polly at her side.

"She's right," Polly said. "We won't let you go. Not unless Davy goes with you."

And just like that, it was decided. We returned to the Crockett's cabin and began at once to gather provisions, planning to leave next morning at first light. My limbs were sore, but my heart was on fire when I sank at last upon my straw-stuffed mattress, prepared for another dream. But my head had scarcely touched the pillow when I heard a soft rapping at the door. I leapt up, alarmed at what this might portend, and swung the door open on the night. And there, ghostly in the moonlight, was the face from my dreams.

"Penn," Little Fawn said. "Please, Penn, we need you. Will you come?"

PART III
HORSESHOE BEND

CHAPTER 24

"I ain't never seen the like."

I STARED, BEREFT OF words. Surely I slept, and Little Fawn had come to me in a dream. But I smelled the sweat of horses, crickets called in the night, and a sickle moon hung low in the sky. No dream had ever seemed so real.

Behind me, Samson barked, Maggie squealed, Davy said, "Well, bust my buttons!" and all three rushed past me, hugging and pawing and dragging this image of Little Fawn into the cabin. Polly and the boys frolicked about in their nightshirts, as thrilled as the others.

When Little Fawn had been welcomed half to death, she turned and eyed me reprovingly. "Well, Pennsylvania McCoy. Are you not glad to see me?"

She seemed to glow in the dark, twice as beautiful as I remembered. I lurched forward then, buried her in my arms and held on tight. If this was a dream, I hoped it would never end.

HUDDLED ABOUT DAVY'S crude hearth, we sipped coffee from tin cups as Little Fawn told of events in the South. Not surprisingly, the news was bad, and much of it revolved around Zane.

"I shoulda killed him," Davy said, and I could not disagree. But Red Eagle had failed to perform the task as well. As had I. It was a mistake I would not make again.

"Once he and Sopath were reunited," Little Fawn said, "Red Eagle wished to make peace, and hoped to persuade other Red Stick leaders to join him. But that was not to be. After blaming the death of Thaddeus Truitt on Red Eagle, Zane approached General Jackson, receiving a commission and command of regular soldiers."

After that, as Little Fawn explained, things got progressively worse.

With the new troops granted him, Zane returned to the Truitt plantation, making his headquarters for a time at the overseer's cottage. Poor Lacy Truitt had once again been a prisoner, until Little Fawn spirited her away to the protection of Red Eagle and Sopath. The one bright spot of news was that Sopath had given birth to a strong-lunged son—named William, after his father.

Since Lacy's rescue, Zane had been on the move. Trading upon his role as Thaddeus Truitt's avenger, he had supplemented his troops with volunteers, attracting some of the most vile and brutal villains in the South.

Zane and his gang of thugs were now striking at Creek villages across the frontier. But instead of attacking Red Sticks, their raids focused on friendlies. Hundreds of those peaceful Indians had already perished, many of them women and children, and the rest left homeless.

"Would Jackson really sanction raids on his own allies?" I asked.

"Maybe yes, maybe no," Davy said, "but it wouldn't trouble him over much. To men like Old Hickory-face, one Injun's much like another."

I understood, and burned with shame for having once shared that opinion. But Jackson's motives were more calculated. To him, the Creeks were both an obstacle to his ambition and a means to achieve it. Zane need merely claim he'd been attacked, and Jackson would look the other way.

"What of your people?" I asked Little Fawn. "Can they ever forgive us?"

She hung her head. "At first, they thought it a horrible mistake. But as the attacks continued, they turned to anger or despair. Delegations to Jackson were given vague promises and sent away. Many of our young warriors have now joined the Red Sticks, and chiefs counseling peace are mocked."

Davy smacked a fist against his palm. "Why can't Red Eagle stamp him out?"

"He has sworn to destroy Zane, and devotes all his efforts to catching him, but Zane makes a point of being where Red Eagle is not. Men say he has adopted the methods of the Swamp Fox, darting from cover to strike and fading back into the wilderness. Meanwhile, as the so-called murderer of Colonel Truitt, Red Eagle has been harried by armies from both north and south. I fear he cannot avoid them much longer."

For several heartbeats, no one spoke. Little Fawn turned her imploring gaze full upon me. "Unless Zane can be stopped, my people have no future at all. Your generals either approve or ignore him. The Red Sticks cannot find him. The settlers think him their savior. No one can stand against him—no one but you, Penn. You and Davy."

NEXT MORNING WE said our goodbyes. Much as I hated to leave, I was anxious to be off before my composure was gone. Polly and the boys hugged us until we begged for mercy. Maggie maintained a brave but brittle smile. Even Little Fawn's eyes were wet. She had talked late into the night with Maggie and Polly, discussing I knew not what, and the three now seemed fast friends. Of us all, only Davy seemed unaffected, but I knew this was merely his way of handling the pain. When we were underway at last, Samson gave a mournful howl, as if even he were loath to leave.

As we rode, I regaled Little Fawn with talk of Kentuck, describing its many attractions in great detail, and shared my visions of the two of us making a life in the new cabin.

"That sounds wonderful," she would say, smiling to show she meant it. But her gaze always stretched forward, fixed on our destination, and she would commit herself no further.

Two days later we passed within sight of Fort Strother. As it appeared nearly deserted, Davy rode down in search of news. Jackson, we learned, had left a week before, planning to attack the Red Stick village of Tohopeka.

With an influx of new volunteers, Jackson's army had swollen to nearly three thousand men, but their mood was tense. On the very day he marched, Jackson had ordered an eighteen-year-old private executed by firing squad. Though charged with mutiny, the lad's only offense was that he had paused to eat breakfast on his way to sentry duty. Davy knew the boy's family back in Tennessee, and was in a savage mood the rest of the day.

Three thousand men left a wide trail, and two days later we topped a rise to gaze upon a bustling camp at the confluence of the Coosa and Cedar Creek. Davy was considering our options when a column of men started from the compound, led by General Jackson himself. We watched from the wooded hilltop as company after company marched out, heading south. Wedged between the bluecoats and the volunteers were several hundred Indians, most of whom Little Fawn identified as Cherokee, her tribe's traditional enemies. When the vast army was a dust cloud in the distance, Davy judged there could be no more than two hundred men left in camp.

Leaving Little Fawn with the packhorse, Davy and I rode in, hoping Jackson had not left orders that we be shot. But the pickets were relaxed, greeting us with grins.

"Howdy, Jacob," Davy said to the first man we saw. "How goes the war?"

"Davy! Wondered when you'd be back." The man tugged a canteen from his shoulder and tossed it to him.

Davy uncorked it, sniffed, and took a sizable swallow. "Rattlesnake oil," he said, smacking his lips, and offered it to me. I waved the stuff away.

"If you're wantin' the general," Jacob said, nodding toward the south, "you'll have to hurry."

Davy shook his head. "Still chasin' Red Eagle's tail, is he?"

"That's a fact. Word is, the varmint's holed up down at Horseshoe Bend with a thousand other red devils, and the general hopes to snuff 'em out in one big blow."

I grimaced at this. Horseshoe Bend, Little Fawn had explained, was a big turn in the Tallapoosa River, where the Creeks had built the village of Tohopeka. It sounded to me like a death trap.

Laying a finger aside his nose, Jacob lowered his voice. "To my way of thinkin', this fight won't be no frolic. I was on a scout down there with General Coffee after that ruckus at Emuck-fau, and I can tell you—them savages built a wall that would hold back the hordes of Hell. Cut down a whole forest of pine trees, they did, and stacked 'em higher than a man can reach. The general's gonna lose half his army afore he gets within spittin' distance. Like most of the others who've seen that place, I volunteered to stay and guard the supply depot."

"Actually," Davy said, "we was hopin' to catch up with Major Zane. Heard tell he's the one rainin' fire and brimstone down upon the Creeks."

"True enough. But he's got crackers with him. Even a few god-damned gougers." Jacob turned his head to spit. "You willin' to ride with scum like that?"

Davy's face betrayed nothing. To cover my own disgust, I adopted a knowing leer. Crackers were so named for their joyful use of bullwhips on their fellow men, and gougers cultivated long, sharpened fingernails to remove their opponents' eyeballs. Such men were as openly depraved as Zane was in spirit. To unleash them upon peaceful Creek villages was a horror beyond imagining.

"Penn's family was at Fort Mims." Davy nodded at me, to which I displayed a most horrific scowl. "And Thaddeus Truitt was a great hero of mine." He patted the rifle in its scabbard. "Old Betsy's eager for vengeance. We ain't killed no Injuns in nigh onto a week, and it's left us mighty wrathy."

Jacob gazed up at him, shaking his head. "War's changed you, Davy. You used to think them polecats was almost human."

"Said it yourself, Jake," Davy said. "War does change a man."

Samson chose that moment to bound out of the brush, a limp jackrabbit between his teeth.

Jacob grinned. "There's a fearsome beast. Yours?"

Davy nodded. "He like enough mistook that hare for an Injun. Red Sticks are his favorite breakfast."

When Jacob stopped laughing, I asked, "Zane going to be at Tohopeka?"

"Can't say," Jacob said, "though it ain't really his style. Last I heard he was somewhere south of the Alabam'. Some of them so-called friendly towns been offerin' succor to the rebels, and he's showin' 'em the error of their ways."

Davy said, "Don't Jackson have Creek friendlies ridin' with him?"

Jacob nodded. "That 'breed McIntosh come up from Georgia with a hundred warriors. The general welcomed 'em, sure enough, but that don't mean he trusts 'em. At the first sign of treachery, he's got half a thousand Cherokees hot to take their scalps."

"Hell of a man, that general," Davy said, and Jacob smiled, as if that were the finest thing in the world to be.

WE VEERED WEST into the woods, skirting around Jackson's column. For an army, they were moving damned fast, but were slowed by their field artillery.

The place Little Fawn had arranged to meet Sopath and Lacy was a canebrake some ten miles west of Horseshoe Bend. The sun was nearing the western treetops when we reached the trail leading into the brake.

Davy was immediately ill at ease. "My dun's nose is twitchin'. He smells blood. Or death." He galloped ahead a ways and quite suddenly stopped, staring down at the ground.

"Which is it?" I called.

"Both." Davy slid from his saddle as we approached, kneeling next to a dark shape.

Little Fawn slipped from her pony to join him. "Harjo!" she cried, and the pain in her voice pulled at my heart.

The form on the ground had been a Creek warrior. Holes in his chest indicated he'd taken three musket balls, but even more ghastly were the purple welts where he'd been tattooed with a bullwhip—and the blood-caked eye-sockets now crawling with ants. There were signs ravens had been nipping at him as well—though not wolves—or more flesh would be missing.

"He was my uncle," Little Fawn said thickly. "And Sopath's. One of the men sworn to protect her."

Kneeling, I put my arm around her. She pressed against me, but her body remained stiff. "Sopath and Lacy. And the child. We must find them."

Davy rode his dun in a wide loop around the body, studying the grass. "Maybe a dozen horses, all shod, an' four sets of boots. They whipped this poor feller from his horse, then came at him on foot. He was likely dead afore he was shot."

Little Fawn choked back a sob.

Davy pointed toward the canebrake. "He came from over yonder, and he came alone."

We rode toward the cane. It seemed wrong not to bury Harjo, but our first allegiance was to the living—or those we *hoped* were living.

At Little Fawn's instruction we left the horses behind a stand of oaks and followed her into the canebrake. There seemed no rhyme or reason to her path, but she picked her way so carefully I knew she followed some route. After a few minutes we emerged into a small clearing with a patch of solid ground.

A glad cry greeted us, followed by another, and two shapes emerged from the cane. Lacy and Sopath. Both wore shifts of mud-caked buckskin, but their natural beauty was undiminished. Behind them came a nearly naked warrior armed with a musket and tomahawk.

Sopath flung her arms about Little Fawn, sobbing, while Lacy embraced me and Davy.

"We prayed you would come," Lacy said. Then her eyes filled, and she glanced toward Sopath. "If only you'd come yesterday."

Davy and I shared a look. Had she seen Harjo die? I waited, fearing to speak.

Sopath sobbed all the harder.

"A group of soldiers spotted us a mile to the south," Lacy said. "We ran, and Ochee, one of Red Eagle's warriors, gave his life to buy us time. But they caught us before we could reach the canebrake." She glanced again at Sopath, and her voice fell to a whisper. "Quanhay," she indicated the silent warrior with a nod, "and Harjo did their best to stop them, but they took little William."

Quanhay's face was infinitely sad.

Davy's face went white. I squeezed my rifle until the wood creaked.

"They could have taken us as well," Lacy said, "but once they had the boy they laughed and rode away."

Davy said, "Was it Zane's men?"

"None that we knew," Lacy said. "But who else could they be? Who else would recognize us, and know the value of Red Eagle's son?" Anguish twisted her features, made them almost ugly. "He should be dead. He killed my father. He burned my home. Why is he not dead?"

She seemed about to collapse, and I cradled her in my arms. "He will be," I promised, "and soon."

We sat on the small patch of earth among the gigantic shoots of cane. When Sopath's sobbing finally ceased, Davy asked, "Does Red Eagle know?"

Sopath shook her head. "He went to Tohopeka to meet with Menawa and the other chiefs. I sent Harjo to tell him of William, and when we heard your horses, we hoped they had returned."

Davy and I hung our heads.

Little Fawn cleared her throat. Her lips trembled, and I laid a hand on her knee. She put an arm around Sopath, hugging her close, and spoke softly as the sun dipped behind the cane.

NEXT MORNING, WE buried Harjo beneath a towering elm and rode for Tohopeka. I had wished to set out the night before, but Davy felt it unwise to approach the Red Stick stronghold after dark.

We were still some distance from the river when Lacy, Sopath and Quanhay left us, to join the Red Sticks' women and children at a hidden camp several miles to the south.

Sopath had drawn Little Fawn aside, speaking urgently in her own language, and the two exchanged hugs. Little Fawn had been torn, she told us, wishing to stay and comfort her cousin, but convinced her presence would help us reach Red Eagle.

I was also of two minds. Much as I wanted her with me, I dreaded taking her into a camp that would soon be under siege. But once decided, she would not be deterred, and we raced for Tohopeka at such speed that Samson panted to keep pace.

Just before noon we found ourselves at the top of a slope overlooking the Tallapoosa river. Though Little Fawn had described Horseshoe Bend in detail, I was still ill-prepared for the sight. The rushing river truly did form a great horseshoe, curling back upon itself so dramatically as to appear man-made. But most startling of all was the great barricade stretching across the neck of the peninsula.

"Thunderation!" Davy said. "I ain't never seen the like."

Nor had I, except in books, and felt a chill just to look upon it. The enormous breastwork brought to mind the walls of Troy, or perhaps the great wall a Roman emperor had built across Britain to hold the wild Scots at bay. It was surely the most un-Indian thing I had seen in this territory, and I sensed the hand of Red Eagle.

The nearer we came, the more astonished I was. The barricade was in all places taller than a man, sometimes stretching as high as eight feet, and marched more than three hundred yards across the peninsula. Huge pine logs had been piled one upon another and packed with earth. Instead of forming a straight line, the breastwork curved inward, so that attackers at any point would be exposed to fire from many places behind the wall. In addition, there were clever zigzags within the curve, providing even more opportunities to catch attackers in a crossfire.

Even with three thousand men, General Jackson would be mad to attack this place. And yet, knowing Jackson, I had no doubt he would do so.

Davy plunged down the slope, urging his horse toward the barricade, while Little Fawn and I raced to keep up. Samson showed better sense, veering off into the nearby woods. When the wall was still two hundred yards away, I could make out painted faces along the top, and saw muskets and bows taking aim at us.

A hundred yards further, Davy halted his horse and raised empty hands high above his head, making a great show of peaceful intent. Little Fawn and I came abreast of him and followed his example.

At this distance, I noted two rows of firing ports running the length of the breastwork, each bristling with arrows and musket barrels. I looked hard at Davy, who shrugged and started forward again. Little Fawn followed immediately, and I rushed to keep pace.

We were fifty yards from the wall when a warrior with a yellow-painted face scowled down from atop the breastwork. His words were faint, lost in the rush of the river passing on either side, but there was little doubt we'd been ordered to halt. We did.

Little Fawn kneed her pony forward another twenty yards, ignoring a second demand to halt. Stopping when she pleased, she answered, her voice calm and clear.

In reply, the yellow-faced man barked an order, and two muskets fired, the balls kicking up dust around her pony's hooves.

My hand itched to draw my rifle, but Little Fawn seemed unperturbed. When spoke again, her voice rang with command.

Yellow Face spat at her, then gestured to others atop the wall. They appeared to hold a conference.

"I told him we had news for Red Eagle, regarding his son," Little Fawn said over her shoulder. "I explained I was of the Wind Clan, and that Davy has mastered the White Drink."

"What did you say about me?" I asked.

"That you are renowned for your love-making," she said, "for that is a skill they admire above all others."

My cheeks were hot before she laughed, and I was doubly abashed for believing her.

The fellow on the wall shouted again, and Little Fawn interpreted. "He does not believe me. He thinks I have sided with the white man, and that you two are spies for Sharp Knife. He is inclined to have us shot."

"Who's this Sharp Knife?" Davy asked.

"Their name for General Jackson."

"Hope he never hears it," I said. "His head's swelled enough already."

Yellow Face jabbered again in Creek.

"We may leave, provided we go at once," Little Fawn translated. "Otherwise, our blood will be the first to feed this ground."

Davy shook his head. "Bunch o' featherbrained idiots. All they gotta do is tell Red Eagle we're here."

I cupped my hands and bellowed. "Red Eagle! Davy Crockett's come about your son!"

I'd barely finished when the air about me buzzed with arrows and musket balls.

"We should go," Little Fawn said sharply. "Now."

Davy shrugged and nodded. We turned our horses, but stopped immediately. Onto the peninsula galloped a party of Red Sticks, at least a hundred strong. At a shout from the man atop the barricade, the new arrivals spread out in a line, barring our retreat.

We had truly stepped in it now, and there seemed no escape. I looked longingly at Little Fawn, a look she returned, and we shared a solemn moment.

A piercing scream spun our heads about. The Red Sticks, too, seemed startled, and all eyes turned to Davy. Stripping the shirt from his chest, he flung it aside and thrust his fists into the air.

"I have been to the land of witches," he roared, "and met the Master of Breath! He says no man can defeat me, and I challenge any o' you jackals to dispute his word!"

A few men murmured approval, obviously understanding his speech, while others looked confused. Little Fawn shouted a translation. Soon all were nodding, their faces bright with excitement.

These men were fighters, and a challenge was an entertainment they could not resist. Even Yellow Face had to smile. He turned to shout into the encampment behind him. A word was repeated, a word that sounded like a name, and it surged through the camp like a wave. The mounted warriors behind us took up the call until it became a chant, growing ever louder and more insistent.

Little Fawn yelled something at me. The noise was too great to catch her words, but her face was taut with alarm.

Leaping from his horse, Davy pranced about before the barricade, waving his arms and howling like a curly wolf.

I wished I shared his confidence. Davy was a skilled fighter, but our survival depended on his ability to defeat their champion. A thought came to me then, and I almost grinned. Who among the Red Sticks was a greater champion than Red Eagle? Davy was betting our lives on the likelihood they would summon their leader to defeat him.

I felt a smile tugging at my lips as the shouts behind the barricade turned to cheers. Red Eagle must be approaching! Then my smile died as a fierce new face appeared above the wall. War cries erupted from both sides of the breastwork. With a brief pause to acknowledge the acclaim, the newcomer hopped over the wall, plummeting ten or more feet to land with a thump that jarred my bones.

My mouth went dry. Before us stood a giant, his arms thick as oaks and his chest wide as a wagon. He raised two anvil-like fists and brought them together with a thunderclap.

Davy retained his outer calm, but his eyes flashed disappointment. His gambit had failed, and this monster would mean our doom.

I swore under my breath. With the aid of his inner demon, Davy might have a chance. But he'd been free of that devil for months, and if he allowed it in now, he might never banish it again.

Even if he managed to win this battle, Davy would be the loser.

CHAPTER 25

"The man is a demon."

DAVY'S STRUTTING AND posturing came to a halt as he stared slack-jawed at the huge figure lumbering toward him.

The Red Sticks laughed. The merriment began on top of the barricade, flowing over us to be caught and returned by the mounted warriors at our backs. The hubbub rose until the great wall itself shook with mirth.

With each passing moment more painted faces appeared atop the breastworks, more eager eyes leered through the double line of firing ports. We'd heard there were upwards of a thousand warriors massed here, but it already seemed twice that number had thronged to see their champion battle Davy.

The Red Sticks' laughter resolved into a chant, a thunderous two-syllable shout accompanied by the shaking of muskets, spears and war clubs. The bloodlust ran so high that should Jackson's soldiers arrive at this moment, I feared the Indians would swarm out and mow them down like so many stalks of wheat.

The giant warrior swelled even larger. He beat a huge fist against his chest and waved to his admirers, driving them to greater frenzy.

Little Fawn's words were lost in the din. I nudged my mare forward and leaned close to her. "Mad Bear," she said. "This is not good."

"I figured the 'not good' part. Who's Mad Bear?"

"When he was a child, a bear attacked his mother. It is said he went berserk, ripping the beast's throat out with his teeth."

I gazed back at the man-monster. While the tale was not impossible, it seemed more likely the bear had attacked his mother nine months before he was born.

Davy caught my eye and grinned. Having recovered from his shock, he now seemed devoid of fear. Turning to face Mad Bear, he made a show of removing the knife and tomahawk from his belt and throwing them out of reach, indicating he wished to fight barehanded.

For a heartbeat, the big Indian just stared at him. Would he cast his own weapons aside, or exploit Davy's foolishness and slice him to bits? At last Mad Bear drew his own tomahawk, gripping it tightly in his fist. He followed suit with his knife, displaying a hideous smile.

The chanting faltered. A few Red Sticks yelped encouragement, but I sensed an air of disapproval. With a laugh, Mad Bear flipped the weapons over his shoulders, causing the warriors to hoot with joy.

The Creeks atop the breastworks put their heads together. Behind us, the mounted warriors did the same. I looked a question at Little Fawn.

"Placing bets," she said.

I was shocked. "Some are betting on Davy?"

"They wager," she said, "on how quickly Mad Bear will kill him."

Davy still wore his grin. This sign of bravado, I assumed, was meant to confuse his opponent. And Mad Bear did eye him strangely, but whether he thought the grinning a sign of confidence or the mark of an imbecile, I could not decide. The giant warrior's bearing expressed utter contempt—perhaps even annoyance—that such a puny creature dared challenge him.

I turned in my saddle, peering into the distance, praying for some sign Jackson was on the way. While the army's arrival would make our position even more precarious, the distraction might give Little Fawn and I a chance to spirit Davy away from certain death. But there was nothing on the horizon but trees. Having prodded his men south like cattle, it would be like Jackson to stop and shoot a few for mutiny before prosecuting the attack.

"Uh, Penn…" Little Fawn pointed at Davy, who had fallen to his knees, his arms stretching toward the heavens. From his lips came the same unearthly cry he'd used when pretending to summon the spirits at Red Eagle's village.

Mad Bear paused in his approach, and the Red Sticks stared, astonished. What Davy hoped to accomplish from this I could not imagine. Should a hoot owl appear and perch on Davy's head, Mad Bear would likely just bite it off, along with most of Davy's face.

In any event, no birds swept down from the sky. No fishes leapt from the river. No wolves or wildcats rushed from the woods. Still, Davy kept at it, twitching and wailing and dripping spittle from his chin. And the Red Sticks began to jeer.

Mad Bear advanced until he towered directly over the crazy man. Turning again to survey his audience, he played to them with an elaborate shrug. And it was then, when the giant Indian was least prepared, that Davy struck.

Surging up from the ground, Davy drove his head into Mad Bear's stomach, folding him in two. While the big warrior gasped for breath, Davy hooked a leg behind the man's knee and toppled him over. Mad Bear crashed to earth with a thud that rattled my bones. Davy was upon him at once, doing a war dance on his breadbasket.

Taking a great bounce from Mad Bear's chest, Davy shot straight up, twisted in the air and came down with both knees plunging into the big man's stomach. Mad Bear's limbs shot straight out, quivering as the air left his body. Davy was up in an instant, one foot planted on Mad Bear's chest, one fist clenched in the air.

"The Master of Breath has favored me," he called. "I now

demand audience with your leader, the mighty warrior known as—"

He was about to name Red Eagle, and I sensed our salvation, but before the words could pass his lips, a huge hand wrapped about Davy's leg, and Mad Bear sat up. Davy leapt sideways, but Mad Bear kept hold of the leg, rising slowly to his feet. The Indian's face was a red-eyed mask of fury. With effortless ease, he raised the helpless Davy above his head and began swinging him in ever faster circles. When Mad Bear finally let go, Davy soared into the sky, limbs flailing in all directions, and crunched to earth thirty yards away.

Davy lay without moving, a heap of arms and legs in no sensible arrangement. The Red Sticks went wild with delight, and Mad Bear puffed up his chest, drinking in the cheers.

Did Davy still live? I turned my mare, intending to find out, but Little Fawn clutched my sleeve and shook her head.

Mad Bear, meanwhile, turned and strode to the great barricade, where he stood with hands on hips, scanning the wall.

"What's he doing?" I asked Little Fawn.

But before she could answer, Mad Bear grasped a six-foot branch protruding from a log, braced a foot against the wall and wrenched the limb free. He turned and stomped toward Davy, swinging it like a club. The branch was thick as one of his massive arms.

Davy lay where he'd fallen, to all appearances nothing more than a pile of shattered bones. But squinting hard, I thought I saw an eyeball peering out from that sorry mass.

As Mad Bear grew near, the Red Sticks wet their lips, eager to see Davy pounded into jelly. I struggled to shut my eyes, but found I could not.

The great club rose. Mad Bear's muscles heaved and rolled beneath his painted skin. His lips peeled back from his teeth. The tendons stood out on his neck.

The Red Sticks held their breath. For a moment the only

sound was the rush of the river. Then the blow fell, plummeting from the sky and striking with a thump that shook the earth.

But Davy wasn't there. Having rolled aside, he sprang to his feet. Before Mad Bear could lift his club, Davy leapt onto it, raced up its length and kicked Mad Bear squarely in the jaw. The crack was loud in the stunned silence.

Mad Bear spat blood and broken teeth but did not go down. Bellowing his rage, he raised his club and swung it like a madman. Davy flattened to the earth as the branch scorched the air above him. He bounced up just in time to avoid another blow, then caught a swipe that tore an angry gouge across his chest. Davy danced away, but his movements were slower, less certain.

The Red Sticks resumed their chant, screaming their champion's name. He had been tried and proven, emerging stronger than ever, while his prey was nearly out of breath. It was time for the kill.

Davy still dodged about, but was beginning to stumble, and the club came ever closer.

Dimly at first, I heard a new voice shouting between the chants. After several repetitions I caught the cadence, and recognized it as a name. "Crockett! Crockett!"

Little Fawn nudged me and pointed up at the breastworks. There, waving a red war club above his head, stood Red Eagle.

Davy heard him then, and as he glanced up, the Red Sticks did also. Their chanting diminished. Even Mad Bear turned to stare up at the wall.

Red Eagle held the war club high until all were silent. Then, nodding at Davy, he flung it up and out, where it turned end over end through the air.

Mad Bear stared dumbly as the blood-red club sailed over his head, but Davy dipped his knees and sprang, soaring up to snatch the twirling weapon from the sky. Still in the air, Davy twisted his body, swung the club and bashed Mad Bear smack between the eyes. The *thonk* of wood upon bone echoed from the wall as Mad Bear rocked on his feet, spinning in small circles.

But, incredibly, he righted himself, took a new grip on the tree limb, and advanced on Davy.

For a heartbeat, no one uttered a sound. Then Red Eagle shouted something in Creek. Mad Bear stopped in his tracks. While the Indians stared, he pointed at Davy, then at me and Little Fawn, and barked a command. With that, he turned and vanished from the wall. The Red Sticks eyed one another, some angry, some amused, but most simply disappointed.

Mystified, I looked to Little Fawn.

"A draw," she said, smiling. "He has declared the fight a draw. And he has invited us to dine."

We urged our mounts toward Davy, where he stood, knees sagging.

"We feared we had lost you again," Little Fawn said.

Davy managed a grin. "That feller's part tornado, part volcano and all earthquake, but 'least I kept my devil stoppered up."

"Would you really have died rather than let it loose?"

Davy's grin melted away. "Would if I could," he said. "But I'm cockeyed thankful we didn't have to find out."

IF RED EAGLE was pleased to see us, he hid it well. We stood guarded by six scowling warriors while Red Eagle and three other Creek leaders engaged in heated conversation a dozen yards away. There had been no further mention of food, but at least we were behind the barricade.

The estimate of a thousand Indians had been no exaggeration, and every one of them was busy at something. Priests danced and waved cow-tail sticks. Warriors wrangled felled trees and brush to bolster the barricade. Further back I saw men guzzling and spewing the White Drink, and the odor alone almost made me vomit.

The glares of the Red Stick leaders left little doubt that we were the point of disagreement. Most of the talking was done by a pair of feather-robed shamans, and directed at Red Eagle.

The fourth man in the group did not speak, but his keen eyes missed nothing.

Unlike most Red Sticks, this silent man had no aversion to civilized attire, though his sense of style was atrocious. His primary garment was a red padded cloak with gold pinstripes. Beneath this he wore a ruffled shirt bound at the neck with a blue ascot. And completing the outfit was a bottle-green nightcap with yellow spots and a bushy red tail whose previous owner had undoubtedly been a squirrel. Any man who dared dress in such a fashion, I reasoned, was either extremely powerful, or mad as a hatter.

I nudged Little Fawn. "Who's the dandy?"

"Menawa," she whispered. "A great war chief."

"Greater than Red Eagle?"

"Red Eagle has much influence, but is not a true chief. Most of the warriors here are sworn to Menawa."

Like Red Eagle, Menawa was fair-skinned and appeared more white than Creek, but was perhaps a dozen years older. His long face was not lined, but weathered, with features so stern they might have been chipped from granite. His cheeks were decorated with red-rimmed blue triangles, almost in the shape of side-whiskers.

The two priests still jabbered away in their guttural tongue. One was clearly superior. His cloak was fashioned entirely of eagle feathers, while his companion made do with the leavings of lesser birds. The first priest's silver-gray hair was bound at the temple with a circlet of gold. His eyes were fierce but intelligent, and his nose and jaw reminded me of George Washington, whom I had once seen in a parade.

"Monahoe," Little Fawn breathed, "the father of all prophets."

The other priest, whom Little Fawn identified as Josiah Francis, had a long straight nose, full lips and a slightly-dimpled chin. Painted beneath each eye were thin horizontal lines, alternating red and blue. His voice was harsh, and he fixed us repeatedly with sour looks. I stared hard at him for a time, but he remained unaffected, and I eventually gave up. Like the others, Francis appeared more white than Indian, and I found it ironic the Creek leaders were those who appeared the least Indian.

"The prophets are baffled that you and Davy still live," Little Fawn explained. "They swore that once behind the wall you would be crushed by giant hailstones or swallowed by an earthquake."

I raised my eyebrows.

"They danced and sang for ten days," she went on, "to lay an enchantment over this spit of land. No white men may set foot here without being struck dead by the spirits."

"I do have a pain in my stomach," I said. "But it's probably just hunger."

Little Fawn's eyes twinkled. "Red Eagle told them you both have Indian blood in your veins. Davy's great-grandmother was a Cherokee, he said, and you are descended from the great Chief Pontiac."

"I am?" I immediately squared my shoulders to better reflect my noble lineage.

The argument among the leaders had grown more animated. With a final burst of invective, Monahoe rose and stomped away from the group, arms waving, eagle feathers streaming behind. Red Eagle and the others turned to face us, and Chief Menawa motioned our guards to bring us forward.

We were six feet away when Menawa raised a hand and pointed at the earth. We sat, Little Fawn in the center, and I was unlucky enough to find myself facing the pinch-faced shaman, Josiah Francis. Close up, he was even less impressive. While the feathered cloak had made Monahoe look majestic, even supernatural, it gave Francis the air of a court jester—except, of course, that he never smiled.

"My brother Red Eagle insists you are men of honor," Menawa said, "but I would have some further assurance. How do I know you are not spies for Old Mad Jackson?"

"Old Mad—?" I laughed, unable to contain myself. "I thought you called him Sharp Knife."

Little Fawn pinched my arm. Josiah Francis scowled. Red Eagle's lips twitched.

"That too," Menawa said. He seemed to focus on me for the first time, and I felt he could see through my skin. He raised a hand, palm up, and a warrior approached, placing something into it. As Menawa's fingers closed, I caught a flash of silver. "Are you men Christians?"

Davy looked uncomfortable. "Not the best," he said, "but tolerable."

I nodded. "I was raised Episcopalian."

Menawa shook his head. "I doubt Pontiac would approve. Nevertheless…" He opened his hand to reveal a silver crucifix encrusted with diamonds. "You will humor me by grasping this and swearing you are not spies for Jackson."

"And if we don't?" I said.

Josiah Francis surprised me. He could smile, after all.

Davy took the crucifix. "I swear it," he said solemnly. "Old Hickory-face ain't no friend of mine." He passed the cross to me.

"I swear as well. I will say nothing of what I've seen here."

Menawa glanced skyward, awaiting lightning bolts. None came. "My thanks, gentlemen." He held out his hand, taking the crucifix. "You may now address Red Eagle."

"We're plumb sorry to bring this news," Davy began, but paused at Red Eagle's stricken look.

"Young William has been taken," Little Fawn said quickly. "Probably by Zane."

Red Eagle's face underwent a series of changes, none of them pleasant. He seemed to be having trouble with his mouth. "Sopath?" he said at last.

"She's safe," Davy said, "or was this morning. But we buried one o' her friends."

"Harjo," Little Fawn said softly. "Ochee is dead as well. Quan-hay is still with Sopath, as is Lacy Truitt."

Red Eagle looked both pained and relieved at the same time. He stared down at his right hand, clenching it into a fist. "Where is Zane?"

Davy hung his head. Red Eagle looked at me. I winced and shrugged.

"Can't say certain sure his men done it," Davy said, "but we'll find 'em. Figgered you'd be wantin' to join us."

Josiah Francis spoke, his voice as grating as his demeanor. "To find this man will take time, a thing we have little of. We are told your Sharp Knife is within a day's ride with thrice our number. Red Eagle's responsibility lies here."

"But this is enchanted ground," Little Fawn said. "You have promised the white soldiers will be struck dead by the spirits. Why do you need warriors at all?"

The shaman bristled. "Your tongue has no place here, woman."

"You require great fighters," she said, undaunted, "because your magic is weak. It failed you at the Holy Ground, did it not? The women say that at the first sign of soldiers, you scampered into the marsh like a rabbit. The men you promised would be struck dead proceeded to burn the town."

Josiah Francis rose to his knees, spittle flecking his lips. He aimed a rigid finger at her. "The Holy Ground fell because Red Eagle allowed two white men and a woman to partake of the White Drink! The magic was broken. I pray your presence has not contaminated *this* ground as well."

"Enough." Menawa said quietly. "You may leave us, Josiah. I believe Monahoe has need of you."

Scowling more bitterly than ever, Francis rose to his feet, dusted his feathers and stalked off, muttering.

"You speak boldly," Menawa told Little Fawn. "A trait I admire. But Josiah is right. Red Eagle is needed here."

Red Eagle rubbed his brow. "Without knowing Zane's whereabouts, I cannot in good conscience leave now."

Davy leaned forward. "Kidnappin' a young'un is a thing I can't abide. We'll get William back for you, or die tryin'."

"We all will," I said, and Little Fawn nodded agreement.

For a moment, no one spoke. We had a near impossible task before us. First to find Zane, and see if he had the boy. Then, supposing he did, to face his army of crackers, gougers and soldiers. Like as not, we would fail with or without Red Eagle's company.

Menawa nodded curtly, indicating our visit was at an end. But as he began to rise, a warrior approached, handing him an envelope. Menawa's eyes widened as the man spoke into his ear.

"A rider brought this letter," Menawa said. "It is addressed to Red Eagle."

Red Eagle stared at him before accepting the envelope. He turned it over in his hand, and we saw it was sealed with wax. Breaking the seal, Red Eagle extracted a folded sheet of paper. He studied the letter for long seconds before looking up. "Perhaps you could read it aloud," he said, passing the sheet to Davy.

Davy hesitated, then accepted the paper. He glanced at it briefly before thrusting it at me. "My readin's a bit rusty. Let Penn do it."

Before I could take the letter, Menawa's hand shot out, snatching it from Davy's hand. "I will read it."

And to all appearances, he did. At least his eyes tracked across the paper several times. Finishing, he looked up, his face dark. "I know not what to make of this, but I suspect treachery of the vilest sort," He shifted his gaze from me to Davy and back. He addressed Red Eagle. "Perhaps it is best that you go. In fact," he said, pushing to his feet, "I command it."

As we just stared, Menawa let the letter float to the earth. He turned then, striding majestically away.

Red Eagle called after him. "And my men?"

"They are needed here," the chief called back. "When your heart is with us, you may return. Not before."

Red Eagle and Little Fawn looked bewildered. Davy's face showed nothing at all.

I plucked the letter from the dirt, and read aloud:

> To the Creek leader Red Eagle: You and your followers have ridden into a trap. General Jackson, with an overwhelming force of soldiers, is on the march to surround your position. I urge you and your fellow chiefs to abandon Tohopeka immediately, or face certain destruction. As a further demonstration of my friendship, I have taken your infant son under my protection. Assuming you follow my advice and escape to fight again, he will be returned to you unharmed.
>
> A Friend

Finished, I gazed into Red Eagle's face, and the sight chilled me. For the first time since we'd met him, he seemed lost in despair.

"What do you make of it?" I asked the others.

"Zane," Davy said. "Almost certainly Zane. But why he'd wish to save Red Eagle from Jackson is a puzzle I can't crack."

"I agree," Little Fawn put in. "The man is a demon, and his motives cannot be fathomed."

"Maybe," I said, "it's what Jackson really wants. Get the Red Sticks out from behind that barricade where he can properly slaughter them."

A heavy silence hung over us until Red Eagle finally spoke. "Whatever course I take, I must rescue my son. Will you help?"

"Of that, at least," Davy answered for us, "there ain't the slightest doubt."

CHAPTER 26

"I will do the persuading."

"**W**HAT DO WE do now?"

"Find William," Red Eagle said. "And kill the men who took him." There were no further suggestions.

We sat our horses halfway up a gentle slope, gazing back at the great barricade. It was no less impressive for having been seen at close range, and I felt a touch of the wonder and dread Jackson's troops would experience when they arrived.

Davy said, "You talk to the feller who brung the letter?"

Red Eagle looked off toward the south. "He is from Nontopiica. Soldiers captured his wife and sons, swearing they would die unless he delivered the letter to me."

"He was a friendly," Little Fawn said for our benefit.

Red Eagle spat. "No longer. He has vowed to remain at Tohopeka and fight Jackson as fiercely as the rest."

"And how would Zane—or whoever—know the letter was delivered?" Davy asked.

"Someone would be watching, the man was told, to see that he passed behind the wall."

Davy rolled his head as if stretching out kinks in his neck, but his keen eyes studied the surrounding terrain. "Watching. And he may be watching now."

I said, "Think so?"

"Maybe not this 'Friend' himself, but surely one of his toadies."

"Then we will find this toad," Little Fawn said, "and persuade him to tell us where William was taken."

"You find him," Red Eagle said. "I will do the persuading." His tone made me shiver.

"We ain't got time to hunt all over creation," Davy said. "We need us a plan." He shaded his eyes, peering up the slope at a stand of cottonwoods. "But since it's nigh onto noon and Penn's lookin' puckish, I say we mosey up there and break our fast."

Red Eagle scowled. Little Fawn frowned at me as if I had done something wrong.

"C'mon," Davy said. "I'm commencin' to get an idea. Tell you 'bout it on the way."

THE FIRE BURNED merrily as we relaxed in the shade of the cottonwoods. Or rather, as we appeared to relax, for we were all eager to begin the hunt for William. While Davy'd been out shooting us a hare, I'd gathered wood and Little Fawn brought water from the river. Red Eagle sat stone-faced throughout the proceedings, arms tight across his chest, the very picture of a man in torment.

Beyond the trees, clumps of dense brush screened us from the countryside, but also screened the countryside from us. It was just the sort of campsite Davy would normally avoid. Still, he appeared quite relaxed, skinning the hare and chatting away about other rabbits he'd hunted. He was in the middle of an amusing tale about a hare who thought it was a dog, when he laughed and said, "But I suspicion I'm borin' you all with this."

I looked slantwise at him, on alert. Once started on a tale, nothing short of a hurricane could stop him.

Davy stuck his skinning knife into the earth and scratched an ear.

Little Fawn nodded slightly and pinched her nose.

Davy said, louder than necessary, "So, Red Eagle, what you aim to do 'bout your son?"

Red Eagle gave no sign he'd heard. His eyes were open, but seemed turned inward, on things we could not see.

Davy clapped his hands. "Red Eagle. Your son?"

Red Eagle shook himself. He turned his head, taking note of us, and once again Little Fawn pinched her nose.

"What choice do I have?" Red Eagle's voice was even louder than Davy's. "If the letter spoke true, I must lead my people away from danger. And I must live, to see my son again."

"And what of the other Red Sticks?"

Red Eagle hung his head. "I fear they will not leave. I will grieve for them. What matters most, even more than my son, is to guard the secret of our peoples' treasure."

Little Fawn burst to her feet. "Enough! You must not speak of that!"

Red Eagle frowned. "Be seated, woman. Crockett and McCoy are my friends, and great enemies of Zane. I trust them in all things."

"No!" Little Fawn stamped her foot. "It is forbidden."

I said, "What treasure is this?" My voice, too, seemed unnatural.

Samson chose this moment to come romping into camp, showing great interest in Davy's hare. Davy eased the hound aside. "Light and sit, boy. You'll eat when we do."

Samson looked disappointed. Then quite suddenly his ears twitched and his head swung toward the thick brush behind the trees.

"Sit," Davy said with more force. "Stay."

Samson remained rigid. The fur along his spine ruffled. Davy grimaced at Red Eagle.

"Samson." Red Eagle flattened his hand and motioned toward the ground.

Samson laid on his belly, stretched out his paws and rested his chin upon them.

I said, "Uh, what was that about a treasure?"

Red Eagle hesitated as if considering his words. "Our people have roamed this land for many generations. We have dealt long with Spanish, French and British traders, and accumulated much gold and silver."

Little Fawn sputtered as if fit to burst, but Red Eagle silenced her with a hand. He leaned forward, addressing Davy and me. "When this war began, the great chiefs decreed the treasure be gathered and kept safe for our children."

"Stop," Davy said. "We heard enough."

"No," Red Eagle said heavily. "I alone know the secret of the treasure's location. And if I should perish in the coming battle…"

"Then tell me," Little Fawn begged, "in private. Not them."

"I will tell you all," Red Eagle said. "The treasure is buried beneath the *chunkey* yard—the sporting field—in the town of Musolagee."

"Musolagee?" I said. "Where's that?"

"On the Tallapoosa. Midway between Ufawlee and Kialega. Zane has already burned the buildings, destroyed the crops and driven the people to seek shelter elsewhere. It is a place he would never think to look. I pray he never does, or he and his men would be rich beyond imagining."

"You honor us with this secret," Davy said. "And we shall keep it for you."

"Thank you, my friends." Red Eagle rose fluidly to his feet. "Now I must return to Horseshoe Bend and get my men—as the letter instructed—before Jackson arrives."

"Stay awhile," Davy said, "the rabbit will be ready directly. Then we'll be off as well. I believe I've had my fill of fightin'. Me and Penn will be headin' back to Tennessee."

THE FIRST PART of Davy's plan had come off without a hitch. Once he'd heard the man sneaking up behind the brush, and seen that Little Fawn had smelled him, we'd launched into our lines. And while our playacting was poor compared to that

I'd seen on stage in Philadelphia, we must have been convincing. No sooner had we finished than Davy signaled the watcher had left us. And as we readied our horses, he pointed out the dust of a rider racing off toward the south.

As we followed, my stomach growled. Little Fawn, riding next to me, eyed me in mock pity, while Red Eagle seemed not to hear. Davy rode far ahead, close on the heels of our quarry. As there'd been no time for lunch, Samson got the hare.

We debated whether the man would rush to inform his master of the treasure, as we wished, or proceed directly to Musolagee, planning to keep the gold for himself. But after several miles, it was clear the fellow was not headed for Musolagee. Our performance had apparently accomplished its end. We now had every reason to hope this man would lead us to little William.

An hour or two later, Davy returned grinning. "He stopped to water his horse, and I was close enough to tweak his nose. It's Zane's skinny nephew, Ned. He's changed his green jacket to blue, but he smells bad as ever."

"So it is Zane, after all," Little Fawn said, something we all knew in our hearts.

As we rode, I told Little Fawn and Red Eagle of Ned's loathsome hobby—an action I would soon regret—and both were greatly repulsed.

Next time Davy returned, the day was growing late. His face was lit with more than amusement. "Boy's goin' like a cat with his tail on fire. Just passed a couple o' sentries, and got waved on. I reckon this is it." He led us away from the trail, under a canopy of live oaks, and finally to the edge of a bluff.

Securing the horses, we crawled forward and lay on our bellies, gazing into a small valley. Below, sprawled out along a narrow stream, were perhaps a hundred men and a like number of horses. Most wore simple buckskin or homespun, the typical attire of volunteers. These lolled in various stages of repose around a collection of cook fires. At the far end of camp sat a tent, and around this stood ten men in blue army uniforms.

Galloping wildly through camp, Ned leapt from his horse and stumbled toward the tent. He was nearly there when a uniformed man in an officer's hat stepped into view.

Next to me, I felt Red Eagle tense. A low growl escaped his throat.

The man in the hat was Zane.

Ned rushed forward, waving his arms and shouting. Almost immediately, Zane clamped a hand over his mouth and dragged him into the tent, barking orders to the bluecoats. As the tent flaps closed, these men formed a solid line between the tent and the rest of the company.

"Like to see old Zaney's face about now," I said.

Davy grinned. "Droolin' like a bear with a honey pot."

Red Eagle's eyes smoldered. "I have not seen William." Nor had I, but did my best not to dwell on it. Zane's letter said the baby had not been harmed, but that meant little.

One of the rough-clad men rose from his cook-fire and strode to the stream, where he proceeded to relieve himself. He was bigger than most of the volunteers, and had a meaner look. A moment later, I understood why. Unhooking a coil of leather from his belt, he snapped it out to full length, where it struck the limb of a nearby tree. As if by magic, an apple leaped from the limb and plopped directly into his hand. That length of leather was no mere *riata*, but a blacksnake bullwhip. Devouring the apple in two bites, core and all, the man scratched his massive belly.

This, then, was one of Zane's crackers—a man who had tired of whipping beasts and turned his attentions to human beings.

On seeing this foul creature, Samson bared his teeth and growled.

Davy looked to Red Eagle. "If Zane hears 'im, it'll spoil everything."

Red Eagle looked hard at the dog, who yawned and lay quiet.

Some minutes later, Ned emerged from the tent and

approached one of the bluecoats, exchanging a few words. This man turned and marched into the tent.

"A lieutenant," Davy said. "Wonder what's up."

This time, the wait was shorter. The lieutenant strode with purpose from the tent, motioning three other bluecoats to him.

"A sergeant," Davy said, "and two corporals."

As the lieutenant snapped out orders, his subordinates hurried off in three directions, speaking urgently to the men on the ground. These stared at them for a time, shaking their heads, draining their tin cups and shrugging. Finally, all but about a dozen climbed to their feet, beat the dust from their britches and went about gathering their belongings. The men still on the ground, including the big cracker who'd eaten the apple, watched lazily as their companions readied horses.

"They are leaving," Little Fawn said. "Have they taken the bait?"

"Let's hope," Davy said, watching.

Zane watched too, from the door of his tent. Strangely, he showed no sign of leaving. A half dozen bluecoats stood about also, as if all the bustle did not concern them.

When the volunteers were at last mounted, the lieutenant and his three companions rode to the head of the column. The lieutenant snapped a crisp salute to Zane, who returned it, then kicked his horse, leading the company out of camp. As they disappeared, we heard hoofs beating off toward the north.

Red Eagle shook his head. "They are not heading for Muso-lagee. That's the way to Horseshoe Bend."

The troops were barely out of sight when Zane strode forth, addressing the remaining men. Aside from a few bluecoats, all were big bruisers, and several had an odd appearance about the hands.

"Kept the crackers and gougers behind," Davy said. "And some of them others are survivors of his old militia."

After Zane's speech, of which we could hear nothing, the

crackers and gougers settled back around their fires. For the moment, at least, they were going nowhere.

Darkness came on quickly, and we kept close watch. Red Eagle's frustration grew until at last Zane's tent flaps flew back, and out pushed Ned, a blanket-wrapped bundle in his arms. After collecting a plate of food from the cook-fire, he quickly returned to the tent. But not before we had spied a baby's face protruding from the blanket.

Little William was alive.

I felt Red Eagle stiffen, and understood. To see his son in the arms of that lunatic must set his blood aboil, but for the moment there was nothing we could do.

WE SPENT A cold night huddled there on the hill, taking turns to make sure Zane—and the baby—remained in place. At last, as the sun lit the eastern sky, the men dismantled Zane's tent, packed their horses, and moved out.

"They are heading straight for Musolagee," Little Fawn said.

Musolagee had been chosen as the site of the imaginary treasure trove because it was one of the friendly towns already visited by Zane's raiders. The homes and tribal buildings had been burnt to the ground, the animals slaughtered, the crops trampled. The town was now uninhabited, so no additional Creek lives would be endangered, and Zane would have no qualms about returning.

We followed at a discreet distance, as Zane led his core group of soldiers and renegades toward the town.

"Makes sense now," Davy said. "Zane don't want Jackson to know 'bout the treasure, so he sent his real soldiers away."

"They still outnumber us at least six to one," I observed. "So how do you figure to get William away from them?"

"Glad you asked," Davy said. "Just happens I got an idea for that, an' it's a real corker." And it was. He laid the whole thing out for us, detailing each of our roles, and by the time he finished I was twice as worried as I'd been before. This new plan was by far the most outrageous he'd unleashed yet.

"Your plan," Red Eagle said, "requires more patience than I possess." He cast an eye at the company before us. "They are spread out now on the trail. If we time our attack right, we can take William and be away before they realize how few we are."

"And he could be hurt," Little Fawn said. "He may be the son of a great warrior, but he is still as fragile as a newborn duckling."

"She's right," Davy said. "This ain't the time."

Gripping his war club, Red Eagle scowled.

"Please," Little Fawn said. "He is Sopath's son as well. She would urge you to caution."

Red Eagle grunted. His shoulders relaxed. "I will wait. For Sopath. For now."

"How much farther?" I asked Little Fawn.

"Three more bends of the river," she said, and when I made an exasperated face, she added, "Not far."

She fell in behind me, and we rode in silence for a while. Then I realized the silence was too great, and spun about. She was no longer there.

Alarmed, I wheeled my mare and hurried back up the trail. I found her leading her pony quietly away.

"What do you think you're doing?"

She favored me with a wan smile. "I will return soon. You need not worry."

"I'm already worried. We agreed to follow Davy's directions, and that Red Eagle would be the one to go."

"You agreed," she said. "I did not. I can do this just as well. And you have seen how he is. We cannot ask him to let young William out of his sight."

"Please don't." I'd reached her side and curled an arm about her slim waist. "This whole plan is mad."

"It may be mad, but it is the baby's best hope." She leaned into me. Her lips brushed mine gently, then fell into place, and we shared a fierce embrace. "I love you, Penn McCoy. And I promise to return." Slipping from my arms, she sprang into the saddle, tapped the pony's sides with her heels and cantered off into the night.

I watched until she was long out of sight. I was still watching when Red Eagle appeared beside me. Even mounted upon Arrow, he moved silent as a wraith. "Where is she?"

"Gone. Gone to do your job."

Red Eagle gazed off to the north. "I would have stopped her. Still, she is a courageous woman. I am once again in her debt."

"Do you think this will work?"

"It seems unlikely. But by one means or another, I will have my son." He turned Arrow back toward the town. "Perhaps the spirits are at work here, removing Little Fawn from danger."

I stared at him. "You really believe in that spirit stuff?"

He flashed me a wink. "Of course. I too was raised Episcopalian."

LITTLE FAWN'S ESTIMATE proved correct. Three bends in the river later, we came upon fields that had once grown pumpkins and corn, and soon sighted a skull-capped pole towering above the treetops. Ahead, we heard shouted commands, and knew Zane's party had reached Musolagee. Red Eagle guided us through the woods to a patch of tall grass where we could observe Zane's men.

As we'd hoped, they appeared fully invested in the search for the treasure. Picketing their horses, they'd spread out over the athletic field, and most were already digging. Only two had shovels, but others made do with tree limbs, rifle butts and even butcher knives. One of the gougers, a man with exceptionally large hands, dug with his fingernails. Zane watched impatiently from a folding camp chair while Ned rocked on his heels a few feet away. Baby William rolled about on a blanket at Ned's feet.

Zane had a score of diggers, but as the field was some three hundred yards long and half again as wide, they had a big job ahead of them.

So far, Davy's plan had exceeded all expectations, and I

wished I felt confident of success. But the next phase seemed so preposterous I could only worry. Little Fawn had risked her life on a fool's errand, I was certain, and I regretted letting her go.

Davy found a soft patch of grass, stretched out on his back and pulled his cap down to cover his eyes. "Wake me if there's trouble," he said, and to my amazement, was soon fast asleep. Samson turned around three times, settled happily beside him and began to snore.

Red Eagle was wound so tight he seemed to vibrate. He stared doggedly at the baby laying at Ned's feet, knuckles white about the rifle butt.

I was caught somewhere in between, too tired to stare but too worried to sleep. I lay on my belly with my chin propped on a fist, worrying about Little Fawn and wondering when Zane would realize he'd been duped. I was saddened, too, by the signs of his previous visit to Musolagee. The town was laid out along the lines of the village near the Holy Ground. The high mound of earth next to the gaming field, once home to their ceremonial round house, was topped by a pile of blackened embers. Ashes swirled about the remains of the grandstands in the town square. And not a single place of residence appeared to have escaped the torch. It was unlikely this town would ever live again.

For the first hour, Zane's men dug with enthusiasm. For the second, they worked with grudging acceptance. But as the third hour waned, and broken sod covered half the field, they became surly. Curses and complaints grew louder and more frequent. At last one of the crackers threw down his wooden stake and stomped toward Zane. He was, I saw, the same man I'd seen whip the apple from a tree. All over the field, the digging stopped as heads swung to watch.

Halting six feet from Zane, the cracker laid a hand on his coiled bullwhip. "I don't dig another inch 'til I get a drink."

"Then get one."

The big man scowled. "We got no whiskey, as you well know. I aim to take a few of the boys and find some."

Zane regarded him calmly. "You realize the next turn of the spade could make you rich as a king?" He swung his head to include the others. "Make you all rich as kings?"

"That's as may be," the cracker said, "but first I get my drink."

Zane shrugged. "And nothing I say can dissuade you?"

The man snarled. "We're goin'." He looked away, nodding to three other crackers, who grinned and dropped their makeshift shovels. And as his head was turned, Zane drew a pistol and shot him in the belly.

The cracker seemed more surprised than pained to see his shirt turning red. "Shit," he said, clutching his stomach, and fell heavily onto his side, where he lay wheezing in the dirt.

Zane calmly set about reloading his pistol. "Rich," he said, "beyond your wildest imaginings. Need I remind you again?"

Those who'd dropped their tools snatched them up, and work resumed. But the mood on the field had changed. In the eyes of the crackers and gougers, there now lurked a sullen hatred.

Red Eagle gave a soft grunt. "If these men turn on Zane, it could be our moment." He stretched out a leg and nudged Davy, who sprang instantly awake. "We must be ready for it."

Davy took in the situation at a glance, and saw me gazing at the northern sky. The sun had dipped behind the western hills, and dusk was fast approaching. "Little Fawn?"

"I worry for her."

"She's as capable as any female I ever seen," Davy said. "Any man, too, far as that goes. She won't be lettin' us down. But it's time I got myself into place. For whatever happens." He scratched Samson under the chin. "Can't take you along, I'm afraid."

Red Eagle patted the earth. "Here." And Samson flopped beside him.

Davy extended a hand. "Best o' luck to you both. If it happens I don't make it, well, I'm powerful proud to have called you friends."

"You are a thief, Crockett," Red Eagle said. "You have stolen my words."

We all shook hands.

"We're all going to make it," I said, exuding a confidence I did not feel. "But I feel the same."

With a tight grin, Davy gripped his rifle and crawled off through the tall grass with no more sound than a chipmunk.

"So," Red Eagle said. "You believe we will succeed."

"Have you forgotten? We Episcopalians believe in miracles."

JUST BEFORE NIGHTFALL, Zane ordered his soldiers to stop digging and build fires so the work could continue. When the fires were going the blue-coated soldiers spaced themselves around the edge of the field, muskets ready to discourage slackers.

Predictably, the effect was quite the opposite. Under the gaze of Zane's soldiers, the crackers and gougers became even more resentful. The sound of the digging slowed, taking on a half-hearted quality. Firelight gleamed from the eyes of the diggers, and it became apparent they were doing more glaring than working.

I leaned toward Red Eagle. "Can you see Davy?"

He pointed. "A few strides behind Zane. In the scrub grass." I squinted. The grass there looked too short to conceal a field mouse.

"You certain?"

Red Eagle frowned. A foolish question.

Davy's plan, such as it was, was to get close to the baby and wait. When the time came he would dart in, snatch up young William and be off into the night. That time would come when Little Fawn returned to do her part. If she returned. And if the situation here remained calm. Davy had not reckoned on a falling out between Zane and his men.

As if in answer to my fears, someone said, "This is bullshit. There's nothing here."

"We've been had," said another voice. "Question is, is somebody playin' Zane, or is he playin' us?"

Zane leaned forward in his chair. "Enough talk. I thought you wanted to be rich."

"We won't get rich diggin' for what ain't there."

"You will dig," Zane said, his voice rising, "or you will be shot." And for the first time, baby William began to cry.

Growling, Red Eagle rose to one knee. I grabbed him arm to prevent him standing.

He gave me a look that chilled me to my toes.

One of the crackers said, "Can't shoot us all. Half at most, if you're damned lucky. By then we'll be rippin' you apart." The man had a point. By my count, there were seven crackers and five gougers.

Zane rose to his feet. "Perhaps I've been too eager. We've made good progress today. We should quit for the night and get a fresh start tomorrow."

The men exchanged looks. Several cursed or growled.

"Better yet," said the big cracker, "we plant you and these costumed monkeys in the ground tonight, and tomorrow we do as we please."

Zane drew a pistol from his belt. "Not you. You'll be dead."

Baby William let out another wail.

I felt Red Eagle's hackles rise. "We must act now. You and I shoot the nearest soldiers, Davy will grab William, and we leave Zane to his beasts."

I sympathized with him. Things were coming to a boil, and his son was caught in the middle. Still, I hesitated. Assuming the crackers and gougers turned on Zane, such a plan might succeed. But they could just as easily come after us, and we were badly outnumbered. Besides, the notion of killing soldiers from ambush, even such sorry soldiers as these, did not sit right. Faced with this new proposal, I discovered a fondness for Davy's original plan.

"Maybe Zane or the others will back down. We should give Little Fawn more time."

"She is overdue." Red Eagle raised his rifle, sighting on the closest bluecoat. "I will rescue my son, with or without your help."

Seeing no way out, I reached for my own rifle.

Someone on the field said, "Where'd that damned dog come from?"

Dog? I patted the ground near Red Eagle. The crushed grass was still warm.

I looked up, following the stares of Zane's men. There, sniffing and pawing at the scrub grass where Davy lay hidden, was Samson.

"Dog?" Zane himself turned, and even from this distance, I saw his features stiffen. Snatching young William up from the ground, he buried his gun barrel in the boy's soft flesh. "Crockett!" he barked above the baby's squall. "Show yourself or the brat dies!"

CHAPTER 27

"Kill me if you wish."

ZANE COCKED HIS pistol. "Now, Crockett. I'm not bluffing."

A coonskin-capped head rose from the scrub grass. "Maybe you are," Davy said, "and maybe you ain't. But I'm a-comin'." He climbed slowly to his feet, Samson dancing happily at his side.

"You will not require your weapons," Zane snapped. "Drop them were you stand."

Red Eagle, still kneeling next to me in the tall grass, aimed his rifle at Zane.

"Don't!" I whispered. "The fall could kill William."

Red Eagle's jaw quivered. His rifle drooped. I had no words to comfort him.

"And Crockett's little shadow," Zane said, "McCoy. I want to see you too."

Red Eagle turned his sad eyes upon me, and I knew I had no choice. I dropped my rifle, knife and tomahawk, scuttled a few yards from Red Eagle, and stood. "I'm here." The two nearest soldiers swung their muskets, motioning me onto the field.

Smirking, Zane pointed to one of his bluecoats. "Shoot that damned dog."

The man drew his pistol and fired, but as the powder flashed, Samson bolted off toward the woods. The crash of the gun only lent speed to his heels.

Zane turned his scowl on Davy, who now stood unarmed before him. "This treasure. That was your invention?"

Davy grinned. "What treasure?"

Zane threw a pointed glance at his men, as if to say, *You see?* "What of that sharp-tongued Indian bitch? Is she here as well?"

"No," Davy said, and his voice carried the ring of truth.

Zane let it pass. "And where is Red Eagle?"

"Last I heard, leadin' his band away from Horseshoe Bend. But I'm a might confused about that letter you sent. Why'd you warn him of Jackson's approach?"

Zane regarded him a long while. "My motives are my own. And as I'm holding the gun, I'll ask the questions. Just what did you expect to accomplish here?"

Davy shrugged. "Hungry wolves always turn on one another. Once you knowed there warn't no gold, we calculated you'd start scrappin' amongst yourselves, givin' us a chance to make off with the baby."

Zane seemed to accept that. "In that case, you should enjoy the irony of the situation."

"Irony?"

"Indeed. For it is you and McCoy who will mend our strained relations." Zane handed the baby to Ned, who quickly returned him to the blanket at his feet. Zane turned to address his diggers. "Here, my friends, are the authors of our wild goose chase! Accept them with my compliments. Do with them what you will."

Bestial growls rumbled over the field. The crackers unlimbered their whips. The gougers flexed their hands, flashed their fingernails. All shambled forward.

"We heard you men was fighters," Davy said, "not cowards! You afeared to face us one on one?"

This brought howls of protest. "No man calls me coward!" one cracker roared. "I'll kill you both myself!" He started forward, tugging at his whip, but a gouger blocked his path.

"Hold on! Why should you have all the fun?" Others echoed this sentiment.

The two jutted jaws at each other, and it appeared they would come to blows.

Another cracker bulled between them. "You can kill each other anytime. I'm more interested in seein' the blood of those two pisscutters." He jerked his head at us, leaving no doubt which pisscutters he meant.

"Draw straws!" another man shouted. "It's the only way." This provoked more cursing and grumbling, but the plan was eventually agreed upon. Ned was delegated to prepare the straws, after which each man made his selection.

The man with the longest straw was a tall, raw-boned cracker with enormous shoulders. He had greasy black hair, a handlebar mustache, and eyes too wide for his face. "The big-nosed one is mine," he growled. "The one who called us cowards."

Davy said softly, "Big-nosed? Is my nose that all-fired big?" I pretended not to hear. This was no time to insult him.

A gouger held the next longest straw. "Big Nose will die easy," he growled, "compared to his companion." This man was bullet-headed and bald, with big yellow teeth and a beard like a briar-patch.

Zane's other villains quickly got into the spirit of things, peppering us with threats and catcalls. I cast a glance toward Red Eagle's position, and thought I saw the gleam of his eyes. I had little hope he could save us, but any hope was better than none.

Our two opponents advanced, and each of us got a push from behind.

Seen from a distance, and amid the others' company, my gouger had not seemed an exceptionally large man. It was only now, in relation to normal-sized humans like Davy and me, that I realized how big he was.

Once, as a boy, I'd paid a penny to see a caged gorilla—brought all the way from Africa, it was said—and found him suitably terrifying. But that gorilla seemed tame as a lapdog compared to the monster before me.

The gouger's hands hung low at his sides, writhing and

squirming into positions that seemed impossible—and vaguely obscene. His hands and fingers were unnaturally large, but the curved fingernails, jagged and long as knife blades, gave them an almost supernatural appearance.

In the light of the fires, those fingernails gleamed like lengths of yellowed bone. I recalled the eyeless corpse of Sopath's man Harjo and felt a loosening in my bowels. I glanced at my own nails, well-suited for scratching my neck or picking nits from my hair, but of little use as weapons.

Davy, I assumed, felt similar shortcomings. The cracker striding toward him had the chest and shoulders of an ox, and the coil of leather in his hand was unlike any whip I'd ever seen. The stock was thick as a man's arm, and the way he held it told me it was likely weighted with lead shot. The lash end was braided and knotted, and as the braids swung free, something caused them to sparkle in the firelight.

"So," the gouger said, "you think to run from me. Who is the coward now?" I blinked, uncomprehending, then realized I had backed up a good ten feet. My body, apparently, was thinking more clearly than my mind. A glance behind told me I could go no further. Zane's bluecoats had taken positions at our end of the field to prevent us running. Still, the thought was tempting. I'd rather take my chances with a musket than face the gouger's deadly nails. But escape was pointless. Zane still had young William in his power, and could demand my return at any time. I had no choice but to stand and fight.

A hopeful glance toward Red Eagle's clump of grass brought me no joy. I saw no trace of him now.

Davy had not moved. Now, I thought—and hated myself for it—would be fine time for the devil to pay a call. But even as the cracker unfurled his whip, Davy just waited, legs spread and knees bent, arms loose at his sides. He looked impossibly calm for a man about to die.

Someone shouted, "Skin him alive, Bo! Just peel the hide and leave the meat for us."

The man called Bo flicked his wrist, and the whip danced in the air like a striking snake. A great looping curve traveled its length until the lash snapped loud as a rifle shot. He had not meant to strike Davy, but merely unnerve him. In that, at least, Bo appeared to have failed.

"Keep watching your friend," the gouger told me. "It'll spare you the sight of your own death."

The man was now a mere ten yards away. I stared at him, seeking some course of action. What would Davy do? That reasoning had helped me with Big Frog, when I'd distracted him by talking. But this fellow enjoyed the sound of his own voice, and was unlikely to be diverted.

If I'd learned anything from Davy, it was to do the unexpected. This gouger expected me to run, as I had unwittingly done already. What he would least expect would be an attack. So, without reflecting on the madness of this strategy, I set my teeth, lowered my head and galloped straight at him.

The gouger, still in the process of terrifying me with his claws, was so astonished he barely had time to react. As it was, I thrust his forearms aside, and with all of my hundred and eighty pounds behind it, drove my skull into his chest. Ribs snapped and gave way, a great whoosh of air burst from his mouth, and I felt him falling back. I pushed away, pulling my head free as he crashed to the earth, his eyes still wide in surprise.

Off to my right, the whip cracked again, and I risked a look. Davy was diving sideways, the braided lash raking the sleeve of his jacket. He hit the ground, rolled, and bounced to his feet, but his jacket was in shreds, the arm beneath streaked with blood. The sparkles in the lash were bits of sharpened steel. For the first time in our acquaintance, Davy looked truly worried.

I doubtless looked the same. Despite his broken ribs, the gouger had regained his feet. And while he was already ferocious, a new element had been added—raw fury. I dashed around him, scooping up someone's makeshift shovel. The length of blackened timber was only four feet long, but it had a rough point, and made a better weapon than my fingernails. I circled the gouger, gripping the stake like a cricket bat and trying to look confident. He merely sneered, plodding toward me. I waited for him to make his move.

He feinted a lunge to my right, then charged left, and I swung with all my might. And hit naught but air, because the attack on my left had been a feint as well. His claws ripped through my shirt, burning like blades as they dug a trough across my stomach. I dodged away, moving instinctively toward Davy. Only together, some instinct told me, did we stand a chance against these modern-day Goliaths.

Davy had removed his jacket and gripped it by the collar, his left arm now dark with blood. Bo's whip curled above his head like a huge and terrible serpent, and Davy began whirling the jacket as if trying to form a shield. The whip lashed out, and I expected Davy to lose half his skin. But the whirling jacket wrapped itself around his arm, and just as the whip arrived, he reached up and closed a buckskin-wrapped hand around the lash end. Holding fast, he ducked and allowed the whip to curl around his arm. Then, before Bo could react, Davy leaned forward and yanked his end of the whip. Bo staggered slightly, surprised but not witless, and set his feet in the overturned sod. If Davy had hoped to yank the whip free, he had failed, and it was now a tug of war—a war Davy was sure to lose.

With the gouger's curses burning my ears, I gripped my stake like a lance and raced straight for Bo. Zane's men shouted warnings, and I feared at any moment he would turn and meet my charge. But his war with Davy consumed him, and I was nearly upon him before he saw me, his mouth forming a toothless O within the beard. He dodged, avoiding a thrust in the belly, but my lance pierced the blubber hanging over the side of his belt, burrowing deep before breaking through the other side. Screaming with rage and pain, Bo dropped the whip and swung his huge arms to crush me. But having skewered him, I let go of the stake and darted out of reach.

Glancing back, I saw the gouger in hot pursuit. Without my

stake, I was again defenseless, and I circled behind the raging Bo, putting him between us. The gouger wheeled, trying to come at me from the other side, but I darted back the way I'd come. The one advantage I had was speed, and as long as I kept Bo between us, the human gorilla could not reach me.

Davy, meanwhile, was reeling in the whip. Did he have a plan? Unable to catch his eye, I kept changing direction, tempting the gouger to follow. My one hope was that he would eventually tire, but thus far his fury had only lent him strength.

At last Davy looked up. Gripping the whip by its great stock, he nodded at me, rolled his head to the right and jerked it left. Near as I could tell, he wanted me to complete my loop around Bo and race across the field between Bo and himself. My lungs burned and my legs ached, nearly spent. But having no better plan, I poured all my energy into that mad dash.

I pumped my legs for all their worth, but the gouger was right behind me, his claws flailing at my shirttails. If Davy didn't act soon I'd be dead.

The gouger screamed. Nails raked my back and I staggered, fearing this was the end. I steeled myself for another slash, then heard a great *crack*. The gouger's next scream was tinged with shock.

I flung a glance at Davy. With the whipstock raised, he was tugging back as if trying to land a fish. And he was grinning, a sign he was still himself.

I spun to find the gouger helpless, wrists lashed together with the end of Bo's whip. I ran at him, mindful of what he and his friends had done to the Creeks, and what he'd hoped to do to me.

"Time you tried your own medicine," I growled. I grasped his head with both hands and dug my thumbnails into his eyes until he bawled like a castrated bull.

The howls of our audience were terrible to hear, but not as terrible as Bo's. He had pulled the stake from his side, and now rushed screaming at Davy. Davy still held the whipstock, but the lash end was tangled around the gouger, and useless to him. He stood rock still, awaiting the enraged cracker.

Bo swung the stake like a broadsword, beginning an arc that would slice Davy's head from his shoulders. Still, Davy did not move. The blackened timber, now gory with Bo's blood, was almost at Davy's neck when he raised the heavy whipstock. The stake hit the stock with a tremendous crack, filling the air with splinters. Then Davy stepped back, swinging the stock like a mace, and smacked it against the side of Bo's skull. The crack of bone was louder than any whip snap, and Bo flopped dead to the ground.

In the sudden silence, I heard William crying, and saw Ned bent over, prodding the baby with his scalping knife.

Then crackers and gougers began to roar their disapproval of the fight, and I heard the baby no more. But with all eyes on Davy and Bo, I looked again for Red Eagle, and this time saw him. He rose like a specter from the grass directly behind Ned. Seeming all of nine feet tall, he wrapped steely fingers around the young man's neck. Without apparent effort, he raised Ned off his feet, shook him until his head flopped at an odd angle, and flung him aside like a rag doll. Then he bent and swept William into his arms.

It all happened in the flash of an eye, and before Zane took notice, Red Eagle had drawn a pistol. He leveled the weapon at Zane, a scant few feet away.

A hush fell over the field, as all turned to eye this new drama.

Red Eagle's voice broke the silence. "I should kill you now, for you have earned it ten times over. But I offer a bargain. Permit me and my friends to leave, and you may live another day. That is the most I can promise."

Davy and I took this opportunity to move to Red Eagle's side.

Zane's renegades hissed and swore.

As for Zane himself, his expression was unreadable. This was a man who hated to show weakness, but Red Eagle had found his weak spot—his own precious hide. At heart, most such men are cowards, and I expected him to break down, to cringe and plead for his life.

Instead, he *smiled.* "Really, my friend, there's no need for such dramatics. Has it not yet occurred to you that you and I are on the same side? Everything I have done, I have done to aid you in your battle against the whites."

I glanced to either side. Red Eagle's face—no doubt like my own—was slack with astonishment. That Zane would believe us so gullible was beyond belief. Davy, however, wore a grim grin, nodding as if this confirmed his thinking.

"True, I forced you to join the Red Sticks, but it was for the good of your people. They needed a wise and crafty leader. It was for that same reason—to commit you to your cause—that I provoked you into attacking Fort Mims. And I burned the friendly villages solely to drive them to your side. In short, I have done my utmost to see that you remain at large, playing havoc with Jackson and his fellow generals."

Red Eagle's brow was furrowed, his nostrils distended. He looked about to explode.

"And why," Davy asked calmly, "would you do all that?"

Zane's smile grew wider. "Because, my friends, I have been working for the British."

Red Eagle's mouth fell open, and I fear mine did the same.

"You are a poor liar," Red Eagle managed to reply, but his eyes were thoughtful.

"As Crockett has no doubt guessed, that letter I sent to Toho-peka was intended to lure you out of that deathtrap. I knew Jackson's plans for the place, and wanted you alive to bedevil him in the future. The longer your uprising lasts, the more the American leaders are distracted from the real threat. While their armies beat the woods for wild Indians, the British are poised to invade on three fronts. Thanks to my efforts, a British victory is all but assured. When they take control I shall be handsomely rewarded." He studied our faces. "Doubt me if you wish, but I have papers to prove what I say."

"So now that you're working for Old Hickory-face," Davy said, "you're playing him for a fool as well."

Zane dipped his head as if accepting a compliment. "An unforeseen bonus. But one, you must admit, that plays to the Red Sticks' advantage. So you see," he said, spreading his hands, "it is my sincere wish that Red Eagle remain among the living."

He turned his head, his gaze seeming to touch every man on the field, and there was something in his face I could not read. And then, all at once, I could. He was amused.

"You've heard this savage's demands," he told his men, "and you have heard my response. We are now all on the same side, and shall permit them to leave. I order you to stand down!"

For a moment, the crackers and gougers stood in stunned silence. Then one snorted, another sniggered, and soon the night was loud with uproarious laughter. The renegades moved forward in a mass, whips cracking, fingernails flashing, to form a circle around us.

I turned to Davy, forcing a grin. "Good thing we already said our goodbyes."

"See you in the Hereafter," Davy said. "If we travel in the same direction."

I felt infinitely sad. I'd accepted the fact we would perish, but thought Red Eagle would live to avenge us. Now he, too, was caught in Zane's web.

Red Eagle had not lowered his pistol.

"Kill me if you wish," Zane told him, "but as you see, I no longer control these beasts. Whatever happens to me, I am afraid you three—and the baby—are fated to die."

"I make no promises."

"**I** THINK NOT," DAVY said brightly.

"And why is that?" Zane asked.

"Like my ol' granpaw used to say. "Every turkey has his Thanksgivin'.'"

Zane bristled. "What the hell is that supposed to mean?"

"Don't you feel the earth shakin'?"

Zane eyed him queerly, while the crackers and gougers slowed their approach, staring at the ground. I thought I felt a rumble beneath my feet. But did the earth truly tremble, or was Davy working some magic on us?

"I feel it," one of the crackers said, peering into the darkness. "And I hear somethin' too."

As did I. The sound grew steadily louder, the trembling more intense.

"What the hell is it?" Zane demanded.

"Horses!" someone shouted. "Comin' fast!" The rumbling had resolved into hoof beats, and seemed nearly upon us. Zane spun about as a new and more terrible sound rose above the thunder. It began as a single war cry—a gut-wrenching scream of bloodlust and rage. But with every heartbeat the cry was joined by another, and still another, until it seemed Hell had opened and unleashed all its devils upon the earth.

"Injuns!" a cracker shouted.

Arrows hissed out of the night. Two men fell. And with no

further delay, Zane's thugs lifted their heels and fled for the woods.

The first rank of riders stormed onto the field, longhaired warriors waving spears and tomahawks and wailing their war cries. I peered hard at each flashing form, and my heart leapt as I spotted a familiar figure—shapely, slim, and clad in a shift of buckskin. Little Fawn.

I started toward her, longing to sweep her from the horse and crush her in my arms, but she merely smiled before raising a war club and plunging after the gang of killers.

I had lost track of Zane, but now spotted him sprinting off toward the remains of the town. Red Eagle saw him, too, and fired his pistol, but Zane did not go down.

Sopath burst into sight, yanked her reins and dropped to the earth, running toward Red Eagle and William. She snatched up her son, hugging him and her husband at the same time.

Davy appeared beside me. "Where's Zane?"

I pointed into the darkness where he had gone. I saw nothing of him now, but Davy nodded as if he did, and took off running.

Red Eagle, meanwhile, had leapt astride Sopath's horse and pounded in the same direction.

Davy had fallen into a long-legged lope. I followed, but try as I might, I could not keep up, and swore under my breath as he steadily widened the distance.

From back in the woods, the shrill war cries continued, punctuated by full-throated screams from the crackers and gougers. Those evil men, who had long reveled in causing pain, were at last tasting it themselves.

As I left the fires behind, the only light came from the sky. I glanced up at the moon, noting that it displayed only half an eye, as if fearing to witness all that transpired here.

Red Eagle quickly passed Davy, and his war cry sent shivers through my bones. I ran on, pumping my legs for all their worth, and was rewarded by seeing Red Eagle leap from his horse.

More screams erupted from the woods.

"Your men are paying dearly for their sins," Red Eagle roared at Zane, "and theirs are nothing compared to yours!"

Then came a shot, and Red Eagle fell to one knee, clutching his leg.

Zane appeared from the darkness, cast aside a smoking pistol and snatched up the reins of the horse. Red Eagle struggled to his feet, but Zane was already settling onto the saddle blanket. The fiend was going to escape us again.

And then he wasn't.

A Tennessee thunderbolt hurtled out of the night, wrenched him from the horse, and flung him savagely to the earth.

Hoofbeats came to a stop behind me, and I turned to gaze at Little Fawn, my heart full of joy. But she looked beyond me, face rigid with dread. "Look. Davy!"

I spun to see Davy jerk Zane from the ground, stand him up and lay him out with a smash to the face. "That's for forcing Red Eagle to war against his will." His voice was queer, almost inhuman, and I shared Little Fawn's alarm.

Zane wobbled to his feet, raised his fists, and took a tremendous uppercut to the belly. "That's for Fort Mims," Davy rasped. "For Penn's folks and Little Fawn's family." As Zane staggered, Davy brought a roundhouse right whistling in to smash against his ear. "That's for Lacy, Nathan and Colonel Truitt." Davy's face was dark, his features contorted, and it seemed his devil was rising—if not already in control.

Zane rose to one knee, and as he pushed off the ground, something glinted in his hand. He lunged at Davy's chest, now wielding a knife. Davy arched his back, watching the blade flash harmlessly by, and hammered both fists on the back of Zane's neck. "That's for Harjo, Ochee and baby William." Davy sounded more animal than man. His face was tight, his eyes ablaze, and my fears were confirmed. His devil had not been defeated, it had merely lain dormant, biding its time. But saddened as I was, another part of me cheered him on. It was somehow fitting that Davy's devil destroy the demon Zane.

Zane's face was in the dirt. But he still held the knife, and while there was life in him, there was hate. He surged up, the blade flashing for Davy's throat. But Davy caught his wrist, squeezing so tight I heard bones snap. Zane cried out. He, too, now seemed more beast than man. As Davy took the knife, Zane's other hand snaked out, his nails seeking Davy's eyes.

Swatting the hand away, Davy's right arm whirled back. Moonlight glittered on the blade as it windmilled nearly to the ground and arced up toward Zane's chest. The force of the blow lifted Zane a yard into the air, arms falling limp as he tumbled backwards, striking the earth with a bone-crunching smack.

Davy stood hunched over, teeth bared, steam pouring from his nostrils, and for a moment I feared he would leap upon the body and sink his teeth into the man's flesh.

A horse snorted, practically in my ear, and I realized we were ringed by mounted warriors. They carried spears, war clubs and tomahawks, and each weapon glistened with fresh blood. A few also carried torches. They had finished with the crackers and gougers and come to witness this final act of the battle.

I could not help staring, for as ferocious as they appeared, nearly all were women—the wives, sisters and daughters of the men fighting at Horseshoe Bend. I'd expected this, of course, but supposed they would be somewhat less terrifying than their men. I was wrong. Davy's mad plan, to summon them from their hidden camp, had succeeded beyond all imagining.

Davy had never intended the women to fight, but merely to surround Zane's men and frighten them into surrender. But fight they had. And it was their courage—and that of Little Fawn— that had saved our lives.

I moved cautiously toward Davy, and felt Little Fawn beside me. I feared he was beyond understanding, for his breath was ragged, his face wolfish and spattered with Zane's blood. As I leaned closer, his eyes blazed. His hands rose from his sides, claw-like, as if he meant to throttle me. Moonlight gleamed from the silver ring on his left hand and I focused on it.

"That ring," I said. "That wedding band! It binds you to Polly, and binds you to life. Think of Polly, Davy, and beat that devil down!"

His fingers twitched, inches from my throat. He clenched his teeth, shook his head.

"Fight it!" I shouted. "Fight it for Polly!"

I felt the eyes of the Creek women upon us, and wondered what they must think of this.

"Davy," Little Fawn said softly, "Polly needs you. Your family needs you." She, too, touched his wedding ring. "Let this be your talisman. Your will is as strong as any I have encountered. That evil spirit is yours to control."

Whether it was my pleading or Little Fawn's I cannot say, but his features gradually softened. He blinked at us as if waking from a dream, and broke into a broad grin. "Sorry to hog all the fun, but Mr. Zane was disinclined to wait for you."

I squeezed Little Fawn's hand. "By God, Davy, we thought that devil'd taken you for good."

"As did I," he said, "but thanks to you, I think I got me a cure." He looked at his hand and caressed the ring with his thumb. "Polly. Polly and the young'uns."

He was still grinning when we heard a groan, then another, and turned to stare at Zane.

"This is sorcery." Sopath said, her voice flat. "The man must be a witch."

Davy's face darkened, but he remained still, as Lacy Truitt slipped from her pony to investigate. Reaching Zane's side, she smashed a booted toe into his ribs. This provoked a louder groan, and there could be no doubt. Somehow, impossibly, the fiend still lived.

Stooping, Lacy tore open Zane's jacket, popping the buttons, and thrust a hand inside. She brought out a thick leather wallet. Flipping it open, she gave it a cursory look. "Papers," she said. "Probably letters."

"Show 'em to Penn," Davy said, pointing, and she tossed the wallet to me.

I caught it gingerly, as if it might bite. The thing was thick as a Prayer Book, and one side bore a deep tear where the knife had struck.

One of the riders handed Lacy a torch, and she held it while I examined the contents.

I carefully extracted the letters, finding them folded and difficult to separate. They too had been pierced with the blade, and to an astonishing depth. Only the last two pages were uncut, and they bore deep indents. It was by this slim margin that Zane survived.

The first letter, addressed to Zane, regarded military objectives and was signed with a flourish by a Lieutenant Colonel of the British army. The others were more of the same. Inquiries as to progress, promises of payment, arrangements for delivery of weapons and powder. It was all there.

"It seems he was telling the truth," I said, "at least about working for the British."

"And about playing Old Hickory-face for a fool," Davy said thoughtfully.

Sopath had been kneeling next to Red Eagle, rocking her son in her arms. She now stood, her face pasty in the moonlight, and handed baby William to her husband. Without a word, she scanned the earth between Davy and Zane, and scooped up the fallen knife. Gripping it in her fist, she stalked toward Zane.

"Wait!" Davy said. "We should ponder this some."

Sopath's head swung to face him, mouth grim, eyes cold. "I have waited long enough."

Davy stepped toward her. "Please. Give me the knife." Instantly, a dozen women leapt from their horses, and Davy faced a ring of spears.

"Whoa!" He backed away, palms forward. "Easy, ladies. I ain't sayin' this varmint shouldn't die. I'm just sayin' we should think on it. It's just possible that, at least for the time bein', he's more useful to us alive."

The women scowled, gripping their weapons more tightly, and looked to Sopath.

She glowered down at Zane, the blade quivering in her hand. "You have been a great friend to us, Davy Crockett, and we will hear you out. But I make no promises."

CHAPTER 29

"Fate will find a way."

WE HEARD THE cannons a mile away. One had a sharp bang, while the other was more of a pop, and Davy identified them as six and three-pounders. With each blast, Red Eagle's expression grew more grim.

Following the rescue of young William, we'd ridden most of the night. Red Eagle felt responsible for the warriors he'd brought to Horseshoe Bend, and was determined to provide them what leadership he could. His greatest fear was that we would be too late, the battle over, and his friends dead before we arrived.

My greatest fear was that we'd arrive in time, and Red Eagle would plunge into the fighting, sacrificing himself on the altar of honor. Little Fawn, after much cajoling, had agreed to stay with the women, and keep Samson with her.

The cannon fire meant the battle was still going. Worse, in Davy's estimation, it meant the real fighting had yet to begin. The field pieces were used to soften the enemy's defenses, and the enemies themselves, prior to sending in the infantry.

It was an hour short of noon when we topped a final rise and gazed down at the besieged town. On our earlier visit, I'd been overwhelmed by the massive wooden barricade. Now, approaching from the opposite side of the peninsula, I was struck with the tremendous size of the battleground. The town of Tohopeka, on the outer end of the peninsula, was the size of a small city, but still occupied only a fraction of the landmass. The peninsula itself looked to cover at least a hundred acres, comprised mostly of brush and trees. Its high banks towered over the river, forming cliffs, and a finger of wooded high ground ran down the center from the town to the barricade, far in the distance. As a battle-field, the place had definite borders, but within those borders was a tangled and varied landscape that would make hand-to-hand fighting a nightmare.

The Indians' plan had merit. It was a strong defensive posi-tion, and they'd prepared canoes at various spots, so if things went badly at the wall they could retreat across the river. What they hadn't reckoned on was the enormous size of Jackson's army. His force outnumbered the Red Sticks at least three to one. With such an advantage, he could assault the barricade and have plenty of troops left over to surround the peninsula, cutting off any chance of escape.

Immediately below us, and fanned out to our left, several hundred Indians covered the outer bank of the horseshoe-shaped bend in the river.

"Cherokees," Red Eagle said, and spat on the ground. "They curry favor with Jackson in hopes of stealing Muscogee land. With them are a few Creeks under the so-called 'friendly,' William McIntosh."

"There's a passel of Cap'n Russell's rangers down there as well," Davy said.

Straining my eyes, I saw activity around the entire bend of the river. Bare-skinned men lay on the banks, others patrolled the wood, while still more tended cook-fires behind the lines.

On higher ground far to our right, several hundred frontiers-men milled about on horses, impatient for the action to begin.

"The Mounted Volunteers," Davy said, pointing at his old unit. "And there's ol' General Coffee himself." He pointed at a mounted figure in a fancy blue uniform, though how he recog-nized Coffee at this distance was a wonder. "They're either hopin' to prevent the Indians' escape, or Jackson fears reinforcements from somewheres else."

Directly below, on our side of the river, one Cherokee hopped onto a tree stump, flapped his arms and crowed like a rooster. Nearby, a group of warriors held a heated discussion. When it ended, three of them strode to the riverbank, where they promptly waded in and swam toward the center of the stream. The current did not appear terribly strong, but the river was wide, at least fifty yards across, and they reached out with long, powerful strokes. They were nearly halfway across when muskets spoke from the opposite shore, and puffs of smoke revealed the Red Stick defenders. The swimmers were undeterred, though one faltered before struggling on, and I had to admire their courage. Reaching the far bank, the first two crawled onto the shore, then dragged their wounded comrade up behind them.

"A brave feat," Red Eagle said, "for the Cherokee. For Creeks, it would have been child's play."

The three Cherokees were on their knees now, peering about. Though the Red Sticks kept up a steady fire, two of the Cherokees simply lowered their heads and ran for the nearest canoes. Dragging them quickly into the river, the two stroked back toward their friends, towing their prizes. The wounded man remained on the bank.

Red Eagle hung his head. "That is one gambit I had not foreseen."

"What?" I said. "The Cherokees stealing canoes?"

"They have discovered the flaw in our defense. Zane was right. This place is a death trap."

We were silent a moment.

"About Zane," I said. "Do you think we did the right thing?"

Red Eagle merely snorted.

"We'll know that," Davy said flatly, "when we see what fruit it bears."

Reaching our side of the river, the two swimmers were hailed as heroes. Then more Cherokees piled into the canoe for a return trip. All along the bank, Indians and Tennesseans jumped into the water and stroked enthusiastically toward the far shore.

More Red Sticks joined the shooting from the opposite cliffs, and more attackers were hit, but most reached their destination, found canoes, and started their return. I began to take Red Eagle's meaning. Each stolen canoe would bring more men to the peninsula, until the Red Sticks' escape plan was ruined, and they found enemies in their rear.

I turned to Davy. "There must be something we can do. Can't we shoot a few?"

Davy's grin was weak. "We could. But there's about half a thousand of them. I didn't bring that much powder. And Coffee's volunteers might take unkindly to it."

He was right, of course. We'd be lucky to get a dozen before the whole force came down on us.

Red Eagle said, "I'm going in."

I felt a touch of dread. "In where?"

Davy laid a hand on Red Eagle's shoulder. "Ain't nothin' there for you but death."

Grim-faced, Red Eagle started down the slope.

"Wait!" Davy hurried after. "What's your plan?"

"I will find what friends I can, and I will lead them from that place."

"How? And how in tarnation will you get in?"

"It is my fate," Red Eagle said stubbornly. "Fate will find a way." And off he went.

Davy looked at me. "Ever figure you'd wind up bein' an instrument of Fate?"

I just stared at him.

"Me neither," he said. "But it seems we been elected."

FROM THE RIVERBANK, the peninsula looked even more imposing. The cliffs rising above the far shore provided an extra line of defense, and gave the Red Sticks a fine perch to fire down upon enemies crossing the river.

We lay in a tangle of brush with a gang of Cherokees to our left and a squad of Russell's scouts on our right. We were close enough to smell fish frying, and my stomach gnawed at me. Our horses were tied in a clump of trees half a mile behind the bend, and with them was a sack of dried meat Little Fawn's friends had given us.

I tried not to think about Little Fawn. She was safe as could be in the company of the other women, but I longed to be at her side.

We'd discussed our options, and they were few. Davy could definitely swim across, and I stood a good chance, but Red Eagle was nursing a bad leg. Davy could fetch a canoe and bring it back, but that would hardly escape attention, and there were hundreds of men eager to cross. We could try piling into a canoe with other fighters, but Red Eagle would surely be recognized.

Davy had one other plan, and while no one liked it, it seemed our only chance. We'd chosen this spot because the groups flanking us were busily ferrying men across. As soon as canoes emptied on the far bank, a man would paddle back for more passengers. One such canoe was now returning to the Tennessee rangers, and Davy nodded to us, indicating this would be the one.

As the canoe scraped the bank thirty paces downriver, I handed Red Eagle my hat, which he jammed down to hide his features. We slid silently into the chilly water, careful to keep our rifles and powder above our heads. The rangers were in high spirits as they clambered aboard the canoe, and failed to notice us in the water. Before they'd gone more than a few yards, Red Eagle and I grasped the near side. Davy was already clinging to the other.

Almost immediately, a bearded face peered down at us. "Here now. What's this?"

I forced a smile. "Just hitching a ride," I said. "We want in on the fun."

The man grunted, not unfriendly, but narrowed his eyes at Red Eagle, whose braids were showing. "And you brung a Injun with you?"

"A friendly," I assured him. "And my cousin to boot. My uncle always had a weakness for squaws." The bearded man enjoyed this, and shared it loudly with his friends as we completed the crossing.

The scouts romped out of the canoe and were climbing the bluff before we emerged dripping from the river. One paddler, who had a battered guitar slung over his back, did a double take. "Davy? Davy Crockett, that you?"

Shaking water from his buckskins, Davy exclaimed, "Georgie Russell! Ain't seen you in a coon's age."

"Sakes alive, Davy. I heard you'd quit soldierin'."

"Had a hankerin' for more," Davy said, "and just in time, it seems."

Under a flat-topped gray hat, the man had a high forehead, wide-spaced crinkly eyes, a stubby nose and an easy grin. His upper lip and cheeks were covered in what appeared to be a permanent stubble. "Mighty glad to have you," he said with a tangy drawl. "But I believe the general wants your hide. You'd be wise to steer shy of him."

"If I was all that wise," Davy said. "I'd be back home nursin' a jug." As the man moved off, Davy called after him, "You take care of yourself, Georgie. One o' these days I'll be wantin' to hear more of your foolish songs."

The man turned and tilted his hat at a jaunty angle. "An' I'll have one ready. Give 'em what fer, Davy!" Then he was gone.

I squinted up at the bluff. "How long before Jackson knows we're here?"

Davy shrugged. "No tellin'. But we're instruments of Fate, remember? Can't let a little thing like a gen'ral stop us."

BEING AN INSTRUMENT of Fate, I soon discovered, was mostly about being shot at. As Red Eagle insisted on finding his warriors, we had no choice but to push on toward the barricade, where the main body of Red Sticks awaited Jackson's attack. That meant skirting the Indian town and clawing our way through half a mile of thick brush and woods, with potential enemies behind every tree. Red Eagle was stiff-legged due to his bandages, and our progress was slow.

Passing the town, we saw women and children run to and fro between the buildings, sometimes accompanied by warriors. The Cherokees and rangers were already setting fire to the outlying houses, and the Red Sticks scrambled to rally a defense.

The first shots whistled past my ears before we'd covered more than a hundred yards. Red Eagle called out something in Creek and got a guttural reply. Moments later five painted warriors came out of a thicket, menacing us with muskets and spears.

"Do you not know me?" Red Eagle asked in English. I noticed he took the opportunity to lean discreetly on his rifle, resting his leg.

"We know you," one answered. "Why do you bring enemies here?"

"These men are my brothers," Red Eagle said. "Do you not recognize Crockett, the man who battled Mad Bear?"

The Indians' eyes widened at this, and they gave Davy extra scrutiny. They nodded with grudging respect, but did not lower their weapons.

"And this," Red Eagle said, sweeping an arm at me, "is the man who bested Big Frog."

One warrior's mouth twitched. Another wrinkled his eyes. A moment later all were laughing, making my cheeks burn. But at least they'd relaxed their weapons.

Red Eagle's men, they advised us, had insisted on defending the center section of the great wall. This group would have escorted us there, they said, but were rushing to defend the town, where some had wives and children.

This scene was repeated several more times, and my embarrassment grew at each mention of Big Frog. But we progressed steadily toward the neck of the peninsula, and at last met a group willing to accompany us all the way to the barricade.

I'd grown so used to the steady pops and bangs of the cannons, that when they ceased, the silence was a noise in itself.

"What does that mean?" I asked.

"Either they're runnin' low on shells," Davy said, "or gettin' ready to storm the wall."

It was then I happened to glance back, and saw thick black smoke boiling up above the trees.

"They are torching the town," Red Eagle said thickly.

"The women?" I asked. "The children?"

Red Eagle shook his head. "They will be spared. But the Cherokees will show no mercy to our men. And they will be coming this way. Quickly."

We hurried on, our small group of escorts leading the way, and this time, despite his best efforts, Red Eagle struggled to keep pace. Moving over the high ground, there seemed no end of brush and tangled trees. From ahead, the Red Stick drums and war cries grew ever louder.

After what seemed an age, we reached the end of the high ground and I stared down at the inner side of the great barricade, staggered by the sight. Hundreds of red painted warriors lined the breastworks, shooting their muskets through the firing ports, loosing arrows over the wall, and screaming for Jackson's troops to come forth and die. Spotting a thick line of trees not far behind the barricade, we scrambled downhill to cover.

Behind us, shouts and shots announced the arrival of the Cherokees. A number of Red Sticks sprinted away from the wall, found cover in the fallen trees, and began firing back at the newcomers. Arrows and musket balls zinged past us on either side.

Red Eagle limped up beside us. "I must accompany my men. I regret I can no longer offer you protection."

Davy gripped his hand. "Gather up your friends, and keep yourselves alive. When I've got me a plan to get you out, I'll scream like a catamount. You can do one of them, I trust."

Red Eagle gave him a withering look.

" 'Course you can," Davy said with a grin. He pointed at a

giant cottonwood on the near edge of the high ground. "When you hear the signal, me and Penn'll be waitin' under that tree."

Red Eagle nodded, then turned to me. "Take care, Penn McCoy. I promised Little Fawn you would return."

I jumped as a musket ball bit a chunk out of the nearest tree. "I made the same promise," I said, "but I'm not sure these folks will honor it."

Red Eagle limped forward, clapping his men on their backs, and their faces lit with joy.

"We can't stay here," I shouted.

Davy grasped my arm and flopped to the earth, taking me with him. "And we can't leave. Leastways, not just now."

From beyond the barricade came a great drum roll, accompanied by hoarse shouts, bugles, and the tramp of a thousand feet.

"There's the charge," Davy said, "likely with bayonets. Jackson *likes* bayonets. Stay down."

Hundreds of Red Sticks crouched atop the wall, loosing their bows until the sky was black with arrows. Still, Jackson's men crashed against the barricade, thrusting musket and rifle barrels through the ports to fire point-blank into the massed Indians. Those shots took their toll, as a growing number of red-skinned bodies pitched to the earth. And all the while, the Cherokees blazed away from behind us. The shots, shouts, screams and curses blended into an ear-shattering din of bestial fury.

Scant yards ahead, Monahoe and other shamans kept up a frenzied dance, whirling their cow-tailed sticks and singing to their gods. Monahoe's cloak of eagle feathers shimmered in the sunlight, and his strident chants rose above the others, lending heart to the warriors. Jackson's troops had yet to breach the wall, and the Cherokees dared come no closer than fifty yards. Sensing things were going their way, the Red Sticks howled like wolves. The prophets had told them they were invincible, and they now had reason to believe it.

Then, with a single musket blast, everything changed.

Monahoe, turning in his dance to momentarily face the wall,

threw his head back and wailed. The roar of the musket cut through his cry, and the back of his head vanished in a shower of blood. For another heartbeat, Monahoe's body hung in the air. The cow tails fell from his hands, his feathers lost their shimmer, and the Red Sticks stared open-mouthed as their mighty prophet flopped backwards and struck the earth. I grimaced, wiping specks of warm flesh from my cheeks.

The war cries stopped. The battle for control of the firing ports was momentarily forgotten, as the warriors gaped at the man they'd thought immune to harm. Monahoe's head was still thrown back, almost facing us. His dead eyes were wide with surprise, his mouth still open from his final scream.

A blue-clad army officer appeared atop the barricade. His face was triumphant as he waved his hat and shouted for his soldiers to follow. The Red Sticks swung back to the wall, aghast that an enemy had scaled their defenses. I understood enough of their thinking to know the death of Monahoe was a bad omen, and many chose that moment to run for cover. Others, including some of Red Eagle's men, leapt to the barricade with renewed fury.

The army officer had scarcely topped the breastworks when a dozen muskets spoke, and a ball struck his head, blasting him back off the wall. But Jackson's men followed his example, and other blue-capped heads appeared.

A second officer sprang up in nearly the same place—a tall, high-headed man shouting his anger at the Creeks. More Indian muskets fired, but he appeared unhit. Smiling with the joy of battle, he leapt to the inner edge of the barricade, preparing to drop inside. But one warrior drew his bow and sent an arrow streaking into the tall man's thigh. His face contorted, he dropped his rifle and plummeted forward into the dirt.

Red Sticks rushed toward him, but pulled back as more soldiers appeared, firing muskets and pistols into the massed warriors. The Indians returned fire, and more blue-coated men fell from the breastworks, but new ones mounted ever faster, and the remaining defenders saw they were now without cover. All along the wall, the Red Sticks began to fall back. Meanwhile the Cherokees, taking advantage of the chaos, crept closer, and began hitting their marks. Unable to move forward or back, the Red Stick line splintered, retreating to either side toward the river.

At last only one Creek stood screaming his defiance—a stocky man in a striped green smoking jacket and red nightcap. Chief Menawa. He held a red war club in one hand and a bloody tomahawk in the other, standing his ground in front of us. The trees sheltered him somewhat from the Cherokees, but he was in full view of the soldiers, and several took aim.

Either Menawa was incredibly lucky, or Jackson's men were terrible shots, because the balls whizzed past him, slapping through the leaves on either side of Davy and me. Then a bullet slammed into his left arm, misting the air red. As he reeled from the blow, another ball clipped his right leg.

"Damned fool," Davy muttered. Bolting from cover, he sprang onto the chief's back and drove him to the ground. As the soldiers watched in surprise, Davy's arm flashed up, a blade glinting in his fist, and hammered down at Menawa. He repeated the action twice more, with obvious fury. At last Davy rose up, straddling the chief's still form, and wiped the blade on the back of his breeches. "Dead!" he roared. "The damned dirty savage is dead!"

Soldiers roared approval as they streamed past us, chasing the fleeing Red Sticks. Davy watched them go, then bent, grasped Menawa's legs and dragged the body quickly back to our place in the trees.

I said, "How could you—"

But that was as far as I got before Menawa turned his head and fixed us with a malignant glare. "You!" he said, his voice raspy. "You pretend to be friends, then attack me from behind!"

I stared at his fancy red jacket, realizing there were no knife cuts.

"What Davy just did," I told him, "was save your danged life, at great risk to his own. The proper response would be 'Thank you.'"

Menawa sneered. "I would have defeated them."

Davy clucked at him. "Don't be tellin' me you swallowed that 'immune to bullets' applesauce. You seen what happened to Monahoe."

"I saw. And I find you two here, ahead of your soldiers, again profaning our sacred ground. Perhaps the prophet Josiah was right, and it is you who bring our downfall."

I could think of nothing to say to that, and while Davy stood shaking his head, the chief pushed to his feet, heedless of his wounds, and darted into the woods behind us.

"What if he's right?" I asked. "What if we really did ruin their magic, and it's our fault they're dying?"

"That's rattlebrained nonsense, as you well know. Question is, how we gettin' Red Eagle out o' here alive?"

I looked back at the barricade. Jackson's men were still coming over, but the stream was beginning to thin. At the base of the wall sat the officer who'd taken the arrow in his thigh, a discouraged looking soldier at his side.

"Pull it out, damn you!" the officer bellowed. "That's an order!"

Bent low, Davy started toward the two men, and I could only follow. Kneeling next to the soldier, we formed a half circle around the injured man.

"I told you, Lieutenant. I already tried. It won't budge." The officer's language burned the air blue, but the soldier remained adamant.

I saw his dilemma. The arrow was wedged firmly in the lieutenant's inner thigh. If the arrowhead was barbed, pulling it out would cause more damage than it had done going in. The only alternative was to cut the arrow out, which normally meant the loss of a limb, if not death from infection.

The lieutenant seemed to notice us for the first time. "What are you two yokels staring at?"

Davy doffed his cap. "A foul-mouthed feller with an arrow through his hind leg. If he was to ask real nice, I might be willin' to remove it."

The lieutenant sputtered at this, and the beleaguered soldier took the opportunity to run off after the Indians.

"Very well, damn your eyes. Could you please do your God damned duty and give me some God damned aid?"

The officer's light sandy hair was brushed back over one one of highest foreheads I'd ever seen. His nose was long and aquiline, and his mouth full. But his most prominent feature was the cavernous dimple in his chin. It was deep enough to hide a rifle ball.

Davy grinned. "Since you ask so nicely, I reckon we'll patch you up. Penn, would you kindly steady this gent's leg?"

While Davy gripped the shaft of the arrow, I took hold of the leg and held on tight.

The lieutenant scowled at me, but made no complaint. And before either of us expected it, Davy plunged the arrow forward, driving the head clean through the man's thigh.

"Yahhhhh!" The officer's yell was long and lusty. He was still yelling as Davy snapped the bloody head from the arrow, grasped the feathered shaft and yanked it back out of his leg.

The lieutenant was stunned. Before he could protest, Davy drew his knife and sliced the leg of the man's white britches. He then tore the fabric into strips, which he knotted together.

"That," the man said, "was my best pair of pants."

"You're welcome," Davy said. "Penn, s'pose you could clean that wound?"

Not far away, a horse snorted. Turning, I saw half a dozen mounted officers rounding the end of the barricade. At their head was the last person I wanted to see.

Davy had spotted him too. "Jumpin' Jehoshaphat," he said under his breath, "this ain't gettin' any easier." The riders were now quite near. We kept our heads down, Davy making a show of tying off the man's leg above the wound, while I busied myself with a canteen and handkerchief.

"Houston!" called a voice I knew too well. "Glad to see you alive."

"And you, General. An arrow just bit me in the leg."

"Takes more than a scratch to stop men like us," Jackson said. "These devils have penned themselves up for slaughter, and I mean to oblige them."

"Be with you directly, sir."

"No rush," Jackson said. "I'm pleased to see some of Russell's rangers have arrived. Good work, men."

"Much obliged, Gen'ral," Davy said, in a voice not his own. He was careful not to turn his head.

I spoke quickly, through the side of my mouth. "Honored, sir."

For a long moment, Jackson said nothing. I could feel his eyes on my back, almost hear his thoughts. *Why do these men look so familiar?*

Davy said, "If you hurry, Gen'ral, you might catch Menawa." He jabbed a thumb over his shoulder toward the far side of the peninsula, decidedly *not* the direction the chief had gone. "He just high-tailed it toward the river."

"Menawa!" Jackson said. "Great snakes, let's be after him!" As the riders turned their horses, he called back, "What of Red Eagle?"

"Wish I knew, Gen'ral. I crave a serious discussion with that rascal."

"As do I, private. As do I."

CHAPTER 30

"You two are devils."

TWO HOURS LATER we were no nearer finding an escape route for Red Eagle. We'd toured the eastern side of the peninsula and succeeded only in getting shot at by more Red Sticks.

After retreating from the barricade, many of the warriors had run straight for the river, expecting to find their canoes. What they found was death. In one instance the Cherokees had left two canoes seemingly unguarded beneath the cliffs. But when the Red Sticks came barreling over the bluff to claim them, the Cherokees swarmed out of the brush and slaughtered them to a man.

Davy and I saw groups of warriors throw logs from the cliffs and jump in after, hoping to hang on long enough to cross the river. But Colonel Coffee's volunteers had lined the opposite bank, and their Tennessee rifles rarely missed at less than a hundred yards. Desperate, still more Creeks dove directly into the cold water. Most were peppered with lead before reaching the other side, and those few who made it were immediately cut down.

The banks were soon strewn with Red Stick corpses. Unable to escape, many scrambled into the caves cut into the cliffs overlooking the river. Rifles could not reach them there, and Jackson's men had yet to find a way of ferreting them out.

Other Red Sticks dared the Cherokee muskets and plunged into the woods. Thick brush and jagged ravines offered many places to hide, and the battle became a deadly game of hide and seek. The bang of muskets, the sharp crack of pistols and the screams of the dying rang from one end of the peninsula to the other.

Davy and I avoided the fighting, taking action only when necessary. When one determined Red Stick dropped from a tree onto my back, Davy discouraged him with a rifle butt to the jaw. I returned the favor as two warriors sprang at Davy with spears. I felled one with a ball in the leg and Davy sidestepped the other to smack his skull with a tomahawk.

On other occasions, we merely tried to slow the slaughter. Spying a soldier about to blast a fleeing warrior, Davy gave the man a hearty clap on the back, and the shot went high. As two Cherokees were about to leap from a tree onto a Creek, I sent a rock crashing through the branches, distracting them long enough for the man to escape.

Davy said little, taking everything in, his mind busy with the problem of Red Eagle. But his brows were still knitted as we gave up on the eastern bank and turned to explore the west.

Entering a clearing, we heard heavy fire and crept forward to find a troop of soldiers surrounding a tangled heap of timber.

"What's goin' on, fellers?" Davy asked.

A man spoke up. "At least a score of the devils hunkered down behind those logs." I thought immediately of Red Eagle. His followers had numbered well over a hundred when the battle began, but had surely diminished. Could this be his final refuge? Davy's face betrayed the same concern.

"Don't fret," the soldier said, "we got a surprise for 'em."

As Davy said, "What?" a man ran up with a torch. Within seconds, three other brands were burning, and men darted forward to fling them onto the pile of timber. The logs were dry, and the brush around them even drier. A sheet of flame sprang up around the Red Sticks' position. As forms appeared through the smoke, the soldiers' weapons began to speak, and

Davy and I could only watch, sickened, as the emerging Indians were slaughtered.

The fire had nearly burnt itself out when the soldiers moved on, rejoicing in their small victory. Stomach tight, I followed Davy forward, examining each of the bodies in turn. Red Eagle was not among them. My feeling was hardly one of joy, for twenty-odd men lay dead before us, men who had been full of life, men whose wives and children would mourn them. Some, quite likely, who were kin by blood or clan to Little Fawn. Still, I was glad we had not found Red Eagle.

A twig cracked and I spun to see a small Indian boy, not more than six years of age, break from the brush and speed for a copse of trees. Having learned the Creek word for friend, I shouted after him. His head turned. And as he gazed back at me, four soldiers emerged from the trees into his path.

Warned by some sound or instinct, the boy turned, just as a black-bearded soldier cracked a rifle butt against his head. The boy flopped loose-limbed to the earth and lay still, as the soldier stood above him, laughing.

Old Betsy swung up to Davy's shoulder, aiming its snout squarely at the soldier. He cocked the hammer, caressed the trigger, and had just begun to squeeze when I grabbed the barrel and pushed it aside. He turned red-rimmed eyes on me and growled.

"I know," I said. "I know. But that's not the way."

"What is?" His voice was like a death-rattle.

I thought sure his devil had returned, but he raised his left hand and jabbed his thumb at the wedding ring. "Polly," he said, and mouthed the words, *Thank you*. So my plea at Musolagee had truly reached him. I nodded grimly, praying the ring would serve as a reminder to keep his demon at bay.

He shook his head, his eyes downcast. I still held his rifle barrel, so he let go and strode toward the four soldiers. A man wearing captain's bars knelt beside the boy.

"Dead," the officer said. "I should write you up for that. We do not fight children."

"Hell, Cap'n." The bearded soldier puffed his chest and glared down at the officer. "He would have grown up to be a Red Stick."

The four looked up at our approach. I kept close watch on Davy, saw him ball his fist and shake it, weighting it with every ounce of his wrath. The soldier saw it, too, and his mouth still gaped when Davy's fist exploded against his jaw, snapping his teeth and lifting him off the ground. Blood spurted over his beard. His eyes rolled back, glassy white. His back hit the earth with a thump.

One of his companions stepped toward us, fists raised, but the captain stopped him with a sharp command. Davy stood tight-faced, staring down at the still form of the boy.

I put a hand on Davy's shoulder. "It's over," I said.

"I agree." The captain's voice was hard as stone. "It's over."

I turned Davy around, guiding him from the scene. We walked in silence for a time. Finally, he said, "Thanks for bein' a true friend, Penn. With your help, an' Polly's," he tapped the ring, "I believe I finally got that devil licked."

THE SITUATION ON the western bank was much like that in the east. The rivershore was littered with painted bodies, and several small battles were underway, where soldiers tried to remove pockets of Red Sticks from the caves. The yells of the Indians, the curses of soldiers and the groans of the dying blended with the staccato gunfire to create a hellish din.

A young lieutenant stood sucking on a pipe as he observed the action from atop the bluff. Davy and I stopped at his side.

"Find any weak spots?" Davy said.

"Weak spots?"

"Holes that need pluggin', where the savages might escape?"

The man beamed as if paid a compliment. "Not a chance. A fish couldn't cross that river without Coffee's men blasting him, and Bean's sharpshooters over yonder are deadly to anyone approaching that island."

I followed the aim of his pipe stem. The trees were so thick that the island had escaped my notice. It looked more like a bump on the far shore than a separate landmass. The island lay roughly opposite the neck of the peninsula, where the Red Sticks had built their barricade.

"Bean?" Davy said. "Jesse Bean?"

"The same. Know him?"

Looking sideways at me, Davy raised his eyebrows and smiled. Jesse was his friend, and mine as well after the gunsmithing we'd done together, but how this helped Red Eagle's cause I could not fathom. Still, for the first time since we'd crossed the river, there was a spark in Davy's eye.

As soon as we were out of the officer's hearing, I said, "What?"

"I'm feelin' neighborly." Davy walked carefully along the edge of the bluff, his eyes darting over at intervals, taking everything in. "Let's pay ol' Jesse a call."

Coming to a notch in the bluff, he stepped over the edge, working his way down through the tangle of rocks and trees, and I stifled a grumble. Almost directly beneath us, floating face down in the river, were the bodies of two Indians. I tried to ignore them, focusing on the canoe beached a short distance upstream.

Reaching the canoe, Davy hefted one end and began dragging it into the water. I hastened to help. We were about to push off when my nape hairs twitched and I cast a nervous glance across the river. Rifle barrels glinted among the trees on the opposite bank. Those marksmen had to be curious—and suspicious. We were not dressed like Red Sticks, but neither were we wearing uniforms. They'd be wondering why we intended to row away from the peninsula, away from the fighting. We could be deserters, or worse, Red Sticks in disguise.

I said as much to Davy, but he was unfazed.

"Those are Tennessee boys, Penn. Think they can't tell friend from foe?"

"From what I've seen of late," I said, "friends and foes look pretty much alike."

He laughed at that, but I remained uneasy as we pushed the canoe off the bank.

Two paddles lay at our feet. Davy tossed one to me, and I handled it clumsily, as rowing was one skill overlooked by my Philadelphia upbringing. But Davy was a good teacher, and I was getting the hang of it by the time the first shots spattered the water around us. While I ducked, Davy calmly set his paddle aside, tugged a strip of white cloth from inside his shirt—a remnant of Lieutenant Houston's trousers—and tied it around Old Betsy's barrel. He raised the rifle above his head, waving the cloth like a flag. The firing stopped.

"Sit on up," Davy said. "If they was fixin' to kill us, we'd be dead." Lowering the rifle, Davy rose carefully to his feet. He cupped his hands about his mouth and yelled, "Jesse Bean! It's me, Jess. Davy Crockett!"

Whether he was understood or not, the shooting did not resume. I heard dim shouts from the island, but the racket of the battle masked his words. In any case, Davy settled back into his seat, and we proceeded toward the island.

Men in loose hunting shirts and leather breeches emerged from the bushes. No rifles pointed directly at us, but all remained at the ready, and I sensed that at the first alarm, they would drill us with lead.

Davy put aside his paddle, and I followed suit. Grinning now, he tipped his hat and executed a seated bow. "How do, gents," he said, "nice afternoon for canoeing."

A familiar figure pushed to the front.

I touched my hat brim. "Good to see you, Jesse."

"Crockett," Bean shook his head, "and Pennsylvania McCoy. Have you two lost your wits, tempting my boys in this fashion?"

"Pshaw," Davy said, "the gen'ral knew you wouldn't shoot a neighbor. Reckon that's why he picked us for this mission."

"Mission?"

"Scoutin' the cliffs." Davy aimed a thumb back at the opposite shore. "Old Hickory-face don't want none of them devils escapin', and craves a first-hand report on their hidey-holes."

"A single-minded fellow, our general." Bean leaned forward and spat into the river. "When he starts to killing redskins, nothin'll do till the job's done."

"We'd be obliged," Davy said, "if you'd sorta not shoot at us. We'd be a might displeased if you sent us to the Pearly Gates before our time."

Another man spoke up.

"I'll do my dangdest not to kill you, Davy." The speaker was Davy's friend Georgie, the man with the guitar on his back. "Case I do, though, could you say howdy to my pa? Tell him I've got three of those snakes to my credit, and itchin' for more."

"You shoot me, Georgie Russell, and I'll tell him you took one look at the Red Sticks and soiled your britches."

JUST PAST THE island, we reached the western end of the horseshoe and spotted the bluff where Jackson had mounted his artillery. Davy peered up at the gun crews milling idly about the cannons.

"I believe I'll swap howdys with those fellows too," he said. Steering the canoe to shore within sight of the gun emplacement, he hopped onto the bank. "Be back before you can say Jack Robinson."

Which wasn't entirely true, but he did return smartly, a stout round keg on his shoulder.

"That's whiskey, I hope."

Davy grinned. "Gunpowder. Told 'em the gen'ral wanted it to blast them redskins out of the caves."

I shuddered. "He would, too, if he thought of it."

"Don't you fret. He won't hear it from me."

We paddled up and down the Tallapoosa for another hour, peering up under the cliffs of the peninsula to support the story we were seeking pockets of Red Sticks. There seemed no shortage of these. Along with several caves under assault by Jackson's men, we spotted three that had so far escaped notice. Gliding past at close range gave me an itch between the shoulder blades.

"Time we was headin' back," Davy said at last. "Our mission here's done."

"Which mission is that? The one you invented for Jesse's ears or the one you've yet to tell me about?"

"Both." Davy displayed his most winning grin. "Don't fret, Penn. I've finally got me a plan by the tail, and soon as it's hog-tied I'll need your help with the skinnin'."

I wanted more, of course, but I knew how Davy's mind worked. He'd reveal his scheme when it was fully formed, and no measure of wheedling would hurry him.

The sun was a good bit lower in the west when we pulled the canoe ashore, directly beneath a large cave mouth. That cave had been under assault when we'd passed earlier, but now lay quiet. Two Red Stick bodies lay sprawled on the cliffside, riddled with rifle balls. More were visible in the cave, one hanging half-out, arms a-dangle, while others slumped behind him.

As we climbed past the dead men, I felt my stomach clench. "Couldn't you have picked a better place to land?"

"I feel for these poor souls," Davy said. "Got snookered into a war they couldn't win. But right now we need to save Red Eagle." He scooped up a bloody blanket, wrapped the powder keg in it and slung it over his shoulder.

"And we'll do that with gunpowder and a blanket?"

"We'll take whatever Providence provides," he replied, and would say no more.

We were halfway up the cliff when a commotion broke out further down the bluff. Soldiers had gathered on the edge, peering over the bank. Below them lay one of the caves still occupied by Red Sticks.

"I'll root those savages out, whether you men help me or not!" A tall figure in an officer's uniform strode to the edge, gripped his rifle and hopped over, steadying himself on the upended roots of a tree. He wore a white bandage around his leg. With a start, I recognized Lieutenant Houston. At once, two musket barrels emerged from the cave mouth, spitting fire. Houston jerked as balls slammed into him, nearly knocking him from his perch.

Dropping the keg, Davy swung Betsy to his shoulder and fired. The shot clipped feathers from the head of one warrior. An instant later, I put a ball past the nose of the other. Both jerked back into the cave, and one of muskets went clattering down the cliff. Blue-clad arms stretched over the bank to tug Houston to safety.

Scrambling up onto the bluff, I was all for seeking the solitude of the woods, but Davy insisted on having words with the lieutenant. We found him on the ground, back against a tree, cursing the man who inspected his wounds. His shirt had been torn open, exposing bloody holes in his arm and shoulder. His blue jacket and hat lay in a pile at his side.

"You two!" Houston's blue eyes went wide at our approach. "It seems I am indebted to you again."

"Does indeed." Davy laid the blanket-wrapped keg aside and knelt. "I'll do the doctorin'," he told the other man. "We'd admire a word with the brave lieutenant."

The fellow looked appealingly at his officer, who nodded. The man snapped a quick salute and rushed off.

Davy worked quickly and efficiently with the bandages, making no pretense of being gentle.

"Forget what I said about being indebted," Houston said between groans. "You two are devils."

Davy winked at me. "You ain't half wrong," he said. "Still, there's one small favor we'd ask."

Houston eyed him with suspicion. "And what might that be?"

"The loan of your jacket," Davy said. "And your hat."

Houston's brows shot up. "Why? What possible use could you make of them?"

"Best you don't know. Suffice to say, we're aimin' to help a friend."

Houston's eyes narrowed. He seemed about to refuse. But his features softened and he gave a short laugh. "A good one, I hope. I've a feeling I may be court-martialed for this."

"If it comes to that," Davy said, "I'll swear we shot you and stole your clothes."

Houston nodded. "If it comes to that, by God, I'll swear the same."

CHAPTER 31

"Is that savage dead?"

HAVING BEEN BREACHED, the giant barricade now lay dark and abandoned. The bodies of soldiers and Red Sticks still sprawled atop the wall or slumped in the dirt. Jackson had not bothered to post sentries, as he still had reserves massed at the neck of the peninsula. Even if Red Sticks managed to scale the wall, there was no place for them to go.

We found cover in the nearest trees. After turning his eyes, ears and nose in all directions to make sure we were alone, Davy cached the keg and Houston's clothes in the brush. He had not yet explained his plans for the gunpowder, and I didn't press him, for I knew it would bring me no comfort. We then headed for the big cottonwood, our rendezvous point

Davy cupped his hands before his mouth and emitted a long, pitiful squall. If I hadn't seen him do it, I'd have sworn we shared the bushes with a cougar.

We listened intently for what seemed an age. From various distant points came scattered gunfire, angry shouts and savage screams, but no answering call.

Davy did it again, this time louder, and even more mournful.

From somewhere between us and the town came an odd squeal, rather like a pig with its tail caught in a crack.

Davy raised his rifle to his shoulder and sighted a line toward the sound. I did the same.

When the squealing stopped, we heard rustling in the bushes, accompanied by a great many snapping twigs.

Davy frowned, and I shared his concern. It was not like Red Eagle to announce his approach. Still, he was lame in one leg, and may have suffered further injury. We waited. The tension made my head buzz.

Still another twig snapped. I sank lower into the brush, rifle steady, waiting for the fellow to show himself.

Davy hissed.

I stared at him, amazed he would give away our position.

He nodded at my rifle and shook his head. Then he pinched his nose.

The first part of the message was clear. I lowered my weapon. But I puzzled over the nose-pinching.

With a great rustle of leaves, a bulky, half-naked warrior came crawling out of the brush, bringing with him a pungent odor. The mystery was solved.

Davy said, "Get up, Big Frog, before some starvin' soldier mistakes you for a hog."

RED EAGLE, BIG FROG explained, had collected more wounds. He was able to walk, but with difficulty, and chose to send Big Frog to the rendezvous. Of the hundred-odd warriors he'd brought to Tohopeka, fewer than a dozen lived. They'd found a blackberry thicket surrounded by many of their dead brethren, and hunkered down to await Davy's signal.

Big Frog held my Pennsylvania longrifle before him as if taunting me. He seemed to understand Davy's instructions, though with all his leering and preening, it was hard to be sure. I had to remind myself he was less stupid than he seemed. He had, after all, bamboozled me out of my most prized possession.

Davy then filled us in on his escape plan, and it seemed a certain recipe for suicide. But as Big Frog appeared even more appalled than I, I declared it to be just dandy.

By the time Big Frog crashed back into the brush, dusk was upon us. It would soon be full dark, and time to put Davy's scheme to work. Fighting on the peninsula had concentrated in fewer and fewer spots. All day, soldiers had been stomping through the trees, searching the ravines and clearing the caves. Hundreds of Red Sticks had been flushed out and killed.

"Now" Davy said. "Time to show off my new duds." He quickly doffed his buckskin jacket and coonskin cap, donning the coat and hat he'd borrowed from Houston. As he strutted about, posing for my benefit, I was impressed. Aside from his buckskin breeches, he looked every inch an officer.

"Once I get them men runnin'," he said, "you trail along behind. I'll rejoin you quick as I can manage."

A dozen questions tripped through my mind, but all remained with me as Davy melted into the night.

I was an instrument of Fate, I reminded myself, or at least an instrument of Davy. Whether it was truly Fate that had brought him to this battle, or merely the whims of Chance, Red Eagle could have no greater champion.

The action began sooner than expected. The distinctive bark of Old Betsy pierced the night, followed by the blast of a pistol. "Red Sticks!" bawled a commanding voice. "To me, damn you! To me! Found a hundred of those varmints hidin' in the town, and they're ripe for slaughter!"

From the darkness came answering shouts and the tramp of many feet. Still barking orders, a blue-coated man in buckskin pants ran past, leading a large body of men away from the western bluff. "Hurry, this might be the last of them!"

The excitement was so contagious I almost darted from cover to join the rush. Men raced from all directions to be in on the climax of the battle.

As the last man lumbered past, I eased into the open and followed. Davy's shouts grew dim in the distance, while the cries of his mob rose to a roar. I followed at a walk, alert for signs of Indians. Sensing movement, I spied shadowy forms flitting from tree to tree and bush to bush. One shadow was thicker than the others, and laboring so hard I heard its breath rasp. Big Frog. He nodded in passing, almost smiling, and I nodded back. In the rear, two swift and silent warriors supported a third. There was no mistaking the tall, broad-shouldered man between them. Red Eagle.

Fearing to call attention to them, I turned back toward the soldiers. The grass was so trampled the trail was easy to spot, even by moonlight.

Davy, of course, had a way of sliding between the moonbeams, and the first I knew of his presence he was at my side. He had reclaimed his jacket and long-tailed cap. "Ready to quit this place?"

"I was ready before we arrived."

Shouts ahead of us now rang with bewilderment.

"Queerest thing happened," Davy said. "That there officer leadin' the troop just up and vanished."

Reversing course, we hurried back toward the barricade.

It was still fifty yards off when Davy grasped my arm and pulled me into the brush. I waited, trusting his senses, and soon heard the snorts of horses. Three mounted figures appeared, trotting after Davy's abandoned followers. All were officers, and the one in the center was General Jackson himself.

"By the blessed eternal," Jackson said, "I hope this is the last of them."

I held my breath as they came abreast, no more than ten yards from our position. Once they passed there'd be no one to prevent us reaching the cache of gunpowder.

An arrow streaked from the darkness, piercing the throat of one officer and knocking him from his horse. Another arrow sliced through Jackson's jacket sleeve. The second officer ducked low, spurring his mount toward two Red Sticks who sprang from the brush and ran for the woods.

The man on the ground was clearly dead. Jackson looked stunned as he fought to calm him horse.

"Ride on," Davy said under his breath. "Ride on, dang it." But Jackson remained.

An Indian broke cover behind him and raced toward his back with a blood-smeared war club. The Indian was Chief Menawa.

The general had no inkling of his peril.

Betsy spat flame, and the chief stumbled. But he kept going, now running with a limp. I raised my rifle. I could hit Menawa, no question, but I'd been trained to kill, not wound. Davy pushed my barrel aside and sprang from the brush on a course to intercept the chief.

Jackson finally realized his danger. Wheeling his horse, he clawed the pistol from his belt.

Menawa was within five yards when Jackson fired. The blast filled the air with smoke. When it cleared, Menawa was aside Jackson's horse, yanking the general from the saddle. Menawa's club rose for the killing stroke.

Between them darted a blur of buckskin. Davy thrust the chief's war club aside, and both men crashed to the earth. First Davy was on top, then Menawa, a whirlwind of thrashing limbs. The grunting and growling was so fierce I feared it would bring a crowd.

Jackson watched as if in a daze. Finding his wits at last, he surged to his feet and drew the cavalry sword from his scabbard. He was about to strike when the roar of a bear issued from brush nearby. Jackson spun about, alarmed. I made to raise my rifle, then recalled Davy's skill at mimicry. Menawa had no such advantage. As he gaped about for the bear, Davy formed a fist and smashed downward. The crack of knuckles against jaw was loud as a pistol shot, and the chief collapsed in the dirt.

"Great balls of fire!!" Jackson beamed at Davy's back. "You've saved my hide, man, and you'll be well rewarded. But where in God's heaven did that bear come from?"

"A simple 'thanks' will do, Gen'ral." Davy turned his head and growled.

Jackson's eyes bulged. He shook his sword and sputtered obscenities.

"It's me, sure enough," Davy said. "What say you forget seein' me?"

"Crockett!" The name exploded from Jackson's mouth. "What the blessed blue blazes are you doing here?"

"As you put it, Gen'ral, I was savin' your hide."

"You're up to something, I know it. So help me, Crockett, when I find out what it is…"

Davy rose, brushing the dirt from his clothes. "No reason to get your tail feathers ruffled, Gen'ral. Did I mention you're welcome?"

Jackson pointed his sword at Menawa's still form. "Is that savage dead?"

"Dead as a squashed frog."

"I don't believe you." Jackson took a step forward, but Davy moved to intercept him. "Out of my way, or I'll cut you down."

"Can't let you do it, Gen'ral." Davy glanced at the brush where I still hid. "Penn, would you see to the gen'ral's horse?"

Confused, I staggered up to join them. Jackson gave me a sour look as I snagged the horse's reins.

"Now, Penn, kindly point that critter off yonder," he nodded toward the interior of the peninsula, "and slap his behind. The gen'ral needs a walk to clear his head."

As I swatted the horse, sending it running, Davy hefted the chief's body over his shoulder.

"Sorry to inconvenience you, Gen'ral, but I got business with this rascal." And with a mock salute, Davy plowed into the woods in the direction of the Red Stick village. I scampered after, as Jackson's curses burned the air blue.

Once out of sight, we circled back toward the river. When Menawa began to groan, Davy thumped him into the tall grass. We stood over him as he blinked and coughed.

"Quiet," Davy said. "We're savin' your life here. Again. Don't muck it up."

Menawa's eyes grew sharp. "You struck me!"

"Thanks for noticin'. Now how 'bout you stand up and follow us quiet as an Injun. Reckon you can do that?"

"And run away? Go if you wish, but I will fight to the last breath with my people."

"Most of 'em have already breathed their last. We're rescuin' all we can, and that includes you."

Menawa's jaw clamped shut. "Never."

IT WAS TIME to put Davy plan into action.

With Menawa bound and gagged in the bushes, Davy retrieved the powder keg, and I set about gathering armloads of dry brush. Davy poured a thin line of gunpowder along the base of the barricade, which we quickly covered with brush.

Kneeling, Davy held his pistol to the ground and dry-fired, igniting one end of the powder line. The brush caught fire immediately, and flames began licking at the logs and branches of the wall. Once the limbs were burning, Davy hoisted Menawa onto his shoulder and we sprinted toward the river.

If all had gone well, Red Eagle and his men would be waiting for us in a cave beneath the bluff—the cave we'd found full of dead Indians, which no one would think to search again.

By the time we reached the river, the barricade was burning merrily. Soldiers shouted in alarm, but had eyes only for the flames, and we slipped unnoticed over the bluff. The river was eerily quiet. The Red Sticks had been scoured from their nests along the bank, and all but two widely-spaced sentries had run off chasing Davy's wild goose.

The footing was tricky here, and Davy slid Menawa from his shoulder. While he grasped the chief's shoulders, I took his feet, and we worked our way down the slope. Menawa was a good kicker, but it got him nowhere and he finally subsided into a determined wiggle. All the while he chewed with enthusiasm on his gag, and I felt lucky to be at the toothless end. If he got through the gag, he'd likely bite Davy's fingers off.

I wondered why the riflemen across the river did not raise an alarm, then realized the blazing barricade had blinded them to the darkness beneath the bluff.

Reaching the river, Davy halted next to the canoe we'd hidden earlier. He guided the chief's head and shoulders over the side, and I pushed his feet in after, giving his ankles a twist to repay the kicking.

Davy peered back up at the cliff. I could barely see the dark patch marking the entrance to the cave, but in my mind I still saw the bodies of the Red Sticks who'd died there. Davy made his cougar call, softly now. An answering call came from the cave, followed by faint sounds of moccasins scuffing the dirt, and black shapes moving against the darkness of the cliff.

Davy was already dragging the canoe toward the river. I caught up the opposite end and pushed. As the cool water entered my shoes, I stepped into the canoe, being none too careful where I put my feet, and got a satisfying grunt from Menawa. Davy thrust a paddle into my hands and dipped his into the river.

"What about the others?" My voice was barely a whisper.

"Already with us. Let's move."

Bewildered, I mirrored his strokes and we quickly shot off from the bank. The inferno at the wall lit the far side of the river bright as day, but the shadow of the bluff cast a curtain of darkness over the river. I'd heard no splash, no slightest gurgle to indicate the Indians had entered the water. But a hand appeared, grasping the side of the canoe. More hands followed, and, straining my eyes, I saw dark heads bobbing in the river around us. Nine in all. Nine, out of Red Eagle's hundred. As we glided toward the island, they swung close to the canoe, allowing our paddles to pass over their heads.

We were barely underway when a challenge rang out, and I had a bad moment. Bean's Tennesseans had been canny enough to avoid being blinded by the flames. After the day I'd had, it would be downright dispiriting to be shot smuggling Indians from the battlefield.

"Hallooo, the canoe. Who goes there?"

"Davy Crockett! Don't shoot, Georgie! Remember what I said 'bout your pa."

"Come on ahead, Davy!"

I shook my head, amazed that yet another of Davy's mad plans had worked, and this one with hardly a hitch.

I was still thinking that when a familiar voice roared, "There they are! Open fire! Kill them all!" The voice was General Jackson's, and it came from the bluff we'd just quitted.

A dozen muskets banged. Lead peppered the river around us. One of the Red Sticks let out a yip.

"Davy! What's happening?" called Georgie Russell. "Ain't that the general?"

"It surely is, Georgie! Must think we're Injuns! He's blind as a mole in the dark!"

Bean's men answered with laughter.

Jackson's bellowing grew fainter as we neared the center of the river. I paddled faster, knowing we had only seconds before the muskets were reloaded.

A second volley crashed from the bluff. This time, fewer balls came near. Luckily, those army-issue muskets had an effective range of barely sixty yards. If Jackson's soldiers had rifles, like the volunteers across the river, we'd already be dead.

We paddled on. More muskets barked. Jackson's force was growing, and the firing became almost continuous, but their shots fell well behind the canoe, and lent strength to our arms.

Bean's men kept waving their hats and shouting. "It's Davy!" they told the soldiers. "Leave off, you lop-eared idiots!" And again, we were fortunate, for without that racket they might have heard Jackson ordering them to shoot us.

As we neared the island, Bean's men threw up a cheer. Jackson's men continued their fire, but we were now well out of range.

Davy steered the canoe parallel to the island, twenty yards

from shore. The Red Sticks all slipped to the opposite side of the canoe, out of sight of the volunteers, and for the first time I spotted Red Eagle himself, grinning in the pale moonlight.

The current carried us now, and Davy took the opportunity to stand. He tipped his hat and took a deep bow, wringing more cheers from the sharpshooters. "We have escaped the deadly fire of Old Hickory's regulars," he said, "an act of heroism to rival the feats of Hercules."

Bean's men guffawed at this. The town-bred regular soldiers looked down on these poorly dressed volunteers, and the country boys returned the favor.

"Our next trick," Davy said, "will be to scoot on upriver before Jackson unlimbers his cannons on us."

"Criminityly, Davy!" Georgie shouted back. "I reckon I'll have to write a song about you!"

Bean's men roared their approval. And to the music of laughter and musket fire, we paddled off into the night.

CHAPTER 32

"A thing I don't take lightly."

AFTER THREE WEEKS of hiding with Red Eagle's people on an island in the Alabama River, it was good to get out. Trouble was, the place we were getting out to was Jackson's new headquarters—modestly christened Fort Jackson—and home to several thousand soldiers.

I missed Little Fawn. The time we'd spent together on the island had been like something from my dreams. I had spoken again of the cabin in Kentuck, and the fine new neighbors await-ing us, but far from my intent, such talk had made her sad.

"I want to come," she'd told me. "You must believe that. But my people need me now more than ever. We must mourn our dead. Rebuild our towns. Learn to live in a different world. Surely you understand."

I did, but understanding brought me no comfort. My heart felt as if it had been ripped from my chest and dragged through a briar-patch.

Red Eagle, Davy and I rode three abreast along the river, with Samson loping along beside. Red Eagle was feeling his old self again. The healing power of Indian herbs bordered on magic, and his wounds had shrunk to scars. Again wearing my hat, he was now clad in a cotton shirt and homespun britches, lessening the chance he'd be recognized from a distance. He'd been the most hunted man in the South for over a year, but the Battle of Horseshoe Bend had raised the stakes. By all accounts, Jackson's desire to catch him had become an obsession.

Jackson had been on a rampage since the horror of Horseshoe Bend, burning Creek villages and destroying their crops. The survivors were starving, and when they tried to surrender, Jackson told them they must first move north of his army, removed from the influence of the Spanish and British. He made it clear there would be no treaty until Red Eagle was either caught or surrendered.

"You're certain you want to do this?" I said.

"Want has little to do with it." Red Eagle rode with eyes downcast, his face in the shadow of the hat.

"The war's over," Davy said, "but the killin' goes on. An' only you can stop it." He, too, wore a battered old hat, along with a cotton hunting shirt in place of his usual attire. It was best *we* not be recognized, either.

Red Eagle glanced up, taking in the country. His eyes, normally dark, looked pale. "This is a homecoming of sorts. I grew up just south of here, and came often to play in the ruins of old Fort Toulouse."

The French fort, we'd learned, had been built half a century earlier at the confluence of the Cousa and Alabama Rivers. This was the site Jackson had chosen for his new headquarters.

"My great-grandfather commanded here," Red Eagle said. "Captain Marchand. At one time I could feel his spirit in the wind, but I feel it no more."

Topping a rise, we got our first glimpse of "Fort" Jackson. Spread out from the crook of the two rivers was an ocean of tents. The ocean seemed to be in flux, but that was the effect of thousands of men and horses going about their business in a confined area. On a bluff overlooking the site, a half-completed building stood amid posts destined to anchor the palisade.

The closer we came, the stronger the stench, even more profound after three weeks among the Creeks. Horse droppings, human waste, sweat, frying meat, and boiling coffee all swirled together to smite the nose like a thunderclap. Red Eagle saw my nose twitch and almost smiled.

If there were sentries, they were either spread wide or sleeping. We rode steadily on. A few heads turned in mild curiosity, but the soldiers quickly went back to their business, which seemed to consist largely of playing cards and napping.

Downriver from the main camp, a cluster of Cherokee lodges stood against the tree line. Red Eagle scowled at this. "Traitors," he said. "Cowards." He turned Arrow's head toward this Indian village, and I believe he would have led us there had Davy not grasped his bridle.

"One hornet's nest at a time" Davy said. "We got Old Hickory-face to worry about."

Red Eagle growled, but resumed the approach toward the center of camp, where a limp flag flew from a makeshift flagpole. This, we knew from Fort Strother, was where we'd find Jackson's tent.

Men pointed at Samson at we passed, and one threw him a gristled bone, which he promptly chomped to bits. His appetite piqued, he leapt over a fire to snatch a hot potato from a spit, bringing a hail of rocks from indignant soldiers. Before matters could escalate, Davy reached into our food sack and tossed the men a handful of plums.

We plodded on, and each new face increased the odds someone would know us and sound an alarm. By the time the command tent came in sight I was clammy with sweat.

We slowed our horses a good fifty feet away. A serious-looking young fellow with bars on his shoulders stood ramrod straight before the tent.

Davy appeared to be thinking the problem over when Jackson's strident voice issued from inside. "Corporal! Fetch me fresh water from the river, and be damned quick about it!"

The young man turned to the tent, hesitating until the voice shouted, "Now!" Tossing a quick salute, the corporal caught up the nearest bucket and bolted toward the riverbank.

I thought this a fine stroke of luck until I spotted Red Eagle grinning.

Davy was all innocence. "Even a instrument of Fate," he said, "needs to cheat a mite now and then."

Urging our horses forward, we dismounted and lashed them to a tent rope. Moments later we slipped into the dim, cool confines of the tent. Samson burst in with us, and was everywhere at once, snuffling and rooting about for food. Jackson and another officer jumped up sputtering and the general rescued a generous haunch of venison from the table.

Jackson was purple with rage. "What in seven hells is the meaning of…" He stopped, staring at the hound. "That dog! I've seen that spotted brute before." Something changed in his eyes, and he gave us careful scrutiny at last. "Crockett," he said, his voice dripping venom. "And McCoy. You dare come here after…" Then words failed him as he stared with widening eyes at Red Eagle. "Y-y-you! You! Ye Gods and Little Fishes! Major Reid, summon the guard at once!"

Davy raised a palm. "Hold your horses, Gen'ral. You'd do well to listen afore havin' us shot."

"Shot? Shooting's too good for you. You'll be drawn and quartered."

"Not just yet, thanks. We got matters to discuss."

Jackson's eyes narrowed. "Such as?"

"You know the old sayin', Gen'ral. 'Those that sleeps with the hounds, ends up with fleas.'"

"And what's that supposed to mean?"

"Zane," Davy said. "Major Gabriel Zane."

Jackson snorted, but some of the color left his face.

"Listen, Gen'ral. We ain't here to make trouble. Fact is, my friend Mr. Weatherford came to surrender."

"You're damn right he'll surrender. And be hanged before sundown."

Red Eagle removed his hat. He grew in size as he squared his shoulders, expanded his chest. The man had the bearing of a king, and even Jackson was taken aback.

"I do not fear you, General. I am a Creek warrior, and fear no man. Though I regret our enmity, I was given no choice. Now I have that choice, and would call in my warriors, but they can no longer hear me. Their bones are at Talladega, Tallushatchee and Tohopeka, and their women and children are starving in the woods. I am in your power, and you may do with me as you will. All I ask is that you let my people live."

Red Eagle stepped back. He'd said what he came to say.

"A pretty speech," Jackson said, "from the butcher of Fort Mims. You can repeat it from the gallows."

Davy waggled a finger. "Beg pardon, Gen'ral. Ain't you forgettin' Zane?"

"Damn Zane. What do I care for a rogue officer? And a dead one at that."

"Maybe he ain't so dead as you think." Davy glanced pointedly at Reid, who listened to this with all his ears.

The general's face darkened. He swung away from us, facing a rear corner of the tent, and his shoulders shook. Samson took this opportunity to retrieve the venison. When Jackson turned back, his features were placid. "Major Reid," he said, "I should like you to gather a squadron of men, good men, and surround this tent. No one is to enter, or leave, without my direct order."

Reid's face fell, but he snapped a salute. "Sir." He glowered at Red Eagle and Davy, even saving a bit for me, and stalked from the tent.

Jackson stepped around the small table serving as his desk and sank heavily into his chair. He had aged since we arrived. "This had damn well better be good."

Davy shook his head. "It's bad. Zane an' his animals was burnin' friendly villages, killin' every man, woman and young'un in sight. You knowed what they was up to, and you 'lowed it to continue." He pulled the chairs from the dinner table, pushed one toward Red Eagle and perched on the other. I sat on the bed. Samson lay smacking on his bone, all that remained of Jackson's supper.

Jackson shook his head violently but without conviction, as if denying the sky was blue.

"You gave him them major's stripes," Davy said, "and that company o' soldiers, and set him to butcherin' defenseless women and children. You."

"That," Jackson said, "is a damned lie. And if you repeat it to anyone I'll have you thrashed like a mule."

"There's more, the part you *don't* know. Zane was makin' a monkey of you." When Jackson merely folded his arms across his chest, Davy finished, "Whilst pretendin' to take orders from you, he was really carryin' water for the British."

In a matter of seconds, Jackson's face went from shock to disbelief, and finally to outrage. "I don't believe it! You're a trickster, Crockett. You'd say anything to save this redskin."

"Maybe so, Gen'ral. On both counts. But that don't change the truth. Zane was helpin' the Redcoats, an' we got proof."

While Jackson sat scowling, Davy related what Zane had revealed to us at Musolagee. The general pursed his lips during the part where Zane took credit for the attack on Fort Mims. "We warn't sure what to believe neither," Davy said, "'til we found his packet o' letters."

"Letters?" Jackson now looked genuinely concerned.

"Like this'n." Davy produced a folded piece of paper from his ammunition pouch.

Jackson stared at it, seemed to shudder.

Davy leaned forward and dropped the paper on the desk.

Jackson thrust his hands under the table as if the thing were a rattlesnake.

Davy waited, almost grinning. Red Eagle might have been made of stone. The only sound in the tent was Samson crunching the last scraps of bone.

After what seemed an age, Jackson brought his hands onto the table and poked at the paper. At last, with trembling hands, he opened the letter and read. When he finished, his face had a yellow cast. He looked up at Davy, almost managing a glare.

"This proves nothing." His voice was hoarse. "A forgery."

"If it is, we got a lot more to keep it comp'ny. Even better, we got Zane, eager to crow 'bout playin' you like a banjo."

Outside the tent, voices rose in anger and confusion. Reid had apparently returned with the guards. And word had spread of Red Eagle's surrender. Among the shouts were "Kill the dirty savage! Burn him alive!" and "String him up!"

Cocking an ear, Jackson smiled. "My sentiments exactly." Refolding the letter, he tore it in half, then again and again. He swept the scraps off his desk. "I don't believe you."

"Figured you'd need convincin'." Davy stood, plucking the brass telescope from the corner of Jackson's desk. "C'mon. Got somethin' to show you."

Jackson followed him out of the tent. Red Eagle remained seated, while I peered out through the flap. It seemed we were now surrounded by half the soldiers in camp. Among them were a number of angry-faced Indians, shouting as loud as the rest.

Davy leaned close to Jackson's ear, pointing off toward a distant hill. The mob quieted somewhat as they strained to follow the aim of Jackson's telescope. After a moment the general's body went rigid. When he lowered the scope, his face was ashen. Without a word to the soldiers, he ducked back into the tent, Davy at his heels.

Jackson slumped into his chair. "What do you want?"

"Only what's fair. Let Red Eagle go back to his family and live in peace. He'll sweet talk Menawa and the others into layin' down their war clubs."

"And what of those letters?"

"We'll hang onto those a spell. And to Zane, 'case you get a notion to crawfish on the deal. 'Long as you leave Red Eagle be, you got my word they won't be used agin' you."

"Your word." Jackson's voice was flat.

"A thing I don't take lightly."

Jackson shook his head. "Damn you. And damn me if I don't

believe you." He hung his head, staring at the carpeted earth, and rubbed the back of his neck. "I agree."

Davy stepped to a chest at the side of tent, corralled a bottle of brandy and several glasses. "Let's drink on it." He poured four healthy drams. When we three held glasses, he placed the fourth on Jackson's desk. Davy raised his glass. "To peace."

We waited. At length, Jackson picked up his own, holding it as if might be poison. "Peace through victory," he said, "and confusion to the British."

"Close enough," Davy said. And we drank.

OUTSIDE THE TENT, bedlam reigned. Davy, Samson and I emerged first. Samson, hackles rising, bared his fangs and snarled. Jackson followed, leading Red Eagle, who faced a surge of curses, boos and waving fists. Men offered various opinions as to his fate, the mildest of which was lynching.

Under Jackson's stern eye, Major Reid's guards formed a circle around us, holding the mob at bay. But they failed to stop a thick-chested Creek, wearing the white feathers and deertail of a friendly, from bursting through. He grabbed Red Eagle by the shirt and held a wicked blade poised above his breast.

Red Eagle caught the fellow's wrist. His other hand grasped the Indian's throat. "Big Warrior," he said. "There is no reason for us to fight."

Jackson watched, amused, as the soldiers egged them on. At first, the two appeared evenly matched, but as they exerted more energy, Big Warrior's face grew slick with sweat. His knife arm bent backward. Red Eagle's lips curled back from his teeth. Davy wasn't the only one with an inner demon.

Davy laid a hand on each man's shoulder. "If you fellers lock horns, more of your people will die."

Big Warrior snarled at that, but Red Eagle nodded. He loosened his grip on the other's throat.

"Crockett is right," Red Eagle said. "We will never be friends, but cannot afford to be enemies."

"You have lost," Big Warrior said, spitting the words. "And deserve only death. You have led our people to destruction."

Red Eagle's face twisted, but he made no argument.

"We must work together," Red Eagle said, "or die."

Big Warrior growled, but released his grip. The two stood back, glowering like dogs after the same bone. The soldiers hissed and moaned, cheated out of a show.

Davy turned to Jackson. "Red Eagle needs time to talk to his people."

"There is but one topic of discussion. Unconditional surrender."

"He knows that. You got 'im in a box. But he deserves a fair shake. Will he get it?"

Jackson hesitated.

Davy whispered, "Zane."

Jackson grimaced. "Yes. He will."

Red Eagle looked to Davy and me. "I am again in your debt."

"Save your people," Davy said, "and raise a strong son. That's thanks enough for us."

"Speak for yourself," I told Davy. "I have something else in mind."

AN HOUR LATER, Davy and I stopped under a sweet-gum tree on the banks of the Coosa. Samson heard a noise in the brush and bounded off in pursuit of lunch.

"I don't see her," I said.

"She's here."

A horse snorted behind us, and there she was. Where she'd been hiding, with two horses and Zane, I could not imagine.

Little Fawn slipped from her pony, dropped the reins of the horses, and ran into my arms. I kept her there a good long while.

When I released her, Davy was looking up at Zane, who swayed in his saddle as the pony munched grass.

"He done his part," Davy said. "High time he was worm food."

"And I pity the worms," I said.

To Jackson, Zane must have looked merely stiff, but close up he was a gruesome sight. The black sockets where his eyes had been gaped at us, and his mouth would have drooped were it not sewn shut. The women had kept him alive, barely, before finally taking their revenge. Then they'd fashioned a high-backed wooden saddle and strapped him to the horse.

Little Fawn steered me toward the bank of the river.

I gazed down at her. "Are you still resigned to stay?"

She plucked a flower from a dogwood and held it to her nose. "I am truly sorry, Penn. I must. Once my people are settled, it will depend on you."

I just stared at her.

"You may find someone else. I would not bind you."

"Too late," I said. "As Davy might say, 'I'm bound tighter than tick to a hound dog's ear.'"

With a half-smile, she stretched up to kiss me, and I squeezed her tight. She moaned, tugging at me, and pulled me down onto the grass.

"Davy's just up the rise," I said. "Maybe we shouldn't—"

She placed a hand over my mouth.

"Shut up, Penn. Just shut up."

And I did.

NEXT MORNING, AS Little Fawn washed herself in the river, I took Davy aside. Before I could even open my mouth, he said, "Told her yet?"

"Told her what?"

"That you're stayin' here. With her."

I gaped at him. "How on earth did you know that?"

"Tarnation, Penn," he said, "I knowed that for months."

I shook my head. "Maybe I did, too, but didn't realize it."

Little Fawn came up the bank and stopped, eyeing us quizzically. Almost at once, her smile grew bright as the morning sun, and she ran forward, throwing her arms around me. Her face, pressed to mine, was wet with tears. "Oh, Penn," she whispered. "I am so glad."

"I suppose you've known for months, too," I said. "I'm always the last to find things out."

Little Fawn pulled away, fixing Davy with an accusing glare. "You told him?"

Davy held up his hands. "Not me! My lips is sealed."

I looked from one to the other, all at sea. "Told me what?"

Little Fawn's smile was back. "It may interest you to know, Pennsylvania McCoy, that you are soon to be a father."

For a moment I was too flabbergasted to speak. Then my knees gave way, and it took both Davy and Little Fawn to hold me up.

When my mouth was working again, I said, "Why didn't you tell me?"

"I could not," Little Fawn. "You are an honorable man, Penn, and would have done the honorable thing. I did not want you to stay for honor, I wanted you stay for *me*."

I fixed Davy with a hard look. "And you knew, too."

"I didn't," he said, "until Polly told me. An' she made me swear to keep it in my pocket."

After that came much rejoicing, and by the time Davy was ready to leave I felt I'd been through the wringer and put out to dry.

Davy laid a hand on my shoulder. "I admire what you're doin', Penn. It won't be nowheres easy, but I know you'll manage."

"I believe I will," I said. "I learned a lot about cabin-making up in Kentuck, and figure I can make one here, too."

"We'll put a roof on your first one," he said, "and hold it ready for you. You two—or *three*—will be always welcome."

I gripped his hand, meeting his eye and nodding my thanks for many things. Little Fawn took his face in her hands and kissed him warmly on the cheek.

Davy said, " 'Pears Samson is payin' a fare-thee-well, too."

And we turned to see the hound squatting on the freshly-made grave, leaving a parting gift for Zane.

Just then, faint hoof beats echoed from across the Coosa.

Davy pointed, and I eventually spotted a group of tiny riders racing down the slope of a distant hill. The riders grew steadily larger, angling parallel to the river, and I soon saw a larger group of horsemen on their heels.

The men in the first group were mostly naked, long braids and feathers streaming behind them. Those in pursuit were garbed in blue. The Indians raced on toward the south and disappeared into the trees. The soldiers were just coming parallel to us, six hundred yards away.

I said, "Remember that shot you made, bringing down Arrow? Do you suppose you could—"

"No," Davy said. "I couldn't. I aim to steer shy of fightin' for a good long while. In fact, I hope never to raise old Betsy again, 'cept to put meat on the table."

He swung onto his dun, nudged it with his heels, and favored us with a parting grin. Samson danced at his side, eager to go.

Little Fawn and I held tight to one another, watching until they were out of sight.

It would be nice, I thought, if Davy got his wish. He'd conquered his devil, and that would help. But as much as he joked about being an instrument of Fate, I had a feeling Fate wasn't quite finished with him.

ALONG WITH DAVID CROCKETT and Andrew Jackson, the real-life players in this novel are Red Eagle, his wife Sopath, Polly Crockett and the kids, Adam Myers, Sam Houston, Jesse Bean, Menawa and the stallion Arrow. A few of the minor characters, such as baby William, Monahoe, Josiah Francis, Big Warrior (real name unknown) and George Russell also existed. The rest are fictional.

Modern historians may quibble with the use of the name "Davy." I've seen no contemporary evidence that Crockett answered to that name during his lifetime, but that's how he's best known today, and I believe it personifies the character I've presented. As detailed in James R. Boylston and Allen J. Wiener's fine book *David Crockett in Congress: The Rise and Fall of the Poor Man's Friend*, the Davy persona was Crockett's invention, meant to endear him to the voters of his rural district of western Tennessee, in sharp contrast to his aristocratic opponents. Sadly, this persona was later used against him, portraying him—somewhat unfairly—as naive and out of his depth in national politics.

Though Crockett exhibits a healthy temper in his autobiography and political writings, there is no indication he actually lost control to an inner demon. This notion springs from his telling of the battle of Tallushatchee, where Jackson's forces had surrounded a Red Stick village. As Crockett describes the action in his autobiography, the killing was brutal, resulting in over 200 deaths, and not limited to Creek warriors. Crockett's line, "We shot them down like dogs," has been taken out of context by pop historians and offered as evidence that he was gleeful about the slaughter. My reading of that passage convinces me he was saddened and disgusted with the killing, and while he may not have discovered a "devil" lurking within him, it's quite likely he saw a side of himself he did not like.

Some sources say David and Polly's third child, Margaret, was born in early 1815, not long before Polly succumbed to an unknown illness. Others say the girl was born in late 1812. I asked the opinion of a pair of gracious members of the Direct Descendants of David Crockett (one of whom is descended from Margaret herself) and their best information favored the earlier date. So for purposes of this novel, baby Margaret has already joined the family.

As noted by Colonel Truitt, the Creek War had no single cause, but the primary instigator was the Shawnee chief Tecumseh, who, at the behest of the British, visited various tribes in his efforts to provoke rebellion. His ideas took root most effectively with the Creeks, who were soon involved in a civil war. The main point of contention was whether or not they should kill the white settlers on the outskirts of their territory.

The term "Red Sticks," meaning those Creeks who favored war, seems derived from the practice of sending a bundle of painted sticks from village to village to announce the date a military campaign would begin. Red was the color of war, and the number of sticks in the bundle announced the number of days until the event.

The attack on Fort Mims was, at least in part, retaliation for an earlier attack by soldiers upon Red Sticks, which became known as The Battle of Burnt Corn Creek. Fort Mims, though, where some 500 people died, escalated the conflict into a full-blown war. Ironically, most of those killed at Fort Mims, including its commanding officer, were of mixed Creek blood, but the fact that white settlers were among the slain spread fear across the frontier, resulting in the raising of armies in several nearby states.

Many Creeks remained opposed to the Red Sticks throughout the war, and some fought alongside the armies of Jackson and other generals against their own people.

Prior to the war, Andrew Jackson's political career had stalled, due at least in part to dueling over the honor of his wife. Mrs. Jackson, at the time of their marriage, seems to have been legally wed to another man. The Creek War rescued Jackson from himself, allowing him to build a reputation as a soldier, leading directly to that of a national hero at the Battle of New Orleans.

Jackson was ruthless in the treatment of his troops, famously executing one young recruit for leaving guard duty to eat supper. The incident of the "mutiny" and the stand-off at the bridge appears in Crockett's autobiography, which inspired a similar scene on the Disney program. In whatever form, it's a good story, and I have made use of it here for my own purposes. Jackson biographers insist that if such an incident occurred, Jackson managed to stop it at the bridge, quelling any notions of mutiny. A more likely interpretation is that Jackson blustered and bullied as long as possible to keep volunteers beyond their terms of enlistment, then gave up and let the men go home.

While most of the events related in this novel are fictional, the battles of Talladega and Horseshoe Bend were real. There is no evidence Crockett came face to face with Red Eagle at Talladega, but he surely would have seen him there. Some 300 Red Sticks were believed killed there, while another 700 escaped. Jackson was furious over the escape and charged one of his cavalry commanders with disobedience, though the case was not brought to trial.

Red Eagle, born William Weatherford, was one of the most fascinating characters of the Creek War. Weatherford's father was a Scottish trader, and because his mother was of mixed blood, some historians believe he was as little as one-eighth Creek. By all accounts he was eloquent and intelligent, despite having no education. A successful planter who bred racehorses and often entertained white settlers at his home, Weatherford was initially opposed to Tecumseh's call to arms. Why he joined the Red Sticks is still in doubt, but one theory is that he may have been coerced by other rebels, possibly by the abduction of his bride Sopath. I have no evidence that he was Episcopalian, but he was surely raised Christian, and that is one faith he may have conceivably shared with a boy from Pennsylvania.

While he did lead the charge to Fort Mims, it's possible Red Eagle merely intended a demonstration of strength, and lost control of his followers when the fort's main gates were found open. There is evidence he tried to stem the killing, and was driven away, only to return with more warriors to enforce his will.

Some sources say Red Eagle's stallion Arrow was black, while others describe the animal as gray. Arrow came to public attention in dramatic fashion following the Battle of the Holy Ground, which took place seven weeks after the action at Talladega. Articles in the popular press described Red Eagle's dramatic escape, in which he and Arrow plunged off a cliff into the Alabama River in full view of the American forces

Red Eagle married Sopath, his second wife, sometime around the start of the Creek War. She was likely about 18, and he 32. Records spell her name variously as Sapoth, Sopoth, Sopath, Sapathe or Softah. She was renowned for her singing voice. In late 1813 or early 1814 she gave birth to William Weatherford, Jr. Some sources say she died soon after, while others indicate she lived another ten years.

The character Adam Myers is taken from Crockett's autobiography. Crockett describes how he fell in with this seemingly friendly wagon driver after running away to escape a caning from his father. He traveled with Myers, assisting in his work for some time and earning a small amount of money before arriving in Baltimore. The story of Myers appropriating Crockett's funds follows that told in the autobiography, and it seemed appropriate for Myers to resurface here as a villain.

The two-man army trick attributed to General Francis Marion is more likely the creation of Walt Disney. Davy used it with Georgie Russell against the Creeks in the first episode of the Disney series, "Davy Crockett: Indian Fighter," dubbing it "the old Crockett charge." Two years later, Marion and his men used the same gambit against the British on an episode of Disney's Swamp Fox series. In both cases the trick was successful. It seemed a fitting tribute to Disney to have Davy credit Francis Marion with the idea.

The White Drink, called the Black Drink by missionaries who witnessed the ceremony, is sometimes referred to as yaupon tea or cassine. The drink was thought to purify the warriors of all sin, fortify them for battle, and even protect them from the weapons of their enemies. Whether the tea actually tasted as bad as Penn thought I cannot say, but it was common practice for warriors to hold it down as long as possible before vomiting.

The Creek War was effectively over in March 1814, after the Battle of Horseshoe Bend, in which as many as 800 Red Sticks, under the command of Menawa, were killed. Menawa himself survived. Lieutenant Sam Houston took part in that fight, and was injured as described. Red Eagle is thought to have been absent from the battle, but the defeat left him without an army, and he soon surrendered. He eventually took a third wife, of non-Indian descent, and established a new plantation in southern Alabama. He died in 1826.

Crockett is believed to have been at home in Tennessee at the time of the action at Horseshoe Bend, but there is no hard evidence placing him there. He did reenlist in September 1814, six months after the battle, to help drive the British out of Pensacola, but saw little fighting.

Following the end of the Creek War in 1814, Jackson was allowed to dictate terms to the Indians. This resulted in them paying an indemnity of 22 million acres, roughly three-fifths of their territory, including all of their best farmland. Creeks who had fought against the Red Sticks received no better treatment than the rebels, and justifiably felt betrayed. Those who could not accept Jackson's terms fled to Florida to join their relatives the Seminoles, some even choosing to fight alongside the British. It would not be long before Jackson took his army south, vanquishing all such foes, and winning nationwide acclaim at the Battle of New Orleans. He was elected President in 1829 and served two terms.

Crockett's wife Polly died in early 1815, and later that year he married the widow Elizabeth Patton, who would give him three more children. After a stint in the Tennessee State Legislature, Crockett was elected to the U.S. Congress in 1826, where he served three terms. Initially a supporter of Jackson, he became one of the President's most vocal political opponents, particularly on the issue of Jackson's treatment of the Southern Indian tribes, and was even touted briefly as a Presidential candidate. When his opposition to Jackson lost him his seat in Congress, Crockett famously claimed to have told his constituents they could go to Hell, and he would go to Texas.

Even before his death at the Alamo in 1836, Crockett had become a character of legend, and the hero of a lengthy series of frontier almanacs.

His fictional adventures had just begun.

EVAN LEWIS FELL under the spell of Davy Crockett at a tender age. He wore a coonskin cap and buckskin jacket. He had two Crockett rifles, one made by Marx and one by Hubley, and flintlock pistols from the same companies. He had a Davy Crockett bedspread, a terrycloth bearskin rug, a light fixture, a saddle-shaped clothes rack and a garbage can. He had books, records, a cereal bowl, jig-saw puzzles and a plastic wallet with a fuzzy coonskin cap on it. He spent countless hours in the basement with an official Marx Davy Crockett at the Alamo playset. Yeah, he had it bad.

Years later, he took an interest in the real Crockett, amassing a stack of biographies, joining the Alamo Society and making two pilgrimages to San Antonio. And he acquired more stuff, of course. Cap guns, coffee cups, a wrist watch and fifty-some versions of "The Ballad of Davy Crockett." Yeah, he still had it bad.

He often felt he heard Davy's voice in his head—sort of like a conscience—so he wrote stories about a modern day descendant of Crockett who suffered from that same condition. Three of those, "Mr. Crockett and the Bear," "Mr. Crockett and the Longrifle," and "Mr. Crockett and the Indians," appeared in *Alfred Hitchcock's Mystery Magazine*. He wrote similar stories of Davy's grandson in the Old West, published hither and yon. And he wrote this novel. He hopes you like it.

Along the way, Lewis received the Mystery Writers of America's 2011 Robert L. Fish Award for his *EQMM* story "Skyler Hobbs and the Rabbit Man," about a man who believes he's the reincarnation of Sherlock Holmes. His *AHMM* story "The Continental Opposite," an homage to Dashiell Hammett, was nominated for a Shamus Award and selected for *The Best American Mystery Stories of 2016*.

He lives in Portland, Oregon with his wife Irene and five dogs, where he blogs about pulps, comics, films and other wonders of pop culture on *Davy Crockett's Almanack of Mystery, Adventure and the Wild West*, at evanlewis.com. He's now hard at work on *Bowie's Gold*, an epic adventure of Crockett's all-too-brief acquaintance Jim Bowie, soon to be published by Steeger Books. He hopes you'll like that, too.

www.ingramcontent.com/pod-product-compliance
Lightning Source LLC
Chambersburg PA
CBHW032228010726
47494CB00002B/400